twenties, Ronni Cooper had a successful career in the club world against a soundtrack of thrusting guitars and r vocals, where outrageous was the norm. She now lives een the UK and LA and writes full-time – but the music, decadence and the thigh-high leather boots are still very to her heart. *Manhattan* is her second novel.

*Also by Ronni Cooper*

Rock Chicks

# MANHATTAN

**RONNI COOPER**

sphere

SPHERE

First published in Great Britain as a paperback original in 2011 by Sphere

ISBN 978-0-7515-4276-9

Typeset in Bembo by M Rules
Printed and bound in Great Britain by
Clays Ltd, St Ives plc

MIX
Paper from
responsible sources
FSC® C104740

Sphere
An imprint of
Little, Brown Book Group
100 Victoria Embankment
London EC4Y 0DY

An Hachette UK Company
www.hachette.co.uk

www.littlebrown.co.uk

To J, B & C.
More than words . . . always.

# ACKNOWLEDGEMENTS

With endless gratitude to . . .

Sheila Crowley, the most inspiring, encouraging agent any writer could have; Emma Beswetherick, who took the first leap of faith; and to Joanne Dickinson, who is just all kinds of brilliant.

Ladies, you rock . . . Rxx

# PROLOGUE

*New York, 1993*

New York Globe – *21 December 1993*

*The stars are expected to turn out in style tonight for the first anniversary celebrations of top New York nightclub Manhattan. Since it opened its doors exactly one year ago today, the venue has played host to famous names from across the globe and garnered a reputation for glamour and excess. It was also the source of much controversy when it was the principal location used in the movie* Disco Drug.

*Manhattan owners Raine O'Donnell, Mei-Lin Yan and Stevie Ross last night paid tribute to the clients who have frequented the nightspot, saying, 'We are incredibly proud of our club and we owe a huge thanks to everyone who has supported us throughout these amazing twelve months. And thank you to the city of New York, because only in this town would three women be able to achieve so much in such a short time in such a crazy industry. Tomorrow night, the cocktails are on us!'*

*It's thought that the celebrities taking the Manhattan bosses up on that offer will include such luminaries as Calvin Klein, Jackie Collins, Janice Dickinson, Diana Ross, Jack Nicholson, Dimitri Krakov, Tala*

DiVinci, Leeane Star, Madonna, Sylvester Stallone, Christie Brinkley and Bruce Willis.

Full details and photographs of what promises to be a spectacular event will feature in our Saturday edition.


*Manhattan, New York, 21 December 1993*

'I haven't been this excited since Sean Penn felt me up on the back fire exit.' Raine covered her grin by taking another sip of pink champagne as she waited for the inevitable chorus of outrage.

Right on cue, Stevie's jaw dropped. 'He did not!'

'Oh, OK, so he didn't,' Raine admitted glibly.

Stevie wasn't letting it go. 'How many times have I told you to stop exaggerating and making things up?'

'A million. You're right. I'm sorry.' She paused. 'It must have been Jack Nicholson.'

The three of them laughed and one by one put their glasses into the middle of their huddle.

Raine offered up the toast. 'Here's to Manhattan and to us. To think they said we'd never make it in this town.'

'That's the worst James Cagney impression ever,' Mei-Lin teased.

Raine nodded. 'I know. Sean Penn taught me.'

After a few moments their laughter subsided and Stevie spoke up, her voice choked with emotion. If her fans could see her now they'd barely recognise this softly spoken, all-American blonde as the biggest female rock star of the decade.

'I just want to say thank you. I'd never have made it without the two of you.'

Mei-Lin leaned over and softly kissed her cheek. 'You would always have made it. It just wouldn't have been this great.'

The others nodded. Mei-Lin continued to speak, her perfect Revlon Red lips an exact colour match of the stunning, floor-length red

2

*cheongsam that skimmed her petite frame. 'You know, when I came to this country my heart was broken, but now, finally, I feel that it is whole again.'*

*Stevie's eyes filled with tears and even Raine executed a very pronounced gulp.*

*Stevie summed it up. 'We all needed each other. And I love both of you so much.'*

*In the distance, a bell started ringing. Raine sniffed loudly and cleared her throat. 'That's the "Too Much Emotion In Here" alarm. I had it fitted especially for tonight,' she joked.*

*Before the others could reply, the phone rang. Raine was closest to it.*

*'This had better be good because you're interrupting a memorable moment.' Her sing-song voice oozed happiness and excitement.*

*'What?' In a split second her face changed. Another bell started to ring, then another. All three heads swivelled to the fire-alarm board on the wall behind them. It was lighting up like a Christmas tree.*

*Raine slammed the phone down.*

*'We have to get out of here. There's a fire on the east side, the west, the basement . . . ' Another light on the board. 'And shit, there's one above us, too.'*

*Despite the urgency of the situation, none of them moved.*

*'This is it,' Mei-Lin whispered. 'He's coming for us.'*

*As trickles of smoke crept in around the doorframe, no one argued.*

# BOOK ONE

# BEFORE THE MUSIC
# STARTED . . .

# ONE

*Raine*
*New York, 1983*

It wasn't the first time she'd watched them.

The first time had been the year before, on her sixteenth birthday, when severe stomach cramps and an aversion to afternoon biology class had caused her to cut the last two hours of school. Since then, she'd encountered them at least a dozen more times – always without them realising that she was there. She didn't understand why the woman brought him here. Didn't the tight-assed bastard have the dough to splash out on a room?

Her eyes flicked to the silk-lined suit that now lay discarded on the cream upholstered chair beside the bed. It looked expensive. Not that she was any expert, but put it this way, it looked more like the kind of outfit that President Regan wore on television, and less like the one her father dragged out for weddings, baptisms and funerals.

Yeah, this joker had the money all right, but he obviously had better things to spend it on. Or maybe that was part of the power trip – fucking a woman in her marital bedroom while her husband was at work. Yeah, maybe that was the kick.

So what was the kick for the woman?

Tiny pores of moisture burst in the palms of her hands.

What she'd give to throw open the door and confront them. To see the shame on the whore's face and the surprise on his. She'd thought about it so many times over the years, immersed in a monsoon of guilt at her lack of action. But . . .

It was a box she didn't want to open. For all their sakes. Because even at seventeen, she realised that the consequences would be life-changing, and it wasn't a call she was bold enough to make.

A moan of pleasure dragged her attention back to the nauseating scene in front of her.

Raine O'Donnell's mom, ladies and gentlemen. Pillar of the community, chapel secretary, the woman who acted in public like she was a miracle and a halo away from sainthood. The one who fucked another man while her husband of twenty years was at work, telling all his buddies how he married the most beautiful woman in Brooklyn.

Sometimes she wished that someone would notice her discomfort, would question why she found it difficult not to sneer when her mother told her that her skirt was too short or that listening to Madonna all night long on her Walkman would warp her for life. Warped? There was only one warped person in this house and it was the one that was lying on her back with her ankles around the neck of a fat, sweating bastard.

The hypocrisy twisted her gut.

Raine silently backed away from the slit in the bedroom door and retraced her steps until she was out in the front yard. She checked her watch. 2 p.m. Her mother would be expecting her home around four o'clock, so she had two hours to kill before she could safely return without the risk of walking in on the most beautiful woman in Brooklyn sucking someone's dick.

The street outside was deserted, the rest of the working class community on this side of Vinegar Hill were either at work, school or inside watching *General Hospital* or reruns of *The Young and the Restless*. Most of the people who lived in the neighbourhood were familiar to her. Predominately second- and third-generation Irish immigrants, it was a community that stuck together, that helped each other out and did its best to keep out the scum, the slackers and the trash.

A bus stopped beside her and on impulse she jumped on and travelled several stops, ignoring the disapproving glances of two elderly ladies who clearly had an opinion on the hissing sound coming from the earphones attached to her Walkman. She turned the volume up even higher. Madonna totally rocked. Only last week her mother had snapped off an MTV show because the singer was wearing a wedding dress and singing a song called 'Like A Virgin'.

There was that hypocrisy thing again.

The following day Raine had taken the cash she'd earned from babysitting the DiAngelo kids next door, gone straight to the record shop and bought the album. She'd fallen in love with 'Holiday', 'Borderline' was stuck in her head, but 'Lucky Star' was her favourite. She'd cut the fingers off her leather gloves, torn the sleeves off her denim jacket and, as soon as she had enough money, dear Lord the hair was going blond. White blond. With any luck it would give her mother a heart attack and that fat bastard would be deprived of his easy lay.

She disembarked at the row of stores that serviced the area. A drugstore, laundromat, a 7/11, a bank and a diner that was always busy on three accounts – it was the only inexpensive place to eat within a ten-block radius, it sold the best bread and doughnuts and it was only five hundred yards from the 84th Precinct, so there was a steady supply of blue uniforms to fill the grey plastic stools at the counter. The mental image that was refusing to leave her head ruled out any notion of eating, but a milkshake would pass the time.

The bell announced her arrival but no one paid any attention except for a couple of construction guys whose hard hats were fighting for space on a table laden with food. Their leers started at her black brogues, then moved up past her thick, black, knee-high socks, her regulation kilt and settled somewhere around the middle of her green cardigan. It was as if the board of governors at St Mary's had conspired to make the uniform as unattractive as possible in order to ward off the potential for sin. Going by the look on those guys' faces, the plan wasn't working. It wasn't the first time she'd been ogled by a couple of middle-aged pervs with a schoolgirl fantasy, but Raine wasn't conceited enough to think they were taken by her beauty. She knew that she'd never make homecoming queen. She may have her mother's Italian colouring and her thick black curls, but she was too tall, too skinny, too gangly – all arms and legs. It made her the star of the school volleyball team, but a complete failure on the dating scene. The only boy taller than her was Jimmy Silva, the high-school star quarterback, and there were way too many pert little cheerleaders flashing their pushed-up breasts in his direction for him to notice the giraffe in the corner.

Not that she'd be interested anyway. Boys her age were far too immature. They were still comparing hickies and jerking off to *Flashdance* posters. Pulling the earphones out of her ears, she clicked off the cassette and made for the nearest empty seat at the counter, rolling her eyes at the nauseating Billy Joel ballad that was playing in the background.

Isa, the counter server, shimmied over to her, an infectious grin beaming across her rotund face. The white of her dentures

10

was matched in brightness by the screaming orange of her hair, a shade that Isa had told her a dozen times was a tribute to an actress called Maureen O'Hara. Raine had no idea who Miss O'Hara was, but if she was responsible for fifty-five-year-old women across America having hair that glowed in the dark then she really needed to rethink her legacy.

'Chocolate or vanilla today?'

'Am I that predictable, Isa?' Raine feigned an exasperated sulk.

'Yes you are, my sweetheart. I'm thinking chocolate.'

'Vanilla,' Raine countered defiantly. Isa let out a hoot of laughter and three cops sitting further along the counter smiled at the exchange before turning their investigative skills back to their burgers.

Raine took a book from her satchel, slid her finger down to the page that was turned over at the corner, flipped it open and started to read. Within minutes she was gone. The Manhattan she was reading about in the book may just be a few miles away, but the characters were living in a world a million miles away from hers.

'Hey, whatcha reading?'

A hand came into her peripheral vision and tipped up the front cover, making her stammer with embarrassment.

'Erm, it's just a book about . . . erm, fabrics. And the textile industry.'

Shirley Conran's *Lace* was slammed shut, and she quickly slipped it back into her school bag, her face giving off enough heat to power up the diner's coffee machine. Death would be preferable to Ricco Dimato knowing that she was reading about the kind of stuff that definitely didn't come with the blessing of Father O'Flynn or the church that – his shifts permitting – they both attended on Sunday mornings.

If her mother's affair was Raine's biggest secret, her feelings for Ricco Dimato came a close second. A cousin three or four times removed, he'd been around her whole life and she'd been madly in love with him for most of it.

Raine, Father O'Flynn and God all knew it was a waste of time.

Despite being only six years older than her, he treated her like she was twelve. It hurt all the more because he was major hot. Major. Ricco in his police uniform could even out-hot Richard Gere in that white suit at the end of *An Officer and a Gentleman*. And Raine should know. The summer before, her best friend Angelica Roberts had persuaded her to blow an entire month's allowance in one weekend at the movie theatre, watching it on a constant loop for two full days.

'You waiting for your dad, gorgeous?' He'd called her that since she was in eighth grade and he'd found her in tears after Jimmy Silva and his bunch of loser jocks had teased her about her height. To cheer her up, Ricco had taken her to see *Arthur* with Dudley Moore and Liza Minnelli and they'd laughed their asses off.

'He's just finishing off some paperwork and he'll be over. Picked up a couple of real scumbags today. Armed robbery. *Sooo* sweet.' The last couple of words came out in a whistle of triumph.

Six months out of the police academy and Ricco made no secret about how great it felt to lock up bad guys. It was an attitude that was all too familiar to Raine, given that she'd grown up as the daughter of Sergeant Patrick O'Donnell, dedicated upholder of the law, minor local hero, several times decorated for bravery and actions above and beyond the call of duty.

'Lookin' at something, guys?' Ricco's attention was momentarily diverted by the renewed stares of the construction guys.

Suddenly they found something on their table that was intensely fascinating and didn't look up again. Raine experienced a surge of something that was definitely more than family affection.

One of the cops further along the counter pushed five dollars in Isa's direction, told her to keep the change and was rewarded with a wink and a grin. Raine recognised him as Danny Docherty, a guy of about thirty who had done his probation with her dad and who'd come over to the house every once in a while in the intervening years. As he passed Ricco, he paused and shook his hand.

'Still OK for tonight, buddy?'

Wow. For the first time ever, Raine thought, Ricco looked ruffled and very slightly shifty.

'Sure. Eight o'clock?'

'Yeah. I'll pick you up.'

There was an awkward silence as Danny headed for the door. Eventually Ricco broke it.

'So how're things going with that squad of dickheads at school?'

Nope, he wasn't getting off that easy.

'You tell me first,' Raine probed playfully. 'What's going on tonight at eight? Football? Dinner? Big date?'

Ricco's discomfort racked up another notch.

'Look, Raine, the thing is . . . '

Oh frigging crap, it was a date. He had a date with some beautiful, non-giraffe-like female and they'd get married, have perfect kids and that would be that. Her heart thudded like a jackhammer, sending blood thumping to her head. The world was over. Done. Finished. No wonder he was practically squirming as he spoke.

'You can't say anything to your old man, OK? But there's a new club opening in the city – Reincarnation over on West

14th Street – and they're paying big bucks for off-duty cops to work the door. It's like seriously easy money. Couple of nights a week and I'll have enough for a new set of wheels in no time.'

Raine fought the urge to raise both hands up to heaven and shout, 'Hallelujah'. It wasn't a woman. Oh dear Lord, thank you. An extra decade of the rosary would be offered up this Sunday. It was just a club. And that was . . .

Oh crap, hang on. How many women would be there? And they'd all be beautiful and glamorous and they'd go nuts for the tall guy on the door with the jet black hair and the green eyes and long thick eyelashes that out-hotted Richard Gere.

But she'd worry about that later. Take small victories, she told herself – he hadn't gone and got hooked up. Thank you, Mary, Mother of God and all the angels.

'Don't worry, I won't say anything.' A shake of the head and a swipe of her hand were added for extra nonchalance and maturity.

'Thanks, gorgeous.' Just when the heart was calming back down his grin ramped it right back up again and – oh God – now he was hugging her. Do not hold on too tight. Do not kiss him. Do not sniff his neck and then whimper . . .

'Hey, Dimato, will you put my girl down before I slam you in a cell with those two reprobates we just picked up.'

Raine jumped. She'd been so busy trying not to have a heart attack, she hadn't noticed that her dad had arrived – a pretty difficult accomplishment given that he was six foot four and built like the boxer he used to be. It used to be the standing joke at the station that he looked a bit like William Shatner when Captain Kirk was in his prime. The guys on the shift laughed about it until a smart-ass perp got wind of it and murmured, 'Beam Me Up, Scotty,' in the middle of an interrogation. The guy got off on the housebreaking he'd been brought in for, but he left with a nose that would never run in a straight line again.

Now, as he walked towards them, his voice was joking, but there was no hiding the tiny hint of warning. It was going to be a brave guy that dated Patrick O'Donnell's daughter because he was officially the most protective dad in Brooklyn. Even the fact that Ricco was the son he'd never had didn't exclude him from certain death if he ever made a move on Pat's princess.

'Don't you worry about a thing, boss. I'm well aware how important my limbs are and I'm planning on keeping them. But I tell you, one day when I'm captain of this precinct I'm coming for her,' he teased.

'And we'll all weep at the funeral for the NY police officer who served the shortest captaincy in history.'

Raine grinned at the banter as she leaned over to hug her dad. 'Shouldn't you be in school?'

'Study time, so I thought I'd come wait for you.'

It was a white lie, but despite Sergeant O'Donnell having the most finely tuned bullshit detector in the five boroughs, it was permanently unplugged when it came to his girl.

'Thanks, baby, but I'm pulling a double shift today. Joe Greenberg's mother passed away last night and we're a couple of men down on sick leave so I'm covering. You have your shake and then get on home and I'll see you in the morning.'

Pat tucked ten dollars into the flap on the front of her satchel and shouted up a coffee and a roast beef sandwich to go. Isa acted like she'd just been given a missive from God. Twenty years she'd worked there, twenty years Pat O'Donnell had been coming in and twenty years she'd had a crush the size of Alaska. No one got served quicker or with a sunnier smile.

Raine thought it was cute and occasionally wondered what it would have been like if her dad had found Isa before he met

Maria. She was fairly sure she'd be going home to milk and cookies instead of a live porn show.

The doorbell dinged again, but Raine didn't bother to turn and see who it was. Big mistake. A few seconds later a hand reached out in the direction of her father.

'Sergeant O'Donnell, good to see you.' The voice resonated with suave charm and confidence.

Pat reciprocated the gesture, delivering a solid, firm hand-shake.

'District Attorney Mayer, always a pleasure.' There was genuine warmth in Pat's voice, riding side by side with an obvious tone of respect. 'I thought you'd already left us to go sort out all those bad guys across the bridge.'

'Another week to go, Pat, and I can't say I'm looking forward to it. I'll miss this place.'

Pat put his hand in his pocket and pulled out his wallet.

'Well I know that will be reciprocated at this end. We've always appreciated your support. This is on me. What can I get you?'

'Thanks, Pat, I'm just in for a coffee to go. Couldn't take any more of the court-house stuff. Don't know what's in it but I reckon more than a couple of cups could kill you.'

Pat laughed and Raine felt every hair on the back of her neck sweep up in a wave of rage as she reflected that if Pat O'Donnell knew that just a short time ago his wife had been screaming at District Attorney Mayer to fuck her harder, the least of the lawman's worries would be the killer coffee.

# TWO

*Mei-Lin*
*Shanghai, 1983*

The first thing Mei-Lin noticed as she woke was the cold. The searing, bitter cold. Every summer she would sweat through the months, praying for relief from the heat, but now, in December, the spirits that controlled the weather took those prayers and laughed as they commanded the ice and winds to wreak the bitterest chill. This year it was uncommonly harsh, with the freezing temperatures reaching lows that didn't normally come until many weeks later. Her mother had thrown an extra rug on the bed she shared with her sisters but still they shivered. She held them close to give them comfort but it seemed to make no difference. At five, the little ones still found it difficult to bear the extremities and it hurt Mei-Lin's heart to see them distressed.

The hills that stood like soldiers above her village were no protection and the rags she tied around her hands as she foraged the land didn't stop the excruciating pains in her joints. For decades her family had made a living from picking the matsutake mushrooms that grew under the trees, but this year's harvest

17

had been poor. Mei-Lin knew why. It was because the gods were unhappy. No matter how many times her mother had knelt by the fire and prayed for more matsutake to come, no matter that they toiled from dawn to sunset, their baskets had remained half empty. Now, weeks after the season for picking the small capped fungi had ended, they were forced to search the land, looking for anything that they could sell, eat or burn. Her sisters cried with hunger and her mother cried with desperation. But not her father. Every evening for weeks he'd sat on the stool in the corner of their home, the anger and sadness oozing out of his pores. She thought he looked older, weaker. Before this winter Mei-Lin could always make him smile with her dancing, or make him laugh with the funny songs she would dream up to pass the day. Not now. He'd grown tired of her. He no longer wanted to engage her in conversation, to teach her, to hear her thoughts and share his with her. His rejection hurt more than the ache of starvation in her stomach.

Mei-Lin made a fire in the sunken pit in the middle of the floor. Their home was one room, made of mud with a straw roof, only three miles from the river that supplied their water. Many years ago her father had made a wooden raft from a tree that had fallen down nearby. In the daytime this was a table around which they ate or talked. In the evening it became the bed for the children, the three or four inches that it was raised off the floor being a small blessing when the insects and the cold came. Just feet away, behind a makeshift curtain, her mother and father lay on a mat to sleep, although lately it seemed that even in the darkness her mother was granted no mercy from the upset that consumed her. Mei-Lin wondered if she was sick. Her cousin Jing Wei's mother had died a few seasons before and she'd gone away to start a new life in the city. Jing Wei promised that one day she would return and they would play together again and Mei-Lin knew that she would come. Her father had taught her that friends always kept their vows to each other.

'Mama, shall I heat more water? The little ones will be up soon.'

Barely awake and still dazed, her mother pushed back the hair from her face and rubbed her red, swollen eyes.

'Add a little more than usual. Uncle Cheung will be here soon and he will be thirsty after the journey.'

A bubble of excitement rose in Mei-Lin's stomach. Uncle Cheung was always a tonic for sadness. When he was young he'd travelled to Shanghai and there he'd found great success. Every once in a while he would return, bringing food and clothes and happiness to the rest of the family. He was a hero, a good man who did everything he could for those still working the land and facing the problems that came with living here. When Jing Wei's mother had died, it was Uncle Cheung who had come to help, rescuing Jing Wei and taking her back to Shanghai to work for a wealthy family who treated her like their own daughter. She would never say it out loud for fear that the spirits would hear her, but sometimes Mei-Lin wondered if Jing Wei's terrible loss hadn't in some ways given her a new life that was so much better than the one she was born to. Here, she'd be expected to toil until she was old enough to marry and have children, who would then join her in the fields. In life, Jing Wei was like the translation of her name – little bird. She wasn't strong enough for this struggle and physical hardship, so if missing her cousin was the price that Mei-Lin had to pay, then it was worth it to know that Jing Wei had the happiness she deserved.

Was it greedy of her to wonder if Uncle Cheung would bring her a gift on his visit? Once he'd bought her a T-shirt that had a bottle on the front that he'd proudly informed her was the famous American Coca-Cola drink. The bottle wasn't as pretty as a flower or a tree but the fabric was so soft that she'd worn it until it was so small it was no longer modest. It belonged to her sisters now. On another trip he brought her a hairclip that was surely the most beautiful butterfly in the world.

He promised that one day he would bring her shoes like the city girls wore. Imagine if he brought them today! Suddenly the can of water that she was scooping from the barrel outside seemed as light as a feather and she didn't even mind that her father ignored her as she took it back inside. She racked her brain to think what she could have done to have earned his displeasure but nothing came to mind. He must have slept badly or perhaps he had a headache. She'd bring him some leaf tea and perhaps that would soothe him. She just wished that she had some rice to boil with it, but there was only a tiny amount left in the bottom of the rice tub and that had to be kept for later in the day.

Chatter from her sisters filled the silence as she went about the rest of her morning chores. Just as she finished rebuilding the fire with twigs and leaves, there was a thundering noise outside the front door. It could only be the noise of the vehicle that Uncle Cheung drove, a burgundy red car that, he explained, was made in Korea and shipped all the way to Shanghai. Mei-Lin could have screamed with excitement but she did not want to displease her father even more, so instead she ushered her sisters back to the table where they waited until their parents had gone out to greet him.

In just a few moments they returned and Uncle Cheung was soon wrapping her in a tight embrace. For the thousandth time, she contemplated that she was so, so lucky to be related to such a kind and successful man.

'You grow taller and more beautiful every time I see you,

Mei-Lin,' he exclaimed as he embraced her. He turned to her sisters. 'And look at you two! Surely the most enchanting twins in the whole of China.'

Mei-Lin's sisters giggled with a mixture of shyness and pride. Uncle Cheung was right. Ling and Suyin were special. Born almost ten years after her, they had come into the world just months before the introduction of the one-child policy and in the year their beloved paramount leader Deng Xiaoping had become the ruler of all of China. Of course, her parents had been disappointed that neither of their new additions was a boy, but the pale-skinned beauty of these little blossoms had soon assuaged their sadness.

Uncle Cheung put down the large bag he was carrying and ushered them all to the table. 'Come, sit, sit. I have lovely things for all of you.'

Despite being desperate to find out what wonderful gift awaited her, Mei-Lin knew her manners. She quickly brought a bowl of leaf tea to the table and was rewarded with another hug from her uncle.

'Thank you, my niece, but we do not need to drink leaf tea today.' He reached into his bag and pulled out a large tin of fine green tea, the kind that they normally only shared on special occasions. 'We will be having this today. And in my car there is rice, a plump chicken and enough vegetables for a feast.'

Mei-Lin thought she might weep with joy. Suddenly all wistful thoughts of shoes were abandoned, pushed aside by the relief that they would all eat well tonight and for several days afterwards. This was truly a special day. She quickly made fresh tea for everyone and then settled on the floor between her mother and uncle. Her father, as always, sat in his seat a few feet away and Mei-Lin could see that although his dignity restrained his celebration and gratitude for the gifts, his eyes welled with emotion.

21

After refreshing his parched throat, Uncle Cheung reached into his bag once again.

'Now, for you two angels I have something especially pretty,' he told the little ones, then produced woollen hats, scarves and gloves that were the prettiest shade of pink Mei-Lin had ever seen. Her sisters shrieked with excitement, immediately grabbing them and pulling the hats on their heads.

'And I thought that these might keep those feet warm at night.'

Well, Mei-Lin wouldn't have been more surprised if he'd pulled rabbits from his bag. The two pairs of fluffy yellow slippers were like nothing she had ever seen before. Soft and pliable like socks, they looked like giant balls of fur and her sisters screamed once again with glee.

'And don't think that I've forgotten about my beautiful elder niece.'

Mei-Lin forgot to breathe for a few moments.

'For you I have many things, but first I must keep my promise with these.'

He handed her a box and when she opened it Mei-Lin gasped. Inside was the most exquisite pair of white shoes, with a small heel and a strap that crossed from one side to another.

Ignoring the cold, she immediately pulled off her thick socks, and slipped them on. They were perhaps just a little small, pinching her big toes, but she didn't care. Never had she owned something so pretty. If only Jing Wei were here to see them she would be so jealous.

Her eyes were so transfixed by her feet that it took a moment to realise Uncle Cheung was holding out a large pile of garments towards her.

One by one she unravelled and held them up. A dress made of pale blue silk embroidered with silver threads that glistened in the light. A white knitted cardigan with a belt that tied around the waist. Pale blue socks that would reach to her knees. And a large sliver hair clasp decorated with many little clear glass balls.

'Put them on, put them on!' her mother encouraged her, smiling for the first time in weeks.

Mei-Lin ducked behind the blanket that allowed them some privacy for washing and emerged looking like a completely different girl. Gone was the fifteen-year-old daughter of a peasant farmer and in her place was a beauty from a fairy tale. She took a deep breath to settle her racing heart and looked at her father for his reaction. To her astonishment, she saw a tear run down his face. It was a tear of happiness, she was sure. Finally she had pleased him and the thought just added to her joy. This day, this moment, was one that she knew she would remember for ever.

She was so busy watching the bottom of the dress float like a cloud when she twirled that she almost missed Uncle Cheung's words.

'Perfect. She will be the most beautiful girl in all of Shanghai.'

It took a moment for his pronouncement to register. Shanghai? She had never been there, and while she had dreams that one day she would visit the city, surely that would not be for many years. They barely had enough money to eat, never mind travel so many miles.

A loud clang interrupted her confusion and she realised that her father had dropped his tea bowl. She ran to pick it up, careful not to let the spilled liquid touch her new shoes.

The ferocity of his expression shocked her, and she was almost relieved when he turned to Cheung instead of focusing his wrath on her. 'We haven't told her yet!'

'My husband, be calm! He was not to know that and it must

be that the fault here is with us.' Her mother leapt to the defence of the brother who had been so kind and generous to them all.

'Mama?'

Her mother reached out and gently took her hand. 'Mei-Lin, you know that we love you so and that the thought of not waking with you every morning breaks our hearts, but the land has failed us this year and we will starve through the winter if we do not find another way to support ourselves. Uncle Cheung has found a job for you in Shanghai with a family that needs a girl to take care of their children. He has told them how well you tend to our little ones and they will pay excellent wages to you – enough to give you a good life and to send some back here to help us.'

'But . . . but . . . Baba?' She looked searchingly at her father, but he couldn't meet her eyes. Suddenly she understood. The moodiness, the subdued behaviour, the sadness, the rage – he knew he was sending her away and the grief was as plain as the tears that now filled his eyes.

Her father's pain was unbearable to her and she knew immediately that she must do something to make him feel better.

'Don't worry, Baba, I understand and I'm happy to do this for us.'

She saw her mother's face flood with relief and Uncle Cheung smile with approval. Yes, she was saying the right thing. All she had ever aspired to be was a dutiful daughter and now the time had come to prove that her loyalty to her family would never falter. She was just glad that her sisters were too busy revelling in their gifts to pay attention to the conversation because if she looked at them now she didn't think she could maintain her composure.

'You are indeed a credit to your parents, Mei-Lin. Let's eat

24

and then we will set off, so that we will be back in Shanghai by nightfall.'

'Today?'

How foolish of her not to grasp that this would happen immediately. Of course it had to. When the food that Uncle Cheung had brought today was done, there was no more to be had, so she must start earning money immediately.

As she washed the vegetables she saw that her hands were shaking and for the first time in weeks her stomach no longer gnawed with hunger. Fear had taken over.

Would she like it in the city? Could she really leave her family behind? Would they forget about her? Would she be lonely? Would the family she was going to really be kind and welcoming?

A voice in her head tried to push away the doubts. Of course they would be kind. Didn't Uncle Cheung say that he knew them personally and that they lived in a big house where she would sleep in her own bed? Her own bed! Imagine!

The thought made her feel a little better, but it was a sudden realisation of something far more wonderful that really calmed her fears and perhaps gave her just a glimmer of optimism about the huge change that was about to take place in her life.

She was going to Shanghai and that meant one of her biggest wishes would come true – she would once again see her beloved Jing Wei.

# THREE

*Stevie*
*Los Angeles, 1983*

Stevie ran her eye across the inside of the guitar case and made a mental calculation. There had to be at least twenty dollars in there – not bad for just a couple of hours. Even after she deducted the cost of the bus fare to Santa Monica, it was more than she would have earned in a day at her usual spot outside the Medical Center in Willowdale, twenty miles inland. There she was more likely to get a mouthful of abuse from a strung-out gangbanger than a dollar for her troubles.

She adjusted the tuning on the D-string on her guitar and broke into her favourite song of all time. Five years before, at the age of eleven, she'd shortened her real name Stephanie to Stevie in honour of her ultimate heroine Stevie Nicks. Now with her long, shaggy blond hair and huge brown eyes, she looked a little like her too. But the biggest similarity was her voice – sharp yet haunting, rich yet vulnerable, sweet but with an unmissable sexy edge.

Two new romantic girls walked by, both with blue, asymmetric, razor-cut hair bouncing against the frills around the collars of their white shirts. One of them threw a few dimes into the case just as Stevie reached the chorus of Fleetwood Mac's 'Dreams'.

Eyes shut, lost in the vibe of the song, she barely registered their approval. After fading out the last few bars she checked her watch. Six o'clock. There was no point going home yet, so she might as well keep going and get the last bus at eleven. Her mother's cleaning shift at the school didn't finish until midnight and there were still plenty of shoppers on the streets, most looking slightly frazzled by the hunt for Christmas gifts. Living in Los Angeles was definitely a bonus when it came to busking. If this was New York she'd have frozen her ass off by now.

A group of older women approached, heading in the direction of the mall. Too over-dressed and highly groomed to be Californian, they were definitely tourists, and given that their make-up was impeccable, their hair huge and their shoulder pads the approximate width of a linebacker, she guessed they were from somewhere in the South. She immediately broke into the opening lines of Patsy Cline's 'Crazy'. It was always a winner. The whole group actually stopped to listen, then every single one of them dropped some cash in the case before moving on, wrapped in the blanket of nostalgia that came free with every verse. It was Stevie's mother Ella's favourite song, although it was difficult to understand why, given that it made her think about the man who'd knocked her up twice and then went out for a packet of cigarettes sixteen years ago, never to return.

For men like that there should be a song called 'I Should Have Killed You When I had The Chance, You Piece of Crap.' Perhaps she should write it, and maybe then one of the music companies she'd sent a million tapes to would listen to her.

In the meantime, she'd stick to crowd-pleasers that brought in the dollars. As she strummed the intro to 'Up Where We

27

Belong' she realised that she had almost enough to buy her mother the new coat she'd been looking at in the JC Penney catalogue. Ella would be thrilled and it was about time she got some payback. It had been years since her mother had bought anything for herself, spending every dime she earned on keeping Stevie and her brother Matt fed and clothed. Now Matt had gone off to college on a basketball scholarship, Ella was bursting with pride and working double shifts to supplement Matt's night job at McDonald's. Between them, they were determined to get him through the four years and into a job in sport or, even better, the holy grail of a career in the NBA.

Stevie was glad that Ella's hopes and dreams for her offspring's success were all on the extra-wide, athletic shoulders of her brother because it was highly unlikely that her daughter would deliver any heady acclaim.

All Stevie had ever wanted to do was write songs, play guitar and sing.

That was it. Growing up, while other girls dreamt of being a princess, Stevie dreamt about being Carole King or Janis Joplin. When her friends were listening to ELO or Kool and the Gang, she was listening to Carly Simon. When her peers were fantasising about boys, she was fantasising about being Debbie Harry.

Her musical appreciation crossed all genres, styles and artists. At any point her record player could have heavy rock, country and even occasionally classical on there. Music was her life, but she was under no illusion about where that path would take her. Everyone knew that it was almost impossible to break into the industry, especially for a girl like her – no contacts, no money and too young to gig in bars and clubs. It hadn't stopped her sending cassettes of her songs to every music company listed in the business directory at the local library, but she didn't hold out much hope of a reply. If she was being perfectly honest, obscurity wasn't the end of the world. Burning drive and ambition just weren't in her genetic make-up. She was pretty chilled about life and just took it day by day. As long as she had a guitar and something to say in a song, she'd happily busk away the years, perhaps travelling as she did it to see the world. She'd heard Europe was cool and one day she'd go there. Busking in Paris in the spring – wasn't that the kind of thing that would give her the material for a dozen new songs?

'You're good.'

Stevie looked up to see a young girl standing in front of her. At least she thought it was a girl. The androgynous apparition looked like a cross between Ziggy Stardust and Steve Tyler from Aerosmith. Only a slash across a white T-shirt that showed a hint of breast pointed Stevie in the female direction.

'Thanks.'

'But do you always play that kinda shit?'

'Nope, I can play any kinda shit you like as long as you've got a dollar for the case.' Stevie smiled without malice or irritation. In truth, she was more than a little fascinated by this strange, confrontational creature in front of her. That kind of individual expression – the clothes, the make-up, the attitude – was definitely some kind of kick-ass statement.

Ziggy Tyler shrugged and flicked over a quarter. 'It's all I got. How about just one verse and a chorus?'

Before she could apply conscious thought or intent, Stevie's fingers took on a life of their own, cranking out the intro to Jimi Hendrix's 'Voodoo Child'. It had taken her months to learn it, and another few months until she felt she could do it justice, but she had never played it before in public. She had absolutely no idea why now seemed like the right time.

Androgynous chick got value for money. Eyes closed, transported to another place, it was more than five minutes before Stevie sang the last line and brought the guitar to stillness.

'Fucking wow! That was amazing,' said her audience of one. 'Look, I don't know if you're interested, but I'm in a band and we're looking for a singer.'

'That sings that kinda shit?' Stevie teased.

'Yep, that's about it. I'm Cally. The band's name is The Bitch of Thorns.'

'Classy.'

Cally ignored the gentle sarcasm.

'Thanks. We think so, too.'

There was a momentary silence as Stevie weighed up the conversation so far. It was intriguing, that was for sure, but being in a band had never been her thing. She just wanted to play her own stuff and let her music develop in its own way, stay individual, no pressure. She had no interest in the inevitable drama of the whole big group thing.

'What happened to your last singer?' Stevie asked.

'Overdose.'

'Not exactly setting out to win me over here, are you?'

It was Cally's turn to smile. 'OK, so it's not the best reference. But we're good. We play alternative rock stuff – you know, everything from Bowie to The Clash.'

Stevie knew who The Clash were – an English band with a really distinct sound. Without conscious thought, she picked out the first few bars of 'Rock The Casbah'.

'Now you're just showing off.'

'You're right.' Stevie knew she should pass, say no, move on, but it was cool to talk to someone with a real interest in music.

'How many are in the band?'

'Three. Drummer, bass and I play lead. We need a really

30

good singer. I can hold a tune but I'm not stupid enough to think that I've got a voice that can sell albums. You do.'

OK, so the flattery was nice – especially coming from such an unlikely source – but the fact was she didn't want to be in a band and this chat was starting to take up a little too much money time. Ella's new JC Penney coat wasn't in the bag yet and there were only a few more hours of earning potential before the shops would start to shut and she'd have to head for the bus stop. Time to wrap it up and politely decline.

'And we've got a record company that's interested.'

The last sentence cut through her thoughts like one of the Jimi Hendrix riffs she'd just nailed.

'Really?'

'Yeah. But they say we need a new lead singer on account of the last one being dead.'

'I can see their point.'

Cally shrugged and kicked at some imaginary crack on the boardwalk.

'Look, just come and listen to us. We're rehearsing tonight over at the drummer's dad's place. It's only ten minutes from here.'

It was a tough call. She'd be giving up probably another twenty dollars and how did she know this girl wasn't a complete weirdo who would totally waste her time or, worse, mug her for her busking cash and leave her half dead in an alley?

'I have a bus to catch at eleven.'

'I'll make sure you're back at the bus station by then.'

Stevie scooped the money out of the case, replaced it with her guitar, and then snapped the clasps shut. Decision made.

They walked in silence along 3rd, slung a right onto Washington Avenue, then a left on 7th. A hundred yards along, Cally dipped into a doorway under a sign that said, 'O'Neil's Hot Legs Bar'.

Stevie paused warily. 'I thought you said we were going to someone's dad's place.'

'This is it. He's the "O'Neil". We practise in the basement. The place stinks of beer, your feet will stick to the carpet and there are entirely too many nipples on show, but the acoustics are fucking wild.'

There was no denying that her safety senses were tingling, but in a way it made sense. In fact, if this was straight up maybe this band were a bit more organised than she'd first thought.

A few moments later she realised that was definitely the case. They descended down a warped set of old wooden stairs to the beer cellar and the first thing she saw, in amongst the huge steel kegs, crates of soft drinks and boxes of spirits, was a spectacular set of red Pearl drums that looked almost identical to a poster ad she'd seen featuring Chester Thompson, the guy who played with Genesis. Behind this set of drums was hair. Lots and lots of shaking, flame-coloured hair, from which protruded two hands, clasping drumsticks that were being struck together in some kind of frantic rhythm.

'Dixie!'

No break in the rhythm.

Louder this time. 'Dixie!'

Finally there was silence, and one stick was used to flick the hair back, revealing a startlingly pretty face so pale it could have been carved from porcelain and framed with piercing blue eyes and black painted lips. The image was somewhere between a pageant queen and the return of the undead.

'What?'

'This is Stevie. She's a singer.'

'Cool.'

The face retreated back into its red bush and the tapping of the sticks recommenced.

Cally rolled her eyes. 'She's a chick of few words.'

'I got that impression.'

'Take a seat over there and let me get set up. Wanna drink?' Cally gestured to two crates of Bud which had been transformed into a bench by placing a thick slab of foam on the top.

'It's comfortable, but if you start to itch it's probably better to stand.'

It took Stevie a few seconds to realise Cally was messing with her and a few seconds more to realise that she liked that. Even if this whole band thing wasn't a goer for her, it wouldn't hurt to have a friend out this way. In fact, it wouldn't hurt to have a friend, period. Since she'd dropped out of school, she hadn't really kept in touch with any of the old crowd. What was the point? They were all into hanging out at the mall, spending money she didn't have and checking out boys she wasn't interested in. All she wanted to do was to play music.

'Hey. Who's the new bitch?'

The voice was a twisted spike of suspicion and aggression, surprising since it came from the mouth of one of the most stunning girls Stevie had ever encountered. Tall, tall, tall. This Amazonian looked like she'd walked straight off the cover of the Victoria's Secret catalogue. It was impossible not to stare at her unfeasibly high breasts, visible through a shirt held together by nothing but a knot, at her tiny waist. Her tanned stomach was almost concave and now that she'd turned to face Cally, Stevie could see that bongo drums could be played on her denim-clad ass. She made everyone in the room look average. Hell, next to her, Cindy Crawford looked average.

'Enough, Lou, play nice. This is Stevie and she's here to check us out. She's a singer.'

Lou spun round to face Stevie, green eyes blazing. 'So sing.'

There was a pause as the two women faced off, one confrontational, the other making no effort to hide her amusement. So this was the last member of the band. Stevie knew her kind – she'd come up against cheerleaders with attitude her whole life, so it would take more than a dose of bitchiness to get under her skin. On the other hand, though, she sure didn't need this shit when she could be out earning money. Sliding off the makeshift seat, she smiled at Cally as she pulled her bag on to her shoulder and picked up her guitar.

'I can see why the last singer checked out.' She shrugged. 'Cally, it was good to meet you but I've got some place to be.'

The only thing standing between her and the door was Cindy Crawford, the psycho bassist. Stevie had handled worse. The whisper was so quiet that the others barely heard what she said as she strolled past.

'Nice meeting ya, Lou,' she whispered sweetly. 'Oh and, bitch, if you're at the store anytime soon, you might wanna shop for some people skills.'

As she went to take the first step up out of the basement she realised her path was blocked by a tall, dark guy wearing a floor-length leather coat and a menacing expression. Probably somewhere around thirty, the steely flint in his eyes and hard set of his jaw made him look like a character in a photo with numbers running across the bottom. Three options sprang to mind: drug dealer, pimp, hood. So much for not putting herself in a dangerous position. If this was an episode of *Cagney and Lacey*, the detectives would spend the next hour notifying her mother that her beloved daughter had been found in a dumpster. Then they'd retrace her last steps before solving the case with the aid of that large group of Patsy Cline-lovin' tourists from the Deep South.

'Going somewhere?' New York accent. Drug dealer now

rose to option number one – unlikely that he'd pimp or steal this far from his territory – a theory that she realised was based on the in-depth criminal knowledge she'd gleaned from watching *Hill Street Blues*.

Her demeanour betrayed no nerves whatsoever.

'Home.'

Stand off. The next few seconds felt a whole lot longer, until the drug-dealing/pimp/hood stuck out his hand. 'I'm Jude Castigan.'

Did drug-dealing/pimp/hoods generally introduce themselves with a smile like that? Stevie decided that civility was the route to go and shook his hand. 'Stevie Ross.'

'Pleased to meet you, Stevie Ross. And don't worry about Lou,' he added. 'Being a bitch is her favourite sport.'

Out of the corner of her eye she saw Lou toss her hair back in fury, then go and pick up a gleaming jet-black Steinberger bass that Stevie had noticed hanging on the wall. It was the new style of bass, sleek, sexy lines and no head. What she'd give to play around on it for a while, but somehow she didn't think Lou was the type to share her toys.

'I brought her here, Jude. You ought to hear her sounds, man, she's got a fucking incredible voice.' Cally turned to Stevie again, her expression apologetic. 'Look, I'm sorry. I know this ain't starting off good but stay a bit longer. Just listen to us, and if you don't like what you hear then you can walk. I'll even get you a cab to the bus station.'

Stevie hesitated. This was a complete bust but she had to admit she was still a little intrigued. And besides, short of tackling this guy out of the way, she still had no idea how she was going to get past him.

'Oh and by the way, that's my Uncle Jude – he's in A&R for Spin Records.'

Spin Records. Stevie had heard of them. In fact, she was sure she'd included them in the last lot of demos she'd sent out.

Amongst others, they represented Della Voight and Meteor Blue. Della had the best soul voice on the Billboard charts at the moment and Meteor Blue were still hot even though their stadium days were probably behind them. Stevie had seen them once, supporting Aerosmith at the Bowl.

OK, so this put a whole new spin on things. *Cagney and Lacey* could probably rest easy, and she was no longer concerned about evading possible death at the hands of a drug dealer/pimp/hood. And besides, what the hell were the chances of this happening? Just a few hours earlier she'd been happily channelling Stevie Nicks and now she was in front of a real-life A&R exec. The gods of stupidity would be lining up to salute her if she didn't at least stick around to see where this went. She checked her watch. 'OK, but another half hour then I'm outta here,' she replied.

Cally grinned, Dixie started knocking out a beat with her sticks again and Lou kicked a case of empty bottles. Stevie pretty much figured that was reflective of the dynamic of this band right there. The cool one, the introvert and the crazy-ass bitch who would end up doing life for first-degree murder.

A screech of feedback blasted from the Marshall amp in the corner as Cally flicked the juice on for her guitar. Dixie counted in the intro and Lou did some weird combination on her bass that sounded freaking awesome. They were barely into the first verse of Bowie's 'Scary Monsters' when Stevie realised they were good. Not perfect, but definitely good. Cally was right about her voice – she could hold a tune but it didn't have that memorable quality they'd need to make them stand out. Dixie was fierce on the drums and Lou was shit hot on the strings. They definitely had a good vibe. Before she realised it, she was harmonising with Cally, who then let her vocals fade into the background, giving Stevie full control.

Shit, did it work.

Even Lou dropped the snarl down from evil to just minor fury.

Jude's expression didn't change and his body language remained inscrutable right up until they faded out the last line, when a glimmer of a smile played on his lips.

'Not bad.'

'Not fucking bad? It was fucking sensational!' Cally bit back. 'That sounded fan-fucking-tastic, Stevie.'

Stevie turned to the others to gauge their reaction. Dixie was nodding her head in agreement while Lou was intently focused on tuning her bass and refused to meet Stevie's gaze. It would almost be worth joining this band just to piss her off.

'D'you wanna think about it?' Cally asked, her words infused with the unmistakable sound of hope.

Stevie turned to Jude. 'What do you think?'

Shit, he was attractive. Why was she just noticing this?

'I think it's raw and the harmonies are a mess . . .'

'Wow, there goes the ego. Hard crowd.' Stevie put it out there with a smile. His verdict was correct, though, and she kinda liked the fact that he wasn't bullshitting them.

' . . . but it could definitely be bankable.'

There was a loud snort of disapproval from Lou that everyone ignored.

'It's up to you, but I think you should give it a shot. You've got somewhere to rehearse, you could sound great, all you need is some really hot material and you could have something.'

'I have that. I write my own stuff,' Stevie blurted, then immediately regretted it. Why the hell had she said that? That was *her* music, to be used on the million-to-one, pigs-might-fly, only-if-there's-a-blue-moon chance that she ever managed to get a record deal. There was no way she was sharing her songs with two girls she met an hour ago and one who looked like she'd take a hit out on her at any moment.

No fricking way. Not for anything. Time to get out of there and hit the road. She'd already wasted enough time and, much as it had been a blast, it was time to move. This went against everything she saw for her future. She'd never imagined herself as part of an ensemble thing, travelling around in a van, forced to spend day and night with other people. Since the moment she'd left school she'd been a free spirit, busking around, only herself to answer to, no pressure other than making enough cash to help Ella out with the bills. That was her scene – this definitely wasn't.

'Well, look, it's up to you. But if you can put something together in the next couple of weeks, I'll let you in on a showcase I'm doing for the board at Spin. They're looking for a new rock act to go up against guys like Decomp and Nuclear Fear. I don't think it's where you're at, but it's good to get the exposure anyway.'

'Yes!' Cally punched the air. 'I've been trying to get in front of these guys for months. You'd think being related to someone in the business would've come with perks before now.'

'If your lead singers didn't keep committing suicide then maybe it would have,' Jude bit back.

Whoah! 'There was more than one?' Stevie exclaimed.

Cally shrugged sheepishly. 'Two. But the first one had issues long before she met us and we were never sure it was deliberate.'

'This offer gets more attractive by the minute.' Jude pushed back his sleeve and checked his watch. Damn, he really was good looking. 'I've got somewhere to be. Cally, call me, let me know what goes down.'

He'd barely disappeared from view when Cally started with the persuasion.

'Did you hear that? It would be crazy not to give this a shot. I know this has all come out of nowhere, but come on, a showcase. People would fucking kill for that.'

'Cally, I don't want to mess with you but this isn't my thing. I'm cool with just doing my own stuff and seeing where that goes.'

Stevie was just about to pack up her guitar again when Lou gave her opinion on the situation.

'Fucking bitch. She's not that great anyway.' Lou dinged the bell at the top of the petulance scale. Stevie would never understand what happened to her at that moment. She would never be able to explain what clicked in her mind. And she would never be sure if it would turn out to be the biggest mistake of her life.

The guitar returned to its spot on the floor.

And she never did make that bus home.

# FOUR

*Raine*
*New York, 1984*

There was a rustling noise from behind the pile of garbage bags in the doorway and Raine had to stop herself from screaming as a rat shot out across the front of her shoes. This was such a bad idea. On the scale of bad ideas it was right up there with choosing to study economics and allowing one of the jocks to give her a hickie at the school prom. He'd automatically taken it as permission to proceed further and she'd had to knee him in the balls thirty seconds later when he'd slipped his hand into her bra.

If she'd hated that crowd of jerks at school before, it escalated to a whole new level of mutual loathing after that. Nothing she couldn't handle, though. She just kept telling herself that they'd still be living in their parents' dens and working the drive-through in five years' time, but she'd be out of Brooklyn and on her way to bigger things. And as soon as she decided what that was, she'd get right onto it.

Anyway, the hassle with the jocks was kid's stuff compared to this current situation. Actually, *that* was the problem. Her dad, her mother, Ricco – everyone insisted on treating her like a kid and she damn well wasn't.

Well, who was the kid now? She was in Manhattan, on her own, and apart from the minor inconvenience of the rat variety, she was doing just fine.

Getting the clothes had been easy. Her friend Angelica's older sister was a wannabe model and the only other girl she knew who hit the height chart at almost six foot tall. She was away this weekend with a guy who owned a sportswear store, fully prepared to put out in return for some catalogue work. The timing had been perfect. On Raine's behalf, Angelica had raided her sister's wardrobe for a black, baby-doll halter dress, a silver lamé jacket and sparkly silver high heels that were currently giving her vertigo. In return, Angelica had wanted to come along for the ride, but Raine had refused. She was going to be in enough shit if she got caught, without incurring the wrath of Angelica's parents, too.

Getting here had gone without a hitch. No one recognised her on the bus, and the Jamaican cab driver that picked her up at the station and dropped her at the end of the street didn't look at her twice, not even when she counted out the fare in dollars and dimes. He did mutter 'whore' under his breath when she didn't tip him, though.

It had all gone according to plan.

But now what?

If she stayed in this doorway any longer she was going to end up with a serious disease.

A bit more forward planning and a tetanus shot might have been a good idea.

A spectacularly long white limo pulled up across the road and she watched Ricco come down the few steps at the entrance and reach forward to open the door, ignoring the long line of people waiting behind the red velvet rope to his left-hand side.

A few of them protested, a few of them booed, but most of them just watched in awe as Dimitri Krakov, the infamous Russian dancer turned actor, and Leeane Star, the notoriously decadent supermodel, emerged from the back seat and strutted into the club.

Reincarnation.

Yep, she'd given in to the notion that had been eating at her since that day in the diner almost exactly a year ago – she'd come to see exactly what Ricco did on the nights he worked at the club. Now she'd been standing in a garbage-filled doorway for over an hour and what had she learned? That he looked even more incredible in his black suit and slicked-back hair than he did in his uniform – and that was a mighty high standard to surpass.

The line of people waiting to get in stretched for about thirty yards along the side of the building, a former cinema that had been transformed into the hottest club in town. From what she could gather, it seemed like two very different sets of people gained immediate admission. Every few minutes a flash town car or limo would pull up and impossibly glamorous people would sweep straight in. And at the other end of the scale, anyone dressed in wacky, outrageous or borderline-pornographic outfits sailed right through, too.

Two guys wearing nothing but G-strings, roller skates and dog collars. A woman sporting a red rubber suit with a ten-foot-long tail. A guy wearing some kind of leather skirt and nothing else except a knitting needle through each nipple. A gaggle of girls wearing plastic dresses that were completely transparent, all of them with their pubic hair dyed a different colour. Raine would never have believed such a world existed. This lot would definitely send her mother screaming to the chapel to pray.

The sight of Ricco looking at those girls, sometimes even laughing with them, made her teeth clench. Yeah, she realised she was acting like a jealous wacko, but it was just so damn tough to watch.

So. Now what? What would Madonna do? She sure as hell wouldn't be standing here when the guy she was hopelessly in love with was only a few feet away, completely oblivious to her presence.

She was mid-deliberation when a buzz-cut dude in a trench coat, who was not a stacked heel away from seven foot tall emerged from the club and whispered in Ricco's ear. Ricco smiled, nodded, then turned and headed inside.

Noooooo. Shit. Shit. Shit.

OK, so the option of standing here all night watching him had now been kicked out of the park, so her choices were down to two: go home or find a way to get inside and check out what was happening.

After all the effort she'd put in to make it this far, going home wasn't going to cut it. And anyway, the whole Ricco thing aside, she was desperate to see more. There was something about this scene that totally fascinated her and got her adrenalin going. Eighteen years old and she'd just seen her first pierced nipple. Maybe she really did need to get out more.

But how was she going to get into the club? She had thirty dollars, the entire contents of her babysitting fund, tucked into her little silver clutch purse, but she had no idea if that would be enough. Problem number two, she wanted to get in right now, not wait in the queue for the rest of the night. Problem number three, if Ricco saw her he'd go nuts. Seriously nuts.

And number four ... OK, there wasn't really a number four, other than the fact that standing here waiting for some act of divine intervention wasn't going to help, so she tentatively stepped out to cross the road and ... Shit, what was that? What just happened? And why was she lying flat on her back with a ... God, her head hurt.

'Are you OK? Oh fuck! Fuck! Giles, you fucking cretin, I told you to look where you were fucking going. Can you speak, sweetie? Sweetie, can you speak?'

Raine tried but no words would come. However, it was nothing to do with the fact that she was now flat on her ass having come off worse in an altercation with a ... a ... oh my God, it was a Rolls Royce. A huge, gleaming, gold Rolls Royce. She'd only ever seen those in movies.

That wasn't even the weirdest thing about this situation. Nope, that was reserved for the fact that the female kneeling in front of her was Tala DiVinci, Hollywood star and renowned bad girl, and the Giles she was screaming at was Giles Corcoran. Giles Corcoran! Raine had watched him a hundred times in a string of Mafia movies that had broken all box office records. He was a legend. A total legend. Only ...

He didn't look particularly iconic at the moment. His floppy brown hair was greasy and dishevelled, his eyes were bloodshot and he was so skeletal he could clearly do with some of Isa's roast beef sandwiches. As for his white suit, he looked like he'd slept in it. For several days. In a ditch.

'What the faaaaaaack ... ?' It sounded so strange in his slurred English accent.

Thankfully, Tala was still at her side. 'You're OK, sweetie. We're going to make sure that you're OK.'

'Can I help you there Miss DiVinci?'

Raine squinted open one eye and realised that the new voice in the picture was coming from the giant at the front door.

'Please, Vincent. Can you just get this poor girl inside and we'll see if we need to call an ambulance. She took quite a hit.

And then perhaps you can have the car moved and check that no one over there in the queue has a camera. Don't want photos of this turning up on page six of the *Post*.'

Raine curtailed her outrage that her rescuer was contemplating negative press coverage despite the fact that she might be lying here with internal bleeding. Temporary inability to form a cohesive sentence aside, she just felt a little dazed, but as she knew from several cases she'd watched on *General Hospital*, you could never tell with these things.

Before she could worry about it she was swept up and carried past the crowd at the door. Yes! This wasn't how she'd considered making an entrance but she was in. She closed her eyes again and resumed the fainting appearance. Acting had never been her thing, but on the strength of this performance perhaps there was a career in it for her. It didn't even cross her mind to be scared. This was the kind of excitement she'd spent far too long dreaming about while she languished in Brooklyn, lying on her bed on a Friday and Saturday night wondering what Ricco was doing, missing him so much she thought she would go crazy.

As soon as they passed the threshold of the club, Raine felt her body start to vibrate to the thud, thud, thud of the music. And the smell. Strangely it wasn't unpleasant – a peculiar mix of body heat, cigarettes, perfume and some kind of incense. The movement changed and she realised that she was being carried up stairs. OK, so now might be the time to bring this to an end. She'd made it inside and, potential internal bleeding aside, she was perfectly fine. Just as she was about to speak up, they entered a room and giant hulk guy laid her down on a soft, furry surface.

Gradually opening her eyes, Raine saw that they'd entered a deep red cavern with a huge bed in the middle. A bedroom? In a club? And it was like no other bedroom she'd ever seen before. The ceiling was tented with silky black fabric and the walls were the same but in red. Over at the opposite side of the room a mirrored coffee table sat in front of a pink leather sofa.

As giant guy backed away, leaving her on the scarlet fur bed cover, Tala DiVinci immediately appeared at her side again.

'Sweetie, can you hear me? Are you OK?'

Stevie nodded as she slowly pushed herself up to a sitting position. 'I'm fine. I think.'

The relief in the air was palpable. 'Oh, thank fuck for that. Honey, you gave us a real fright there.'

A dull ache was working its way down from Raine's hip to her toes. The car hadn't caused serious damage but it had definitely given her a glancing blow. She had a feeling the pain was being anaesthetised by a combination of adrenalin and excitement and that it would hurt like a bitch tomorrow.

'I thought Giles was going to spend another night in the cells.' Tala was still talking and now that her face was just inches away, Raine could see that she was both spectacularly beautiful and spectacularly wasted. Her eyes were red-rimmed and glistening, her nose was slightly inflamed at the end, and unless she was wearing a very unusual perfume, she smelled like she was heavily tanked up too.

Yet her expression and voice came off as almost maternal.

'How can we help you, sweetie? Is there someone we can call for you?' Sure, it was the voice of someone who was on the wrong side of the bottom of a bottle, but either Tala DiVinci was genuinely concerned or she was a better actress than her appearances in the cheeky comedies *Action Woman* 1 through to 6 had shown.

Raine thought the question through. If Pat O'Donnell got a call to say that his beloved princess was in a Manhattan nightclub instead of at a sleepover with her best friend, he'd be down here in under an hour with the whole NYPD behind him, then she'd spend the next decade confined to her bedroom.

'Honestly, I'm OK. I just want to … to … go find my friends. They're in the club somewhere. I was … erm … going to meet them when you knocked me over.'

In the background, Giles Corcoran groaned. Raine pushed herself up and saw that he was now sprawled on the leather sofa in front of a huge red curtain that stretched from one wall to the other. She realised, too, that he was curled over six long lines of white powder that had appeared on the coffee table, chopping into them with what looked like a gold razor blade.

Tala, obviously satisfied that Raine wasn't going to snuff it in the next five minutes, stood up with a languorous stretch and staggered slightly as she went over to join Giles. On the way, she stopped at a mirrored bar that sat against one wall and grabbed a large silver wine bucket containing a couple of bottles of champagne and two long-stemmed glasses. She plonked them down on the coffee table. Giles paid no attention to her at all until she took a hundred dollar bill that he was holding between his teeth, deftly rolled it up and snorted one of the lines in a smooth, almost elegant movement. It was difficult for Raine to process the fact that this wasn't a scene from a movie. She was definitely there, she was definitely in a room with Tala and Giles, they were definitely off their faces on liquor and booze, and there was definitely a huge tank of a guy standing at the door, waiting for further instructions. Most bizarrely of all, the three of them seemed to have completely forgotten she was there.

Eventually, after making two lines of the white stuff disappear, Tala waved away the incredible hulk, 'Thank you, Vincent, but I think we're fine now. Tell Jason …'

At that moment the door swung open and in walked a short

47

Asian man with a pencil-thin moustache, wearing a full tuxedo and a top hat and carrying a silver cane.

'Did I just hear my name mentioned, my darlings?'

He moved over to greet Tala and Giles with air kisses and screeches of welcome. Raine watched the whole thing in silence, unsure whether to stay, go, or just blend into the background and hope no one noticed her. She knew who this guy was. Since Ricco had come to work here, she'd scoured the newspapers looking for any mention of Reincarnation, and Jason Tang's name was always at the centre of every story. The son of a former Chinese envoy to the US, he'd caused major controversy back in his homeland by staying on in New York after his family had returned to Beijing, something only made possible because his father had pulled strings with his visa. Now he owned Reincarnation and several other businesses in Manhattan, and he had a reputation for being as flamboyant as he was ruthless. The business community treated him with suspicion, but despite several investigations his affairs appeared to be squeaky clean. Jason Tang, the papers claimed, was untouchable. Her father said he was a crook. Shit, if he found out Ricco worked here they'd have to put Pat in restraints for his own good.

'And who is this little poppet?' Jason was staring at her now. 'Well, isn't this just the perfect thing to make a dick hard?'

Raine gasped at his words. Clearly his mouth didn't match up to those squeaky-clean standards. For the first time since she'd set off tonight, she had a twinge of . . . what? It wasn't fear. It was more of a slight concern that she could have got herself into a situation she couldn't handle.

She pushed the thought to the back of her mind. She could do this. All it needed was a bit of smarts and her brains hadn't failed her yet.

'Behave, Jason, she isn't for playing with. Giles almost

fucking killed her with the car so we brought her in with us.'
And shall I have her removed now that we can clearly see she's
still alive?'

Raine's hackles rose. So far she'd been used as a racetrack by
rats, frozen, knocked down and then carried up here like a lump
of wood, and she still had absolutely no idea what Ricco was
doing. Now some arrogant little shit was dismissing her as
though she was a piece of crap. Yes, he was the arrogant little
shit who owned the place. And she was, technically, too young
to be here. And she hadn't paid to get in. But still . . .

She pushed herself off the bed and took a step towards the
door.

'I'm just going to go . . . '

'Ooooh, it talks. And so tall, too. Uncle Jason likes them like
that.'

Eew, this guy was seriously creepy.

'Don't go, dear, the entertainment is just about to start.
Come here, my darling, and have a little drinkie with us.'

He plopped himself down on the sofa next to Giles, who was
midway through hoovering up another line. Tala was lying on
the thick red carpet now, her eyes glistening even brighter, with
pupils that covered almost her entire retina. 'Who's going up
tonight?' she murmured, pressing a button on the table that acti-
vated a mechanism at the side of the curtains. Silently and
smoothly, they parted, allowing Jason to turn and peer out of
the window at something of interest down below. 'We've a new
exotic bird. Arrived here this morning and she's very keen to
get ahead.'

For the first time, he addressed Raine directly, 'Now come
on, my little chicken, don't be afraid.'

He patted the space beside him on the seat and Raine cringed
inside. Unless she was going to tackle Vincent the tank to the

ground and step over him to get to the door, she had no option but to comply. Suddenly she had a longing to be back in Angelica's room, gossiping and watching reruns of *Magnum PI*.

With unsteady steps she made it over to the sofa and experienced a jolt of surprise as she looked out of the window. As her disorientation lifted, she could see exactly what they were talking about.

They were obviously in a room that had been constructed on the gallery level of the old cinema. To her left she could see at least a dozen other rooms like this, to her right just one or two – it was hard to tell. Some had the curtains drawn, some had the windows open, some were in total darkness. Thirty feet below them, there was a sea of thousands of heads, all bobbing up and down to the thudding beat, their arms raised in some sort of frantic, mass homage.

But it was the action on the stage about a hundred feet in front of them that made her eyes widen and her heart beat just a little bit faster.

There was a huge wooden cross, at least twenty feet high, and strapped to it was a naked black girl, her eyes closed, her mouth wide open as if screaming to the heavens, her body painted with streaks of white. As Raine watched silently, the cross was hoisted upwards towards the elaborately painted black and gold ceiling.

Tala snorted up another line of coke then crawled over to press another button at the edge of the wall. The window automatically slid back, assaulting them with a ferocious blast of noise and humidity.

'UP, UP, UP, UP!' the crowd chanted, like some kind of religious mass of madness. There was an unexpected sound beside her and she turned to see Giles, still slouched on the sofa but eyes fixed on the human sacrifice, not even attempting to conceal the huge bulge that had appeared under the zipper of his trousers.

Neither Jason nor Tala reacted with any surprise. Instead, Tala smiled slowly and moved towards him, pulling herself up on top of him like a feline slowly pouncing on her pray.

Oh frigging hell. Frigging. Hell. Every one of Raine's senses was screaming at her to leave, yet she remained absolutely motionless, paralysed by a strange combination of shock, fear and fascination. In the scale of shocking sexual and erotic behaviour, this blew the whole jock/hickie thing right out of the water.

She watched wordlessly as Tala slid her dress up, then straddled Giles's hips. He reached up and brought her face down to his, kissing her with an intense ferocity. His hands slid down, massaging her breasts through the sheer fabric, until eventually he tore it down and she shuddered with pleasure. He licked one nipple first, then the other. Tala moaned, before grabbing his hair and pulling his head back, allowing her to kiss him again. Only when the noise from outside became deafening did they turn their gaze to the girl on the cross in front of them. It was like some kind of real-life porn flick and they were definitely getting off on it.

The most bizarre thing was that no one seemed to think it was in any way odd or strange. Just your normal, everyday movie stars making out in a room overlooking a warped biblical scene, while being watched by a club owner who seemed to find the whole thing mildly amusing.

This was seriously messed up. And yet . . . Raine couldn't run, didn't want to. In fact, she was feeling a tingling in her stomach that she'd only ever felt when Ricco was around. No other guy had ever done anything for her. Eighteen years old and still a virgin. Not even a decent feel or a hand job to show for her years. Yet here she was in a full-scale erotic scene and – creepy guy aside – she was finding it strangely hot.

She took the glass of champagne that Jason was holding out to her and threw it back in one go.

'That's more like it,' he purred. 'Now come sit here with me and watch the show. Uncle Jason doesn't bite.'

Raine had a very strong feeling that he probably did.

'I'm a watcher, not a fucker. Isn't that right, Vincent?'

The guy at the door nodded silently.

'It's all far too unhygienic for my tastes. Vincent, you can get back to the front door now and make sure none of those unbearable yuppy types are getting in. Send someone up in half an hour to escort me back downstairs.'

Half an hour. She could do this. Raine picked up another glass and took a large gulp from that too, feeling the fizz go straight to her head and make it spin in a warm, fuzzy way.

She knew that she should probably be afraid, yet of all the strange emotions she was feeling, fear wasn't one of them. What could happen to her here? It wasn't like they were going to harm her physically and she believed Jason when he said he wouldn't touch her. Best thing was to let this play out and just go with the flow. Shit, she was going to have one mad-assed crazy story to tell Angelica tomorrow.

'Up. Up. Oh yes, baby, she's beautiful. Oh my God . . . ' Tala was still straddling Giles, his fingers now lost under the hem of her dress, his hand moving backwards and forwards while her cries ascended in volume in direct relation to the noise of the crowd outside. Raine watched as the cross slowly continued its rise to the skies, the audience chanting more feverishly with every pull. The girl's head was lolling from side to side now – either in pain or ecstasy, it was hard to tell – her mouth echoing the chants of the room. Up. Up. Up.

Jason took a small gold case out of his inside pocket, extracted a tiny spoon and inhaled the powder on the end. He offered it to her. No way. She'd never done drugs. Never. They were as easy to get a hold of as apple pie at school but it just wasn't her thing. But then, neither was hanging out in a New York nightclub at 1 a.m. with movie stars and club owners.

What. A. Frigging. Blast.

A tiny urge of temptation took her by surprise.

Hadn't Tala taken some coke? And if she was going to try it, shouldn't it be here when it was guaranteed to be decent stuff? Her dad had drummed into her time and time again that street drugs were cut with all kinds of garbage, but this had to be better quality than that.

She leaned over, trying really hard not to look like it was the first time she'd done this. Covering one nostril, she inhaled deeply with the other and waited for the rush.

She knew what to expect. It wasn't like she hadn't read about cocaine or heard the kids at school talking about taking it. There would be the rush of blood, the pounding heart, the fantastic feeling, the . . .

No. None of that was happening. Instead she felt like she was floating, like the rest of the world was moving backwards into another place, one that she could see but couldn't touch. She was vaguely aware of Tala and Giles, both of them chanting now, Tala looking almost possessed as she swayed, topless, to the rhythm of the crowd. She could see that Jason was smiling at her, but it was as if she wasn't there, as if nothing could touch her world.

A bubble – that's what this was like – being in a lovely, warm, safe, bubble that was keeping her warm and safe and happy. Nothing could harm her here. Nothing could spoil this feeli—

'Boss, Vincent sent me up to replace him. Anything I can do for you?'

Ricco? Was that Ricco's voice? Jason Tang stood up, picked up his cane and said something about leaving.

Lift. Head. Must. Lift. Head. Slowly, Raine found strength in her neck muscles to raise her chin, and pushed her hair back from her face.

Ricco. Her Ricco. But ... Why was he looking at her like that? Didn't he know her? Didn't he know that she was here to see him? I love you, Ricco. I love you. Don't you know that? Somehow she was saying the words but they weren't coming out of her mouth.

No, this wasn't real. This was a dream. A wild, fucking dream. Tala DiVinci and that guy from the Mafia movies were in it and ... who was the little ringmaster? Ricco didn't like him. Nooooo. Her Ricco was shouting at him and baring his teeth and there was white spittle coming out of his mouth and ooh, he looked real, real mad.

But the ringmaster wasn't scared.

The ringmaster was laughing and that was making Ricco even more crazy. Now Ricco was coming towards them and the ringmaster was telling him to stop, but Ricco kept coming and kept coming and ... what was that? What happened there? The silver cane came up and it sliced through the air and now it was all red at the end. Lots of red. Dripping onto the carpet and immediately disappearing. Ricco's shirt was red too and he was pressing his hands against his stomach, letting the deep, thick liquid squeeze through his fingers. What was wrong with her Ricco? Why was he moving backwards? Why wasn't he coming to hug her and tell everyone they were friends? She loved him. She loved her Ricco. Maybe she should ask him if he loved her, too. She would. She'd ask him right—

Falling. Why was Ricco falling down and lying on the floor? Why?

Was Ricco tired? That must be it. Ricco was tired. He just needed a nice long sleep.

# FIVE

*Mei-Lin*
*Shanghai, 1984*

*Dear Mama and Baba,*

*I hope this finds you well and that the sun continues to be kind to you this winter. It is difficult to believe that a whole year has passed since I left. The time flies by so quickly. Be assured that although I don't often find the time to write I am well and very happy. The family I am living with continue to spoil me with their generosity and kindness and the children are a delight. Their playfulness and curiosity grows and they are learning well. I do so long for my sisters, though. Please hug them tightly for me and tell them that they are never far from my thoughts.*

*As always I have enclosed a gift for you, my cherished parents. I hope that this will keep the rice barrel full and the home warm.*

*I miss you both more than I can say, but please do not worry for me as I am doing well and Uncle Cheung is always on hand with care and support.*

*With eternal love until we can be together once more,*
*Your devoted daughter, Mei-Lin.*

Mei-Lin had barely written the last letter when the hand came crashing down on the back of her head. 'Do not fucking smudge that ink with tears, you selfish bitch!'

The urge to scream or cry was almost too difficult to subdue but somehow she managed it. In the early days she had screamed with the pain of every blow, sobbed at the sound of every harsh word, but she had soon realised that this only incurred a mightier wrath. It was far better to remain silent and accept the punishment. Uncle Cheung called it 'behaviour correction'. If it truly was, then the girls who were kept in this house had taken enough beatings to correct the behaviour of every person in Shanghai.

She folded the letter to her parents and pushed it across the table. Uncle Cheung would mail it and soon her parents would have money for the market, safe in the knowledge that their daughter was thriving in her role as a children's nanny. The thought gave her a small crumb of comfort. There could only be one thing worse than the situation she was in and that was if her parents found out the truth. The shame of it would kill her. The dishonour. She would never be able to face them again, never be able to return to them, and when she lay in the dark waiting for sleep to come that was the only thought that gave her the strength to live another day.

One day she would go back.

One day.

The sound of retching coming from along the corridor snapped her out of her self-pity.

'That pathetic whore!' Cheung's mouth twisted with contempt. How had she never seen that he could be such a man? It was hard to believe now that she had once worshipped him, revered him as her benefactor. She no longer thought of him as her uncle. He was nothing to her – nothing more than a jailer and a pimp.

'Go tend to her and make sure she is ready for today. You lazy bitches have cost me enough money with your stupid games this month. Do you think I'm a fucking charity? Do you think I can just send money to every peasant cunt in China? Go! Go see to her and you'd better fucking make it up to me this afternoon. A very important guest is coming today and I want him so well taken care of that he'll open his wallet and let winds of cash blow our way.'

Mei-Lin knew better than to argue. Cheung's temper knew no mercy, and if he were riled then the punishment would not only be on her head, Jing Wei would suffer too. And wasn't she already suffering enough?

On the way out of the room that served as their kitchen, Mei-Lin grabbed a small bowl of tea that she'd made earlier for Jing Wei. As she walked along the corridor she ignored the sounds coming from the rooms above her. Several of the girls had guests at the moment. Guests. That was what they were forced to call them. In the deep recesses of her mind, Mei-Lin called them something very different. They were the devils and her uncle was the most evil of all.

It hurt like a knife through her soul to remember the optimism and openness of the girl who'd set off from her home a year ago. Cheung had remained the loving and caring uncle for many hours, his mood changing only as they finally entered the crowded streets of Shanghai. Mei-Lin had barely noticed, so entranced was she by the masses of people and the array of buildings. This was like nothing she had ever seen before and as different from her village as night and day.

The car had come to a stop in a street that was narrower than the others they'd travelled along. It was darker too. The only illumination came from a strange blue light that sat above the door. Who could have believed that such a thing existed? Blue light? She'd only ever known the yellow light of the fires that lit and heated their home.

Her home.

She would not cry. She would not. No matter how deep the ache she would not cry. For all their sakes. If she could go back to that last moment she would change so much. She just wished that instead of losing herself in excitement she had taken another moment to look at the sky, to breathe the air, or even to run and never stop, but then how could she have known that when she entered this house she would never again leave it?

Wearily, she pushed away the dark thoughts. There was no point in thinking about what could or should have happened. Right now she must be strong to deal with the day ahead of her. Bumping the door open with her hip so as not to spill a single drop of the tea, she saw that Jing Wei was lying on a blanket on the floor of their room, her body like a collection of bones inside a brown sack. Her head was against one wall of the small cupboard space, her feet against the other, leaving just enough room for a pot in the corner, a small wardrobe behind the door, and one more slender body to lie on the floor. The girls were used to it now. In fact, holding each other tight at night was one of the few things that brought them comfort. Falling to her knees, Mei-Lin slipped her arm under Jing Wei's head and raised it so that she could drink the tea.

At first they'd thought her ails had been caused by an infection or disease. With thirty girls living in the same house and an endless procession of guests, germs grew and spread, often affecting the weakest like Jing Wei. She'd been in a terrible state when Mei-Lin had arrived, and it was only by sharing her food, sneaking a little extra into Jing Wei's bowl, that Mei-Lin had managed to build her strength back up. Until now.

The sickness had come two weeks before and it had been

relentless. A week ago Cheung, furious about the loss of income, had called in a friend who had once been a doctor before his fondness for the poppy had ruined his health and mind. But even to his drug-addled brain the diagnosis had been obvious. Jing Wei had fallen to the one thing that all the girls dreaded more than anything else. She was thirteen years old and she was pregnant.

Cheung paid him in baijiu, the potent, harsh liquor that they normally kept for the guests who were paying the lowest of rates, and sent him on his way. Before he was even out of the door, Cheung delivered the consequences of Jing Wei's actions. This time no doctor would be called.

Mei-Lin tried to coax some of the lukewarm drink between Jing Wei's lips. 'Drink it, please, my little bird,' Mei-Lin begged, using her pet name from the childhood that seemed like so long ago. It was difficult to know if Jing Wei's lack of thirst was due to the nausea or to the fact that her lips were so swollen it pained her to sip. Her own family would struggle to recognise her. Cheung had left her with a face that was black and blue, her eyes swollen almost shut, and lips that looked like they'd been stung by a thousand bees.

'Mei-Lin, I can't do this. It hurts so much.' A tear dropped from the corner of each eye. Heart breaking, Mei-Lin used the sleeve of her jumper to gently wipe them away.

'The doctor is coming back today, Jing Wei, and it will all be over. The baby will be gone and you will soon feel much, much better.'

They both knew she was lying. As long as they were in this hell it would never be better, but the only way to get through each and every day was to hold on to the promise of a happy ending.

Mei-Lin soothed Jing Wei with tender strokes and gentle

words until she slipped into sleep, then she took off her jumper, formed a makeshift pillow and carefully eased it under her cousin's head. Leaving her was excruciating, but if she wasn't ready for the arrival of the important guest the repercussions would be horrific for both of them.

The dressing room was empty when she reached it. Situated next to the stairs at the very end of the damp, dank basement it was the room where the transformations took place. The girls entered as waifs, but inside they washed, applied make-up and chose underwear and a dress from the rail that was covered in clear polythene to protect the fine fabrics. They weren't allowed to wear the same outfit more than once in a week. The men who visited didn't pay good money to see girls who looked shabby or cheap. The clients were being sold the dream by those who were living the nightmare.

With every layer of powder she applied, with every swipe of lipstick, she became another girl, a gilded butterfly who looked exquisite but felt nothing. Numb. For Mei-Lin this was part of the process that allowed her to deal with what had happened to her, removing all traces of the person she was and putting on a mask of anonymity. The stranger looking back at her in the mirror felt nothing.

The stairs creaked as she climbed them and at the top she had to summon all her strength to push open the heavy mahogany door. It was like entering a different world. Rich walnut wood covered the floors and the walls were lined in pale green wallpaper that was etched in olive with woodland flowers. Overhead the corridor was punctuated with lights that hung in little glass beads like raindrops falling from the sky.

The room Mei-Lin used on this floor was very different from the one in the basement below. This bedroom was elegant, the kind of room that Mei-Lin imagined a wealthy woman would occupy. There was an ornate bed against one wall, covered in gold brocade and framed by a canopy draped with soft red silk. Nearby, sat an elaborately carved sideboard, finished in black lacquer and painted in russet and gold with scenes from ancient folklore. On top, a tray of beverages – tea, brandy and whisky – left there by Tai Tai, the old lady paid to keep the rooms clean and ready for business. Mei-Lin sat on the edge of the sumptuous red damask armchair, her stomach heaving with apprehension. The waiting always filled her with anxiety, even when the client was already known to her. Best case scenario was that it would be Mr Kasaki, a businessman from Hiroshima who travelled to Shanghai one day every fortnight and visited her on most of his trips. As clients went, Mr Kasaki was by no means the worst. He was the first man she had been forced to lie with and he told her that he'd paid handsomely for her virginity. He'd never struck her, never harmed her and never treated her like a whore. However, she feared her time with her Japanese client was over. A new girl had just come in from Hangzou and today was to be her first day of working. The poor little mite didn't look much more than twelve, but she would be the biggest earner in the house this month. Cheung had been touting her virginity for several weeks, and she knew that Mr Kasaki would be given the option to make her bleed. He would undoubtedly come up with a sum that matched Cheung's greed.

Perhaps, then, today's guest would be Mr John, the Englishman from the embassy. He had only three specifications: he'd insisted that she was free of all body hair, he demanded that she call him 'father', and she must always lie on her front and let him take her from behind. In return, he often bought her gifts of perfume and small pieces of jewellery that were immediately handed over to Cheung.

With every passing minute, her anxiety rose. If her very important client did not show up, Cheung would require her to accept whatever guests came without appointments, and as the day turned to night they would get drunker and rougher. Covering the bruises was never easy afterwards. A group of Russian men who were working on some kind of pipeline had visited every night for two weeks and one of them was far too brutal and quick with his hands. If she did not satisfy Cheung this afternoon, she would undoubtedly be the first to be offered to the Russian ogre that evening.

The door suddenly swung open, making her jump up to a standing position and automatically bow her head in deference.

'Here's my little Mei-Lin,' Cheung announced. Only when he'd moved forward into the room could she see who he was talking to. It wasn't one of the regulars. However, it must be someone really special because Cheung had on the suit she recognised as his very best, the one he kept for greeting council members and big spenders.

The man who followed him did indeed have a look of importance. His jacket and trousers were well-fitting and made of the kind of thick navy wool that cost many Yuan. His hands were smooth and she could see that his nails were clean and perfectly shaped. On his head was a dapper fedora and, most unusually, he carried a silver cane. Mei-Lin had never seen such a thing.

He was Asian, definitely, but it was still a surprise when he opened his mouth and his accent was from the Beijing region. Over the last year she'd become attuned to such things and realised that usually men of this wealth came from Hong Kong or Singapore.

'You were right, Cheung, she definitely is a beauty.'

Cheung beamed with pride like the doting uncle the bastard used to be.

'Turn around,' he ordered, his tone firm but not aggressive.

Could he hear the thudding of her heart as she obeyed his command? This was the first time any man had inspected her so closely, most of them glanced quickly at her face and then immediately made her work, usually on her back, occasionally on her knees. This was different, almost like he was surveying a new piece of furniture before deciding whether to purchase.

He moved towards her and inspected her skin, her hair, then asked her to walk across the room. She moved with grace and elegance, the way the older girls had shown her when she'd first arrived.

'And she's smart, you say?'

Cheung nodded. 'The smartest one we've ever had. Already she can master some English, some Russian and she's almost fluent in Japanese.'

Only fear and incredulity stopped her from laughing at Cheung's exaggeration. The language skills she'd acquired were very basic and even then she was almost positive that most of those words and phrases could not be used in polite conversation.

'Then I will accept her. But I warn you, Cheung, if she is thick as a pig or riddled with disease then I will return and you will have more than just mah-jong debts to worry about.'

A frown of confusion furrowed Mei-Lin's brow. Accept her? This man made it sound like he was taking her somewhere, but this couldn't possibly be so. It was true that every day and night since she'd arrived she had prayed for her freedom, but the most important part of that wish was that she be allowed to go home and take Jing Wei with her.

A glance of warning from Cheung made her bite her tongue.

'Have her belongings packed and have her sent to my car in ten minutes.'

The relief was written all over Cheung's face as he nodded his agreement. 'You won't be disappointed, Mr Tang. Mei-Lin is a special girl.'

'She'd better be.' Tang didn't even glance back in Cheung's direction. 'Nothing lives for very long when it's floating in the Yangtze.'

As soon as his footsteps told her that he was out of earshot, Mei-Lin turned to her captor. 'Uncle? What is he talking about? Where am I to go?'

Cheung rounded on her and she instinctively recoiled backwards, then yelped as she caught her hip on the arm of the chair. Cheung grabbed her hair and pulled her out of the room, dragging her along to the dressing room that she had visited just a short time before.

'Two dresses, one pair of shoes and underwear – although the Gods know that a whore like you won't keep that on for very long.'

He pointed to a canvas bag in the corner. 'Put it in that bag and then Tai Tai will give you a coat at the door.'

'How long?' she screamed.

He ignored her, instead using all his strength to swing her across the room, sending her crashing into the rail of dresses.

'Uncle, how long?' The fear of what he could say was sending tears streaming down her face.

His mouth contorted into a sneer. He was enjoying this, she realised. He loved the pain. For the first time in her life, Mei-Lin realised that she could happily kill another human being.

'You won't be back here,' he crowed. 'After tonight you'll either be fish food in the river or you'll be far from Shanghai.'

'Nooooo!' she wailed, falling to her knees. 'Uncle, please. Please do not make me leave Jing Wei. Please, I beg of you. She cannot survive without me here and . . . and . . . ' She frantically grasped for a way to break his indifference to her argument. 'And Uncle she makes you money. Jing Wei is very popular with the Japanese men and will continue to profit you in the coming years. We will work so hard, Uncle Cheung, I promise you. We will make twice as much as before and we will never give you a moment of trouble. Just please, please don't make me leave.'

Watching him standing there in his best clothes, his hair greasy, his fingers stained yellow from the Marlboro cigarette that was always in his hand, Mei-Lin's urge to kill grew, becoming almost irresistible when he spat out his answer.

'That bitch will make nothing for me. Doctor Pang has just told me she'll be dead by nightfall.'

# SIX

'For God's sake, Lou, don't bend over or I'll be giving your OBGYN a call with an update.'

Dixie and Cally laughed at Stevie's perfect summation of the situation, leaving Lou – as always – to take the defensive.

'Fuck off, Little Miss Prissy,' Lou fired back. 'Do you really think the jerks that will be coming here today are pitching up for your insightful lyrics and melodic screech? Because if you do, you're as fucking stupid as you look.'

Cally rolled her eyes and resorted to her default setting of dry and sarcastic. 'Jeez, we get more wholesome than the Osmonds every day.'

Cally took a long drag on a ridiculously long spliff and then passed it around to the others. Stevie took a quick hit and passed it on. It wasn't her thing. If she so much as went near drugs, she heard Ella's voice in her head, threatening to whip her ass and ground her for ever.

In the beginning, the rest of the girls had teased her for being so straight, but they didn't even notice now, especially since it never stopped her from having a good time.

Stevie still couldn't get over the fact that it shouldn't really be like this. Weren't bands supposed to struggle? Weren't they supposed to cross the country, stealing drugs, sleeping in the back of a beat-up van, wasted out of their faces while inhaling the vomit of a fellow band member?

That just wasn't how The Bitch of Thorns rolled.

For a start they didn't have an old, battered set of wheels. Courtesy of Lou's father's need to over-compensate for the fact that his career as a pioneer in the field of rectal surgery had taken him abroad for most of her childhood, they had a Winnebago that was a few years past its prime, but which still ran like a dream and allowed them to sleep in any one of six fairly comfortable bunks.

There was also a never-ending supply of free booze and rehearsal space, courtesy of Dixie's old man's bar. But it was Cally's mother that had been the biggest revelation. Cally: short, awkward, social belligerent, styled by the influence of renegade rockers, attitude by anarchy. Cally's mother: a tall, blonde, typically Californian ex-swimsuit model with a free spirit and a generosity that extended to sharing her extensive reserves of weed with anyone who asked. And they frequently did.

Oh, and the big-shot A&R uncle couldn't be overlooked either.

This was breaking into the music industry rich-bitch style, and Stevie still thought it bizarre that she'd managed to hook up with these chicks when she had nothing to bring to the party but her songs, her voice and, unlike her predecessors, no obvious suicidal tendencies.

'Nervous?' Stevie realised that Jude was standing right behind her, so close that she could smell the spearmint chewing gum on his breath.

'Nope,' she replied honestly. It was true: singing never made Stevie nervous. Leaving home did. Hanging out with the other girls 24/7 did. Changing her style and her sound to suit a band definitely did. But singing? That was the reason she got out of the camp bed in the Winnebago every morning.

'Good.' He checked his watch and then had a quick look at the pager that never left his side. 'No cancellations or delays so we're going to be good to go at four o'clock.'

'Man, I could puke,' Dixie murmured.

'Yeah, well just don't do it on the drum kit,' Cally replied. 'By the way, it's looking shit hot over there.' Cally gestured in the direction of the stage and Stevie spotted just a hint of tension in her face. Cally was definitely a deep river while Stevie preferred just splashing in the puddles.

It was no surprise that anxiety was overtaking the room. This was the day they'd been preparing for all year – the showcase for Spin Records. Turned out Jude had been using the carrot and stick approach when he said they'd be meeting the record company a few weeks after they got together.

It was a good move on his part.

It had given them the motivation and drive to progress, while delaying the showcase for a whole lot longer than he'd originally promised had allowed them the time to find their feet as a band. Their sound had evolved since that first rehearsal back in O'Neil's. They'd taken a definite step towards a harder rock sound, reminiscent of bands like Van Halen and Aerosmith. The general dress code was anything black (Cally), anything denim (Dixie) and anything that had been shredded so that it exposed areas of anatomy that qualified as erogenous zones (Lou). Stevie was the stand-out in terms of fashion. Beat-up black leather motorcycle boots were a given, but the rest of her outfit could range from a fishnet vest and skin-tight Lycra pants to a gossamer tunic dress that wouldn't have looked out of place on one of the twelve apostles.

It was this sense of individuality and style that set them apart visually, but it was Stevie's music that defined their sound. Pounding beats with hardcore lyrics about love, pain and survival, blended with massive power ballads that ripped out the heart and kicked it from one end of the stage to the other.

They were confident that they'd become the band they were meant to be – the question was whether there was a place for them in the music world amongst the more pop-orientated sounds that currently sat at the top of the Billboard.

Cally checked out the clock that hung on the wall behind the bar. 3 p.m. One hour to go. They were in Amp, a club just off Sunset, a ten-minute walk from Spin's west coast office. It was pretty dark and dingy in the daylight but attracted a decent crowd at night and had yet to lose the favour of the hot crowd that dictated which clubs were in and out in LA. The company had a deal with the owner that allowed them to use the club when it was shut to the public in return for an occasional free gig by one of Spin's acts.

It was the first time The Bitches of Thorn had been on stage there. Stevie hoped it wouldn't be the last.

'OK, ladies, let's hear what you've got.'

The band hit the stage and launched into one more run-through of their three showcase songs, this time watched over by Jude. They opened with the self-titled 'Bitch Of Thorns', a foot-stomping declaration of hatred for a cheating lover with an anthemic chorus that stuck in the brain and refused to shift. Next up was 'Run Or Die', another up-tempo number with painfully raw lyrics about an abusive relationship. Finally there was 'Tragic', a haunting, soul-baring ballad about a lost love that Stevie Nicks would have sung the shit out of until the end of time.

As soon as the last note ended there was an uncomfortable silence and the pulsing vein in the side of Jude's neck betrayed his concern. Stevie knew it hadn't gone well. Dixie was all over the place, Cally was so nervous that she couldn't get her flow on, Lou was so freaking hyper she was hogging the stage and Stevie just wasn't finding the depth that normally came naturally to her.

Perhaps she was a bit wound up after all. Fuck, what had happened to them? And what a shit time to discover that pre-show nerves were an issue.

They all had very specific roles in this band and they'd just fallen out of them. Cally was always intense, Dixie specialised in detached crazy, Lou was the thrusting sex goddess and Stevie was the laid-back one with a simple outlook who saw the good in everyone, who didn't take anything too seriously and who always delivered. It would seem that when one of them was off their game the others followed them right off the field.

How the hell could this have happened?

This was the seminal moment in their careers and they'd prepared for this opportunity for months. They'd conquered egos and disputes and Lou's penchant for not turning up to rehearsals because she was screwing some married guy with a perpetually open wallet. They'd worked with Dixie's shyness until she could actually open her hair a couple of inches and reveal some of her face when she was playing. And now that their big moment had come they sounded like crap.

'Cally, any more dope?' Stevie could hear the overtone of tension in Jude's voice.

To his obvious relief, Cally nodded.

'Good. Take Dixie and Lou out onto the fire escape and take a hit – don't come back in until you're chilled enough to get it together. Stevie, can I speak to you out here?'

Unsurprisingly, Lou pouted at the fact that Stevie was being treated differently from the rest of them, but she knew better than to argue when Jude was in business mode.

They headed out into the corridor and as soon as they were out of the eyeline of the others he grabbed her hand and pulled her into the ladies washroom. Inside, his lips pressed down hard on hers, his hand slipped round to the back of her neck and offered her no chance of escape. Not that she would have taken it. Her Jude-crush had been burning in the background for months, but she would never in a million years have acted on it first. Every time they talked about it, her mom told her to let him do the running and she wasn't arguing. If Jude wanted a sexually forward, predatory female he'd have given in to Lou's weekly propositions before now. Yeah, trusting her mamma's advice had paid off big time.

He kicked open the door of the first cubicle and they stumbled inside, his free hand already frantically caressing her black leather mini-skirt. She had – she just realised – dressed to make an impact today. The white chiffon shirt would have been a virginal contrast to the skirt if it weren't for the fact that it was completely transparent and she was wearing only a sheer nude bra underneath.

Sexy. Suggestive. Smokin' hot.

It seemed Jude had definitely noticed.

'Oh fuck, I've been dying to do that for months.'

'Really?' He'd hidden that well. In fact, she'd been pretty much certain that it was strictly a one-way crush. But then, her mom's advice aside, she didn't exactly have a wealth of

71

experience in relationships to fall back on. There had been a couple of guys in school. A long-haired Led Zeppelin fan who'd lasted about six months until she could no longer stand the fact that he only showered once a fortnight. She'd lost her virginity in a quick, unsatisfactory interlude with her music teacher. He'd promised her they were star-crossed lovers who were destined to share a lasting bond. In reality, all they shared was a fifteen-minute sexual experience on his marital bed while his wife was away at a scrap-booking conference in Torrance. And he had the cheek to give her a B in her next exam.

Finally, a couple of months before she'd left home, there'd been a brief relationship with the only other guy she knew who wanted to be a professional musician. Caleb was a classical pianist who was a year older than her and available for weddings, funerals and bar mitzvahs. On the bright side, he showered every day and wasn't married. On the negative, he was already set to leave on a music scholarship to Juilliard and he couldn't tell his parents he was seeing her because they were very orthodox and believed their son should only hook up with girls of the Jewish faith. She had long come to terms with the fact that her skills in choosing men needed work.

Perhaps that situation had just changed.

Jude's breath was warm on the side of her neck as he kissed his way from her ear down to her shoulder, then ... holy crap, this was hot.

'Are you kidding me? You are one completely fuckable babe,' he murmured, interspersing the words with more kisses.

She could feel a definite tingling in her nether region and her nipples were awake and standing to attention. 'But Jude, what about ...'

'Forget them,' he replied, pre-empting her question before bringing his mouth back up to hers and pressing down hard again. His tongue flicked across her teeth, then probed deeper, his hands cupping her face, his groin pressed into hers.

Every bit of her wanted him and wanted him right now, except ... Nope, it wasn't right. The first time they had sex wasn't going to be while her ass was freezing off on top of a cistern in a washroom that smelled of pee. The kissing was insanely hot but this wasn't how she wanted it to go down. An apt thought considering he'd fallen to his knees and was busy pushing up her skirt while nudging her legs apart. Tempting. Definitely tempting. But ...

'Not now,' she gasped, slipping her hand under his chin and gently easing him back to his feet. His puzzled expression told her this wasn't a reaction he normally experienced in this situation.

'Jude, not here. Later, I promise, but not here.'

For a moment she saw something flare. Lust? Anger? Irritation? Confusion? Hard to tell. But then a soft smile broke on his face and he leaned in to her.

'I totally understand, baby. I do. Fuck, you are incredible. When you're ready we are so going to get it on, but you need to know that this is something bigger than that. This is more than just a quick fuck, babe – way, way more.'

Oh. My. God. How completely unbelievable. This was the kind of selfless guy that only usually featured in romcoms and very occasionally in her songs. The crush just slid up another notch.

One of his hands slipped down and took one of her nipples under the sheer fabric of her blouse and began to rub it between his fingers.

'Jude! Oh God, Jude, that feels so good.'

How was she supposed to stop this? Every pore of her being was screaming at her to hitch up her skirt, open wide and go for it.

He pulled back – if this were a song on a record player the stylus just scratched right across the disc. 'Later, I promise, and it will be so right. Let's go and get this gig done. They're going to think you're the sexiest chick that ever walked that stage and they're going to fucking love you.'

Ready to explode with longing, but thankful that he'd listened to her, she slid off the cistern and pushed him back against the door. 'So what was that then? My free pep talk?' She giggled. He grinned and kissed her again. 'Absolutely. Shit, Stevie, I'm sorry, I just couldn't help it. Soon as this showcase is done we've got some serious talking to do. And ... erm ... that other stuff.'

A bolt of electricity shot right across her reproductive organs.

As soon as it had subsided enough to allow her to regain the power of thought, she realised this was going to be tricky. His timing was appalling. All those endless, monotonous nights on the road together and he chose right now to tell her he wanted to get it on?

The girls couldn't know about this. She didn't want any accusations of favouritism, especially when – through no fault of her own – she already had more than her fair share of the spotlight.

Still kissing, still groping, still breathing hard and fast, they worked their way out of the cubicle until she got a peek of her reflection over his shoulder. 'Jesus, I'm a mess. How long have I got to fix myself up?'

The overhead fluorescent light was definitely not her friend.

He checked his watch and shook his head. 'No time – they'll be here.'

'No!' Oh crap. Crap! This was the most important moment of her life so far and she was sure she must look like she'd been ravished sideways for days.

This wasn't going according to plan.

But apparently Jude had other ideas. He straightened up his clothes, rubbed his face, ran his fingers through his hair, then pulled open the washroom door and led her out, not even giving her time to stop at the mirror and attempt some damage control.

When they got back into the bar, every face in the room spun to look at them. The rest of the band was already in their positions, looking surprisingly cool about the fact that she'd done a disappearing act. Even Lou just looked relieved to see her.

Standing a few feet away from the stage were the three men their future depended on.

Cole Presley, Jo Santos and Vic Susso were legends in the music scene. As part of the preparation for today, Jude had filled them in on the men's backgrounds. Cole Presley was the president of Spin, a former drummer with a hard rock band back in the early seventies, his long hair, beat-up boots and jeans still lived on more than a decade after he'd hung up his sticks. Jo Santos was an east coast legend in rock circles, former road manager for Cole's band and lifelong friend of the top man. Vic Susso was the money man. A Harvard graduate, this guy could make a profit on a dime, declare nothing and still convince the tax man that he was due a rebate. On a day-to-day basis, the latter two men handled the business and finance side of things, while Cole Presley focused on the acts.

Stevie was relieved when Jude let go of her hand and gestured for her to take her place at the mike. Excellent – introductions averted. Music first, small talk later. That plan worked for her.

While she climbed onto the stage, Jude made his way over to shake hands with his bosses.

'Sorry, guys, just a last-minute bout of nerves there. Stevie's great but she just needed a little reassurance.'

They didn't look entirely convinced, but neither did it seem to be a problem. These were seasoned music guys so it was a fair bet that they'd been there, done that and bought the T-shirt saying, 'I Screwed The Singer'. It didn't stop Stevie's face burning with embarrassment, though. She covered it up by setting up her guitar and swapping hopeful glances with the rest of the girls.

Jude was still selling them up to his bosses. 'I promise you, you'll be blown away. I really think these girls have got something.'

'I hope so, Jude, 'cos I've been paying you plenty and you've come up with jack-shit lately.' Cole Presley obviously wasn't going for any kind of commendation for tact and diplomacy. Jude flushed but then covered it with a confident smile and a nonchalant shrug of the shoulders.

Up on the stage, Stevie took a deep breath. This was it. This was what it all came down to. A sudden longing to call Ella came over her. She just wanted to hear her mom's voice, to tell her what was going on and get that boost of confidence that only her mother could give.

Instead, Stevie met Cally's gaze and gave her a hint of a nod. Behind them, Dixie recognised the exchange and began softly beating out a rhythm on her sticks. Lou got on board with a soft twang of an intro, before Cally and Stevie brought in their guitars, adding to the gentle sound. All in, the volume ascended over the next eight bars, nudging the song into life before ... cut. A pause. Then all hell let loose as they banged it up ten gears and rocked into the first verse of their signature song, 'Bitch Of Thorns'.

The impact of the sound was as stunning as it was instant and Stevie watched as the record company guys' expressions instantly flicked to interested. Suddenly she no longer felt like an unprepared wreck who'd been wasting time making out in the toilets when she should have been setting up for a major event.

Adrenalin surged through her and in an instant, the rush of the audience, the rush of the moment and the rush of the music combined to give her the biggest high. Stephanie Ross from Willowdale was long gone and in her place was Stevie, wild and wanton rock goddess who had sex, drugs and rock and roll written all over her mascara-smudged face.

They smashed out of the first song and went straight into the second, with Lou blowing it away on the bass as the dark, thunderous intro to 'Run Or Die' filled the room. Lou: stunning, beautiful, talented. Yet, still Stevie noticed that the stares of the record company chiefs remained on her.

Before they lost interest, she cranked out a killer riff on her guitar and launched the angry, bitter rant of betrayal and devastation.

The hands that stroked now deal the blows
The piercing stab of pain in the place that doesn't show
My heart is bleeding, love and trust
I'm leavin' you now, gonna put myself first

Stevie criss-crossed the stage, demanding attention for a song that worked on so many levels. It could be a goodbye to a lover or an indignant declaration of independence, or perhaps it was a condemnation of a father who left his children only for them to free themselves of the longing for his return. It was not in any way inspired by an introverted but gifted guy called Caleb who was afraid of his mother.

It was as if there were three people inside the one body. One was the innocuous, naïve teenager who didn't have much experience in relationships and whose natural instinct was to avoid anything too intense or heavy, the other was the songwriter who could pull out emotions and lyrics that belonged in the soul of someone who had lived and lost and suffered and known what it was to truly love. And then there was this rasping, pulsating rock chick who could deliver a song and put on a hardcore tornado of a performance that set the room on fire.

And right now she was giving off heat.

By the time the third number faded out Stevie was soaked in sweat. The energy of the first two songs had left her so spent that as Cally took them into 'Tragedy' Stevie returned to the centre of the stage, stripped off her guitar, and just stood in one spot and sang. Closing her eyes, she disconnected from the room and went to that place of pure emotion, feeling every word, delivering each line with utter believability, her heart breaking with sorrow and regret for a love that was gone.

Not one person in the audience moved, no one made a sound. For three and a half minutes the room was spellbound as the men who would determine their future watched, listened and made decisions.

When the song was finally over, all was still for more than ten seconds before Cole Presley started clapping a slow, rhythmic demonstration of his approval.

Stevie realised that Jude's tactics had worked. By relaxing the band and distracting Stevie from the anxiety of the situation he'd created something truly special.

The question was, did the chiefs of Spin Records agree?

# SEVEN

*Raine*
*New York, 1984*

> Amazing Grace, how sweet the sound
> That saved a wretch like me
> I once was lost but now I'm found
> Was blind but now I see

The haunting sound of the pipes cut through the drizzle that clung to the mourners as they watched the coffin lower into the ground.

Father O'Flynn spoke with authority and the kind of solemn surety that only God could provide on a day like this.

Ricco had been a good man, he told them, cut down in his prime, his loss a devastating blow to the community. He was with Jesus now, looking down on them, asking them not to mourn his loss, but to celebrate the life he had lived here on earth.

Raine knew that was bullshit.

If Ricco was looking down on them right now he was mad as hell.

Beside her, her father stood tall and steady, only his face

betraying the searing devastation he was feeling. Men like Pat O'Donnell didn't cry. They fought, they raged, they swore that justice would be done, but they didn't cry.

Raine wondered if knowing the truth would change that.

Pat O'Donnell and everyone else standing in the Holy Cross Cemetery on this freezing December day thought they knew why Ricco Dimato was being lowered into a hole in the ground. Danny Docherty, a fellow cop, had been in the club that night and had spread the word. He and Ricco had been enjoying a little down time. Not working there, you understand. No, that would be against department policy. They were just chilling out, having a few beers, when a fight had kicked off. Some guy, out of his mind on liquor, had started beating up his wife. Ricco, stand-up guy, had of course stepped in. Before his buddy could help, Ricco was on the ground, stabbed twice – once through the stomach, once through the heart. The warring couple had yet to be found and there were no other witnesses. You know how it is in these places – no one ever sees anything.

Raine knew exactly how it was.

She'd woken up in an alley as day broke over Manhattan, no clue how she got there and only a vague memory of some horrible dream. By the grace of some higher power she'd found a cab to take her home and managed to slip into bed before anyone realised she'd been gone. The next day she told Angelica that she hadn't made it into Manhattan and had just gone home instead. She told her parents that she'd come in at midnight and went straight to bed. But the dream, the dream just kept on coming.

It was just before noon when she heard that Ricco was dead and realised that the dream was reality. Telling the truth was her first reaction, but she realised it would be futile. Danny Docherty, the cop who got Ricco into the club scene, was spreading the wife-beater story to save his own skin. If anyone knew that he was involved in putting Ricco there his career would be over. And anyway, if she told the truth it would be her word against his and what credibility did she have? Who would believe her? She'd already lied. She'd have to admit that she was there, and she'd have to confess to the drugs, too.

Movie stars making out in front of her? A club owner giving her dope? Jason Tang, multi-millionaire entrepreneur, sitting behind some of the best lawyers in the country, would tear her apart. It would be months of pain and it would achieve nothing. At the moment everyone knew Ricco died a hero. It was true. But if she admitted the facts there would be a stain on Ricco's record when it transpired that he was working for someone like Jason Tang. His parents, Riccardo and Caroline, didn't deserve that.

But the biggest reason she could never tell was standing right in front of her, buckling with pain. If he knew that she had caused this it would break his heart all over again. It would destroy him, destroy their family's name and Pat would never recover. The thought of hurting him even more was too much to comprehend. She'd already killed one man she loved; she couldn't do that to her father too. She just couldn't.

But Raine knew the truth. And so did at least one other person.

Ricco wasn't up there asking them to celebrate his life. He was screaming down at her to make this right, to get justice, to make someone pay for taking away his future.

At that moment she made the decision: if it took every minute of the rest of her life, that was exactly what she was going to do. Somehow she would make Jason Tang pay for what he had done.

'I promise, Ricco,' she whispered as she stepped forward and threw a white rose on the casket that now sat in a gaping hole in the ground. 'I promise.'

# EIGHT

*Mei-Lin*
*Shanghai, 1984*

As the lights of the city faded to black, Mei-Lin's face was a frozen mask of grief. She would not cry. Not ever again. Nothing could be worse than the pain of leaving, knowing that her family did not know where she was, knowing that she was leaving everyone she loved behind, knowing that she had failed Jing Wei. She should have taken better care of her. She should have protected her more, found a way for them to escape.

Now she was on her way to a new life.

She had no idea who her new owner was, but she had already realised that he was a man of much power. They had travelled straight to the airport and there he had taken her into an office where the officials had bowed and grovelled to him. They'd issued her with a book they called a passport. It wasn't in her name, the photograph didn't even look much like her, but apparently she needed it to board the thing they called an aeroplane.

All of this she gathered from listening to their conversations. No one spoke directly to her. No one told her anything. When she attempted to ask Mr Tang where he was taking her, he simply acted like he couldn't hear her, as if she didn't exist.

When she got on the plane he warned her to speak to no one. Only when they'd taken off did she hear a voice coming from the air, welcoming them on board and telling them that they were travelling to Hong Kong.

In Hong Kong they boarded another flight, a larger aircraft with soft seats and chattering families and couples in smart clothes who laughed as they pushed their big bags and jackets into boxes above the seats.

It was all so completely alien to her and the strangeness of it somehow helped her deal with the fear. In the many hours that they were travelling, she did not sleep, but sat in contemplation. There was comfort in the bodies all around her, a safety in knowing that nothing could harm her while so many eyes could see. The freedom from immediate danger allowed her mind to clear and she realised that it was time to accept the reality of her situation.

She would never see her family again, she knew that now. Uncle Cheung would fabricate some story, give them a reason for her disappearance, something that would allow them to sleep at night without worrying about her. Perhaps he'd say that the family had taken her off to a new life abroad. And later, when he stopped sending them money every month, he would say that she had forgotten them and they would shake their heads in sadness at the thought of the daughter who had deserted them.

The thought of their disappointment caused a tightness in her heart and made her breath come in quick shallow gasps.

Her dream of returning home was over. Now she must find a way to deal with whatever path she encountered. Hadn't her father always told her to be positive and not to worry about problems until they arose?

Underneath his brusque indifference, perhaps her new owner was a kind and good man who would treat her well. Yes, that was what she would choose to believe for now. Glancing sideways at his profile, she looked for signs of evil and saw none.

Maybe the gods had sent him to save her from the hell in which she was living. In the name of those Gods, she would choose for now to believe that Mr Tang was a man of honour and integrity who would bear her no harm. He would educate her and give her a life that was free of danger and fear. Perhaps he would marry her and come to love and cherish her as her father had cherished her mother every day of her life.

She would forever mourn the loss of her family and her beloved Jing Wei, but she had to find a place in her heart to put that loss so that every moment wasn't consumed with pain.

Shanghai was behind her and she didn't know what was to come. But she had to believe that in the hands of the man who sat beside her, it couldn't be worse than what had gone before.

# NINE

*Stevie*
*Los Angeles, 1984*

By nine o'clock on the morning after the showcase, The Bitch of Thorns had accepted an offer to sign with Spin Records and Jude Castigan had been appointed their manager.

As they gathered in the Spin offices, the electricity ricocheted off the walls. They'd done it. They'd actually done it. It struck Stevie that she should probably discuss the contract with someone outside of this room, but she decided not to rock the boat. Jude was on their side so she knew he'd have it covered and that he would have done everything to get them the best possible deal. He'd already said that the deal would give them fifty grand up front, ten grand for each of the band members and ten grand for him as a retainer. That wasn't bad money to kick off with. Ella would be getting the contents of several pages in the JC Penney catalogue, gift wrapped and on her doorstep before the day was out.

'I'm telling you, little lady,' Presley announced as he pushed the contract across the desk, a pen sitting on top of it just waiting for their signatures. 'We are going to make you the biggest rock star in America. Sky's the limit, baby. Sky's the limit.'

A sudden chill shot through the air.

True to form, Lou was the first to react. 'What?' Her beautiful face was twisted with anger and uncertainty. 'We're a band – she's not a fucking solo act.'

Presley's retort was seamlessly charming. 'Of course you are, darlin'. Same goes for all of you. We're gonna make sure every guy in America gets a hard-on just thinking about you girls.'

Presley scored a direct victory, hitting Lou in her vulnerable spots of adulation and sexual gratification. Smooth. Real smooth.

The other girls took it in turns to sign, with Stevie being the last one to be handed the pen.

As she signed the contract, buzzing with achievement, she ignored the niggling feeling that she now belonged to them and the knowledge that they'd been in the business long enough to know exactly how to get value for money.

She pushed aside the thought that this was never how she'd seen it working out for her. Gone was the girl who just wanted to sing her songs and live the life of a free spirit, just her, a guitar and the music. In her place was a product, a rock and roll image just waiting to be sold.

It would be fine. Great. It had to be.

Because now that her name was on the dotted line it was too late to change her mind.

# TEN

*Raine*
*New York, 1985*

She watched them.

Just watched.

This was the third night in a row that she'd stood there, cold but too pumped on adrenalin to care.

Just watching.

After a year in New York, Raine was used to a solitary life, but just for a moment she wished that she had someone here with her. Friends were in short supply these days.

She'd tried to stay in Brooklyn, she really had, but the familiarity of everything just hurt too damn much. Everyone had something to say about Ricco. Or questions to ask about Ricco. Everywhere she went she saw somewhere she and Ricco had been.

Ricco. Ricco. Ricco.

It gnawed at her, compounded the grief and the anger. It reminded her every day of the promise she had made and the fact that she had done nothing about it. Nothing. Jason Tang was alive and well and – according to the press – getting more successful and prominent by the day, while Ricco rotted in the ground. The guilt consumed her, ate away at her soul until she realised that she was slowly going insane. The day she dropped out of college, she thought her father was going to have a stroke.

It was more drama she couldn't handle. In the end, she'd packed a bag, travelled to Manhattan and used the money she'd saved for a room in a fleapit motel. Every day she'd pounded the pavements looking for work. On the fifth day she found it: fifty hours a week in Manzo's, a midtown pizza parlour, paid cash, no questions asked.

In twelve months, her entire circle of new friends had come to consist of the old lady who worked in the library near her home, the sisters who were the official tenants of the apartment she now lived in and the maintenance guy who looked after the building. The apartment was right above a dry cleaners and during busy periods the fumes made her head hurt. It was cheap, but it was also small and logistically challenging. The sisters were air hostesses working for Virgin Atlantic, so they were both away around fourteen nights out of every month. They had a fluid arrangement. The apartment had two beds in one room and a sofa in the lounge. Factoring in shifts, holidays and overnight stays with boyfriends, there was usually at least one bed free for Raine. If not, she slept on the couch.

She didn't mind. It was in Greenwich Village, a long but doable walking distance to work when money was low and, most importantly, it was in the vicinity of the reason she was in Manhattan in the first place. That was everything. The reason for waking up in the morning, the reason she lay awake at night and the reason that kept her going through the shitty daily shifts in the shitty pizza joint. And the reason that she didn't have much time to find someone to hold her hand when things got rough.

Right now, it was about as rough as it could get.

Reincarnation. The backdrop to all her nightmares.

Three nights before, on the anniversary of Ricco's death, she'd come here. She'd told herself that she would strut straight in like she belonged there, but in the end she didn't have the guts. Trepidation had frozen her brain. What was she going to do? What if she saw Tang? What was the point of being there? And how was she going to get in?

In the end, she'd retreated to that doorway across the street, waiting for her moment.

Now she realised that it had come.

A large group of weird characters had just poured out of a bus in front of the door. Raine had no idea where they'd come from, but she guessed it was Freaksville, USA.

Every one of them was dressed in a completely bizarre style. There were a couple of Catholic priests, who were on a path to excommunication if they were genuine because when they turned round they revealed costumes that left them holy on the front, naked on the back. There were at least three rubber-clad dominatrices. There was a guy in full wrestling costume and four schoolgirls – one of them six foot three inches tall with a full beard.

This was a crowd she could blend in to.

There was a bittersweet irony in the fact that her outfit for tonight had been inspired by Ricco. The New York clubs thrived on shock and awe, and Raine had realised that she had to serve that up if she had even the smallest chance of free and automatic entry.

Cue shock. Cue awe. After months of planning, Raine had transformed herself into a crime scene. Black Lycra bodysuit with black patent boots that added six inches to her already towering frame. Face splattered with red dye to give the appearance of blood. A fake knife she'd picked up at a fancy dress store jutting out of her heart. And the crime scene tape, bright yellow, wrapped around her body.

Now it was time to make it work.

Quickly and quietly, she moved across the street, being careful to look out for a speeding Rolls Royce, and joined the back end of the Freaksville crowd.

The big guy on the door waved them right in. They were in the middle of the foyer when a voice cut through her thoughts. 'I saw that, cheeky.'

Raine had a horrible feeling the voice was addressing her, and when she turned to find its source she realised she was right. She also realised that this young guy was so tall she was in the unusual position of being able to look him directly in the eye. Although, this was a little difficult given that she was heavily distracted by his Wonder Woman costume, complete with what appeared to be a spectacular set of breasts. His hands went to his hips and Raine realised he was waiting for a reply.

'And you plan to deal with this situation by . . . ?' Her highly arched eyebrow gave the clue that she was unimpressed by his interference. If he had the audacity to reveal to the security guys that she wasn't a legitimate member of their crowd, he'd be dealing with a lot more than the wrath of an eyebrow.

Thankfully, after a moment of thought, he had a better idea. 'OK, I'll forget all about it if you buy me drinks, ply me with drugs and if the mood takes me I might ask you to spank me.'

Cute. Smart. Just for fun, she decided to play along with the game. 'And what if I were to tell you that I charge for those services?'

'Then clothing aside – and incidentally that outfit is fucking genius – you'll definitely fit in with this crowd because we give nothing away for free. I wanted to put a sign on the bus saying "Rent Boys' Night Out", but I was over-ruled.'

'I like that. Good marketing. Gets word of your services out there.'

His laughter was high-pitched and contagious.

'Oh, it's already out there, darling. I'm the most overworked boy in Manhattan. So. What's your name?'

'Raine.'

'Storm,' he shot back instantly. 'That's what we'll call you. Raine Storm. I like that.'

'Raine Storm.' She mused over that for a few seconds and realised that she could live with it too. Right then she'd live with him calling her Doris if it gave her a free pass inside.

'And what brings you here, Miss Storm?' he said in the voice of a doctor waiting to dispense happy pills and bad advice. The question stumped her. I want to avenge the death of someone I loved. I want to set the place on fire and watch it burn to the ground. I want to murder Jason Tang in cold blood. I want to take back what happened and change that moment so that I can still hear his voice every day.

'I'm not sure. I guess I just wanted to see what it was like.'

'Then let me show you.'

He held his arm out like a courtier tending to his queen. Raine definitely had the feeling that it should be the other way around. He accompanied her along the corridor, every step taking them closer to the throbbing sounds coming from behind the massive red curtain in front of them.

'Your name! You haven't told me your name.' She shouted in his ear so that she could be heard over the ascending riot of noise.

'Didi DeMille, darling.'

Of course it was. Because he was never going to be Hank from the Hamptons.

Didi pulled back the curtain and, as the immediate blast of noise and heat hit them, Raine realised that they were going into her equivalent of the lion's den.

And it felt good not to be doing it alone.

# ELEVEN

*Mei-Lin*
*New York, 1985*

Mei-Lin felt as if her head might explode. The thumping beat of the music was assaulting her ears and the man sitting next to her found the need to shout, his spittle hitting her face with every word. There was only one way to react to such a vile assault on her senses: she smiled and slipped her hand between the buttons of his shirt, letting her fingers rub against the damp hairs of his chest.

God, she hated him.

'It's such an honour to be with such an important man,' she said, retaining a demure posture while raising her voice just enough to be heard.

She could gladly poison that drink that he held, and then sip a cold drink while he died.

'It always pleases me to speak with you and learn from such an important man.'

Or she could stab him. Straight through the heart. Perhaps with one of the stiletto heels that squeezed and deformed her feet until she honestly felt that she could weep with the pain.

The imbecile in front of her puffed out his chest and slid his hand further up her thigh, letting it slip under the short black cheongsam that Tang insisted she wore every night. He said it was her signature.

Mei-Lin smiled encouragingly and continued to stroke the chest of the fat pig in front of her. After she'd killed him she could take the stiletto and put it through the eye of Jason Tang.

Who could ever have believed that she would be capable of such thoughts? She, who could not even harm a worm in the fields she worked as a child. But this was her survival. Two lives. One a physical life, played out in the nightclub Tang owned, working every night, presented as a gift to the most important guest in the club. 'Do anything you wish with her,' he would say grandly. 'She's yours, with my compliments.'

The bastard made it sound like he was giving them a free drink or a bowl of nuts. That was all she was: a freebie. A cheap perk. Albeit one that was dressed up and groomed to look like she was as expensive as they came.

The most important thing in the world to Tang was image. The club's image. His image. And that vanity extended to his whores. There were five of them living in a tiny flat a few blocks away that they called the United Nations for obvious reasons. Whore number one: Tatiana, Russian, 22. Number two: Makalo, African, 19. Number three: Suzy, English, 20. Number four: Ami, Japanese, 21. A girl for every occasion and taste, all of them bought and paid for with fear, desperation, threats or promises.

How ironic that she'd once had a glimmer of hope that coming here could be an escape to a wonderful life. This place was as steeped in immorality and debauchery as it was possible to be. When she'd first arrived, the shock of what she saw almost stopped her heart. The people, the sex, the craziness, the money that changed hands. The price of one drink would feed her family at home for a week. It was incredible to her that such a world existed. Yet, much as the life she'd been taken from and the one that she'd come to were completely different, the fundamentals were the same – new scene, same whore.

Although, if she were to look at it objectively, she supposed that some things were an improvement. She was no longer living with the physical cruelty of Uncle Cheung and the animals who came to him. Here, the clients were all people known to Mr Tang, high rollers and VIPs, so they were usually clean and violence was rare. The other plus was the working hours – night time only, when the club was open, so at least every waking moment wasn't consumed with pleasing the pigs she was farmed out to. There was less sex too. Many of these men just wanted to be entertained while they were in the club, before going home to their wives. Sometimes they just wanted to watch her dance, or to perform with one of the other girls. On the occasions when they did want the partying to continue after the club closed, they were often staying in beautiful hotels where the bed was comfortable and the showers were warm.

Her days were spent cleaning the apartment, cleaning the club and grooming, grooming, grooming. Mr Tang expected them to have the most beautiful appearance, to have flawless skin and nails, perfect hair, stunning clothes. Image. It was all about image.

Leaving wasn't an option. Mr Tang was a powerful man and he'd left them all in no doubt what would happen to them if they dared to disappear. He knew where their families lived. He had contacts all over the world. There would be repercussions. And when he found them – which he would – they'd be beaten like dogs, then they'd be turned over to the authorities because none of them were in this country legally. Mr Tang had the stories all worked out, he'd told them. Who would believe two-bit whores over a successful, well-connected businessman?

Running was a foolish option. Hopeless. The American dream for the lowest of the low.

And anyway, where else did she have to go? The options were prison or the streets, and if the price of avoiding them and keeping her family safe was to act like she had an iota of interest in the devils she was forced to pander to every night, she would take it. For now.

Two lives. Yes, she had the day-to-day indignity of being treated as a possession to be passed around but there was another life that kept her from screaming with the despair of it all; there was the life that she was planning in her mind.

As far as she could see there were only two ways out of this. The first was that she meet someone who wished to marry her, treat her well and who had the money and power to release her from Tang's grip. Apparently this had happened to the girl she replaced. Ying had been given to a very famous musician, who had decided that she brought him luck and had paid Tang much money to take her with him. Occasionally, when the musician was playing in New York, she returned to the club with him and acted like the girls didn't exist. As far as Ying was concerned, she was above them now. Detached. Mei-Lin didn't blame her – wouldn't she give her soul to be in the same position?

However, since there was no imminent chance of being swept away by a client, she worked on a backup plan. This option was trickier and required more thought and much patience. She listened.

That was it. She listened to everything the men she was with told her or discussed with each other when she was there. And when she got home she wrote everything down in a journal she had slipped from Tang's office when she was cleaning it.

At the moment she had no idea what she would do with the information, but she hoped that one day the gods would direct her to the answer, and that answer would bring her freedom.

She had names, preferences, deals, secrets – it was amazing what you could learn when people treated you like you were invisible. And in the meantime, she hated every one of them.

His hand was kneading the inside of her thigh now, hard and demanding, and his smell told her that he was starting to perspire. Perhaps the fat pig would have a heart attack and die in front of her. Wasn't she due a bit of luck?

# TWELVE

*Stevie*
*Phoenix, 1985*

When Stevie woke up the first thing she realised was that her head hurt. The second thing was that she had absolutely no idea where she was.

When had one town begun to merge into another?

The first few months had been so exciting. The thrill of living on the road and getting paid – albeit not much – just to sing every night. As a naturally solitary creature who enjoyed her own company, she'd been surprised how much she loved hanging out with the rest of the guys.

Add in her relationship with Jude and the promise that success was just around the corner and she was grateful that Cally had found her that day in Santa Monica. Nothing could spoil this for her. Nothing.

'Hey, bitch, you look like shit.'

Almost nothing.

Stevie opened one eye and saw that Lou was already up and dressed: a tiny white vest that stopped just under her bra-less tits and skin-tight jeans that sat so low on her hips they defied the laws of gravity. Given that none of her erogenous zones were actually on show, this was fairly conservative for Lou.

She would never admit it to her but Stevie admired Lou's sexual confidence. Here was a girl who knew what she wanted and who made no apology for getting a thrill from the adulation of others. Lou didn't give a damn what anyone thought of her.

Stevie was way too sensitive for that kind of arrogance. It went against the stereotype of the egotistical lead singer, but she really would rather blend into the background and save the attention for when she was on stage.

To her left, Stevie heard a moan as Cally stirred on the twin bed next to her and struggled up to a seated position. 'Where are we?' she groaned.

'No idea,' Stevie replied with a smile. 'D'you think Mötley Crüe wake up every morning like this?'

'If Mötley Crüe wake up next to sights like you two then they need to go back to rock star school.'

Cally chucked a pillow at Lou, but she dodged it and instead it landed on a mound in the corner. The red bush on the top of it confirmed it was Dixie.

'Rich coming from you, Miss Prissy,' Lou announced. 'There's a clean-living, sexually repressed, sober, drug-free gospel choir out there just waiting for your call.' She snatched up her bag, giving all of them a free view of most of her buttocks. 'Anyway, I'm going over to the bar. The manager there was cute. Said we could get in early to set up and get free drinks all night if I blew him.' Lou applied another coat of lipstick as she spoke, then flicked back her auburn curls and headed for the door.

'Another moment of dignity.' Cally didn't even try to hide how she felt about Lou's promiscuity. Sometimes Stevie wondered just what Cally's thing was. Months on the road and she'd never seen her hook up with anyone. Even Dixie had managed to get bombed enough to pick up a couple of one-night stands.

Of course, they probably weren't too impressed with her relationship status either. Her thing with Jude had become open knowledge, although they didn't ever flaunt it in front of the rest of the band. Stevie didn't want to make anyone feel uncomfortable, so public displays of affection were out and Jude was careful not to give her special treatment.

At the door, Lou clutched her heart and delivered a line in her best Scarlett O'Hara voice. 'Oh no, please don't say that, Cally – I can't bear it. Please say it ain't true.'

Cally closed her eyes and exhaled deeply. 'Fuck off.'

They heard Lou's laughter all the way down the corridor.

'I fucking hate her.'

Stevie rolled over so that she was facing Cally and propped herself up on one elbow. 'Don't get so wound up, babe, you know she gets a thrill out of annoying you.'

Cally's expression of fury descended into a minor scowl as she took a cigarette out of a packet on the bedside table and lit up. 'I know, but honest to God she's an irritating bitch. She's like Satan's child or something.'

Stevie reached over and took the cigarette from Cally's hand, inhaled, then handed it back. 'I know she's a pain in the ass but she's harmless really. It's all for show – just for a bit of attention. Underneath that evil exterior there's some good. There has to be.'

'Yeah, they say that about serial killers, too.'

They lay in comfortable silence for a while until Cally stubbed out her cigarette. 'S'pose we better get Dixie up and get over to the bar before Satan's spawn sucks that guy's dick clean off.'

Stevie didn't argue. The sooner they got over to the bar, the sooner she'd see Jude, and that was a prospect that was pretty hard to resist.

Jude was hot, he was smart and he played it cool in that really infuriating way that guys who knew they were a catch always did. That wasn't a problem for Stevie, though, because she wasn't sure that she was in love with him.

That wasn't what this was about.

The man that she would fall in love with would touch her soul, would make her feel the words that she wrote in her songs. Jude made her hot, made her horny, made her laugh and made her feel like she had someone there for her no matter what. But love? She wasn't feeling that yet, though maybe that was still to come. How could they get to that level when they were with other people almost twenty-four hours a day and their entire relationship consisted of quickies in bathrooms, dressing rooms and anywhere else that they could be alone for ten minutes?

Maybe one day they could get away on their own for a while, just them, and chill out and get to know each other as two people on an even footing, not as a boss and a product that was there to be promoted.

In the meantime, she'd take what she could get. And right now she wanted to see him, hang out for a while and work on a new song that had been playing in the back of her mind for the last couple of days.

The walk to the bar took ten minutes longer than it should have because Dixie insisted on stopping at a coffee shop for doughnuts. The girl was the skinniest chick Stevie had ever seen, yet she existed on a staple diet of Jack Daniel's and doughnuts. While she was topping up her carbohydrate levels, Stevie spotted a pay phone and quickly pushed in a quarter and called Ella.

'Hey, baby girl, how's your week going?'

'Fine, ma. We've got a gig tonight. No idea where we are, though. I know it's a cliché but the towns are all starting to look the same.'

Ella's soft laugh reached her ear. 'Just you enjoy it, my love. Make good choices, laugh and don't waste a minute.'

It was a familiar lesson. Ella would never admit it but she had suffered having two children when she was only a child herself, then working three jobs to raise them. Stevie knew that the one thing Ella was proud of was that Stevie had choices. The beeping sound signalled that her quarter was done already. 'Call you tomorrow, ma. Love you.'

'I love y—'

The line went dead just as Dixie reappeared with both cheeks bulging. They moved on and were almost there when Cally had a bolt of realisation. 'Phoenix. We're in Phoenix.'

'Cool.' It had been so late when they'd arrived the night before that Stevie had missed the official tourist information.

They walked on, ignoring the stares of the people that passed them on the streets. Mothers pushing babies in prams. Kids going home from school. Businessmen rushing to meetings. There was a whole world out there and they felt and looked alien to it. It was like living in a bubble where homes and bills and groceries and normal lives didn't exist. And she wouldn't swap it for anything.

'Henry! Henry, come over here!' An overweight red-haired woman in her forties grabbed a bespectacled child of around twelve and pulled him to her side as they passed. Yeah, the kid definitely needed to be protected from the sight of three pale, skinny, leather-clad females walking down a street in mid-afternoon. Thank God Lou wasn't here or she'd have flashed them.

'Is that it there?' Cally pointed to a neon sign that spelled out the words 'Hog's Head'.

'Yep, think it is. Jude said it was the only bar on the main street and I don't see any others.'

Cally kicked a can twenty yards along the road. 'You realise that Aerosmith are probably playing to sixty thousand people in a stadium in Brazil tonight? Where are we? Playing to three men and a dog in the Hog's Head in Phoenix. Put me out of my misery and shoot me.'

Stevie threw her arm around her and hugged her. 'Honey, it will happen. And what's the point in stressing out until it does?'

Cally groaned. 'If I didn't love you, your never-ending optimism would really fuck me off. Don't you ever get down? Don't you ever want to punch someone until they bleed?'

'You talking about Lou again?'

'Maybe.'

They were still laughing when they pushed the door of the bar open. The first thing that struck them was the smell. The second thing was that their feet were sticking to the floor as they walked. Perhaps Cally had a point – this might not exactly be their finest hour.

There was a guy of about sixty polishing glasses behind the bar.

'Tell me that's not who Lou had to blow off?' Cally hissed in her ear.

Trying not to giggle, Stevie shouted over to him. 'Excuse me, we're the band that's playing here tonight. Where are we setting up?'

'Through that back curtain there.' He motioned over to a tattered purple piece of fabric that was nailed to the back wall.

'Shoot me. Please shoot me,' Cally mumbled.

'Look, just be happy. It could be worse, we could—'

'Stevie.'

Cally's voice was flat, with just a hint of danger.

'What?'

She caught up with her and followed Cally's line of sight.

A jukebox. A pinball machine. Two legs. Shit, no, four legs sticking out from between them. Oh, crap – they'd interrupted Lou in full action with the guy who owned the bar. Time to back out gracefully. Maybe they wouldn't notice. Maybe they wouldn't care.

Hell, how rock and roll were they? Sex on the floor in the middle of the day. This particular floor wouldn't be her first choice, but it was still pretty edgy stuff. She made a mental note to have the condom conversation with Lou again.

'Oh. OK, let's back up,' she whispered. There was still a chance they could get out of there and avoid an awkward situation. 'We can come back again in ten minutes and pretend like this never happened.'

'Stevie, I don't think so.' Dixie this time. She'd caught up with them, and even through the tiny gap in the front of her hair Stevie could see that she was looking confused.

'Sure we can.'

'Oh yes, baby. That's it. Right there.'

*Noooooooooooo.* Too much information. Time to leave. Right now. This second.

'Oh yes, that's it. Harder. Harder, Jude. Harder, baby.'

Stevie froze.

The bar owner's name was Jude? Or . . . no. Just no.

For the first time in her life she realised how it felt for time to stand still.

Jude and Lou. Oh man, she hadn't seen that one coming.

'Cally, I think I just found another use for that gun.'

'I'll do it for you, honey.'

Two choices. Stay. Go. Actually, there were three if you included 'go over there and kick the crap out of them'.

Head shaking, Stevie walked towards them.

'Yes, baby, yeeeeeeeessss.'

She reached them right as they both came. The sound of a smashing glass next door suggested the old guy in the front bar got the memo, too.

'Lou! Lou! Oh f— Stevie!'

Her back to her, Lou immediately stopped grinding and Stevie got a small rush of satisfaction that she'd spoiled the moment. 'What the hell did you just call me?' Lou demanded.

Jude didn't answer. Lying flat on his back on the floor, trousers round his ankles, he had a clear view of Stevie over Lou's shoulder.

'Stevie, don't be pissed, I—'

Lou suddenly clicked on to what was happening and turned round just in time for Stevie to see a glimmer of satisfaction cross her face. That changed everything.

Whatever she was about to say, however she was about to react, that tiny gesture stopped her in her tracks and bumped her over to another path. She would never allow Lou to think she'd got one over on her. That bitch would never get under her skin because she wouldn't let her. Fuck her. Clearly, Jude already had.

Make good choices, her mother had said.

Choice number one: Freak out, go crazy, give Lou the satisfaction of knowing she'd scored a direct hit.

Choice number two: Walk away, head held high, be a class act, say goodbye to something that was probably never going anywhere anyway.

Only one choice worked. Leaning casually on the pinball table, she blanked Lou altogether and addressed Jude. 'Hey, babe, you might wanna get checked out by a doctor, because after fucking Lou I've a feeling it's gonna hurt when you pee.'

With that she winked, turned and headed back out, past a grinning Cally and Dixie. 'You know, Cally, I think we got it wrong. I reckon this kinda shit happens to the Crüe guys every day.'

# BOOK TWO

# OPEN FOR BUSINESS . . .

# THIRTEEN

*Raine*
*New York, 1987*

'See ya later, Raine.' The two cops slid off their stools and headed for the door. They'd be back tomorrow. Ever since her dad had called an old friend in the precinct that covered this area to ask him to keep an eye on his daughter, word had spread and the place had become a hangout for cops looking for a good cup of coffee and a discount on calzone. Occasionally the younger ones took their lives in their hands and hit on her. Invariably she brushed it off with a smile and a large slice of pie.

'Three pepperoni, one margherita and a four Diet Cokes.' Raine slid the plates onto the counter and called out the order in her brightest voice. Four Japanese tourists, their necks weighed down by cameras the size of shoe boxes, took the plates and glasses from the other side of the metal barrier and disappeared off into a booth.

'You're pretty good at that, you know.'

The voice came right out of left field and made her jump, then laugh at her own reaction.

'Jeez, Pa, you scared the shit out of me there.'

'Hey, language, please. Let me live in the hope that all those years at St Mary's paid off.'

As he pulled himself onto one of the stools in front of the counter, Raine realised that he was starting to look his age. The last couple of years had been hard on him and it showed in every crevice and vein on his face. Captain Kirk had definitely been beamed up and in his place was an older, weaker version. His hair was almost completely grey now – still short back and sides and swept back at the top in the style he'd worn since his twenties – and jowls were forming around his once-taut jawline. Teamed with the florid complexion and thickened waistline that caused the buttons of his uniform to strain, he was starting to get the look of a man who liked a whisky or six.

And it was all her fault.

The familiar knot of guilt began to twist around her gut.

'Good to see you, Pa. Coffee?' She was already pouring, so by the time he nodded she was ready to nudge it across the counter. 'So, usual speech or are you here to surprise me with something new?'

He returned her grin. 'How did you get so smart with that mouth? To think we prayed for you when you were a kid and look how you turned out.'

'I turned out just fine, Pa,' she said softly, more a reassurance than an argument.

A flash of sadness crossed his face as he took a sip of coffee, and for a moment Raine thought her heart might break.

'You did, sweetheart. But, you know, your mama misses you. Ain't it time you came back home?'

'And there it is,' Raine said with a rueful smile. The speech. The one that she'd been listening to twice a week for almost three years now.

'Mama doesn't miss me, Pa, you do,' she replied wearily.

Pat emptied two sugars into his coffee and topped it up with cream. 'Why do you always give your mother such a hard time? There isn't a day goes by that she doesn't talk about you.'

Raine had to bite her tongue not to argue. There was no point. Not once in three years – not *once* – had her mother made the trip over here. Raine went back on birthdays and holidays, but Maria O'Donnell loved her only daughter so much that she hadn't managed a twenty-minute train ride in three years. Probably too busy screwing some random prick to notice she wasn't around.

Raine realised that all she wanted to do was reach over and put her arms around him, but that wouldn't help. And besides, a big strong Celt like Pat O'Donnell didn't do public displays of affection. That didn't stop her feeling sick about the injustice of it. He was a good man and although he didn't realise it, every single important person in his life had betrayed him. His wife was banging other guys. His partner died while secretly working off the clock. His daughter. Oh dear God, where to start with his daughter.

Raine knew that her betrayal was the worst of all. She'd caused Ricco's death. Her own selfish, stupid behaviour had caused a man to die. If her father knew the truth he'd walk out of here right now and never look back.

When his coffee was done, he pushed the cup away. 'Thanks, sweetheart. See you next week. Come over for dinner on Sunday if you can.'

'OK Pa, I will.'

They both knew that she wouldn't.

The rest of the shift passed in busy boredom. Manzo's sat on the corner of 41st and Broadway, where the customers were mainly tourists who had someplace else to be and no time or inclination to talk to the polite but subdued girl behind the counter. That suited her just fine. This was work, plain and simple. It wasn't a Brooklyn diner where the customers liked to pass the time of day with some gossip and banter. Gino and Paulo Manzo, the two other staff that worked out front with her, were cousins of the owner – both in their forties, rotund and happy to leave the majority of the work to her. They prattled away in Italian all day long. Raine felt no need to tell them that, courtesy of her Sicilian mother, she understood every word they said. It was flattering but a little unnerving to know that they thought she was cute and that they discussed a longing to screw her at least once every few days. On the other hand, they also agreed that she was a moody bitch and probably thick as shit.

It was after 8 p.m. before the busiest period of the day was over and she had time to clean down the counters. Time for a bargain with God. 'Dear Lord, if you arrange for no more customers to come in between now and closing, I'll say a Hail Mary every day for a week.'

The door opened and in walked a tall guy, wearing a thick cord jacket and a beanie hat pulled down low to protect his ears against the cold.

'Was it something I said?' Cute grin. Not that it mattered.

Raine looked at him questioningly. 'Pardon?'

He was already peeling his jacket off as he sat. 'You rolled your eyes when I walked in the door. Either I've offended you in some way or it's a new guest relations policy. If it is, then I'm not sure it'll pay off.'

It was only when he removed his hat that she realised who he was. Large ham, sausage, mushroom, thin crust, mineral water, roughly once a fortnight, always at this time of night, often with a gorgeous girl, never the same one twice. Raine had him down as either a fitness trainer (great body), a male escort (again, great body) or a pimp.

110

'Sorry, it's not you,' Raine blustered, tripping over her words. What the hell was wrong with her? Dear God, first you toy with me, now you deprive me of the gift of fluent speech.

'Don't take it personally, but it's half an hour till I knock off so I was hoping no one else would come in tonight.'

'Shall I go? Only the last time I ate in the deli next door I had food poisoning for a week.' Raine laughed. 'Well, you'll have to stay then. Can't have that on my conscience.'

Raine took a note of his order (exactly as she'd predicted), posted it through the steel hatch, then went out front to stack the chairs on the tables so that she could clean the floor. She was on the third one when she realised he was helping.

'You don't have to do that, I'm fine. I mean, thanks, but er, it's er . . . OK.'

What was wrong with her mouth? Dear God, you are obviously twisted. I've decided to take my business elsewhere. I've heard the Buddhists are recruiting.

'S'OK, I've got nothing else to do other than sit there staring through the hatch at that guy who's making my pizza. Do you know he sweats a lot?'

Raine nodded. 'I *had* noticed that,' she told him, her mock seriousness making him smile.

He held out his hand in introduction. 'Shay. Shay Smith.'

Raine wiped hers on her apron before reciprocating.

'Raine O'Donnell.'

When the last bright orange plastic chair was on top of a table, she slid back behind the counter. Somehow washing the floor around him just didn't seem right so that would have to wait. It would add ten minutes on to the end of her shift, but she didn't mind. It was actually quite nice to talk to someone, even if he was a chick-magnet/personal trainer/male escort.

'Don't look now but sweaty guy is watching you.' Shay

whispered the warning in a voice that had all the drama of an action-movie hero. This guy was funny and cute. Not a bad combination.

'You're right,' Raine replied, mimicking his tone. 'He's trying to pass on the classified and highly sensitive information that your pizza is ready.'

She broke off from conversation to retrieve it and laid it down with a flourish.

'Want to join me? There's no way I can eat all that by myself.'

'You eat all that by yourself every time you come in here.'

'Aaah, so you've noticed.' His grin was playful and exposed perfect white teeth. This guy was full of contrasts. The whole preppy-perfect smile, sharp jaw and great body were an interesting dynamic against the battered jeans, the hobo cardigan and the beanie hat.

'I remember all my customers. That's what makes me great at my job.' It was a big fat lie but Raine was determined not to add to his confident cockiness.

'Let's see, the blonde you were in with last time was a Caesar salad, no dressing. The brunette the week before was a mineral water. The Native American girl with the waist-length black hair – she's beautiful incidentally – was a fresh fruit salad. I've just realised what you do for a living – you run a WeightWatchers class.'

Raine knew she was being a smartass but he seemed to find it amusing so she figured he could take it.

'I'm a photographer. They're models.'

Ah, good explanation. Although she had no idea why that revelation pleased her. This guy was nothing to her. It wouldn't matter if he was screwing the whole of Tribeca. OK, so she was a bit stumped for words now. Come on, God, a smart reply. Just one. Gimme something to make up for earlier and we'll call it quits.

112

'Cool.'

Mother of frigging God! Cool? *Cool?* Buddhism was looking better by the minute.

She wondered if he was telling her the truth or just spinning her a line. There had been a couple of 'photographers' in here before, giving her the chat about how they'd love to photograph her and telling her that they could see real potential. Yeah, right. Maybe she had the height for it, but that's where the model comparisons began and ended. What those jerks really meant was that if she took her clothes off they might be able to get her a couple of pages in a porno mag. They soon got the message when their pizza was accidentally dropped on the erections they tried to conceal under the tables.

Shay swallowed his first bite and washed it down with some water. Nice hands. Soft. Clean. Do not stare. Do not stare. Oh shit, she was staring.

He didn't seem to mind.

'Listen, I know I don't know anything about you and I could be some kind of mass murderer ... '

'A mass-murdering photographer?'

'Yep. There's one of those in *Hill Street Blues* every week.'

He ran his fingers through his hair. Man, he was sexy. The realisation caught her off guard. Why was she even thinking about this kind of stuff?

'But if you can overlook the whole homicidal thing, would you like to grab a coffee when you get off?'

It had to be said this was definitely tempting. Not so much for the whole boy-meets-girl thing, but just to have a chat. Talk. This guy was quick with the banter and she liked that. It reminded her of how she was with ... with ... Ricco. The thought caused a sharp inhalation.

There had been no one since. She was twenty years old and

had racked up nothing more than a dozen one-night stands, no emotion involved, and no follow-up plans accepted. Rejecting any kind of romantic relationship hadn't been a conscious decision, just a by-product of a solitary life and a mission that pushed thoughts of personal happiness to one side.

She hadn't come to Manhattan to meet a guy, get married, have two point two kids and move back to the 'burbs. She'd moved here because it was the only place that she had any hope of atoning in some way for what she'd done. The only place where she could even begin to get some kind of justice for what had happened to Ricco.

And she wasn't going to achieve anything if she got distracted by cute guys with a great line in chat.

'I'm sorry,' she said, her tone of regret surprisingly genuine, 'but tonight there's somewhere else I have to be.'

# FOURTEEN

*Mei-Lin*
*New York, 1987*

'But no, I don't believe you're a day over forty,' Mei-Lin purred in his ear.

Urgh, he couldn't pass for under forty if he was in a dark room and she had the sight of a half-blind bat. The idiot swelled with pride and took this as a sign to slip his hand up further. Thankfully her dress was so tight that he couldn't quite get where he was aiming for. At least, not yet.

This guy had been here a few times before. Cole Presley was in the music industry and Mr Tang always made sure that he was well taken care of: private room, free drinks, at least one girl, two if they were quiet. Suzy would be seething that she hadn't been given to him. Unlike Mei-Lin and Ami, she worked for Tang through choice. It was her ambition to make it as a famous singer and Tang had promised her that this was a way of meeting the right people. Not this time, though. Tonight the music guy had been given the oriental double act and he seemed thrilled with the choice. She glanced over at her Japanese companion. Ami was her favourite of all the girls: sweet, shy, always willing to help. It made her a target for the stronger girls. Suzy and Tatiana treated her like their personal slave when they were in the apartment.

Ami's story was as depressing as her own. Orphaned when she was six, her grandfather sold her to Yakuza, the Japanese crime organization, for enough money to keep him in sake and food for the rest of his days. Over the years, her ownership had changed hands many times, until she was bought by Tang as part of a deal with a Japanese diplomat who had tired of his shy little concubine.

Mei-Lin cast a glance over to her and saw the despair in Ami's eyes. It was clear that Ami was finding it more difficult here with every passing day. In some ways she reminded Mei-Lin of Jing Wei: fragile, sweet, always hopeful that the day would come when she would follow Ying and be rescued and swept away to a life of happiness and contentment.

Lately, however, it seemed that a light had gone out inside her and a couple of the regular clients had stopped requesting her. Tang had warned her twice in the last month that unless she changed her attitude she'd spend the next five years rotting in a jail cell or worse.

Mei-Lin wasn't sure that Ami cared any more.

There was a knock at the door and Vincent, the man in charge of Mr Tang's security, entered in front of a waitress carrying a large bottle of Scotch, a silver bucket with ice and three glasses. The girls were expected to drink with the clients. After all, it was a party, wasn't it? The only rule was that they never consumed to excess and that they were always sober enough to perform their duties.

Vincent cleared his throat and the gesture caught Mei-Lin's attention. She made eye contact with him, only for him to turn his gaze to the top right-hand corner of the room. She knew what that meant. As far as the clients were aware, the small black box high up on the wall was a speaker that pumped the music into the room. They were half right. What they didn't realise was that it also had another purpose.

Ami poured the drinks as Mei-Lin let her hand slide down further, lightly massaging as she went, causing the bulge in Cole Presley's trousers to grow even bigger.

'What would you like to do with us this evening?' Mei-Lin asked, wishing with all her heart that the choice was left up to her and that there would be some miraculous way of disposing of his body afterwards. 'I was thinking that perhaps you would like us to begin dancing for you?' This was all part of the script: they danced, stripped, involved the client. Even if they were just here for the company and attention, not one of them had ever been able to resist two beautiful girls offering to fulfil their wildest dreams. And not one of them had ever noticed that a little red light had appeared in the corner of the speaker on the wall and that the girls kept their backs to it the whole time.

Ami's eyes widened. She knew the drill. Involuntarily, her eyes flicked up to the speaker in the corner, before she caught herself and focused once more on what she was doing. As she handed over Cole's drink, her hand shook just a little.

Cole didn't notice.

'Dancing works,' Cole murmured, then groaned as Mei-Lin took her hand off his erection and stood up. He made a playful grab at her, but she was too quick, smiling indulgently at him as she backed off a few feet, swaying her hips as she moved towards Ami.

Mei-Lin saw the panic in Ami's face and realised that she wasn't handling this at all. Ami hated the dancing, she hated that yet another act of humiliation and indignity was being caught on film.

The shakes that made her hands vibrate started to spread through her whole body and she froze, just standing there, beads of sweat forming on her forehead.

Out of the corner of her eye, Mei-Lin glanced at the little red light. Tang was watching now. He was sitting in his office, in front of a bank of television screens, watching the action in the private rooms playing out in front of his eyes.

This was not good, not good at all. Ami had already been warned about her performance and if Tang saw her now there would be no mercy.

Mei-Lin slowly, provocatively, wrapped her arms around Ami's neck.

'Now that's the kind of dancing I like,' Presley leered.

The whisky bottle cracked against the table, the jagged edge in his neck, jugular vein split, death in seconds. Mei-Lin parked the fantasy to one side. Right now the most important thing wasn't her hatred of the man on the sofa, or her loathing of the one behind the camera. Right now all she cared about was helping Ami.

Slowly, sensually, she licked the side of Ami's face, tracing a line with her tongue from her neck to her ear. To the camera it would look like the act had begun. They wouldn't be able to see that Ami was as rigid as a board, unable to move. Mei-Lin felt her own panic rising. This wasn't good. She should have realised that Ami's increasing unhappiness and despair was rising to breaking point. She'd seen this back in Cheung's brothel in Shanghai. Between the fear of the new girls and the numb acceptance of the ones who were resigned to their fate, occasionally there came a point where the reality was too much to bear. One of two things happened. The girl quickly got a grip of her feelings and got back on track before the punishment kicked in or she simply broke.

Snapped. A chill ran through Mei-Lin at the thought. She would not lose another friend, and right now Ami was the only one she had.

'Come on, my darling, you can do this. Just move with me, Ami, please,' she whispered, ensuring that neither Presley nor the microphone attached to the camera was able to pick up her words.

She threw a smile over to Presley, just checking that he was still engaged, entertained and oblivious to the problem. The glazed expression and the hand that was rubbing his crotch told her that he was.

Ami didn't move. Rigor mortis had set in to the living. Mei-Lin pulled Ami's hips to hers, holding them tightly, making them sway in time to the beat of George Michael's 'I Want Your Sex'. It was a huge favourite in the club and Mei-Lin knew that the crowd in the main hall would be going crazy right now, dancing with much posturing and graphic moves, singing the words to strangers they'd just met minutes before. Despite her own occupation, Western promiscuity and blatant sexuality was something that never ceased to amaze her.

There was a moan from the sofa and Mei-Lin saw that Presley had unzipped his trousers, releasing a fairly insignificant but solid penis, and was pleasuring himself as he watched. That was good news.

Tang would be very happy with that and hopefully it would detract his attention from what was going on with Ami.

Something had to be done and quickly.

Mei-Lin moved behind her now, positioning herself between Ami and the camera, her front pressed against Ami's back so that Tang could see nothing of her friend. The show still went on as Presley had full view of her hands as they wrapped around Ami's body, slowly moving up and down, caressing her stomach, tracing a teasing path across her breasts. This was nothing new. They'd performed girl-on-girl stuff countless times, both of them putting in performances that meant nothing but would have been worthy of an acting award. Never had those skills of pretence been more required. The eroticism of the scene was in screaming contrast to the panic she felt inside. Still moving, still giving the impression that she was nuzzling Ami, she moved her mouth in close behind her friend's ear again. 'Ami, please, you have to help me. Please don't do this. Come on, my lovely, just move. Just help me pretend and then tonight will be over and I'll take you home.'

Nothing. Not a single movement. Mei-Lin would give anything to stop this, to put an end to the pathetic farce and get Ami out of here, but they both knew that wasn't how this worked. There was no union, no health policy, no legislation covering their working conditions. There was only one way non-performance could end and Ami was moving further towards it with every moment.

Fear rising, Mei-Lin continued to dance, maintaining eye contact with Presley, desperately hoping it would prevent him from realising that Ami wasn't participating in any way. There had to be something she could do. This was terrifying. It was as if Ami wasn't even there, as if she'd become a ghost inside a body that was still breathing, still inhabiting the space. Nothing moved, nothing responded, nothing touched her.

George Michael was still boldly demanding that he be given what he wanted when Presley's eyes suddenly moved to Ami and for the first time Mei-Lin saw a flicker of puzzlement cross his face. The hand that was jerking off slowed to a stop.

'Ami! Ami,' her hiss was more urgent now. She had to stop this going wrong. The angle of the camera was perfectly poised to capture Presley's expression – wasn't that the whole point? –

and if Tang was paying attention he would now realise something was amiss.

There had to be something else that she could do, something that would ...

Ami went down as if a sniper's bullet had just taken her out. A faint could perhaps be put down to illness, to a bug or dehydration, but this was no ordinary collapse.

George Michael was drowned out by an explosion of screams so tortured and blood curdling that Cole Presley jumped up in surprise, his penis shrivelling and dangling pitifully from his zipper.

Ami was on her knees, rocking back and forward, her lungs still pushing out a noise that was barely human. There was no hope of covering this up now.

Mei-Lin fell to the ground and wrapped her arms around the shape of misery, her endearments louder now, more urgent, hushing her like a mother would comfort a hurt child.

'It's OK, Ami, I'm here, I'm here. It's going to be OK. We'll sort this. Just come back to me, Ami, please come back to me.' The tears were pouring down her face. It was almost like the ghost of Jing Wei was in the room. This couldn't be happening again. It couldn't. She could not lose another friend.

But wherever Ami had gone to, there was no return.

'This is bullshit, man. Fucking bullshit. What the fuck's wrong with her? Is she fucking tripping or something? I didn't even fucking touch her. Nothing to do with me. No fucking way. Nothing to do with me.'

Mei-Lin was incredulous. Who did the pig think he was speaking to?

'Get me some water. Now!' Mei-Lin shouted. Suddenly, as abruptly as it started, the screaming stopped and Ami slumped against her, her head lolling from side to side as if her neck muscles could no longer support it. Mei-Lin quickly moved her arm to help, cradling Ami to her chest. Ami's eyes were wide open, but they reacted to nothing. She was still breathing, yet it was as if she was dead. Her body lay there, but Ami was no longer inside.

Cole Presley ignored Mai-Lin's request for water, instead busying himself by tucking his dick back inside his pants and pacing from one side of the room to the other, muttering to himself.

'Nothing to do with me. Nothing. Didn't touch her. What's wrong with her? Must have taken something. She's trippin'. Trippin'. I didn't give her anything. Nothing. No dope on me. Nothing to do with me.'

On and on he went until the door swung open and Vincent strode in, followed almost immediately by Tang. She'd known they would come, but the reality of it sent a freezing chill coursing through her body. She would hold on to Ami. She wouldn't let her go. As long as she held her they couldn't touch her, couldn't get to her, couldn't harm her.

Vincent lifted Mei-Lin up as if she were lighter than a feather and tossed her to one side. Ami's head banged on the floor, but she didn't even whimper.

Leaning down, again with absolutely no effort, he scooped up Ami, threw her over his immensely wide shoulders and carried her from the room.

'Cole, I can only apologise. That was rather, erm, unfortunate. Why don't you let my little Mei-Lin and this little gift make it up to you?' As he spoke, he snapped open a silver cigarette case to reveal a layer of white powder, then grandly placed it on the coffee table.

Mei-Lin pushed her hands behind her back to hide the shaking and forced every muscle in her face to move into a smile.

She had to keep it together. If Tang was feeling merciful he might forgive Ami if this situation was resolved and the client pacified. However, if she caused another scene now there would be no hope of Tang cutting the girls any slack.

Understanding and empathy were two characteristics that were missing when the gods made Jason Tang.

Presley looked uncertainly from Mei-Lin to Tang to the coffee table and then back again to her. Mei-Lin knew that he would refuse the offer. He was seriously freaked out and anyway, what kind of guy could possibly think about sex, drugs and partying after what he'd just witnessed?

'You know what? I might just do that.' The way his lip curled into a smug leer made Mei-Lin want to fall back on her plan to cut his neck and watch him bleed out in agony.

Yes, the naïve little Chinese girl had grown up and developed thoughts that she would never have believed possible. Not that they mattered. All that she cared about right now was minimising this problem, rectifying the drama caused by Ami's meltdown and then getting home to see if her friend was there. She prayed with all her heart that Tang's punishment would be swift and lenient with no long-lasting repercussions.

But then again, Mei-Lin knew that when she prayed the gods rarely listened.

# FIFTEEN

*Stevie*
*New York, 1987*

Stevie knew they had to do something to mask the air of desperation. It wasn't attractive – not in a woman, not in a man and not in a band that knew this was their last shot and if they didn't get it right they could wave goodbye to any hope of a future.

Three years. Three long years of touring and gigging and playing every shitty festival from one end of the country to another. They'd recorded an album that had bombed, failing to make even the lower gutters of the Billboards. It was so difficult not to rage against the infuriating injustice of it all. This should have been their year. The rock genre was smoking hot with record sales going through the soundproofed roof. Established bands like Whitesnake, Mötley Crüe and Kiss were doing great again. Van Halen's *5150* had come out the year before and sold over six million copies. Jeez, even Aerosmith were back. She and Lou had almost come to blows over a copy of *Permanent Vacation*.

The thing that pissed them off most, though, was that they seemed to be missing out completely on the boom-time-baby for new bands. A whole wave of new guys were rocking the charts and they weren't getting in on the act. There were some guys from New Jersey called Bon Jovi who had broken out big time with an album called *Slippery When Wet*. The things that Stevie wouldn't do to that lead singer could be written on the back of a stamp.

One of the conversations that had kept them going during long nights on the road was the big debate as to which of the new acts would go furthest. Cally reckoned that Bon Jovi had one more album in them but that they'd get pummelled in the long term by another group of east coast guys called Poison. Lou, meanwhile, was obsessed by a crew who'd been working the LA scene with them for a while. They were hardcore maniacs, but their music rocked and their lead guitarist was sex with a six string. Slash. What kind of name was that? Freaking genius. Their album title was brilliant, too: *Appetite For Destruction*. If they didn't kill themselves or each other, Stevie reckoned they were in with a real shot at making it huge. For her, though, this year had been all about the Steel Spikes. Straight out of some hole in Pennsylvania, they'd signed to AC Records and she reckoned they would go on to blow that label's big established acts, Nuclear Fear and Decomp, right out of the water.

Stevie had no idea who he'd had to sleep with to get it, but Cole Presley had somehow managed to get them on a gig at Madison Square Garden. Decomp were headlining, the Spikes were supporting and The Bitch of Thorns were a filler in the middle. It was the second gig on Decomp's Rehab Tour, inspired by the fact that the lead singer Randy Storm had been forced to go sober after a scandal that ended in the death of two hookers at his LA home. The guys were dry now and as a supporting act, The Bitch Of Thorns had been forced to sign an agreement stating they wouldn't bring alcohol or drugs to the gig. Stevie didn't need it. She was getting the biggest high ever from sheer adrenalin, topped up with a buzz of fear.

Was this it? Was this going to lead to the break they'd been working for? It damn well had to be because they didn't have another month of unremarkable mediocrity in them. It had been a rough ride. Her sunny disposition and karmic calm had worn off somewhere around the middle of the second year on the road, when the monotony began to wear them all down. If they had a dollar for every time some two-bit promoter or journalist said there was no room for a hard-core female rock band, they'd have enough to upgrade the Winnebago to a jet.

Now she was standing with Jude and the rest of the band at the side of the stage watching the Spikes rock out to twenty thousand screaming fans. The Bitch Of Thorns were going to play a five-number set between the Spikes and Decomp. Cole Presley had flown in from LA to watch them and they knew that he was there to decide whether or not to bring down the guillotine blade and cut the head off a band that had become his money pit. This was their last break, and if they didn't work this crowd and find their groove they could pack up their amps and go look for real jobs.

It was the last-chance saloon for desperate musicians.

Stevie had spent a lot of time thinking this through and she knew she could survive outside the band. She could go back to busking or gigging in bars. But 'could' and 'wanted to' were two very different things. They were so tight now that if it all failed she'd mourn the loss of three years of her life spent trying to make it. And she'd mourn the loss of her sisters, too. For someone who'd always lived a fairly solitary life, she'd become used to Cally's love and to those moments when Dixie broke out of her shell of hair and said something remarkably astute or interesting. Hell, she'd even miss Lou threatening to kill her in her sleep.

126

Nothing said 'I love you' more than a crazy bitch promising to take you out before daybreak.

'You ready for this?' Jude was looking cool today, dressed in his trademark floor-length black leather coat, his stubble giving him that aura of cool danger the chicks seemed to love. Or at least, the kind of chicks that congregated around Jude.

Unsurprisingly, she and Jude had never hooked up again after that day in Phoenix. The easiest thing to do would have been to lose her temper, go nuts, to kick the crap out of both of them and quit the Thorns. But somewhere in amongst the hurt and surprise of that moment, she realised that the people who would suffer most would be the rest of the band.

Instead, she'd gone back to her mom's for a weekend and spent most of the time snuggled up on the sofa with Ella, eating popcorn and watching movies. Her mom didn't push her to do one thing or another. Instead she just listened, then reminded Stevie that she was doing something that could give her an incredible life that only a few ever achieved. It honestly didn't matter to Ella – Stevie knew that all her mom cared about was that her daughter was a decent happy person. By the Sunday night, somewhere after accompanying her mother to church and in between *Prizzi's Honor*, *St Elmo's Fire* and back-to-back reruns of *Charlie's Angels*, Stevie realised that she didn't want to quit. Something happened to her when she stepped on a stage that she couldn't explain or come close to in any other activity in life. It was where she belonged, the only place where she felt truly alive, and she wasn't going to be the only potential music star in history to have their plans derailed over a quickie under a pinball table. Jude and Lou's behaviour reflected on them, not her. She'd done nothing wrong and still had everything that was important to her: her mom, her brother and her self-respect. And her band. Yep,

The Thorns were an integral part of the package and they'd come way too far to give up now.

Decision made, it was easy to go back on the road and refuse Jude's pleads for another chance. They were definitely done.

It wasn't like they were Romeo and Juliet, and let's face it, she should probably have seen it coming. Jude was too good-looking and arrogant to be faithful. Rising above Lou's bitchdom hadn't been too tough, either. Lou's need to do anything she could to get one up on any of them was a flaw in her soul that would stop her from ever being happy or content. Stevie actually felt a bit sorry for her, but she wasn't about to fuck up her own life, and the band, just because Lou had decided to mess with her, so she blanked it. Got over it. Acted like it never happened.

No hard feelings. And she made it clear that she didn't even care if they carried on getting it together. They were welcome to each other.

Now, a million gigs later, Jude and Lou still had a casual thing going, although they were both so volatile that the status changed on a daily basis. At the moment it was off, so Jude was hitting hard on the Spikes' manager, a terrifyingly intimidating Amazonian female called Lori who dressed in a black rubber catsuit and had a reputation for chewing nails for breakfast. Stevie reckoned he had about as much chance of scoring with her as she had of waking up the next morning in a sexual sandwich between Eddie Van Halen and Jon Bon Jovi. Now there was a thought . . .

'Hey, you're in another world.'

His nudge brought her back to the present.

'Sorry, just . . . just . . .' What? Terrified? Nervous? Desperate to make this work? All of the above, but with another overriding emotion. ' . . . can't wait to get out there.'

'Stevie, I wanna change the set. I think we should play "Heaven".'

The other three girls spun round to face Lou, all of them high on the shock factor.

'What? Are you kidding me? We're not changing the set now, it's five freaking minutes before we go on. You're a fucking maniac.' None of them had ever seen Cally so wired and pissed off.

'Hey, hold on! Hold on.' In a bizarre role swap, Stevie took over Cally's position as peacemaker. 'What's going on, Lou? Why do you want to sing it?'

Lou shrugged. 'I don't know, it just … feels right. Can't explain it.'

'Heaven'. The most poignant, heartbreaking song and far, far from their usual material. She'd written it the year before, after the death of Cliff Burton, the bass guitarist for Metallica and the hero love of Lou's life. When the news broke that he'd been killed Lou had shut down, refused to eat, refused to sleep, even refused to deal out her usual litany of crap to everyone around her. Eventually, the novelty of Lou's silence had worn off and Stevie recorded 'Heaven' on a portable cassette and posted it under Lou's bedroom door. The next day Lou came out, resumed being the queen bitch and never mentioned it again from that day until right now.

Stevie stared her out for a couple of seconds and then nodded. God knows they needed everything they could get on their side right now, and if that included a rock god who'd left this earth, they'd take it.

The Spikes were rounding up now, playing out with their killer track 'Act of God'. The adrenalin kicked into overdrive. Yes. This was it. Cally, Lou and Dixie were pushed up against her back now, Cally dangling a reefer the size of a salami from her mouth in a desperate attempt to chill out. If anyone from the Decomp camp saw that there'd be hell to pay. Back on stage the Spike's lead singer, Sly Rammer, was announcing them. Pitching up somewhere between a young Mick Jagger and Jim Morrison from the Doors, he would definitely be invited in on that sexual sandwich too.

'Now kick it up for our favourite Bitches ...'

Crowd goes wild.

'Here we go. Stevie, you cool?' The nervous tick in Cally's jaw throbbed as she spoke. Stevie hugged her. 'Baby, it's gonna be great.'

Back on stage ... 'The Bitch Of Thorns!'

Considering they were relatively unknown, the crowd's response showed an encouragingly lukewarm enthusiasm, sending another surge of adrenalin to Stevie's nerve endings. She could hear a few roars from the guys in the crowd and was glad she'd dressed to please. Their style hadn't changed too drastically over the years. Cally and Dixie still went for a combination of black T-shirt, jeans or leather. As ever, Lou was in a denim skirt that allowed the entire front row to get to know her intimately. Stevie had gone down the more suggestive route: black leather trousers with her trademark white sheer shirt giving a tantalising view of what was underneath. She'd dropped a dozen silver chains of various lengths over her head and her hair was a blonde homage to Slash from Guns N' Roses – a wild frizz that looked awesome.

A hard, demanding chord combination way up high on Cally's fret board hushed the crowd and focused their attention on the stage.

'Are you ready for us, New York?' Stevie yelled, fists punched high in the air.

A semi-enthusiastic response indicated that New York was mildly curious and prepared to give them a shot.

Stevie launched into the thumping vocals of 'Your Heart

Runs Cold', a song she'd written in one of their very first sessions as a band. They didn't stop for breath at the end, taking it right into 'Jealous', then back up to the relentless rage of 'Pass In The Night'. With every bar, every chorus, every verse the crowd's reaction grew. By the time they opened on 'Garden Of Love', there was a unified mass of bobbing heads and frissons of electricity shooting between the band and the head-banging teenagers who were getting seriously into their sound.

Lou and Cally moved up to either side of her, both of them drenched in sweat, jamming out hard, their faces alive with the sheer intoxication of the moment. The three of them sparked off each other, Cally and Lou coming in on the chorus, their harmonies pitch perfect. Lord knows, they'd practised them enough. Stevie could see that the crowd were digging it. They were really, really digging it.

As the last bars faded, a massive wall of noise hit them.

'Jesus, I swear I'm getting a hard-on,' Lou yelled in her ear. Stevie didn't have time to reply because she was on the move. It was unplanned. It was completely spontaneous. It was absolutely fucking crazy. But if this was their last shot she was going to make it a gig that not one single person out there would forget.

Running as fast as she could, she charged over to the side of the stage, jumped up on an amp and used it as leverage to get on to one of the steel columns that supported the massive lighting rig above them.

Then she climbed.

'Bitch. Of. Thorns.' The crowd were chanting now, loving the madness, astonished by her actions.

There were forty feet between her and the floor when she stopped at a small platform, about twenty inches in diameter, designed to give access to some of the stage sidelights.

She let go and raised her arms again, giving the impression

that she was ready to swallow dive to the ground. Over in the VIP hospitality area, the vice president of the stadium's insurance company winced and began to rub a pain that was developing on the left-hand side of his chest.

Stevie looked down on the receding shapes of the people below her, every face turned upwards, the atmosphere cracking with amazement and anticipation.

'I'll ask again, are you ready, New York?' she shouted, savouring every second, because even in her insanely buzzed-up state, she knew that when this was over she'd look back and be insanely terrified about what she had just done.

Stop looking down. Whoa! Stop looking down. It was a shit time to test whether or not she was afraid of heights.

Instead, she pulled her head up, threw it back and raised one arm in the air, holding the mike with her other hand. One gust of wind and she'd be the first person to perform a forty-foot dive in Madison Square Garden.

Someone got the VP of the insurance company a seat and a glass of water.

> 'When you left, you said goodbye.
> I didn't even try
> To stop your love from leaving,
> Big mistake.
> The heart stopped, it was still
> The killing hand of fate.
> And now, my love, we know the truth
> Heaven. Heaven Can't Wait.'

No drums. No strings. Not a sound except the soaring, incredible vocals of love and pain, completely captivating and commanding the attention of every single person there.

132

Up in the VIP box, no one noticed the insurance guy slump to one side.

Down on the stage, the rest of the band fell to their knees, heads bowed.

A cappella to a crowd of heavy rock headbangers?

Crazy. Insane. Never gonna work.

Yet as she sang the last line of the final verse and her head dropped to her chest, the audience roared. The floor vibrated as everyone in the seated sections stood up and let their stools snap back. Stevie slid back down the rig and, at the bottom, turned to the crowd, absorbing the incredible vibe. This was one of those seminal moments that no one watching would ever forget.

This was their moment.

And if it was the last one they ever had as a band, then it was some way to play it out.

Cally, Dixie and Lou ran to her side and together they turned to face the audience and bowed. Still the thunder continued.

On. And on. And on.

It was a full minute before they took the final bow and finally left the stage, all of them soaked in sweat, glazed and euphoric.

'Fucking incredible. You. Were. Fucking. Incredible!' Even Jude's stable state of cool calm cracked, allowing a rush of excitement to burst through.

Stevie hugged him, then felt a hand on her arm, pulling her round to face the other direction. When she turned, she saw that it was Cole Presley.

'Where the hell did that come from?' Cole Presley blurted, pure astonishment dripping from every word.

'Just somethin' we knocked together,' Stevie replied, still channelling the kind of pure ecstasy that no drug could manufacture.

'It was totally sensational, man. It's got hit written all over it.'
This was good. Really good. But was it good enough to make Cole give them another shot?

'Jude, call me tomorrow. It's time we came up with a new strategy to make it happen for these guys.'

*Yes!* Stevie looked around for the other Thorns to share this, but they were chumming it up with Decomp as they waited to go on stage. She was about to offer Cole her first-born child in thanks when someone else got in there before her.

'Yeah, well you should, because if you don't then I might just have something better to offer.'

For the first time, Stevie noticed the man standing just off to the left of them. She knew who he was. In fact, everyone who was in any way connected to the music industry knew who he was. Short guy, stocky, his beard as grey as his thinning hair. This was Ari Covet, infamous manager of the Steel Spikes, Decomp and Nuclear Fear. Major cokehead. Ruthless bastard. Notorious in the music industry. He was the kind of guy that gave the business a bad name, but his acts made serious money and there wasn't a wannabe musician in the country that would knock him back if he came calling with a contract.

Cole's shoulders immediately went back, his chin went out and a defensive attitude took command of the situation; he was like some kind of alpha gorilla determined to protect his pack.

'Fuck off, Ari, these girls are mine.'

Stevie tried hard to suppress the smile that was playing on her lips.

'Oh yeah? And when was the last time you paid them or invested in them to give them a hit record?'

Everyone but Cole could see that he was being played here, and everyone but Cole kept quiet because they knew that it was totally deserved. He'd pretty much ignored them for the past year and this was payback time.

'It's coming, Ari. Don't you worry about that.'

Ari nodded his head thoughtfully. 'OK, man, I'll take your word for it. And hey, you know that poaching acts isn't my style. In fact, I tell you what, I'll help you along. Decomp don't have a full-time support band on this tour because the Steel Spikes are going off to record their album.' He leaned over and winked at Stevie, then said in a stage whisper, 'That's what happens with my bands – they tour, they record and we all get richer.' Shit, this guy took patronising to a whole new level.

Cole turned so red there was a danger that spontaneous combustion would become a distinct possibility.

Ari turned back to address Cole again before that happened. 'So what do you say we put your girls on the tour? Give them real audiences to play to, a bit of exposure and a chance to make some serious cash. Have you got material ready to release?'

'Sure,' Stevie nodded. Stay cool. Stay cool. Do not freak out. Act like this happens every day. 'We've already recorded it. Just waiting for a release date from Cole.'

If squirming were a sport, Cole just qualified for the Olympics. Ari turned his attention back to Stevie.

'Well, I'm not looking to interfere here, but I think you've got something special going on, so I'm gonna give you a break. If you're up for it, I'll sign you on the tour.'

'We're up for it,' Stevie interjected. This was a slam dunk, so she didn't even have to discuss it with the rest of the band. Cally and Dixie would be totally hyped and Lou would orgasm at the very thought of it.

Ari nodded. 'Cool. And if this man hasn't made you little ladies stars by the time we're done, I reserve the right to make you all mine.' There was no doubt that this was some kind of fucked-up, music-mogul pissing contest. Covet was shooting furthest and he knew it. His expression sat somewhere between a smug jackal and a predatory reptile.

Yet right at that moment Stevie loved him more than any man on earth.

This could be it. This really could. Touring with Decomp was a huge deal and if it shook Cole up a bit and got him back on track with them, even better.

'Hey, don't I get any say in this?' Jude spoke up for the first time, having sensibly chosen to keep his mouth shut until now. No good was ever going to come from getting stuck in the middle of the two powerhouses.

Cole didn't even look at him. 'No.'

Jude flushed but didn't argue. Ouch.

'Excellent,' Covet said, rubbing his hands together. 'I think this is gonna work out just great. So what do you say we all go and celebrate our new collaboration?'

Oh God. Stevie had heard nothing but wild things about this guy. All she wanted to do was get the girls and go out and celebrate on their own terms, but refusal clearly wasn't an option here.

'Sure, sounds good.'

'Excellent. Cole, I'll have my guys call your guys to get the details organised. So, ready to hit the town?'

On stage, Decomp had just been announced and Randy and the guys were running past them to another crescendo of noise from the crowd. Man, she loved this. Loved. Every. Moment. She was finally getting close to everything she'd always dreamed of and there were no words to describe how great it felt.

'Aren't you going to wait and watch the band?' Stevie asked.

Ari shook his head. 'Heard those dickheads a million times before. OK, let's go. And you can bring Darth Vadar over there.'

He tossed the last comment out to Jude and Stevie couldn't hide her laughter. Maybe it was time he lost that black leather coat.

'And what about you, Cole, are you in?'

'Where we going?' Cole was clearly irritated and his internal struggle was written all over his face. Getting a gig with Decomp was a major prize for any new band, which would inevitably spin off into album sales, so there was no way he could knock this one out. On the other hand, he was letting his band near a guy who was as ruthless as they came.

'Let's hit 21 and then head over to Reincarnation.'

Was it her imagination or did Cole just grimace? Now he was checking his watch, looking flustered.

'Look, I've got a flight to catch so I'll take a rain check. Get your people to contact us tomorrow, Ari.'

Wow! What the shit was that about?

Stevie was pretty sure he'd said he wasn't heading back to LA for a few days. No time to ponder that, though, because Ari Covet had his arm around her and was steering her away from the stage and back towards the dressing room.

'Let's get those girls together and get out of here. We're about to have the night of our lives.'

Ari Covet. Reincarnation. New York City. This was serious rock and roll.

As she stepped into a limo for the first time ever, she knew this was gonna be one of those nights that would change the rest of her life.

She wasn't wrong.

# SIXTEEN

*Raine*
*New York, 1987*

Raine caught her reflection in the window of a fabric store as she walked past. If her dad could see her he'd lodge a formal complaint with the board of St Mary's because right now her language would be the least of his concerns.

Actually, it might not come to that because in this outfit she doubted whether her pa could pick her out in a line-up. And if he did, he'd be more concerned about her dying of hypothermia than anything else.

She sped up, hoping the exercise would keep the circulation going. The floor-length purple fake fur coat might have been a protection against the elements if it wasn't open and flying behind her in the wind. At five dollars from a thrift shop in the Village, she hadn't stopped to argue about the lack of buttons.

And anyway, this was a personal statement not a comfort statement because the whole point was to reveal what she was wearing underneath. Or rather, what *wasn't* underneath. She thought of it as her Batman moment. Bruce Wayne went into the bat cave and came out as a rubber-clad action hero. Raine

O'Donnell spent her days as a mild-mannered pizza waitress, but at night she became something different altogether.

Her breasts were covered by two strategically placed strips of her trademark crime-scene tape, and on the bottom half of her body, sitting well below her belly button, there was a tiny yellow tutu that stopped anyone getting within twelve inches of her hips or ass. Underneath, a black thong was clearly visible, and when the coat came off her butt cheeks were displayed in all their resplendent glory.

It was shocking by any standards, but as far as Raine was concerned, the clothes alone didn't go far enough. This was about acceptance – not by society or family, but by the guys on the club scene she now belonged to. The only way in was to push boundaries, cross lines and aim for the top of the shock scale, thus her trademark look had developed further. Her hair was pulled back into a flesh-coloured rubber cap that made her look bald. The fake blood that was drenched all over her body took her from wacky to seriously messed up. It was sick, twisted, vile. It was absolutely perfect.

Onlookers in the real world recoiled at the sight, but in club land she'd become one of the elite. Raine Storm: member of a gang of wild and crazy party people who were popping up all over the New York club scene, each one more outrageous than the next. It was all about sex, drugs and hedonism, about refusing to conform and indulging in every fucked-up fantasy a warped mind could come up with.

Raine was one of them now and frozen buttocks were a small price to pay.

'Hey,' Stormie chick, Didi and Choo were lookin' for you – they're in the VIP room.'

'Cool, Vincent. Thanks.'

Her six-inch heels clattered off every step leading up to the front door. In her side vision, she saw the astonished expressions of the civilians waiting in line to get in. Guys in suits and women in high heels and big hair, hope written all over their faces. By the end of the night half of them would blow anyone just to get in and the other half would go home and come back again tomorrow night, desperate to get past that red velvet rope. Right at the start, she'd realised that drastic measures were required to separate her from the crowd who lived in hope that they could experience a tiny snapshot of this life. It wasn't about standing in the cold, waiting to be admitted to a magical world. It was about being in the centre of that universe, about realising that nothing could be achieved by being an outsider. It was about putting herself in a position of trust within the ranks of the enemy.

Maybe her pa would be proud of her. This was the kind of undercover work that usually came with a badge. As she approached the door, it never failed to make her smile that Vincent, head of security, had no idea that she was the same chick from the suburbs who'd been at the centre of that night of hell three years earlier. No idea at all.

'Oh and Storm, need someone to go up tonight – you in?'

'Maybe, Vincent, give me a shout later.'

It was a badge of honour in their crowd, going up on the cross, reigning victorious over the crowd in some kind of Messianic ritual. That wasn't how she saw it. Sick. Humiliating. Debasing. A power trip that exploited those who didn't have the guts or the sense to refuse. It wasn't for her. By playing cool and giving the kind of casual rain check she'd just thrown out, she'd so far managed to avoid it without anyone realising.

As always, Marilyn was behind the cloakroom counter when she dropped her coat in for checking. Just over five feet tall and weighing about eighty pounds, layered with white foundation, red lips and platinum hair, Marilyn had changed her name from

Clara when it had come to her in a dream that she was the living presence on earth of Marilyn Monroe.

Marilyn Monroe. Aged sixty-five. After a life of excess. The woman had a lifetime of experience that had left her with a heart of gold and a coke habit that would bring down a man three times her size.

Raine threw five dollars she couldn't afford into the tips bucket at the side of the counter.

'Thanks, baby girl,' Marilyn purred in a voice that came straight out of *Some Like it Hot*. 'Marilyn not happy tonight,' she went on, with a petulant pout thrown in for emphasis.

'What's up, honey? Who's messing with you?'

'Didi is hijacking my look tonight an' that bitch ain't no movie star.'

Raine went for earnest empathy. Marilyn was notoriously unstable when riled and she didn't want her to kick off. She leaned over and delivered a hug. 'Don't you worry, babe, I'll sort him out. Won't happen again.'

Marilyn sniffed and nodded, like a mollified child. 'An' you can tell him I said he was a bitch.'

'I will, honey, don't worry.'

All kinds of crazy, Raine thought. But then, anyone looking at her in her crime-scene tape and tutu costume would probably come to the same conclusion.

Janet Jackson's 'Control' boomed from the speakers as she entered the main dance hall, straight into a sea of bodies pulsating and writhing to the beat. The first time she'd come here it was to see Ricco. The second was to revisit the scene of the crime, to take a step towards revenge on the twisted fuck who reigned supreme. That was still the driving force behind every single night spent here, but along the way something else had happened to her: she'd realised that she belonged in this world.

Everything about it – the danger, the excitement, the vibe, the craziness – combined to make this the closest thing she'd ever felt to belonging. Even if the Tang situation didn't exist, she would still be a club chick, she'd still spend every night hanging out with these guys in this altered existence because this was more real to her than her old life in Brooklyn, than watching her mother fuck government officials, than serving up pizza to cops on the day shift. The club world had got under her skin and she couldn't imagine ever wanting to leave this pulsating, heaving madness.

Pausing at the bottom of the stairs, she checked out tonight's scene.

At first glance it was easy to see the cliques. The trannies were living it up over on the raised area near the corridor to the toilets. They never liked to be too far from somewhere to touch up their make-up. A group of about a dozen model types were posing just a few feet to the left. They never liked to be too far from somewhere to throw up. The centre of the floor was one third gays going wild, one third serious dance chicks showing their moves and the rest were just tanked up civilians who'd be passed out in the toilets by the end of the night and who would then spend years recounting the tales of their wild night in Reincarnation to anyone who'd listen.

She slid along the black rubber-clad wall to the right, between two rows of mirrored pods, ignoring the long line of predatory lizards standing there in their best suits, drinking twenty-dollar cocktails and scanning the dance floor to see what chicks looked drunk enough to fall for their shit chat-up lines. As Raine passed, not one of them spoke to her. Their reaction was either a wide-mouthed, astonished ogle or a sneer and aversion of the eyes. That was the thing that had surprised her most when she adopted this style. She spent the whole night half naked yet not one normal guy ever hit on her; they were all too repelled, intimidated or terrified. She wondered how her day-time colleagues would feel about her night-time look. Maybe one of these days she'd go into Manzo's in this outfit and revel in the sheer terror of her darling co-workers' responses. Somehow, she had a feeling that their urge to bang her might flatline.

As she climbed the stairs to the mid-level VIP room, she cast her eye along the line of windows that fronted the private rooms. She didn't let her focus go as far as the second one from the far right-hand side. The last time she'd been in there had led to Ricco's death, so the only way to deal with it was to block it out.

Running her gaze along the row of booths, she saw that some were blacked out, some had lights on and a few were already populated. In one of the middle rooms, the curtains were open, the lights were on and a perfectly formed tanned, naked Adonis had another perfectly formed tanned, naked Adonis bent over the sofa and was taking him from behind in full view of anyone who chose to look up at them. Reincarnation – where the most shocking thing was the fact that nothing shocked any more.

'They're right inside, Storm. Told me to tell you to come find them.' At the entrance to the VIP room, Joe, a Somalian bouncer so tall and wide he filled most of the corridor, passed on the information while pulling a heavy black door to one side to let her slip in.

The VIP room was almost identical to the private rooms, just on a much larger scale. Blood-red walls, leather sofas, mirrored tables and ceiling, with a window that stretched for about forty feet along the whole length of one wall, giving a panoramic view of the club below. Over in the corner, topless male bartenders in white leather shorts dished out bottles of champagne and phone numbers to anyone who could get them an

143

acting job, modelling work, or a session providing private entertainment in return for serious cash. Raine had heard that one of them was living with a world-famous pianist in a New York loft, while the pianist's wife remained utterly oblivious in her Upper East Side condo. On any given night you could see a dozen of the country's biggest celebrities in here. Stars like soul icon Della Voight, Dimitri Krakov, Leeane Star and Tala DiVinci lounged on the sofas, feasting on the standard trio of excess: cigarettes, champagne and cocaine. And no, Tala didn't recognise her as the girl her ex-boyfriend once mowed down with a Roller. Giles Corcoran hadn't been in for a while due to the fact that he was serving six months in an LA jail for roughing up a Sunday school teacher he mistook for a hooker. Turns out her father, a judge, wasn't big on the concept of divine forgiveness.

The biggest name she could see at the moment was slouching on a sofa by the window – Ari Covet, head of AC Records. A real piece of work. Raine had come across him a few times before, always loaded, usually with a dominatrix chick. Not tonight. Four or five young girls surrounded him and Raine was guessing none of them had been asked for ID at the door. Ari was holding a champagne glass up to the mouth of a blonde girl and there was a whole lot of giggling going on. She just hoped they knew what they were getting into.

'Where the fuck have you been?' Didi shot to her side and was dangerously close to taking her eye out with the ten-inch cigarette holder that he was waving around like a magic wand. 'Hours, I've been waiting. Hours!'

'You know, I'm glad you're not a melodramatic, wired-up drag queen 'cause that would get real old real quick.'

Didi's irritation was immediately dispelled in a cackle that came out like an AK47 discharging into a brick wall. The now legendary Didi DeMille – only a couple of years on the club scene and already he was calling the shots. It had been a testimony to luck that Raine had latched on to him that first night and been indoctrinated into his crowd. Within a couple of months their numbers had grown and now Didi was the central figure in Reincarnation's alternative scene, the go-to man for anything from fetish to deviance to dates that charged by the orgasm.

'By the way, you have to drop the Marilyn tribute, otherwise our favourite cloakroom attendant will take you out.'

'But I do it so much better than she does. Go on, say it. You know it's true.'

Raine sighed. 'OK, so the choice is a sixty-year-old cokehead or a twenty-five-year-old freak from Poughkeepsie. Somehow I don't think Marilyn is up there congratulating herself on a job well done.'

'Jealousy, darling. Jealousy. Just because I've got better legs.'

Raine smiled as she took the cigarette out of his hand and inhaled deeply. Where's Choo?'

Didi flicked his eyes over to the corner, where a heavy bald guy wearing a Captain America suit was licking the face off a Boy George lookalike. Choo, the one working the superhero theme, had been Didi's lover for two years, but unsurprisingly there were no rules or boundaries in their relationship. At first Raine had viewed these creatures as nothing but a way to get into the in-crowd, but after a while she'd realised that under the make-up, clothes and debauchery, they were actually just guys who had never really fitted in and had now found a way to use that to their advantage. She might not get off on the same stuff that they did but they didn't lie, they didn't steal and they didn't fuck each other over, and that was more than could be said for half the so-called 'respectable' people she'd come across in her life.

In the early days she was sure that they would bomb her out

145

because of her reticence to completely give herself up to the wild side. If there was any coke going, she'd occasionally take a line, but as far as mind-altering substances went, that was it. She was here for a bigger purpose than just to get wasted and she needed to stay in control. The need to focus also ruled out the mass debauchery that was their gang's main hobby, so she avoided the orgy scene by being incredibly bitchy about the options on offer. Fortunately the costumes, the dance and her ability to throw out a killer one-liner had kept them entertained and onside.

'You're looking on fire tonight, baby.' Didi did an exaggerated head-to-toe scan.

Amused, Raine raised a cynical eyebrow. 'What, in a massacred ballerina kinda way?'

'Absolutely. Like Margo Fonteyn meets Carrie. It works.'

Raine felt a little surge of satisfaction. A style compliment from Didi was the equivalent of Vidal Sassoon announcing that her hair looked great.

He grabbed her hand and tugged her towards the door.

'Hey! I'm not dancing, let me get a drink first.'

'We're not going to the floor, divine child. We've been granted an audience.'

Raine's heart stopped. Unless the actual pope was in town – and if she wasn't mistaken there had been at least two papal hats on the dance floor, both of which were attached to half-naked dancers – Didi was paying homage to the leader of a whole different kind of religion.

Leaving Captain America to deliver another soul into the hands of decadence, Didi grabbed Raine's hand and dragged her behind him as he strutted – never forgetting his catwalk swagger – towards a door at the far corner of the room.

The two goons that flanked either side of it didn't budge and for a split second Raine was glad. She wasn't ready for this. Not yet. For the last three years all she had thought about was finding a way to take Jason Tang down and she knew that there was only one way to do it – power. She had to have power in the world in which he operated. And right now she had the sum total of a few weirdos and a grasp of the scene – not exactly enough for a military coup.

'Open, you big gorgeous Sesames,' Didi purred at the bouncers. One of them actually growled in his face.

'Ooooh, feisty. I like that.'

Dear God, he had a death wish. The contemplation of Didi being turned into steak tartar at any moment did at least take her mind off the nausea swirling in her stomach.

It always had to go down like this, she knew that. They'd been trying to get in front of Tang for months – Didi, because he wanted to promote his own night and thereby take another step towards his inevitable rise to the throne of the Manhattan club scene. Raine, because she needed to get a handle on what made Tang tick, to get close to him and find the ammunition she needed to bring about his downfall. However, fantasising about this moment was a lot easier than the reality of it.

One of Tang's goons brought a radio up to his mouth and murmured into it. Didi faked a yawn, then let his face slide right into an impatient purse of the lips. After a few seconds, a change in the hired muscle's facial expression indicated that he was listening to something in his earpiece. Satisfied, he stepped to the side, pulling the door open as he went.

'Straight down the corridor, first door on the right.'

Raine was more than happy to let Didi go first. The contrast between the environment on the other side of the door and this couldn't be more stark. Out there it was all luxury and lavish opulence – in here it was concrete floors and grey stone walls with a fluorescent light running the length of the ceiling above.

Didi stopped at the first door, knocked and waited.

'Ready, divine child?' Didi was like a kid on Christmas morning, hyped up on anticipation.

Breathe in. Breathe out. They can't hear your heart beat. Breathe in. Breathe out. Raine's brain drummed out commands to her failing functions.

After a minute or so the door opened and an Asian chick nodded to them. Raine had seen her around. Word was that she was a hooker Tang pimped out to his high-class, sick friends, but Raine wasn't convinced. The girl was breathtakingly beautiful – almond eyes, flawless skin, glossy hair styled to perfection and a body that could only have been designed by God on a good day – but she looked too perpetually miserable to be a good-time girl. Unless she was one hell of an actress in front of the johns, there was no way this chick was going to show anyone a slice of happy heaven.

'Come.' Miss Asia walked back across the room and slid onto a Queen Ann chair in the corner, and for the first time Raine got a look at Tang's office.

Holy. Fuck.

This might just be where French royalty came to die. Every single piece of furniture looked like an antique riot of curves and gilt. On the wall were oil paintings, most of them featuring nudity, framed in ornate gold. The only nod to the present day was the wall to the left, a bank of twenty small television screens, all showing different pictures. By the time her gaze had reached the third screen, Raine realised that the images were inside the club. By the time she got to the fifth, Tang had picked up a large remote control from his desk and snapped them all off.

The desk. That warranted a 'holy fuck' all of its own. Raised up on a platform, Tang sat behind an almost laughably large slab of carved pink marble atop a deep rosewood base.

Only somehow Raine wasn't giggling.

Behind the altar of ego sat Tang, wearing a gold suit with black lapels, cut as always in his signature ringmaster style. He looked every inch the flamboyant nightclub entrepreneur: rich, gilded, ostentatious. Raine wanted to reach across and slam his head against that pink marble desk until his face was roadkill.

'Mr Tang, thank you for seeing us.' Jesus, Didi was practically curtseying to the bastard.

Raine couldn't look at him. She just couldn't. Since she started coming to Reincarnation she'd seen him many times, always at a distance, always with dozens of people between them. Now he was feet away, right there, and in three or four steps she could touch him. Ricco's killer. The man who was responsible for every tear Ricco's family had shed, who'd taken him away from her when their lives had barely begun. It took every shred of control she had not to go for him, but she'd already thought this through and knew it would achieve nothing. If she attacked Jason Tang she'd lose. Security would have her out of there in minutes and all the effort she'd put in so far would be wasted. There was no other option, she had to keep it together. She pushed her shaking hands behind her back and concentrated really hard on trying not to vomit as her eyes searched for something, anything, to stare at.

The girl. The Asian chick. Raine's gaze settled on her and a jolt of realisation coursed through her. Sitting off to the side of Tang, she was staring at him with undisguised intensity. That chick was obviously seriously in love with Tang because she never took her eyes off him. The thought sickened her even more.

'So how is my favourite freak?' Tang's voice came out in a clipped staccato.

Didi clearly took that as a compliment.

'I have a business proposition I'd like you to consider.'

Even through the panic, Raine could see that Didi was stick-ing to the script. They'd discussed this many times. If they ever got this opportunity they were going to go in direct and let Tang see that they were more than just doped-out wackos.

'Listening.' A hint of a tolerant smile played around the edges of Tang's mouth.

'Sunday nights. They're slow. We'd like to take them over. Run a club night. We can bring in the people – we get the door, you get the upturn in the bar.'

Tang sat back, his fingers twiddling his silver cane like a majorette warming up her joints. A sick, evil, bastard majorette.

'How many will you bring?'

Marilyn would have been proud of Didi's confidence, espe-cially as it was based on nothing but optimism and sheer balls. 'A hundred in the first couple of weeks, four hundred by week six.'

'And how do you plan to achieve this?'

'There's a movement, Mr Tang, and we are at the front of it.'

OK, slight exaggeration. Was Didi known all over the New York club scene? Yes. Did he have a legion of followers waiting at the end of the street ready to storm the building? No. The only person chasing him at the moment was a homicidal cloak-room attendant with identity issues.

What he did have, though, was a growing reputation in the underground alternative world, contacts in most of the other Manhattan clubs and big dreams. Didi wanted to be the Andy Warhol of his generation. He was convinced that he was a pio-neer of his times. And if it got her closer to Tang, no matter how painful that might be, then she was determined to go along for the ride.

'Theme?'

'The Beautiful and the Damned. I'm sure Mr Fitzgerald

wouldn't mind me borrowing his line. We're going to bring together the glamour and grime and set it against a music vibe that's so fucking sexy they'll be creaming it on that dance floor. Haylo and Master V have already agreed to come in on the decks.'

Tang raised an eyebrow at this. Haylo and Master V were two of the most sought-after DJs in the city. Thankfully Didi had been blowing Haylo off since they were both new innocents in the big city, and Master V was a distant cousin. Still, for Didi to deliver them was a major coup.

Tang's pensive manner told her he felt the same. Eventually, he spoke.

'Three months. I'll give you three months, all promo costs are yours, you subsidise any comp on the drinks. I'm not having you buying numbers using free booze from my bars.'

'Deal. And I need a presence on the door.'

'Who?'

'Storm.'

Whoa, first she'd heard of it. But . . . she realised instantly that it was perfect. Whoever controlled the door controlled the club. If she wanted a way into Jason Tang's business, running his door was the perfect place to start.

Tang rose from his chair and came around to the front of the desk, stopping just inches in front of her. For the first time she thanked God for her height as it meant she was too tall to feel his stinking breath on her face. For a second she experienced a rush of fear that he would recognise her then dismissed it. On the night Ricco died she'd been an over-made-up, sparkly eighteen-year-old playing dress-up in someone else's clothes. Now she was an outrageous persona, apparently bald, with freakish make-up and fake blood dripping down her face and body. No one would ever put those two incarnations together.

'A beauty. Not my taste but some people do like the wild and dangerous, don't they, Mei-Lin?'

The Asian girl's voice was as dead as her eyes. 'Yes, Mr Tang.'

'Mmm. Are you sure you don't want to come and work for me, freak girl? I have some very generous friends.'

Raine pulled herself up to her full height and wondered what it would feel like to take that cane and stick it so far down his throat that it came out of his ass.

'I. Don't. Work. For. Anyone.'

The malice in her voice surprised him almost as much as it shocked Didi. Raine could see that he was looking at her quizzically, probably wondering if she was tripping, horrified that she could be on the verge of blowing this.

The tension in the room ramped up as she got herself into a staring match with Tang. She knew it was a dangerous move but she couldn't help herself. He'd taken everything. He'd taken her life, her plans . . . he'd taken Ricco.

Tang was the first to blink, his face creasing into a slow, satisfied smile.

'Good choice, Didi. She's got balls. Fearless. I think this one will do just fine on the door.'

Didi almost fainted with relief. 'So, one month from tomorrow OK as a start date?' he said, desperate to seal the deal before she did anything else to screw it up.

'That works.'

'Fucking awesome. Good decision, Mr Tang, you won't regret it.'

As they strutted victorious out of the room, Raine made a vow to herself that this would be the biggest regret Jason Tang ever had.

# SEVENTEEN

*Mei-Lin*
*New York, 1987*

Ami was gone. When Mei-Lin had got home to the apartment the night before, Ami's stuff was still there, but her friend hadn't come home. This morning she'd come in early to clean Mr Tang's office and used his phone to call all the hospitals nearby. None of them had an admission by that name.

Every time. Every time she got close to someone she lost them. But it was not herself that she felt desperate for. This wasn't a time for self-pity and mourning. Ami was out there somewhere and Mei-Lin knew that she would be scared and she would be hurt.

Where was she?

Had Tang turned her in to the police? That was the threat he always held over them, but she wasn't sure he'd gone through with it because no one from the police department had come to the house or club.

So if Ami wasn't at the hospital, the police station or home, where was she?

When the answer came to her it was so simple she almost

smiled. She was here. In the club. The building was cavernous, with many corridors and levels, so she must be here somewhere.

But where?

It was difficult to contain her anxiety as she sat in the office watching while the two strange people spoke to Tang. Mei-Lin had seen them both many times in the club. The man who was dressed as a female was crazy, unpredictable, always at the centre of the crowd. But the girl . . . she was different – the blood on her face, the tape on her body – and there was a detachment, a wariness about her eyes and an intensity that looked almost like anger. It was probably just the drugs. That whole crowd were always stoned out of their heads on something. Spoiled brat kids who didn't even realise what a great life they had.

The thought threw up another wave of anxiety for Ami. She had to find her.

As soon as the two strange people left, Tang picked up the remote and the security screens came back to life. Sometimes Mei-Lin wondered what her father would think of all these gadgets in the modern world. She doubted that her family had a television or even electricity in their home yet. She had a fantasy that one day she would go back and introduce them to all the technology that enhanced Western life, but she knew that it was nothing more than a pointless dream.

There was no going back.

She had shamed them and there could never be any forgiveness or acceptance of what her life had become.

Fighting back the lump in her throat, she scanned the screens. The front door to the club. The back alley. The corridors leading to the washrooms. The vanity area inside the washrooms. She quickly passed over the ones showing the action in the private rooms. How she'd love to tell every one of those people that they were being filmed.

The dance floor from the north, south, east and west. One, two, three, four, five fire exits. The cellar. The . . .

The cellar.

The camera was focused on the two doors in the basement corridor, deep in the bowels of the club. One was a store cupboard that housed cleaning materials and bar supplies, the other was the locked cellar containing all the liquor stock and beer pumps.

It was the only place Ami could be.

But how could she find out?

She had no clients at the moment so technically she was free. When Tang received a call that Ari Covet was on the way, he'd reserved her time for the record boss. Usually Covet came with an escort, then took Mei-Lin to boost the numbers. Pig. He loved watching a performance – all the more if it involved pain and suffering. She'd been relieved when he'd shown up tonight with a whole gaggle of girls and her services had not been required.

This hiatus would not last long. Since she'd come to work here, she could count on the fingers of one hand the number of times she'd gone a whole night without been sent to entertain.

When the phone rang, she jumped. Tang didn't notice as he picked it up and barked, 'What?'

It was impossible to hear what was being said, but Tang didn't look happy.

'How many has he had?' he snapped. 'Fucking parasite. OK one more but that's it. And if he doesn't like it, call me back and I'll deal with him.'

The phone was slammed back into the receiver and Tang immediately turned to the TV bank and fixed his stare on the screen showing the VIP room. Mei-Lin watched, too, as seconds later a bartender took a silver bucket on a stand over to Ari

Covet and proceeded to produce a bottle of champagne and top up the glasses. Tang was clearly pissed. If the man had an Achilles heel, it was riding higher than most of the human race, somewhere up around the pocket that held his wallet.

'Mr Tang, they are costing you many dollars. Why don't I go and pay a visit to the room and see whether or not I can encourage some of our other regular guests to be a bit more liberal with their cash this evening.'

It was the first thing Tang had taught her when she arrived. When a guest is buying, always ask for champagne and make sure he buys a whole bottle.

Tang considered her request, his thirst for dollar signs blocking any suspicion about Mei-Lin's sudden desire to go out there and engage the customers. Enthusiasm had never been one of her key strengths before now.

'You may as well – better than sitting there on your skinny ass costing me money.'

'Yes, Mr Tang.'

Head bowed, she didn't breathe again until she was out in the corridor. OK, what now? She had to get down to the cellar, and there was only one person she could think of with access to every area.

Vincent.

But first there was the small matter of convincing Tang that she was doing her job.

Moving quickly to the VIP room, she immediately went to the corner in which the camera was mounted. Tang would be watching, without a doubt, so the only thing she could do was to make him think that she was where she was supposed to be.

On a sofa directly under the camera sat Dimitri Krakov, the Russian ballet dancer turned actor and legendary drinker. A fondness for straight vodka ensured that he would never pirouette again. Krakov was wild but harmless with a generosity that was almost as impressively abused as his liver. Every call girl, every escort, ever two-bit starlet knew that if they got in front of him he was a meal ticket to a great night – one that could last for weeks, until he sobered up, dumped them and went off to lick the wounds on his bank balance.

'Mr Krakov, so lovely to see you. Are you alone tonight?'

'Little China girl! It's been a while. Come, sit. Miss Star will be here in a moment and I'm sure she will be thrilled to see you.'

Ah, so the romance was back on. They broke up on a monthly basis, then reunited in a blaze of passion. There were whispers that it was all done for the sake of publicity, but Mei-Lin wasn't so sure. Why would someone cause themselves such heartache just to get their names in the newspapers? And why would someone want the embarrassment of having their lives played out for all to see? It was so undignified, she couldn't possibly believe that it was anything other than genuine, a tempestuous passion that was impossible to tame or control.

'I would love that but unfortunately I am just on my way to visit another client. Please give Miss Star my regards and perhaps I can be of service on a future visit.'

Thankfully, none of that publicity had ever mentioned that one of the sources of the couple's disagreements was her love of pussy on the side – often paid for, sometimes in public and occasionally Mei-Lin.

'But in the meantime, shall I have Miss Star's favourite champagne sent to the table?'

'You're fucking good, do you know that?' Krakov winked as he opened his wallet and pulled out a credit card.

'Thank you, Mr Krakov, I'll just leave this behind the bar as always.'

Some guests received complimentary drinks, some had a credit limit that required a card, some had to pay cash because their bar tab had reached a level that could purchase a small island. Krakov accepted that his gross overindulgence had caused a slide from the top category to the middle.

As she walked to the bar, Mei-Lin made sure that she gave Tang a full view of the card and her actions. That would satisfy him.

'Chad, Mr Krakov would like a bottle of champagne. Please charge it to this card and then ensure it doesn't run dry.'

'No problem Mei-Lin. I'm on it.'

OK, next step. Her larynx closed up and she struggled to breath or speak. She could do this. She must.

'I'm just going downstairs, is there anything you need while I'm there?' Please say yes. Please. She needed an excuse to go down there and this was her only chance.

Chad did a quick sweep of the bar. 'Only problem is the draught beer. I think the keg's done on pump four. I was just about to go down and fix it but we got a rush on.'

She just hoped he didn't notice the relief on her face.

'I can ask someone downstairs to check that for you. Who would be able to do so?'

Chad flipped tops off bottles of Grolsch as he spoke. 'Any of the security guys down there, they all know how to change a keg.'

Mei-Lin gave a thought of thanks for Tang's tight behaviour. Instead of employing a full-time cellarman, he'd made it the job of the security staff downstairs to change kegs and bring up stock when a busy night depleted supplies. Hell, even she knew where the case of ten-grand-a-bottle special edition Louis XIII brandy was kept, having been sent to retrieve one on a couple of occasions.

But that wasn't important now. She had a quick peek at

Chad's watch. Midnight. Perfect. Tang called Beijing at this time every evening to speak to his mother. He'd be busy dolling out the lies and the false platitudes for at least the next half hour.

Calmly, like it was the most natural thing in the world, she walked back over to Krakov and whispered in his ear that the champagne was on the way. Directly under the camera, she'd be out of Tang's line of vision now, so he would think that she'd sat down to entertain the Russian. Instead, she took a few steps to the left and ducked out of the door, everything crossed that he was so engrossed in relaying his latest triumph to his mama that he hadn't noticed.

OK, what next? Stairs. There were no cameras on the stairs so she moved down them quickly and slipped out to the entrance foyer. Right, camera on the cash desk and on the door, so she kept her back against the opposite wall so that she couldn't be seen.

All she needed now was a bit of good . . . yes! Vincent was right there with his back to her, talking to three other doormen.

'Vincent?'

He turned when he heard her voice and immediately came over. The staff in the club knew that if she was sent it was usually on Tang's orders so she automatically took priority.

'Hi, Mei-Lin, what can I do for you?'

The warmth in his tone was genuine and it didn't surprise her. Vincent was a shrewd guy with great contacts in the police force he used to work in, but he was also a bit of a player who'd had a crush on her for a long time. Sometimes, when she was with clients and he was around, she saw the irritation on his face, the clench of his jaw and the pulse of a little vein on the side of his neck.

She just hoped that would be enough for what she was about to do.

'Vincent, the top bar needs a keg changed and they're too busy to come down. I've come all the way down here and just realised that I've forgotten a cellar key. Can you help me?'

'Sure. Guys, I'll be back in ten minutes. Buzz me if there's a problem.'

He tapped the receiver in his ear to emphasise the point.

Once again, Mei-Lin prayed Tang was still engrossed in his call because otherwise he'd freak at Vincent leaving the door at the busiest time.

He followed her down to the basement and as soon as they got through the door she took her moment.

She paused before they moved into range of the camera that covered the corridor and he stopped with her. She bowed her head and sniffed, shaking her shoulders a little to add to the effect.

'Mei-Lin, what's wrong? Are you OK?'

She shook her head before looking up at him with tear-filled eyes.

'I'm so sorry, Vincent, it's just that I'm so ... so ... lonely.'

Her heart refused to beat for a moment, halted by apprehension that she may have misjudged his feelings. But no. Two huge, strong arms came around her and as she turned her head up to his, he brought his face down and kissed her. The feeling was alien to her. She very rarely kissed and if she did it was being forced by the other party. This was the first time in her life that she had willingly given her lips to someone, albeit for a motivation that didn't involve true emotions.

'Vincent, I've waited so long for you to hold me. Please, can we go somewhere? Now?'

His breathing was coming hard now and she could feel the erection bulging against her stomach.

'Mei-Lin, I had no idea.'

Oh for all that was heavenly, now he wanted to talk?

'Somewhere private?' she put the emphasis on 'private' and that seemed to focus his mind.

'The cellar.'

'Yes!' she gasped, then followed it up almost immediately with, 'No! The camera, it will see us go in there together.'

Vincent thought for a moment. Come on, come on. She didn't want to have to spell this out for him, but if he didn't get this soon they were going to be missed.

He flicked the keys out of his pocket and handed them to her, then stretched his right hand up to grasp the camera.

'Go on ahead. I'll move this a little until you're in and then move it straight back.'

Finally his brain was working as well as his penis.

As soon as the camera slid to the side she ran to the door, her palms sweating as she tried two wrong keys before getting the right one. Ten seconds felt like ten minutes until she felt the door open and she burst through.

She flicked on the light and scanned the room. Nothing. Or rather, no one. Her whole body sagged with disappointment. She'd been so sure that Ami would be in here, so convinced that she could rescue her, and now she'd risked everything for nothing. Nothing! This time the tears that filled her eyes were real.

'Oh, baby,' Vincent murmured as he came through the door, looking at her with undisguised lust.

Damn! All that, no success and now she would have to screw Vincent as well. This was not good, but there was no option but to finish what she had started, so she turned and slid her hands up his chest, then brought them back down, unbuttoning his shirt as she went. After dragging him here she knew she had to make this a pleasing performance or it could affect how he treated her in future. It was never wise to wrong anyone who had Tang's ear.

Her first thought was to sink to her knees – wasn't that the act that all men loved the most? – but Vincent seemed to want to kiss her, to caress her just as she caressed him.

She went along with it, allowing him to unzip her cheongsam and let it fall to the floor, then lift her up and place her on top of a stack of boxes that sat directly behind her.

'Mei-Lin, you're so fucking beautiful.'

There was a strange sensation in her stomach and it took a moment to realise that it was a tug of emotion. Never before had someone related to her for who she was – Mei-Lin. She'd always been a commodity, a bonus, a toy for a customer to play with then discard.

He was surprisingly gentle, kissing her tenderly, moving downward until he was almost bent double to take her nipple in his mouth, first one then the other. At the same time, he slipped his hand between her legs, then pushed them wide apart. Their breathing was heavy now and Mei-Lin could feel his body temperature rise. One hand was massaging her pussy, his damp fingers alternating between slipping inside her and rubbing her clit, while the other opened his trousers, releasing a dick that was almost purple with urgency. Both hands moved around to her ass now and he pulled her hips towards him, thrusting his penis into her with a low, ecstatic moan.

'Oh, baby, that feels so good. My dick is on fire.'

Mei-Lin almost groaned for completely different reasons – why did he have to be a talker? They always took longer and expected more than just a vacant orifice and a willing partici-pant. Time to help him along and get this moving.

'Fuck me harder, Vincent. Harder. Oh, yes that's it. Harder, baby.' As she spoke she tightened her vaginal muscles so they held him like a vice, then ran her hands up her body and began to squeeze her own tits, throwing her head back, murmuring variations of this being the most amazing fuck of her life. The sweat on his body was smearing her with moisture now, making her even more determined to be done. While he pummelled her, she brought her legs up high, moving her hands to her ankles and holding them out wide, like a gymnast performing a movement that required almost elastic flexibility.

The resulting position allowed him to go even deeper, his balls slapping against her ass, until she decided she'd done enough and clenched her vagina so tight he roared as he spurted inside her. As soon as he came, he crumbled, holding her so close it was difficult to breathe.

'Mei-Lin, that was amazing. Oh my God, that was so good. It was . . .'

Gratitude. Another unfamiliar experience. This man was actually grateful that she had chosen to allow him to have sex with her. He was thankful for something that he knew other men got for free. This was a difficult notion to understand.

'But the other men and the job that I must do?'

He was kissing her neck now, his fingers kneading her buttocks. It struck her that he might be just having a break, giving himself time to get hard again before going for another round. That was madness. If Tang hadn't noticed they were missing already, then he soon would.

'I don't give a fuck about the others. Look, I know he makes you do it, but this . . . this is different.'

What a fool. All these years he'd seen her be abused, pushed around, whored out and he'd done nothing to help, yet he professed to have feelings for her? What kind of man could do that? A weak one. A fool. A wave of hatred swept across her, closely followed by such anger that she startled herself. This was astonishing to her. After years of keeping a lid on her feelings, remaining detached and aloof, acting like a zombie so the pain couldn't penetrate, she was now running the whole gamut of the emotional spectrum.

'You . . . ' she was ready to spit, to tell him he was nothing, castigate him for being such a pathetic excuse for a human being when she heard the noise.

A scratch. Like a rat running across the wall.

'What was that?' she gasped.

'What?'

The fool was still nuzzling her neck and yes, she could feel the stirring of another erection. She had no idea what drugs Vincent was on but they were clearly working well in the genital area.

Another scratch.

She pushed him backwards and slid off the boxes, grabbing her dress from the floor and slipping it over her head as she crossed to the wall furthest away.

There was another stack of boxes there: potato chips, napkins, cocktail stirrers.

'Help me!' she yelled at Vincent, who was following her lead and scrambling to pull his clothes back on. 'Mei-Lin, what the hell . . . '

A door. Behind the stack of boxes was another door and now she could clearly hear more scratching from the other side of it.

'Your keys! Give me your keys!'

Disorientated, he searched around and finally found them lying just inside the door. He threw them over. 'I've no idea which key . . . '

Mei-Lin went for the obvious choice – the skeleton key that opened all the cleaning supply cupboards. Surely that would be too easy? Surely this would require a special key, one that only Tang would hold?

Click. Again Tang's frugality had allowed her to prevail.

Vincent helped her pull open the door, then both of them paused as their eyes adjusted to the darkness inside.

After a few seconds she spotted a pile of rags in the corner. After a few more seconds she realised they were moving. Only when she dropped to the floor and desperately pushed away the sacks on top of the mound did she know for sure that it was Ami.

'Help me get her out!'

Looking over her shoulder, she realised that Vincent was frozen to the spot, staring at them, his brain unable to compute what he was seeing. Mei-Lin had no idea why he was surprised. He'd seen Tang do things like this and much, much worse before now.

They half lifted, half dragged Ami out into the light and Mei-Lin wailed when she saw her. It was like the worst kind of flashback to her beloved Jing Wei.

Ami's face was swollen, battered and bruised, her clothes torn, her eyes wide with suffering.

'Oh, Ami, what has he done to you?'

'Look, we have to get out of here. Tang will go fucking crazy if he realises we've been in here. You have to put her back,' Vincent blushed.

Ami didn't even have the strength to scream.

'You fucking creep!' The viciousness of Mei-Lin's voice took them both by surprise. Her mind was working fast, fuelled by sheer adrenalin and fury.

'Get me a bottle of orange juice from that box over there, then give me your keys and your wallet.'

'No way, I'm not . . . '

'Do it! Now!'

'Mei-Lin, don't be so stupid, he'll . . . '

She looked up at him and pure venom shot from her eyes. 'You will do as I tell you or Mr Tang will hear about how I found you in here, selling booze out of the back door. He'll also hear that you told me Ami was here.'

'But I didn't know that.'

'Do you think he'll believe you? I'll tell him that you found her and came and told me. Oh yes, he'll know that you can't be trusted and I can be very believable when I put my mind to it. Or you can help me and I'll make sure he never finds out you were involved. Want to take the risk?'

It didn't take him long to make up his mind.

Ami was coming around now, finding her way back to the present. The orange juice helped, as did the relief and the comforting sound of Mei-Lin's voice.

'We're going to get you out of here, do you hear me? You're going to be all right.'

After a few moments, Mei-Lin pulled her to her feet. 'Give me your jacket.' Vincent didn't even begin to object. It drowned Ami, but at least she was warm.

'OK, here's what we're going to do.' Mei-Lin turned and pointed to the delivery doors. 'Vincent, go out that exit, down the alley and get a cab. Give the driver the address of your apartment and give Ami your keys and some money.'

'But ...'

She treated his feeble objection like the insignificance that it was.

'Then you will walk back round to the front door, wait ten minutes, then call Mr Tang down on some pretence. While he's out of the office and on the way down, I'll use that time to get back upstairs. He'll find out Ami is gone but he'll have no idea how she managed it. In fact ...' Her gaze was drawn to a window up high in the cupboard. 'Open that window. He'll

166

never understand how she reached it, but we can lock the door again and he'll have to assume that's how she got out.'

Ami's head slumped against her shoulder. 'Ami! Ami, honey, can you do this? Do you understand? You're going to Vincent's house and when he gets home he's going to take care of you. Aren't you, Vincent?'

'You fucking bitch.'

'You're right,' she replied. 'But I'm the fucking bitch who doesn't have a key, who had no reason to be in here and who will – how do you say it – *fry your ass* if you mistreat her.'

He didn't say another word, just picked up Ami and carried her out into the alley. Tang would have no idea. The same alley contained a massage parlour frequented by certain city officials, so Tang had been refused permission to put a camera on that side of the building.

This was one puzzle the beast would never solve, and that gave Mei-Lin a real satisfaction.

However, there was something else that was giving her an even stronger sense of triumph. Since the day she'd walked into that Shanghai brothel, her body had been used to give pleasure to men, to fulfil their needs and boost their egos. She had been a victim from that day until this.

Tonight was different. Tonight was the first time she'd used sex for her own gain, as a manipulation for her own ends, and she'd just realised the power that gave her.

This life with Tang had become a battlefield. And sex had just become her weapon of choice.

# EIGHTEEN

*Stevie*
*New York, 1987*

So this was what it was like. This was how real rock stars behaved and this was where they hung out.

Stevie threw back another shot of tequila and then squealed as the sour taste hit the back of her throat. Sure, she'd had liquor before, but this was something else. She shouldn't even be in here. It was another year until she turned twenty-one, so she should have been asked for ID and refused at the door.

Yeah, like that was ever gonna happen. Not when they were with Ari Covet. They'd been welcomed to Reincarnation like they were royalty and greeted like personal friends by the tiny Chinese dude who owned the place. Weird dresser, too. You'd never get this kind of heavy glam scene in LA. California was way too laid back for this.

But here?

Insane.

She just had to look around to see how wacked out this place was. That Russian actor had been dry humping Leeane Star on a sofa in the corner for the last hour. She was pretty sure that

Donnie Cray and Brody Revel, two of her favourite movie stars, were knocking back drinks at the bar surrounded by at least a dozen half-naked women. Over on the other sofa, two dudes that she could swear were in the Rolling Stones were smoking reefers the size of cigars. And as for the outfits? Man, they were seriously freaky. Standing just behind them, a six foot guy dressed like Marilyn Monroe had been deep in conversation with a woman dressed in a skullcap, bright yellow tutu and crime-scene tape, who was covered head to toe in what looked like blood spatter.

Yep, seriously freaky.

In fact, Ari Covet had probably been the biggest surprise of all, given that he'd turned out to be a pretty all-round good guy. They'd dumped Jude somewhere along the way in one of the five or six bars they'd visited before they got here, and in every place Ari had bought the drinks and told them brilliantly indiscreet stories about his other bands.

She was pretty sure that no one knew that Sly Rammer, the lead singer of the Steel Spikes, had a raging heroin problem, or that the girlfriend of Dax Rice, the lead guitarist, had a hard-on for Sly.

Or the lead singer of Decomp had a pain fetish and loved it most when it hurt real bad.

Wow, this whole industry was seriously wacked and to her surprise, even though she'd never been one for drama or scandal, Stevie was finding the whole thing totally fascinating.

It might have something to do with the fact that she was more loaded than she'd ever been in her life. Jeez, her ma would kill her if she saw her now. Ella would march her out of here, send her to bed, ground her and then pray for her at church tomorrow morning. This was one of the very few things that she was going to have to keep a secret from her mom. One little blip wouldn't hurt – not when it felt this great.

The rest of the girls were feeling no pain either. At the end of the sofa, Dixie had passed out, slid to the floor and was sound asleep, wedged between the sofa's leather arm and a table of drinks.

Cally had gone to the ladies' half an hour before and had yet to come back. Lou was on the other side of Ari, but her attention was focused on Brody Revel, who had left the harem at the bar and was talking to her without taking his eyes off her tits. Perving aside, how smokin' hot was he? In his latest film he'd played the young twenty-something one-night-stand of a middle-aged model who was going through some kind of 'finding herself' trip around the world. Brody was the highlight of the English leg of the trip and it was a fair bet that tourism figures from the US to the UK had jumped after that, especially in the thirty-to-fifty-year-old female bracket.

Now he was sliding down the age scale and was having an in-depth conversation with two very pert 34DDs.

That left Stevie with Ari, but she didn't mind. He was OK really. Not that she had anything to compare it with, but he was kind of fatherly, telling her how great he thought she was and how he was going to look after them and give them a real shot at success, starting a couple of weeks from now on the Decomp tour.

A worldwide tour. God, that felt good. It looked like she was going to get to Paris after all, and not by busking. This was going to be first-class travel and tour buses, cool hotels and decent wages. She could even fly Ella over and they could go up the Eiffel Tower. She had no idea why that thought was making her giggle.

This was it. This was how it felt to stop playing at being a rock star and start acting like one.

'Hey, what you laughing at?'

'Just happy,' Stevie replied, giggling again.

Ari handed her another glass of champagne. 'Got this one especially for you, honey. The best there is.'

'Aaaw, thank you. You know, you're really a pretty nice guy. I'm glad I didn't believe everyone who said you were a dick-head.'

Covet roared with laughter at that one. Shit, she couldn't believe she'd said that out loud. What was she thinking? Wow, and why did the room keep moving out of focus like that? Man, she had to stop drinking. There was 'wasted' and there was 'sleeping on the floor while a guy who bore a resemblance to a Rolling Stone flicked cigarette ash on your head' wasted and it looked like one member of The Bitch of Thorns already had that one covered.

'Listen, d'you want to go and see the main floor? You can't come to Reincarnation and spend the whole night in one room.'

'Sure, I'd ...' Wow, the room was slipping out of focus again. 'Cool. Definitely cool.'

And definitely no more drinking. This chick had had enough for one night.

Ari pulled her up and then caught her as she half-slipped back down again. Shit, this was embarrassing. She had to get it together. Ari Covet was an important man and there was no way she was going to do anything that would screw up getting this tour.

No way.

It was a good thing he was walking in front of her, though, because it meant she could hold onto the wall with her other hand.

Outside the VIP room, they paused for a moment and a wave of noise, heat and a sticky pungent smell hit her senses, sending her wobbling on her heels. Bad footwear choice. She knew she should have worn shoes that were easier to walk in. Ari's hand slid round her waist now, supporting her as they began to walk again. So sweet. He was such a lovely, lovely man.

They turned left into a corridor, then right ... Or was it right and then left? She wasn't sure. But she was beginning to feel real thirsty. Water. That was what she needed. A big glass of water and she'd be back on top again.

Left. Right. Left. Then into a room. A room that was – freaking shit, she could see the whole club from here! There was a window right in front of her and it looked down on hundreds, no, thousands of people dancing, all of them grinding it out. Erasure were setting the place on fire with 'Victim Of Love'. Yeah! One of her favourite songs ever. Instinctively, she started moving and it felt real good. The best. From her toes to the top of her head all she felt was ... happy. So, so happy. This was the best night of her life and nothing could spoil it. Nothing could take away this feeling of pure, unadulterated bliss.

And ah, there was Ari again. What a sweet guy. He was holding out another glass of champagne for her. She shouldn't take it but ... perhaps just one more because she was so thirsty. That would help. Champagne was just like water really, but with bubbles.

She liked bubbles.

She liked Ari.

She liked it here.

This was just so great. The best night of her life.

Ari liked her, too. He had his arms around her now and he was kissing her neck. Lovely, Ari. Lovely man. She loved Ari.

Oh that felt so good. She was dancing and Ari was taking off her shirt now and he was telling her how pretty she was. She felt pretty. And now he was pouring more champagne in her glass and ... on her! It poured all over her neck and down over her breasts and she was laughing now and so was he. It tickled so bad.

Ari was licking it off now and his lips were around her nipple and oh, that felt good. That felt so, so good. Her head fell backwards and she laughed again.

'Feel good, baby?'

'Real good.' Whose voice was that? It didn't sound like her. That sounded like Lou's voice, all sexy and purring like a cat. The thought made her laugh again. She'd stolen Lou's voice. There'd be a riot if she didn't give it back.

More champagne and this time she felt it pour down her stomach. Her trousers were open. How did that happen? She must have forgotten to close them last time she went for a pee. Or maybe Ari had done that. Maybe he wanted to see what she looked like under those leathers.

Ari thought she was pretty. He kept telling her that. Pretty girl.

More champagne. This time it was right down her stomach, onto her thighs and ... where were her clothes? She had no clothes on now. Where had they all gone?

Didn't matter, this felt really lovely. She was still nice and warm and cosy. It was because Ari was cuddling her. She was sitting on his knees now and he was cuddling her and kissing her and it felt so incredibly nice. Thirsty. She was still thirsty. And ... sleepy. Ari wouldn't mind if she went to sleep, would he? No, he just wanted to be her friend and take care of her. He'd told her that lots of times tonight. Just a little nap. Just a few minutes. She'd sit here on Ari's knees and she'd just have a little ... sleep.

Sleep.

Sleep.

Sleep.

The noise. What was that noise?

It was hot now. Hotter than she'd ever felt before. Humid. She could feel beads of sweat pop out all over her body. The noise. She just had to open her eyes but they were so heavy.

Moving. She was moving. It was as if she were flying yet she couldn't move her arms or her legs.

And still the noise, like thousands of people chanting all at once.

'Up. Up. Up. Up.'

What did that mean? What was up? Maybe it was her. Maybe she really was flying. Eyes. Had to open her eyes just a little and . . .

She was flying. All those people looked so little down there, and they were all looking up at her and chanting and she was flying above them like an angel. Was she an angel now?

Her arms felt weird – they were out to each side and they wouldn't move. Why? Why wouldn't they move? Didn't angels have arms?

Wings! They had wings! That was how she could fly because she had wings and she could go anywhere now.

So thirsty. So tired. So hot.

'Up. Up. Up. Up.'

Sleep. Maybe she'd just sleep a little longer. Just until she felt all better. Angels had to sleep, didn't they?

Sleep.

Sleep.

Sleep.

'Stevie!'

Sleep.

Sleep.

'Stevie, wake up you lazy cow.'

Sleep.

174

'Stevie! What the fuck was she drinking last night? She's totally out of it.' Lou's voice.

'Don't ask me.' Dixie was speaking now. 'I was senseless by the time we got to Reincarnation. Does anyone know why I've got ash in my hair? And some dude has written "Mick Jagger" on my arm. What weird kinda fuck does that?'

Stevie felt a wave of relief. She was with the girls so that must mean they were back in the hotel.

Forcing open one eye, she had a quick look then slammed it shut again. Yep, the hotel.

'Hey, sleeping beauty stirred there. Come on, prima donna, we've got rehearsals to go to. Apparently we're preparing for a tour.' Cally's voice. And she sounded so happy.

The tour. They were going on tour with Decomp. That was so fantastic.

This time Stevie managed to get both eyes open, earning a round of applause from her band mates. Wearily, she tossed a pillow at Lou's head. Unsurprisingly, it missed.

'So how'd you get back here last night then?' Cally asked. Stevie shrugged. 'No idea. The last I remember I was ... I've no idea. Talking to Ari, I think. What about you guys?'

Lou beamed with pride and satisfaction. 'Brody Revel. His hotel. Sex all night long. Frickin' A. Maze. Ing. That guy knows what he's doing. Better than doing one of those work-out videos. And he says he's going to come and see us on the tour.'

Stevie smiled in what she hoped came over as a congratulatory manner.

'What about you guys?' she asked Dixie and Cally.

Dixie shrugged. 'No idea. But if I ever find out what bastard wrote Mick Jagger on my arm, I'll be having a conversation. Can't get the fucking thing off.'

Her forearm was red and raw now but she carried on scrubbing it with a wet facecloth from the bathroom.

'Cally?' There was no disguising the hopeful tone in her voice, but Cally was no help.

'Dunno. I hooked up with a dude in the bathroom and we split. I just got in an hour ago.'

'Ooooooooh!' Lou and Dixie went for a full-scale tease. Stevie just winced and held her head to stop it exploding.

'Ari Covet must have brought me back to the hotel then.' A horrible thought suddenly hit her and she immediately grabbed at the sheet and held it up, checking underneath. Phew. Still fully dressed in last night's clothes.

Her actions brought on the closest thing to a smile she could manage. She had no idea why she'd just done that. As if someone like Ari Covet was going to have sex with her in the state she must have been in last night. Nope, she couldn't remember a thing. That was definitely the most wasted she'd ever been in her life.

She should really drop Ari a line to say thanks for getting her back. Or maybe call him? Was that the correct thing to do under the circumstances? Maybe not. It felt a bit weird. And let's face it, Ari Covet had been in the music industry for decades and managed some real hardcore bands. Surely there was nothing he hadn't seen. One young girl drinking too much in his presence and then passing out was hardly going to scandalise the man.

No, she'd just leave it and casually thank him next time she saw him.

In the meantime, she just wished she could remember anything that had happened last night. How incredibly stupid of her. She finally makes it to one of the most famous clubs in the country, gets into the VIP section, mingles with all sorts of . . .

shit, she wished she could remember who was there. But there were definitely famous people. Definitely. Anyway, she gets to the very pinnacle of New York nightclubs and she can't even remember being there, leaving there, or anything that happened in between.

Pathetic.

She'd made a complete idiot of herself, fallen asleep in the company of one of the most important men in the industry, forcing him to abandon his night to take her home.

Not her finest moment. In fact, it was thoroughly mortifying.

Pushing herself up into a sitting position, she grabbed a bottle of water from the bedside table and finished the lot in one go. That felt better. A few Tylenol and she'd be over it.

No point in brooding, dwelling on it or beating herself up. She'd fucked up but it was over now. Finished. No long-term harm done and by the looks of things the only people who knew what she'd done were Ari and her. Scrap that – only Ari. And he wasn't the kind of guy to go blabbing about a stupid girl having too much to drink.

The whole thing was best just forgotten about. It was over. She would chalk it up to inexperience and then just forget about it.

Done. Dusted. After all, even if she did get a bit wild, it wasn't as if anyone else saw what she'd got up to . . .

# NINETEEN

*Raine*
*New York, 1988*

Raine let out a long, low whistle as three new customers strolled through the door. 'You have got to be kidding me. The Miss Universe contestant from last week almost tipped me over the edge but these girls are your best yet.'

The two tall Barbie-like dolls giggled uneasily, both of them looking at Shay questioningly.

'Don't worry, ladies, this is Raine. She's harmless. Mostly. But check your food before you eat it.'

'Heed that advice, Mr Smith. Heed that advice.' Raine laughed as she slipped some menus in front of them. Ten bucks said she could write the order already. Two green salads, dressing on the side. Two mineral waters. Shay's usual pizza and a full fat Coke.

In the meantime, she tried not to stare. These two were like honest-to-God dolls. Long blond curls to the waist, huge blue eyes and a breast-to-waist ratio that should ensure they toppled over when they tried to walk.

'We're just going to pop to the washroom.' They giggled. Why? Oh lordy, they were that kind of chick – the ones that did the girly giggle after every sentence. 'Could you order us up a couple of green salads and some water?'

Raine smiled sweetly. 'Of course I can. My pleasure.'

They wiggled off, still giggling.

Shay nodded to her pad. 'Well?'

She held it up and let him read it. '2 G. Salads. 2 Water.'

'You're seriously good at that.' The way his eyes creased up when he grinned just never got old.

'I'm fifty per cent detective. It's in the blood.'

'And the other fifty per cent?'

For a moment she contemplated giving him an honest answer, but she had the feeling that viewing her as fifty per cent whore would affect their friendly banter.

There was no getting away from the fact that she was incredibly attracted to him. He made her laugh, he was smart, they had that kind of easy rapport that all good friendships needed, and there was no denying that he was easy on the eye.

'So is there any point in asking you again?'

One year, one week and three days since he'd first asked her out, and since then he'd repeated the question at least a dozen times. She wouldn't be human if she hadn't thought about saying yes. He was gorgeous, funny, smart and there wasn't a female with 20/20 vision who could deny that he was major league sexy. She'd found herself looking forward to him coming in and being disappointed when he didn't appear. But in the end, she knew her complicated life left only one answer.

'Nope. None at all. And anyway, what the hell is the matter with you? You're in here with most guys' idea of a wet dream and you want to ask out the quirky-looking Italian girl behind the counter. I can't possibly go out with you on the basis that you're clearly insane. You should be spending every spare second trying to come up with ways to get Barbie and Cindy naked.'

Shay shrugged. 'Already. But not in that way. Torrelli Tyre calendar today – they're June and July.'

'Great. So you've seen them naked. You're dead to me. Dead.' Harsh words, breezy tone, delivered with a smile.

He picked up a knife from the cutlery set in front of him and mimicked stabbing himself through the heart. 'Can't take it anymore. Don't try and stop me.'

'If you bleed out on that floor, I'll freak out – I've just spent twenty minutes cleaning it.'

The knife went down and he put his hands up in defeat. 'OK, OK. But I'll wear you down and you'll be so sick of me asking that you'll go out with me just so I'll stop bugging you.'

'Nope, that's what restraining orders are for.'

The giggles alerted her to the return of the killer Barbies. They sidled up on either side of Shay, all wide-eyed and flirty.

Her teeth automatically began to grind. Sure, the scene in front of her hurt just a bit but she couldn't complain because it was of her own doing. There was only room in her life for one man, and he was long dead.

'Ladies, help me out. What can I do to get Raine here to go out with me?'

Barbie and Cindy looked at her with undisguised astonishment, layered with just a hint of an irritated sneer. She knew what they were thinking and she didn't come out of it well.

Eventually Barbie, or maybe it was Cindy, realised that they should really play along if they wanted to get Shay's attention.

'Go on, babe, live a little. Get a little wild. You might even like it,' Cindy purred in Raine's direction.

For a moment she was tempted to tell them just how wild she could be.

\*

'Female in white shoes, nope. Guy who looks like he's borrowed his dad's suit, nope. Cheerleader girl is fine and don't let that rocker guy anywhere near me – that beard is infested.'

Vincent nodded with each instruction and then carried out her wishes, politely refusing everyone except a female on roller skates wearing nothing but a short skirt and two strategically placed pompoms.

The rocker guy started to argue but she cut him off with a definitive, 'Fuck off,' before producing a camera from behind her back and quickly snapping his face.

'For the cops,' she said with a sweet smile. There was a moment of stunned hesitation before he called her a fucking bitch and stormed off. The camera usually did the trick. No one wanted their mugshot taken before they'd actually committed a crime.

Vincent shook his head and suppressed a smile as the Led Zeppelin tribute guy stormed off down the stairs. He'd once admitted to her that he'd initially struggled to accept her presence and opinions on the door, but he'd got over himself after a couple of weeks when he realised that she was fair, firm and took no crap from anyone, including him.

In truth, her outfits were usually intimidating enough that only the very drunk or the very self-important argued with her.

Tonight she was wearing her favourite: black latex pants with a row of metal spikes protruding from her ass, finished off with her trademark looks – bald cap, crime-scene tape around the torso and lashings of fake blood streaked across her face and body.

The Sunday club night had been running for a year now and it had taken off big time. The queues were long, the reputation was fierce and the takings at the door regularly broke records. Didi had been true to his word – he'd brought in the trendies from all over the scene. Her ruthless door policy had kept the numbers down in the beginning but people soon got the message. This wasn't for tourists or corporate nights out, this was hardcore party and only those who made an effort were coming in.

They came in droves.

In the beginning the attraction was the DJs and the novelty value of a new outlet, but recently Raine had begun to notice a change.

She checked the clicker in her hand. Eighteen hundred. Capacity crowd.

'OK, Vincent, shut it down. No one else gets in unless they're on the guest list. Buzz me if there are any problems.'

'Will do.' He signalled to the rest of his guys that the door was shut, prompting a collective groan from the waiting crowd.

Raine dipped back inside and made her way up to the back of the stage. She kicked the cross that lay there as she passed it. That had been rule number one – none of that pseudo-religious shit on their club night.

Ignoring a couple who were getting it on in the shadows just behind the DJ booth, she used her key to slide open the catch on the back door of the glass room and ducked inside. Haylo was pumping up the crowd and they were giving it back to him.

However, she could sense straight away that the atmosphere was off. In the beginning this had been all about a celebration of freedom, a gang of misfits and party people who came together, and it was all about music, sex and style.

Somewhere over the year there had been a subtle shift.

Up in the gallery of private rooms, she could see people dancing, drinking, and there were a few rooms where the action was very obviously X-rated. Up in the VIP bar, she knew the beautiful people would be indulging in every excess they desired.

But it was down on the ground floor that she could see a

change. On the dance floor, the frenetic moves of the cocaine and ecstasy generation reigned supreme, but in the shadows at the side, where the lizards used to scope their prey, now there were zombies. And every week their numbers were increasing.

Reincarnation was being taken over by something new.

Ketamine was getting a grip on their crowd and Raine knew exactly who was to blame.

One hand on the deck, the other on the left cup of his headphones, Haylo grinned and winked at her as she ducked back out of the box. He'd been a brilliant investment. In a city where anyone could get five minutes of fame, Haylo's pulling power showed absolutely no sign of diminishing. This was his night and people came from all over the state to see him, a draw that had been boosted by his appearance on Leeane Star's first music video. It wasn't often that actresses made the transition to music, but the fact that she could hold a tune and never wore anything more than fishnet stockings and a leather bra and knickers had assured her video was one of the most played on MTV.

Raine slinked through the crowd to the east staircase, taking the steps two at a time up to the VIP room. Hopefully she wouldn't bump into Tang. It was getting harder and harder not to punch the little prick's lights out, but she knew she had to be patient. Payback was coming – she just had to figure out where, when and how.

Patience.

Hadn't her dad always told her that the secret of a successful operation was patience?

The VIP room was thick with smoke and a sweet, intoxicating perfume. Raine recognised it straight away. Dior's Poison. Apt for this place.

She scanned the room for Didi but couldn't see him anywhere.

Exasperation took hold. He was getting more unreliable by the week. This was his job – to stay up here, schmooze the VIPs, keep them coming and the masses would follow. How fucking hard could that be?

Rubbing the back of her neck brought her blood pressure back down a notch and she chided herself for getting annoyed. It was exhaustion. Working full shifts in the pizzeria, then spending every waking hour promoting this night was taking its toll. Sure, they were making good money, but they didn't have any time to spend it. Cancel that thought – *she* didn't have any time to spend it. Didi on the other hand . . .

She caught a horizontal flash of red over in the far corner and realised she'd just found her partner. It was a depressingly familiar sight.

Smiling at every well-known face on the way, she crossed the room, praying that nothing would kick off before she got to him. Or her. It was difficult to tell which gender Didi was going for tonight, with his red rubber hot pants and basque over black patterned stockings and vertiginous heels. So far so female. It was the red rubber gimp mask that threw the look.

He was sprawled across a sofa, absolutely dead to the world. Great advert for the club. But right now, that was the last thing on her mind.

Her Didi. How had he got to this?

'Storm, can you let Didi know that the guys downstairs are looking for some more stuff. Been a busy night tonight.' The nonchalance in Joe, the security guy's voice said it all. When had Didi stopped being a promoter and started being a dealer?

She looked at him again, completely comatose, dribble running from the side of his mouth.

And when had he stopped being a dealer and started being a user?

'Well, it looks like the shop is shut so he'll just have to fucking wait.' She instantly regretted taking it out on Joe, but she was just so pissed with this whole crappy situation.

It took every ounce of effort, but – ignoring the glances of the regulars – she dragged Didi upright. 'Don't just stand there, give me a hand.'

The urgency in her voice kicked Joe into life and he used some kind of fireman's manoeuvre to get Didi onto his shoulder.

'Take him into the back corridor. Where's Tang?'

'In one of the private rooms with Tala DiVinci and that bloke from the Bond movie.'

Excellent. If Tang saw Didi like this the little bastard's wrath would be unleashed. Ironic really. He was the one that supplied the K, giving Didi a cut of the profits, but he'd hit the roof if he saw him like this again. Final warning, he'd said last time. Despite the fact that they were making him money, she knew Tang would cut them out in a heartbeat.

Didi was too big and heavy for Joe's shoulder to support, so he manoeuvred him round so that it was more of a dragging situation. A group of actresses from a sitcom stared in undisguised disgust as they half carried/half pulled Didi past them. It was OK for them to ingest large quantities of Columbian talc up their nasal passages, but passing out? Well, that was to be sneered at. Raine wanted to toss the lot of them out, but she knew she was just misdirecting her anger. Why the fuck did he have to do this? Watching him killing himself over the last few months had been agony. He'd always liked his cocaine and ecstasy, but this was a whole different ball game. Hallucinations. Mood swings. Irrational behaviour. And when he mixed it up with straight tequila the paranoia and schizophrenic behaviour kicked in.

Yet he wouldn't stop. Said it was the wildest ride. And Raine knew that Didi never, ever got off a roller coaster.

The corridor was dark and as the door slammed behind them Didi stirred. 'What the fu—'

He wrestled his arms free from theirs, slamming Raine against the wall as he fought to escape them.

'Didi, it's OK, it's me. It's . . .'

'GET THE FUCK AWAY FROM ME!'

Even in the dim light she could see that his eyes were wide and saliva was spraying with every word. Shit, he was really gone this time. If she didn't get him out of here, he'd—

'I know what you're doing!'

SLAM! Every time she tried to stand up he slammed her back against the wall.

Joe reacted quickly, got him in a headlock and pulled him back.

'Get the fuck away from me. Fucking murderers! You're all fucking murderers!'

Every second of this felt like a chisel was chipping away another piece of her heart. Her wild, crazy, sweet Didi. Where had he gone?

Joe was struggling to restrain him as Didi fought against him. At the far end of the corridor a door opened and Raine panicked. It would be staff on their way back to the bar from their break. If they saw Didi like this Tang would hear about it in no time. Much as she'd come to realise that every person on the payroll hated him, it wouldn't stop the more two-faced employees trying to brown-nose the boss by keeping him in the know.

'In here! Get him in here!'

She opened the door behind her and all three of them stumbled in. Shit. Only when she hit the floor did she realise it was the last place she wanted to be. Tang's office. Fuck. Fuck. Fuck.

Thank God there was no one—

Wait.

From down behind the desk a head appeared, with a face that looked as terrified as she felt.

The Chinese girl. What was her name? She'd only ever heard her called China Girl.

'What are you doing here?' The voice was high, fearful, yet the English was almost perfect.

Raine decided the answer was pretty obvious. Joe was on top of Didi now, sitting on his chest as he thrashed from side to side, eyes glazed, face contorted in something between pain and evil.

Raine quickly clambered to her feet.

'Tang! Where is he?'

The Chinese girl immediately scanned the monitors. 'Just leaving room twenty-four. He'll be here in five minutes, less if he doesn't stop to check the takings in the VIP bar.'

'Shit! You've got to help us, please!'

For a moment Raine was sure that China Girl was going to refuse.

'Please!'

The perfect, oval face and slanted brown eyes turned back to the monitors. 'He's in the VIP room now. I will go and find a way to keep him there. But you must get your friend out of here quickly.' She picked up a radio from the desk and spoke into it.

'Vincent, this is Mei-Lin. We have an emergency on the back stairs. Come alone and quickly.'

Only the fact that Didi was still thrashing around, screaming like a maniac, stopped Raine from throwing her arms around this girl and hugging her.

'I will go now. Get your friend through there and down the stairs.' She motioned to a doorway at the back of the office.

187

'Vincent will meet you on the way and help you. It leads to the basement and there's a door from there to the alley outside.'

Before Raine could thank her she was gone.

Didi was bucking now, lying on his back, thrusting his hips upwards, determined to get Joe off him. How the hell were they going to get him under control?

'Cunts! You murdering cunts!' His screams cut through her hesitation.

'Knock him out!'

There was a moment's hesitation as Joe looked at her quizzically.

'We'll never get him anywhere like this. You have to knock him out.'

The punch landed with a sickening thud and suddenly Didi was still. Raine's stomach tightened even further. Joe read her mind and slipped two fingers to the side of Didi's neck.

'Don't worry, he's OK. Pulse is on overdrive. But he'll have a fucker of a headache tomorrow.'

Raine quickly glanced up at the security screens and saw that China Girl was talking to Tang in the VIP bar, guiding him over to talk to some female who looked like Melanie Griffith. Or was it Meg Ryan? The angle and the clarity of the picture left room for doubt.

'OK, let's go. Can you drag him?'

Joe nodded and hooked his hands under Didi's armpits. Raine held the door open and they pulled him through. As soon as they were in the stairwell, she picked up his feet and they got him down the first flight of stairs. She was fit, but even so her heart felt like it was going to explode by the time they got to the second landing, so it was a huge relief when Vincent appeared.

Between the three of them they got him down to the bottom

of the stairs and Vincent kicked open the first fire door they came to. As China Girl promised, it led to the alley at the side of the building.

The cold air hit her like a bolt of electricity. Motion sensors outside the massage parlour further down the alley kicked on and flooded them with light.

'What the fuck happened?' Vincent ran his fingers through his hair and tucked his shirt back into his trousers as he spoke, clearly not enamoured with the situation. Joe was bent double, his hands on his knees, taking huge deep breaths. Didi lay in a heap, his bizarre costume a flamboyant contrast to the garbage bags and dumpsters behind him.

'I'm sorry, Vin, but he went crazy and I couldn't let Tang see him like that. It would be the end for him.' Raine pleaded with him for understanding. Over the last year, she'd built up a good relationship with Vincent, but she had little doubt where his loyalties lay. He was Tang's man through and through.

'Come on, Vincent, China Girl said you'd help.'

Something in his face changed and he nodded, almost defeatedly.

'Joe, get back upstairs. This never happened. Get it?' His voice was calm but firm.

'Sure, boss.' Surprise was written all over Joe's face, but he didn't question Vincent's command. Many of the guys Vincent recruited were ex-service or guys who, for one reason or another, had been kicked off the force. They were used to following orders and keeping quiet.

'OK, so what next? How am I going to—'

The sentence stuck in mid-air as Raine realised that, a few feet away, Didi had stumbled to his feet.

He was clearly dazed and disorientated, but he was up and moving.

'Didi . . . ?'

Slow. Calm. Taking a step towards him, she held out her hand.

'Didi, it's OK, I'm here. We're going to get you home. You're gonna be fine. Just—'

'NOOOOOOO!' The scream and freaked-out expression proved he was still wired, still wasted. He was backing away from her now.

Christ, he'd been knocked out, sat on, dragged down four flights of stairs and he was acting like he wasn't in the least bit hurt. He must have taken enough K to tranquillise a fucking elephant.

'Didi, it's me. It's Raine. Take my hand, honey, and I'll come home with you. It's OK. I won't let anything happen to you.' Another few inches and she'd be in grabbing reach. If she could just hold him, just make him feel safe, he'd calm down and she could get him out of here and then they were going to do something about this. It couldn't go on. He had to get straight and she would help him.

'NOOOOOOO!' It was like the wail of pain from a trapped animal. He was looking at her like he didn't recognise her and there was something else. His gaze kept going into the middle distance, like he could see something there, something that was terrifying him.

Touching distance. Almost touching distance and then . . . crap!

She almost had him when he span round and started running, his bare feet pounding off the tarmac. The red stilettos he'd started the night in had been discarded somewhere between the VIP room and here.

'Fuck!' Vincent and Raine started after him, Vincent taking the lead almost immediately. They had to get to him before he reached the end of the alley. The front door and the line of people waiting to get in were right around the corner and the last thing they needed were more witnesses to this. As it was, the chances of keeping it from Tang were getting slimmer by the second.

They were so done. But right now that didn't matter. All she cared about was getting Didi home, getting him to safety.

'NOOOOOOO!' This time it was her voice. Didi reached the end of the alley first, but he didn't turn right towards the door. He didn't turn left towards the cab rank. He kept on going, straight into the road.

The thudding noise seemed like the loudest sound in the world. The screams came straight after. In the seconds it took Raine to reach him, she realised they were coming from girls in the queue, None of them were coming from Didi. He was quite still, other than the very shallow rise and fall of his chest.

'He came out of nowhere! Nowhere! I didn't even have a chance to brake!'

The cab driver was out of his vehicle, but she didn't even reply.

'Didi, stay with me. Stay with me, honey. It's all going to be OK. It'll all be OK.'

She pushed his hair back off his face and kissed his forehead, rocking him back and forth, but there was no answer.

'Someone get an ambulance. Someone get a fucking ambulance!'

Now the only person screaming was her.

# TWENTY

*Mei-Lin*
*New York, 1988*

Mei-Lin thought that her heart would surely stop when the crazy people burst in. For a split second, she'd thought it was Tang and that she had been caught. How could she possibly explain being on her knees behind his desk, rifling through the documents in the bottom drawer?

At least it hadn't been wasted activity. Right at the bottom of the drawer she'd found a small tin and when she opened it she saw that there were several hundred dollars inside. But that wasn't the big prize. She'd dropped it back into the drawer and that was when she realised that the sound was wrong. Taking it back out again, she knocked the bottom panel and felt it move.

Gently, she'd probed around the edges, until she pushed a spot in the corner and the false bottom angled enough to allow her to slip her fingers down the raised side and flip it up. Her gasp had come from somewhere deep inside.

A book, full of notes written in Mandarin. The symbols looked familiar to her but she had no idea what they meant.

Since she'd arrived in the US she'd worked hard to teach herself to read their language, but back in China she'd had no education at all, other than the evenings when her father passed the time by teaching her the symbols that related to numbers. Tucked inside the front cover was a key, but there was no clue as to its purpose.

Underneath the book was a sheet of strange paper, like papyrus, almost fabric-like in consistency. It was tattered around the edges and looked like it could disintegrate at the slightest touch. Gently, delicately, she unfolded it and her brow furrowed in confusion. It was an old Chinese leaflet, with a picture in the middle of a very beautiful baby. Underneath was some more writing and then a row of symbols that she did understand: 24 10 45.

It took a few moments for the pieces to fall into place. Jason Tang. Born 24.10.45. Underneath were two other pictures, a man and a woman. His parents. There were more numbers and then a long narrative that took up both sides of the page. She had no idea what the text meant but she could guess. This was a Chinese astrological chart. She'd heard of these before – predictions drawn up by experts on the occasion of a new arrival. Her eyes were drawn back to the numbers under Tang's picture and suddenly Mei-Lin felt a wave of amusement well up. He told everyone that he was thirty-three but here it was, plain as day. Forty-three. Oh, the vanity of the man was almost laughable. The moment of satisfaction would have lasted longer if it had not been so abruptly spoiled by the crazies. She'd only just replaced everything and closed the drawer when they'd burst in. For a moment she'd considered refusing to help them, but there was something about the girl. Over the years she'd seen all of that gang drunk, high and acting insane, but she realised now that she had never seen the tall girl out of control. She had no idea what made her want to help, but instinct told her it was the right thing to do. She would soon find out. If Tang got to hear that she'd been snooping in his office then a lesson would be learned.

Out in the VIP room, distracting him had been easy.

'Mr Tang, I've noticed that those gentlemen over there don't have any entertainment at the moment. Would you like me to take care of that?'

He didn't even try to contain his surprise as he reached out and grabbed her chin, squeezing it just enough to send a message of control, but not enough to hurt. 'Well, my little Mei-Lin, I do believe that you are finally learning to use your brain. About time you used more than just that delectable pussy. Who is available?'

Stopping her hand from shooting out and slapping that smug grin off his face had been almost too difficult. One day. One day soon.

'Only me. Suzy just joined Mr Takamani and his entourage in room six. All the others are with the Arabs in eleven and twelve.'

Tang nodded thoughtfully and headed over to a horseshoe-shaped leather sofa on the other side of the mirrored bar, where Brody Revel and Donnie Cray, two of his most regular clients, were demolishing a bottle of Jack Daniel's.

'Gentlemen, a pleasure to see you.'

Revel didn't even bother taking his boots off the table.

'Hey, Jason baby!'

Mei-Lin sensed Tang bristling, but his expression never changed. For once the smile on her face was genuine. Tang hated overt informality, especially from two young, good-looking, successful guys such as these.

'I trust that you are having a good night?' The impeccable manners of a perfect host won the day.

Revel was too hyped up on bourbon and arrogance to notice. 'Sure. Some tail wouldn't go wrong, though.'

Donnie Cray dissolved into drunken giggles at that. Tang ignored him.

'Then I have the perfect solution right here.' He gestured to Mei-Lin, who put her hands together and bowed in their direction. 'Wow, Asian chick. Never had one of those before.'

'Then allow this to be the first.' Tang smiled magnanimously. 'Enjoy, gentlemen. I'm sure you'll find Mei-Lin very accommodating . . . to both of you.'

The loaded implication wasn't missed by the men who both hollered like cowboys at a rodeo. Mei-Lin wondered if her hatred of creatures such as these would ever subside.

Gritting her teeth into a fixed smile, she sat down between them and automatically refilled their glasses.

'So what's the deal here then?' Brody Revel got straight to the point. 'I'm guessing that fucking you in the middle of this bar ain't the done thing.' Over the years, she'd become attuned to accents and colloquialisms, and Mei-Lin realised that his drawl belonged to men born in the UK.

She decided that a direct question deserved a direct answer.

'If you so wish, I will stay here with you all night and entertain you with conversation and dancing. If you wish to have private time with me, we can go through to the rooms on the balcony and your credit card will be charged by Mr Tang.'

'Well, fuck me dead.'

'I can also perform that service but it's very expensive – lots of lawyers afterwards.'

Both of them roared with laughter. 'Hey, that was pretty quick – I like that. What about if I like it so much that I wanna keep you all night?'

Mei-Lin lifted his glass from his hand and took a long, provocative sip, never breaking eye contact.

'That, too, can be arranged. We can go back to your hotel and if you so wish I can have someone very beautiful meet us there so that your friend is entertained also.'

Please say yes. Please say yes. She kept her expression blank, despite a whole lot riding on his answer.

In the end, Donnie answered for him. 'Fuck, yeah. This place is like, seriously full of weirdos tonight anyway. Can you ask your friend to meet us at the Plaza?'

'Of course. Do you have a car outside?'

Revel nodded as she knew he would. All these actors had cars and drivers written into their contracts when they were shooting in town.

'Then I will call her from the car. Unfortunately, her fee must be in cash as she is not employed by the club. Two hundred dollars. Is that acceptable? I can promise you that she is worth every dollar. She is a very talented girl.'

By this time Donnie Cray was so turned on and geared up for it that she doubted his ardour would have cooled if she'd told him it was a man in drag.

'Hell, yeah. Is she another Asian chick?'

Mei-Lin nodded. 'Fucking ace!' was the suave, romantic reply.

'One moment, gentlemen. I shall just let Mr Tang know that we are leaving.'

The gaze she left with Revel was full of promise. These guys never failed to amaze her. They could have any woman in this club and yet they were prepared to pay for it. One very famous actor had told her it was easier that way – no fuss, no promises, no lingering expectations and they could demand anything they wanted. She supposed there was some logic to that.

Tang was behind his desk when she entered and her first reaction was fear that he somehow knew she'd been through his drawers. But no, he didn't look troubled in the least.

'Mr Revel wishes me to return to his hotel with him.'

You could almost hear the dollar signs dinging in his eyes.

'Good work. Fast. About time your little peasant pussy brought in some cash.'

'Yes, Mr Tang. I will report back in the morning.'

He waved his hand, already bored with the conversation and returning his attention to the screens. Mei-Lin glanced quickly at them. The orgy in adjoining rooms eleven and twelve was in full swing, and her eyes settled on one of the girls doing a very flexible act with two men at the same time. Over in room six, Mr Takamani had his naked ass sticking in the air and his head buried between Suzy's legs. That was his thing. The bites took a while to heal but he tipped well.

It was time to get out before Tang changed his mind. Without even stopping to pick up a jacket, Mei-Lin headed back to the bar where Revel and Cray were waiting, Jack Daniel's bottles in hand. As others turned to watch them, she wondered what it would really be like to live a free life and have a boyfriend like this. Someone wealthy, handsome, successful, someone who would treat her well. She didn't miss the irony. Here she was dreaming about being attached to the kind of guy who went with hookers. What did it say about her life that right now that seemed like a good option?

Downstairs they climbed into the limo, and Revel immediately pulled her onto his knee, unzipped her cheongsam and pulled it down, letting her breast spring free while he stuck his tongue down her throat. The taste of cigarettes and Jack Daniel's assaulted her. There was nothing pleasurable about this, absolutely nothing, but at least it was better than some of the fat sweating bastards who stank of BO and fish. Normally she avoided kissing at all costs, but in this case she didn't want to do anything that would make him turn the car around and deposit her back on Tang's radar. Freedom. That's what this was – a tiny, bittersweet moment of freedom. Going back to clients' hotels was the only time she wasn't under the eye of the devil or one of his servants.

Revel's hand was squeezing her nipple now, like the dial on a TV. He maybe a famous heartthrob, but this guy knew nothing.

'Hey, man, either cut that out or share.' Donnie Cray lit a cigarette and ran his fingers through his wavy, jet-black hair. Sharing wouldn't be her first choice of options.

'If I may use the phone I will arrange for my friend to meet us.'

Cray snatched up the black receiver from a fake wood panel that was sunk into the arm of the white leather upholstery. Mei-Lin dialled a number. 'Hello. Plaza as soon as possible. Room . . .'

'Three four five,' Cray slurred.

'Three four five,' she repeated.

'Paarrrrr-teeeee', Cray hollered, then chugged back some JD straight from the bottle.

'Man, I need some head,' Brody Revel whistled. Mei-Lin decided that there was already enough of a bad taste in her mouth without adding to it. Instead, she slipped onto the floor and simultaneously slid down both mens' zippers. As soon as they realised what she was doing, they hollered like teenagers and high-fived each other.

Mei-Lin's provocative expression belied her complete and utter distaste for these cretins. They both let their heads slip back on the leather seats as she jerked them off, Donnie Cray coming first in a chorus of 'fucks', Revel following suit moments later, just as the Plaza came into view.

Thanks to light traffic all the way up 6th, they'd made the journey in less than fifteen minutes. The carnage of bottles, cigarettes and the hole Cray somehow managed to burn in the leather seat would take a lot longer to clear up.

The concierge swung the door open outside the Plaza, then acted like he absolutely could not see that the Chinese girl was zipping up her dress and Brody Revel and Donnie Cray were cleaning off their jeans. A twenty the actor pressed into his hand as he passed ensured that he wouldn't suddenly remember later.

Walking across the lobby heads swung to watch them. Everyone knew who Cray and Revel were. They'd just played brothers in the biggest grossing movie of the year, a film about two Vietnam vets who went back into the jungle to search for their missing brother. It had a happy ending – the brother was found and it grossed forty million dollars in the opening weekend.

Mei-Lin held her head high and walked with a confident stride. They had no idea who she was so just for a moment she could pretend to be someone else. Someone free. Someone who was used to living a life of luxury. Going on her performance, she deserved an Oscar more than the actors did.

The suite was as lavish as the rest of the building. A navy and gold Aubusson rug stretched across the walnut floor. The deep, overstuffed pale blue sofa sat behind a beautifully carved rosewood coffee table, which co-ordinated with all the other fine pieces in the room: a stunning bar, a TV unit, a desk, two occasional tables. The effect was utter class – and totally wasted on these two assholes.

Revel picked up the remote and flicked on MTV just as the opening bars of Robert Palmer's 'Simply Irresistible' thundered from the speakers, then he pulled another bottle of Jack Daniel's out of the bar and poured triple measures for him and Donnie. He didn't bother offering anything to Mei-Lin. Instead, he flopped on the couch and beckoned her over. 'Come on then, Sweetcheeks, show me what makes you worth the money.'

Already the bulge in his pants was as wide as his languid grin. What these guys didn't have in class or manners was obviously compensated for by stamina. Mei-Lin didn't even hesitate. One thing was for sure, if she went over there on her own then the night would take a different turn. They were both horny, arrogant and wouldn't hesitate to get their rocks off, even if it meant they both fucked her at the same time. Hand jobs were one thing, but a threeway with these two was bound to be messy and painful. She had to stall this out until her partner got here. There was business to be generated and money to be made.

Mei-Lin rose from the beautiful Louis XV chair, and in two steps she had kicked off her shoes and was up on the coffee table, to the appreciative hollers of her clients.

The strip tease began. Without embarrassment or modesty, Mei-Lin moved her hips slowly, provocatively, letting her hands trace her body from her chest to her hips. Their eyes didn't even flicker to the tall, beautiful, slightly bored-looking models in the Palmer video now. Reaching up her back she slowly pulled down the zipper on her dress once again and this time let it fall to the floor. Brody Revel gasped. They'd discovered back in the car that she was bra-less, but now they realised that underneath she was wearing nothing. Nothing at all. Her high, firm breasts and rose-pink nipples glistened with tiny specs of body powder. Every inch of her torso and ass was perfectly toned and when she slowly, teasingly turned around so that they could get a full frontal view, an involuntary groan came from Revel as he fixed his gaze on her perfectly manicured, tiny black heart of pubic hair. Hips still swaying, she walked her fingers back up her body, stopping to lightly trace a circle around her nipples, moving up to her shoulders, her neck, her head. Keeping her hands up high, she closed her eyes and moved to the music before gently slipping the long clasp from the back of her hair and letting her raven locks tumble down past her waist.

'Fucking hell,' Revel murmured. 'My dick is about to explode.'

'Simply Irresistible' faded into 'Need You Tonight' by INXS. Mei-Lin continued to dance a slow, hypnotic seduction. A couple of times Brody reached over for her and she playfully swerved out of his reach. Donnie Cray was rubbing his own hard-on now, sipping his JD, not taking his eyes off her for a second. The relaxed, ice-cool contours of her face showed no trace of the anxiety that was rising within her. Come on. Come on. Come ...

The doorbell rang briefly, almost apologetically. Donnie was the only one who moved towards it, obviously more than ready for the room service he'd ordered.

Mei-Lin slid off the table and moved towards Brody, sliding on top of him and straddling him. He immediately slipped his fingers inside her and she let out her very best groan of enjoyment. It was almost amusing how a few token sounds of appreciation made them even hornier.

Mei-Lin gently eased Brody Revel's fingers from her pussy, and took them to her mouth, sucking them one by one. Behind her she heard the door open and Donnie whistled low and long. Heels on the wooden floor, then silence as the wearer reached the rug.

'Good evening.' Imperfect English, with an almost imperious tone.

'Good evening, Ami.' It was impossible not to smile. Her friend couldn't look more different from the night they'd rescued her from the basement at Reincarnation. Now she was once again groomed to perfection, but this time in her own style. A red wrap dress, cut low to her waist, revealing enough of her perfect breasts to be jaw-droppingly sexy, but still classy. Her black patent stiletto heels added four inches to her height, and another couple were added by the classic bun on top of her head. A black clutch purse completed the look. Class. Expensive class.

'Gentlemen, this is my friend Ami.'

Donnie Cray let Ami's hand go and slid his hand around her waist instead. He just about managed a grunt, making Ami giggle.

'Pleased to see you, gentlemen. I see you've started without me.' She leaned over and gently traced a finger down the side of Mei-Lin's arm.

'Holy crap. I'd want to see these two fuck each other right now if I didn't need to come so bad,' Brad said to no one in particular.

Donnie had other ideas, too. 'Let's you and me go right on in here.' He was pulling Ami urgently towards the doorway that led to one of the bedrooms. Before she even got out of sight he'd pulled the tie that held the dress together, so the last thing Mei-Lin saw before the door swung shut was Ami's naked ass being squeezed. She smiled, and of course Brody thought that was directed at him. For maximum benefit, it was important to judge the next stage correctly. So far neither man had pulled out any coke, which wasn't surprising. Everyone knew that both these guys had been involved in a major scandal while they shot the war movie that had resulted in them getting arrested in a Baltimore motel. It was big news that the studio they worked

202

for were now drug testing them while they worked on the sequel.

For Mei-Lin this was a huge bonus on what was turning out to be one of her better nights. Brad was already seriously wasted, so all she had to do was …

On a hunch, she moved in to kiss him, then twisted round so that she was straddling him with her back against his chest. He brought his free hand round her to grab her breast, but she leaned forward, putting it out of his reach. She swept round to the side of him now, leaving her ass tantalisingly high in the air. He got it immediately. Pulling himself up onto his knees, he entered her from behind, pounding her hard, but nothing she couldn't handle. The dog position served two purposes – he could have sex with her without having to waste time on kissing or words, and she could pass the time by watching TV while satisfying the client. It was what she believed the American businessmen called a 'win/win situation'.

'Oh fuck, oh fuck, I'm gonna come.' He was slamming her hard now, forcing her to hold on tight to the arm of the sofa, both of his hands on her hips, adding force to every thrust.

Slipping her hand between her legs, she grabbed his dangling balls and began to massage them. Once. Twice. Thr—

'Aaaaargh!' If anyone was passing the room door at that moment they would be in no doubt as to what was occurring inside.

Mei-Lin pulled her vagina in tight, finishing the job quickly while Brody's groin spasmed beneath her.

'Fucking hell. Fucking hell. That was fucking incredible.' Clearly his friend Jack Daniel's was giving him an altered perspective on events. He slumped back on the couch and reached over to the side table for his cigarettes, his limp dick shrivelling as it left her. The cigarette was already lit before Mei-Lin gently pulled herself around and reached for the T-shirt he'd discarded. Slipping it on, she made her way over to the bathroom. He didn't notice. The volume on the TV had already been turned up and he was staring in a vacant, zombie leer at the screen, watching Debbie Gibson confessing that she just couldn't shake someone's love.

In the bathroom she switched on the shower, and then stood under it for a long time, her eyes closed, letting the warm water cascade down her back. One day this would end. One day. If anyone ever wrote the story of her life, that is what it would be called.

One Day.

It could have been five minutes later, it could have been twenty, when there was a gentle rap at the bathroom door.

'Come in.'

Ami's steps were silent on the marble floor as she crossed the room, wearing only a white fluffy robe with the hotel crest on the front. She sat on the closed lid of the toilet and pulled her knees up to her chest.

Mei-Lin twisted the gold taps, switching off the shower. 'He's sleeping?'

Ami nodded. 'Like a teenager. Five minutes and it was over. Thank you for tonight.'

'You're welcome.' Mei-Lin smiled softly.

Ami's hand went into the pocket of the robe and took out a bundle of notes.

'Four hundred dollars,' she said.

'You must have been good. I told him your rate was two hundred.'

'I know. He doubled it when I promised to stay until tomorrow. My rent is paid for this month already. It's a good feeling.'

Finding a place for Ami had been a huge gamble. Vincent

had started to seriously sweat as the weeks after her escape passed and she was still on his couch. It was a good position for them – made him more amenable to lending them the five hundred dollars they needed to rent an apartment on the outskirts of Hell's Kitchen for Ami to live in. To Mei-Lin's surprise, Ami announced that she wanted to stay in the same line of work. Not that she had many other options. With no green card, no passport, no family and no means, there weren't a whole lot of other avenues she could pursue. So they'd come up with a plan. Mei-Lin would find the clients, and they'd both work them and just pray that it never got back to Tang. So far, so good.

The apartment was a dump in a bad area, but within a few days it was clean and she'd furnished it gradually as Mei-Lin pulled in the after-hours clients. That was the deal. Tang would get his minimum fee, and all extras would be pocketed by Ami and used to fix up the tiny two-roomed closet. Mei-Lin would live there one day, too. Despite the fact that she had only seen it once, during a snatched hour on the way home from screwing two Italian businessmen at the Waldorf, she already thought of it as home.

'Put that in the usual place and we will sort it out later. You know I can't keep it in case Tang finds it. I think Suzy searches my things at the house when I'm out.'

Ami nodded. 'Mei-Lin, it must be time. Why can't you leave and come to our home now?' Her voice was pleading, her forehead furrowed with concern.

They'd had this discussion many times over the last few months and Mei-Lin's shoulders slumped just a little as she replied.

'You know I can't. So many reasons. This arrangement is the best way for us to get access to clients who pay top rate. If I leave now we'll have to start from nothing to build up customers. Tang will come after me, and then he may find you, too. I'm not ready, Ami. I don't have enough on him yet. I need to find ... something. I'm not sure what. Just something that will protect us in the future and prevent him from looking for us.'

Ami switched on the cold water faucet, then filled a glass that sat on the marble unit behind the sink. 'I worry about you there.'

'I know. But I'll be fine, I promise. Did you speak to the girl you told me about?'

Ami nodded. 'She's Russian, as I thought, and she would like to take us up on the offer.'

Ami had mentioned meeting a girl they were both familiar with from Reincarnation when she was out running. Tall, blonde, lips like pillows, she was one of the classiest hookers that worked the club and she had regular clients. Tang had approached her to work directly for him and she'd refused. The decision came with a price – no entry to Reincarnation; and she'd be refused at the door if she tried. She'd called him a cunt and stormed off.

Now Ami had offered her a home and a service. She could work her own clients and keep the cash, but she would also work any clients that Mei-Lin referred to them through Reincarnation. After rent and bills were paid, Mei-Lin got a twenty per cent cut in cash, which she handed over to Ami for safe keeping.

After saving Ami's life, Mei-Lin was trusting her to repay the favour with honesty and integrity. So far she hadn't failed.

'Remind her that she must keep my part in this absolutely confidential,' Mei-Lin warned. There were too many big mouths in the club scene. All it took was for one person to shout their mouth off, Tang to hear that Mei-Lin was drumming up outside business and she had no doubt she'd be wearing cement boots in the Hudson by dawn.

The towel she used to wrap around her hair was as soft as silk and the robe she took from the back of the door smelled of lemons.

'Come,' she held her hand out to Ami, who stood up as she took it. Together they went back into the lounge where Brody Revel was snoring like a hog on the sofa. If the women of America could see him now they might rethink that whole heartthrob thing. Jeans at his knees. Limp dick flopped on his thigh. Drool dripping from the side of his mouth and a noise that sounded like approaching aircraft.

They peeked through to the bedroom to see Donnie in a pretty much identical state. Excellent. Neither man would trouble them for the rest of the night.

Quietly they padded into the second bedroom and Mei-Lin picked up the phone and ordered hot drinks and sandwiches for them both.

'Just leave it outside the door, please – I don't want to wake my boyfriend.' The staff were trained to accommodate.

Fifteen minutes later, she peeked out and the food was sitting there waiting. She picked it up and took it back to the bed in the second room, where she sat with Ami, their voices hushed, talking and laughing as they ate their supper.

It was one of the very few snatched moments of happiness she had in her life.

'I wish it was always like this,' Ami said wistfully, before swallowing the last bite of her chicken sandwich.

'It will be, my friend. One day. One day soon.'

# TWENTY-ONE

*Stevie*
*Houston, Texas, 1988*

'Thank you, Houston – you fucking rock!'

The noise of twenty thousand people going crazy filled the Houston Astrodome. Up on the stage Stevie bowed, waved, then turned to her right just in time to see Lou rip open her shirt and flash the audience. Cue a whole new level of crazy.

The adrenalin coursed through her as she ran off stage, her hair stuck to her face with sweat. The first thing she did was flick open the button on her pants and slide the zip down. One thing was for sure, whatever fool decided that black leather trousers were going to be the rock star's dress code hadn't thought it through properly. Sweat. Heat. Sticky fabric. It would take an army of roadies to get these off her.

'Holy shit, that was amazing,' Cally whistled, throwing her guitar to the tech who was waiting in the wings for it. Yep, they even had their own techs now. This is what happened when you had a number one album.

It had come out of nowhere, starting within days of the Madison Square Garden gig with Decomp. Two things combined to make the big stuff happen: Ari Covet released a tape of the gig to MTV, who played the live performance of 'Heaven' over and over until every kid in America that loved rock was crying out for more. The second factor was that the radio-station DJs and music journalists in the audience had raved about the performance. Suddenly every magazine had pictures of The Bitch of Thorns, radio stations from one coast to another were playing their songs and Cole Presley was smart enough to re-release the album.

Meanwhile the girls completed the Decomp tour and spun straight into headlining their own gigs. Presley took a gamble and went for the small stadiums. People were prepared to travel to see them and he wanted them pulling in big numbers. It paid off. In less than a year they went from unknowns to stars, and the album that had struggled to sell a thousand copies was now multi-platinum, with 'Your Heart Runs Cold', 'Jealous', 'Pass in the Night', 'Garden of Love', and especially 'Heaven' becoming the songs a whole generation would identify with the summer of '88.

The album was their *Slippery When Wet*, their *Appetite For Destruction*, their *Rumours*. Their time had come and they were the biggest sensation of the year.

Stevie crashed back into the dressing room, headed straight for the fridge and pulled out a bottle of champagne. They were usually in a car and out of the stadium before the lights went up, but not tonight. This was the last gig of this leg of the tour and Presley had arranged for the concert to be filmed and for them to be interviewed backstage afterwards. He'd set up full catering and told them to invite whoever they wanted to a final night party in the stadium's hospitality suite. For someone who had paid them little attention when they were struggling, he'd definitely upped his game.

There was a commotion behind her as the rest of the band and the camera crew fell in the door. As usual, Lou was giving them more sexy stuff than their censors would ever pass, Cally was trying to explain the deeper meaning of their music and Dixie had slumped on a sofa and was sitting perfectly still, hoping it would make her invisible and that no one would pay any attention to her whatsoever.

The room was filling up and Stevie was just wondering if she could sneak away for a shower when a familiar face appeared.

'Mom!' She threw herself into Ella's arms, and it didn't go unnoticed that her mother was wearing one of the many jackets JC Penney had delivered to her door over the last few months. She'd had her hair done, too. And her nails. A stranger would be able to spot that they were mother and daughter now – the same eyes, the identical heart-shaped faces, the same blond hair, albeit Ella's had a little help from some expensive styling. The money Stevie was sending her allowed her to treat herself for once. But the real difference wasn't in the material things, it was in the glow of pride all over her face.

'Oh, baby, you were amazing. I am so, so proud of you. I can't believe that was you up there. Where did that come from?'

Stevie laughed. 'You, Ma. You were obviously some kinda showgirl in a past life.'

Ella blushed and squeezed her tighter and that's when Stevie noticed that she hadn't come alone.

'Damn, you got even bigger.' Releasing Ella, she reached up to hug her brother. Was there another couple of inches on there or did it just seem like she had to stretch even further than she remembered? Matt had to be at least six foot eight, maybe more, and he was a complete contrast to her, with their father's dark hair and sallow skin.

'Lovin' the cap, bro,' she said, flicking the front of his hat with the purple and yellow insignia. The Lakers. Matt had realised the dream and been selected for the squad straight out of college. Her mother had said it was one of the proudest moments of her life. Something inside Stevie hoped that tonight came close in the maternal pride stakes.

'OK, sis? You were great.' He'd always been a boy of few words. 'This is, erm . . . ' Matt moved to the side and allowed another man to take his place.

'Jinx Daley.' Stevie finished for him. Even a sports ignoramus like Stevie recognised one of the greatest players ever to pull on a Lakers jersey. His career in Los Angeles had been stellar but short-lived, due to a major, highly publicised and ultimately unsuccessful contract negotiation. Now, though, after a couple of successful stints with other clubs and a change of heart by the bean counters, he was back at the Lakers playing out the last stage of his on-court career.

'Hope you don't mind, but when I heard Shorty here was your brother I persuaded him to let me tag along. I'm a fan.' As he spoke, Daley shook her hand and at the same time leant down to kiss her cheek.

Stevie took a slight step backwards. 'You don't want to do that. Serious sweat been going on here.'

Jinx laughed at her honesty. 'That ain't always a bad thing,' he said, grinning.

Stevie felt an automatic flush of attraction. Jinx was even taller than Matt, maybe six foot ten. Unsurprisingly, he had a perfect physique, but it was the brown eyes and razor sharp cheekbones on his beautiful black skin that gave her serious goosebumps. Actually, that might just be the after-effects of cooling down while wearing wet leather trousers.

For the first time ever, Stevie just wanted to stare for a while. Just look. Drink in every bit of him. The force of her reaction took her completely by surprise and it was a few moments before she snapped out of it with a smile.

'No, I guess you're right.'

'Stevie, can we have a few words with you now?' The journalist who was running the interviews was Australian and notoriously belligerent.

'Of course.' She turned back to her mum and guests. 'Sorry about this. I'll be about fifteen minutes with these guys. Why don't you have a drink and then we can split from here as soon as I'm done.'

'That would be great, honey,' her mom replied. 'We booked into the Hilton like you suggested. Maybe we could go back there and have something to eat? You're so skinny now it's time you got a proper meal down you.'

Stevie threw her arms around her mom. 'God, I've missed you, Ma.'

Ella raised an eyebrow, 'Stephanie . . . ' The reprimand was light-hearted and threw Stevie right back to her childhood. Ella had never allowed any kind of blasphemy in the house.

'Sorry, Ma!' Stevie was laughing hard now. 'I should have said, 'Holy shit, I've missed you. Ma, you do know I'm a rock star now and we're supposed to be all messed up and crazy?'

Ella playfully pinched her cheek. 'I brought you up better than that, baby girl. And you're never too big for me to ground you.'

'Stevie?' The impatient journalist cut through the hilarity.

'You're right, Mom. Be back soon.'

Kissing her mother on the cheek, she headed off in the direction of the film crew. They placed her on top of a desk, the portable lighting system geared up for maximum flattery. Not that she needed it. With her gleaming eyes and flushed skin she'd never looked better. Even Lou would have serious trouble matching up to her.

There was something else in there, too. A coyness. A modesty. A flirtatiousness. The camera crew saw it, but they had absolutely no idea that it was because the whole time she was answering questions she was aware that Jinx Daley's eyes never left her.

It was a huge relief when Mr Belligerent Journo called it a wrap and she could head back with them to the hotel.

'Let me just grab a quick shower and I'll meet you in the bar. Will you order me a club sandwich please, Mom?

Her mother beamed as if her very presence had single-handedly saved her daughter from certain starvation.

Twenty minutes later she made it to the bar, hair still wet, no make-up and wearing a pair of low-slung, ripped-up jeans, a white T-shirt and battered cowboy boots. The effect was unintentionally dazzling.

Well, perhaps it was a little intentional. She was banking on the fact that Jinx was a basketball player who was constantly surrounded by glamorous, impeccably groomed girls, so maybe it was time for some normality. And for the lead singer of the biggest female rock band in the country right now, she was pretty normal.

'Thanks, Mom.' She slid the club sandwich in front of her and took a sip of the fresh orange juice next to it. Wow, a balanced meal and a fruit juice. The guys from Guns N' Roses would kick her ass off Planet Rock for this. Lou told her on a weekly basis that she was the worst rock star that ever lived and it was true. No drugs, barely any booze, no scandal, barely any sex and she had never even been arrested. What kind of hell-raiser was that? Note to self – must do better. As long as her mom didn't find out or she'd be confined to her bedroom for a decade.

For the next hour they were like any other normal family,

swapping stories, asking questions, catching up. Yes, Ella had cut down to just one job now, but she didn't want to quit it because working with the kids at the day-care centre made her happy. Yes, Matt was tipped for a regular place in the first team if his scoring average stayed up, no, he didn't have a girlfriend and yes, he knew he had to stay away from gold-diggers and hookers. Ella slapped Stevie for the last reminder.

No, Jinx wasn't married or seeing anyone, yes, he loved his mother and five sisters and yes, he planned a career as a commentator when he quit playing.

And no, Stevie hadn't met anyone special yet.

'What do you expect? How are you going to meet a nice, normal guy with the life you lead?'

It was more of an observation than a criticism from her mother.

Stevie laughed. 'Mom, maybe I don't want a nice normal guy.'

Her mom feigned surprise. 'Really? And there was me thinking that if I had a plumber as a son-in-law then I might just get the faucet in the bathroom fixed. Damn thing has been leaking for a decade.'

'Ma, I'll send a plumber round and it's on me. It'll be much cheaper than springing for a wedding.'

The other guests – four tables of couples enjoying a late-night drink – turned to see what the group at the bar were laughing at. Every one of them recognised Stevie, and all the guys and a couple of the women recognised Jinx, too, making them even more intrigued.

Ella decided to call it a day.

'Honey, I'm bushed.'

'No problem, Mom. I'm heading off to the sack, too.'

There was a pause as Ella slid down from the bar stool and bridged the eight-inch gap between her feet and the floor.

Another hug.

'Did I tell you I'm proud of you?' Ella asked.

'You did, Ma.'

'OK, well I'm telling you again. Now, honey, what are you planning on doing for the next couple of weeks? Didn't you say you had a break?'

Stevie nodded. 'Yep, we don't head over to Europe for another month.'

'So wouldn't you think about coming home for a little while? Let me fatten you up?'

'Can't do it, ma. Can't afford to buy a whole wardrobe of leather trousers in a bigger size.' She couldn't help noticing that Jinx was amused by the banter. She liked that.

In truth her priority had been to get to the end of the US tour and then start preparing for the next leg. She hadn't given a thought to what she would do in between. Hell, she didn't even have a house to go to. She'd been so busy on the road that sorting out an apartment for her gap month had been the last thing on her mind.

'Just think about it, OK?'

'I will, Mom. And thanks for the club sandwich.'

'Don't thank me, I charged it to your room.' Ella disappeared in a cloud of cackles.

There were a few moments of easy silence as they watched her go, then Stevie yawned.

'I'm going to head off, too. It's been a real long day.'

Matt stood up. 'We'll walk you to your room. Don't want you getting mobbed by hysterical fans. What floor you on?'

'Nineteen.'

'Cool. Same as us.'

They chatted about the team all the way there and Stevie could see that Matt loved it. She was happy for him. It felt great to see him achieve so much. They'd been brought up by a single mother who worked day and night and they'd both turned out pretty good. Ella had done a great job.

At her door, Matt leant down to hug her.

'Do I get to do that, too?' Jinx asked.

'Sure.' Stevie replied, reaching up. She couldn't even get her arms all the way around him. This guy had shoulders like a linebacker but without the padding.

They hugged and then the boys wandered on down the corridor as Stevie opened her door.

Inside, she leant against the wall. Had she misread that? She could have sworn that Jinx was giving off interested signals, but he hadn't followed through on it. Maybe all those basketball guys were just naturally charming and flirtatious and she'd completely misunderstood.

It wouldn't be surprising. Life on the road had been pretty barren when it came to chalking up experience with guys. There had been a couple-of-months thing with one of the road crew who seemed like a pretty decent guy, but he'd turned up one too many times wasted and it began to get boring. All she wanted was someone . . . good. Not a deadbeat like her dad. Someone who was decent and reliable and sober and . . . she realised she was coming up with a list of all the things Lou hated in a man.

In the meantime, she was still human so . . . argh, what was she going to do about the severe dose of the horn that her flirtation with Jinx had left her with?

She checked her watch. 1 a.m. The rest of the band would be out somewhere, getting into serious trouble for the next couple of hours at least. They'd developed a habit of gatecrashing strip joints and tipping the girls big bucks. If the stripper society of America ever decided they needed official patrons, The Bitch of Thorns would be pretty high on the list.

She was way too wired to sleep. Maybe she could track them down, page Jude and find out where they were hanging. But . . . Could she really be bothered? Another bar, another assault on the liver, and the club sandwich was already sitting a little uneasy on top of that bottle of champagne she'd got through in the course of the day. She was sensible, not a saint.

The knock was almost imperceptible on the first rap, but a little more pronounced on the second. In one smooth move-ment she reached over, opened the door and Jinx walked in.

'I thought you'd never ask,' he joked.

A smart-assed reply was on the tip of her tongue when he slid his arms around her and kissed it away. No further conversation required. They didn't even make it as far as the bed. They pulled at each other's clothes, desperately trying to get to the bodies beneath, their mouths never breaking away, their eyes open as they slid to the floor. Only then did he pause, stretch up and drink in every inch of her. 'You're incredible,' he whispered, and Stevie smiled as her heart thudded in anticipation, desperate for every sinew of his perfectly formed torso to bear down on her, aching to feel him inside her. She flipped her legs up and twisted her ankles behind his back, then pulled him down towards her. When he entered her she gasped, her pelvis tilting up to accommodate the sheer size of him.

Every inch of his body was rock hard, yet Stevie had never felt anything so tender, so gentle, as his elbows slid to either side of her head and his hands cupped her face.

'I've been waiting for you,' he said, his eyes burning deep into hers. In that second, she knew exactly what he meant.

'I've been waiting for you, too.'

It was no flippant line thrown in to ramp up a soulless quickie. The realisation that this was absolutely true sent another level of ecstasy coursing through her. Her hand reached up to him and she traced a line across his lips, their eyes locked on each other. He began to move, slowly at first; they explored each other's bodies, playing with the bliss of it, until neither of them could contain it any longer. Without speaking, they both knew it was time, and their connection suddenly became more urgent, the intensity of her need for him building and building until she felt the first orgasmic wave rise up and consume her, the release of it making her scream. Suddenly Jinx was there too, calling out her name over and over as he came, until eventually he stopped, held perfectly still, his body appearing to float above her.

Still their gaze didn't falter. Stevie had no idea what she was feeling. This had never happened with Jude or with any of the other guys she'd dated over the years. This was terrifying, intoxicating, fear, peace, and . . . right. It just felt right.

'This is something,' he told her, his beautiful face absolutely serious.

'It is,' she agreed. Man, this was movie stuff. A ballad. A fairytale. A dream. A perfect, perfect moment.

Still inside her, he eased himself down, taking all his weight on one elbow, their faces only inches apart now.

'Glad we got that down. So what are you going to do for the next couple of weeks?' he asked, a smile playing on his perfect lips.

'What are you offering?'

He laughed, still maintaining eye contact, still full body skin on skin.

'I have ten days on hiatus and a beach house on Hawaii.'

'Then I guess that's where I'm going.'

It wasn't even up for debate. It was insane, irrational and completely foolhardy, but refusing wasn't an option.

They made love twice more, once in bed, once in the bath,

before they finally crawled under the sheets, locked into each other perfectly, despite the difference in height.

It was getting more and more difficult to believe that this was her life. A year ago they were about to play their first major gig after years in obscurity. Now she was a household name, building up some serious cash and lying in bed with Jinx Daley.

Even if it all fell apart tomorrow, she would remember this moment for ever.

Not for a second did she think that would happen, though. Nope, this was just the start and life was going to get even more incredible over the next couple of years. Starting with ten days on Hawaii.

Beside her Jinx was snoring softly, so when the phone rang she quickly snatched it from the cradle so as not to disturb him.

'Hey, baby.' It was Jude. And he'd obviously been indulging in some serious chemical substances. 'There you are! Been looking all over.'

'Hey, Jude, whassup?'

She said it as quietly as possibly so that Jinx wouldn't stir.

'All good, baby, all good. Listen, you gotta come out and meet us.'

'Not happening tonight, babe, my family is in town.'

'Look, dump the family, this is important man. I've got someone here that wants to see you.'

'Who?'

'Your favourite Mr Covet. Says he's got something he wants to talk to you about and that you'll want to hear what he has to say.'

# TWENTY-TWO

*Raine*
*New York, 1989*

Only one of the nurses at the work station looked up as she passed, a Philippino girl called Lilly who had the sweetest temperament and just as much time for the families and friends as she did for the patients.

'Hi, Raine, go on through. No change, I'm afraid.'

No change.

One year of visits, one year of hearing, 'No change.'

In Didi's room, she rinsed out the vase at the side of his bed and put in the sunflowers she had brought for him. They always seemed like the right choice – a tiny ray of happiness where there was absolutely none.

His eyes followed her everywhere she went but he didn't respond to her idle chatter.

Raine would have been astounded if he had.

No one knew for sure whether it was the after-effects of the crash, or the drugs, or some kind of neurological breakdown that would have come anyway, but since the night he was rushed to ER after a head-on meeting with a cab, he hadn't said a word. Not one word.

After four weeks in ICU the doctors had come to the conclusion that there was no longer anything physically wrong with him and he'd been transferred to the psychiatric wing of Bellevue Hospital.

Since then, no change.

He watched, he listened, he could move when forced to by the nurses, but he'd never spoken or engaged with anyone in any way. He sat in his chair, his mind in another world, far away from the one he'd left.

He didn't even look like Didi any more. The make-up had gone and so had the crazy, razor-cut hairstyles and colours. His hair was medium brown, trimmed by a lady who visited the ward once a month and by Didi's mother Marge, who came all the way from Poughkeepsie to visit him every week with her husband Dave. They knew little of Didi's life before the accident. On one of the many times that their visits had overlapped, Marge explained that David junior had left home at sixteen, headed for New York and never come back, calling every few weeks to reassure them he was fine. They'd tried to persuade him to come home, they'd even scoured the streets of New York looking for him, but he was lost to another world – one that a nurse and a tyre fitter would never understand.

As always, Didi was sitting on a bedside chair, so Raine flopped onto the bed and took his hand, then chatted away for twenty minutes, telling him all the gossip from the club. He always loved the weird stuff, so she told him about the sixty-five-year-old woman who'd twice been caught supplying blow jobs to businessmen in the fire-exit corridors. She told him about the vicar, whom they assumed was a stripper in costume but who was actually a fire and brimstone preacher from the

221

South who attempted to storm the stage and give a sermon about how they were all damned and only he and God could save them. The old Didi would have loved the story about the two transvestites who got into a bitch fight about which one of them looked more like Cher, unaware that the real Cher was on the guest list that night.

When it was time to go she leaned over and kissed him.

'Goodbye, my gorgeous boy, I'll see you next week. And I haven't forgotten ... He'll pay, Didi, I promise you.'

She whispered the same thing every week, but it had no impact on him whatsoever. It struck her that perhaps he was losing faith in her words. Or perhaps he didn't blame Tang for what happened to him. It didn't matter – she did, and that was all she needed to keep her motivated, to keep her in there, to keep her looking for some way to avenge the damage he had done. That focus was behind her decision to continue running the club nights after Didi's injury. Tang hadn't even looked up at her when she'd gone to his office and announced that she was taking full charge. He carried on writing something in a note-book on his desk, and said, 'Fine. Takings go down, you're out.' He really didn't give a damn and that was OK by her – the less notice he took of her the better.

Raine gathered up her things and headed towards the exit, smiling at Lilly as she passed. At the main door, she pulled her collar up around her neck, put on her gloves and checked her watch – eight o'clock. She'd be home by nine, then it was bath and bed and maybe even some TV if no one else was there and hogging the remote control. Tuesdays and Wednesdays were the only nights she wasn't at the club and she was usually in bed asleep by ten. Work, sleep, work, sleep – that was her existence. It sometimes occurred to her that she should just give it all up and go back to the suburbs to a life of domesticated normality, but . . . she couldn't do it. This was who she was now and she wouldn't quit until she'd had some kind of payback for Ricco – and now Didi. After that? It was impossible to think that far ahead.

'Excuse me, can I speak to you for a moment?' The guy stepped out from the shadows of the main gate, blocking her way. Raine surreptitiously felt for the personal alarm she always kept in her left pocket. How ironic. She'd bought it because she regularly walked home through Manhattan at four and five o'clock in the morning when all the crazies and criminals were out. Yet the first time she was contemplating using it was eight o'clock on a Tuesday night in a well-lit public facility.

'No,' she said flatly, stepping aside to go round him. Just then another man appeared and her heart began to beat a little faster. The one in front of her was wearing jeans, boots and a leather bomber jacket; the other one was younger, maybe late twenties, and slightly smarter in slacks and a jacket with an open-neck shirt.

In the far right of her peripheral vision, Raine spotted a security guard. If she set off the alarm now, she reckoned he was too far away to help, but at least he would see enough to alert the police and give a description of these guys.

'Miss O'Donnell.'

It wasn't a question, and it *was* enough to stop her in her tracks.

One of them slid his hand into his pocket, pulled out a black wallet and flashed it in her face. She knew enough about law enforcement to see that it was genuine.

'My name is Ralph Connor and I'm with the DEA.'

Oh. Fuck. Her first thought was that this wasn't going to end anywhere good. Her second was that if she was being accused of anything her dad would find out and it would be the biggest disappointment of his life. Her mouth wouldn't work so she just stood there, staring blankly at him.

'We'd like to talk to you about your friend David Callum. He's in a pretty bad way in there.'

She wanted to blurt out that she didn't need them to tell her that but growing up in a cop's house had taught her that hostility wasn't the best course of action at this stage. Instead she just murmured, 'I realise that.'

Ralph Connor gestured to the double doors behind her. His partner still hadn't said a word. 'Look, they have a canteen through there. How about we go back in and have a coffee?'

'Does your friend have a name? Only it's rude not to introduce people.' OK, so maybe a little hostility was healthy. Set the boundaries. Establish that she wasn't a complete pushover.

Connor looked mildly disconcerted at her outburst but his partner couldn't suppress a smile.

'Sorry, this is Eric Tosca, also DEA.'

She kept her expression neutral. 'OK, we'll talk.'

If they were going to bust her they would have done it by now and besides, what could they have on her? She had deliberately stayed away from all the shit at Reincarnation and guilt by association wouldn't wash in court.

They walked back inside in silence and it wasn't until they were sitting in a stark dining room that smelled faintly of disinfectant that he got to the point.

'David Callum was a dealer at Reincarnation,' Connor said.

Her face remained impassive. 'I don't know anything about that and I think you'll have a tough time questioning him.'

'Don't be a wise-ass.'

'Just stating the truth,' she said with a shrug. His attitude didn't phase her. Pat O'Donnell had a reputation for being the toughest interrogator in Brooklyn and she knew the drill. Go in hard, put them on the back foot, get the fear up, then go in for what you really want. His sidekick still hadn't said a word. Raine guessed he was in his first few months on the job, probably transferred from some small-town force and thrilled to be up playing with the big boys now.

'We know who you are. Took us a while to piece it all together. There we were, watching Didi, trying to get a hit off one of his connections, and you turned up. It was a bit of a surprise when we worked out that you're Raine O'Donnell. You've got Eric here to thank for that – he met you in the pizza joint once when he was still in uniform.'

'Congratulations on such stellar investigative work. But you could just have asked me. I've got nothing to hide.'

'Really? So what's with the act at the club then? Those costumes you wear are a pretty good disguise.'

They'd been watching her at Reincarnation then. Wouldn't be hard. As she'd continued to run the party night every Sunday, she was on the door in plain sight of the street and she was invariably at the club every other night it was open, too.

Good cop/bad cop shuffled in his seat, his smile almost malicious.

'Just part of the scene. It's not like it's a big bad secret.'

'Sure about that? So what are you saying, that your dad knows all about this life you lead? Pat O'Donnell, one of the most straight up cops in the city. Pillar of society. Does he know his daughter is a big shot in the club his partner got killed in?'

There it was. The proverbial kick to the metaphorical crotch. It was all she could do not to wince because they both knew that she was backed into a corner. Instead a flash of anger . . .

'Don't you fucking dare bring Ricco into this. You know nothing. Fucking nothing. Not about me, or Ricco, or my dad.

225

Don't you dare mention them. Don't. You. Fucking. Dare.'

'Hey, hey, hey . . . ' His hands were up in the surrender position. This felt wrong. Everything about it was off. She'd been brought up her whole life to trust the cops, to go to them when she needed help. Much as this dickhead in front of her was pressing her buttons, there was a part of her that wanted to tell this guy everything but she knew she couldn't. No one would ever know what happened that night in Reincarnation until she'd made it right on her own terms.

'Look, we're not here to antagonise you or mess with you. I'm sorry.'

The lack of sincerity in his voice made it clear that he wasn't. He was enjoying this.

'So your point is?'

'Look, it's not you we're interested in.'

Ah, here it comes.

'Tang. We want Jason Tang.'

The urge to punch the air was almost irresistible. The DEA were going after Tang. It had crossed her mind to let the cops know about his drug dealing, but she'd dismissed it as pointless because she knew that Tang had big-assed lawyers that could get him off on just about anything with a slap on the wrist. And besides, she had no proof of anything on him. What was she going to say? He's a bad guy and he provides drugs and sex to his customers. Good luck with finding anyone willing to testify to that in court. His lawyers would have him off on petty drug and vice charges before the judge had time to spend the bribe.

But this was different. These guys were serious shit and they had resources. If they were already monitoring the club, that meant this wasn't just one or two minor misdemeanours he could wriggle out of. They must be committing serious budget to the operation and that could mean only one thing.

'You want to take Jason Tang down?'

Connor nodded and hunched over towards her. 'I'm going to give it to you straight.' Oh for fuck's sake, what was with the dramatics? This guy had been watching way too many episodes of *Columbo*.

'We know you're in with him, but here's the thing, you're wasting your time. One way or another we're going to get him and you're going to be out of a job. If you help us you'll come out of it OK. If you come over to our side we'll pay for information. So I guess you have a choice. You can run back to Tang and tell him all about this conversation or you can do the right thing and stick with us. I just hope your daddy taught you well enough to make a good choice.'

For several moments, she just stared at him, until the interrogator started to look a little uneasy. She guessed he had a whole lot riding on this back at the office and she was almost pissed off enough to tell him to go fuck himself just for fun.

Eventually Raine took a deep breath, sat up straighter and pushed her chin forward just a little in an expression of unequivocal strength that came directly from her father's genes.

'Number one, don't ever mention my father or Ricco Dimato to me again. They are fuck all to do with you. Number two, you know dick shit. Because if you really did know anything about me or about what goes on at Reincarnation you'd know that I am most definitely not "in" with Jason Tang.'

Connor's face clouded and he opened his mouth to speak.

'Don't interrupt me,' she said quietly in a deadly tone that probably made his balls curl up into the foetal position.

'Number three, and make sure you're listening carefully, I will do anything your organisation wants in order to bring down Jason Tang – not for money, not because it will look good and not for my family, but because I hate his fucking guts. So you just let me know what you need and when you need it. Contact me on this number.' She took out a pen, jotted down the number of her pager service and slid it across the table.

'Oh, and number four. I may call you Columbo from now on. It suits you better.'

It took a few seconds for him to recover.

'I want you to come into the office tomorrow and I want names, faces, photographs. We'll need the full day. I want to know every single thing you know about that operation.'

'No.'

Columbo reeled like someone had hit him.

'I work tomorrow. I'm off Thursday, I'll come in then.'

Audible sigh of relief.

'And I'll tell you everything I know, but I have questions. Why now? Why you guys? And what are you going after him for? He's got half the city in his pocket and he's always kept himself squeaky clean. The drugs in Reincarnation don't seem like a big enough story for you guys to be involved. So why's he really in your sights?'

Columbo looked at the sidekick, obviously not sure how much he should give away. She gave him a hand to decide.

'And if you don't answer my questions, I walk. I'm not getting myself in the middle of something I don't understand or trust.'

He picked up a sugar packet from a white ceramic dish on the table and idly flicked it between his fingers. Anxiety was a bitch.

Eventually he put it down. 'Importing.'

*What?* Man, she hadn't seen that coming. She'd assumed that Tang had a supply chain in the US that he connected with his people in the club and that was it. But if he was importing . . .

'It's not just Reincarnation. He's supplying gear to half the clubs in New York. Sure, he's detached from it, but it's got his name written all over it. It comes in from Shanghai and goes out through a network. Ketamine, Coke, Quaaludes, Ecstasy, Meth, Brown. All of it. Your friend Didi there set up the supply chains to the other clubs.'

Raine felt her stomach twist just a little tighter. It disappointed her more than surprised her. Didi had contacts all over the scene, and if Tang had asked him to use them he would have done, especially in his later months at the club when he was so out of it he'd have doped up his own mother. She just wished she'd seen it, stopped it, helped him more. But Didi was his own person and she couldn't be with him 24/7, not when she had a job to hold down and bills to pay. Seemed like he was doing what he had to do to pay his too.

Why hadn't he told her? Actually she already knew the answer. It had been the one secret between them, the one thing they weren't in sync on. He knew how she felt about the drug scene and he'd deliberately kept the whole deal from her.

Being mad at him would be easy, but all she felt was unbearable sadness.

'The hookers and the dope in Reincarnation, we know about but, like you say, that's chickenshit. Importing is a whole other ball game.'

There was silence as Raine thought the new information through for a moment.

'I didn't know about the other clubs but I can see how that makes sense. I'll come in on Thursday, I'll tell you everything I know and we'll get this moving. Believe me, the sooner this all comes down the better.'

Columbo was smiling now. After a few dodgy turns this was going better than he could ever have expected. He slipped a card across the table. Raine picked it up and slid it into her pocket.

'Ten o'clock, Thursday morning. The address is on that card.'

The chair screeched across the tile floor as she stood up. 'Done.'

She'd taken a couple of steps from the table when she turned back and looked at Connor's sidekick, who was still standing against the wall directly behind his boss.

'And you know, Eric, if we're gonna be going on dates like this, you really need to come outta your shell a little.'

A grin crossed his face as she winked at him, then she turned and headed for the door.


The whole way home on the subway, the adrenalin pumped through her veins. She was a long way from victory, but this was the starting pistol on a race that was going to end with Tang's ass being fried and Raine couldn't think of a single thing she wouldn't do to make sure that happened.

This was it. Five years after Ricco died she finally had something to work with. Just thinking about Ricco stopped the adrenalin in its tracks and as she climbed the subway stairs and headed towards her home, she felt her shoulders sag and a huge come-down overwhelmed her.

Twenty-three. She was twenty-three years old and what the fuck had she got herself into? Drugs. Vice. Death.

Her pa had told her that Angelica Roberts was about to qualify as a teacher and was planning her wedding to Tony Porcello, the son of family friends and the guy she'd been dating since school. In a couple of years' time she'd be a wife, a teacher and no doubt living in a beautiful house on the outskirts of the old area with a kid on the way. What would Raine be doing? Who knew?

Normal. Sometimes she just had a longing to be normal.

'Hey, there.'

It took her a moment to realise that the voice was directed at her. What was this, scare-the-shit-out-of-Raine night?

She leaned against the post at the bottom of the stairs up to her building and looked at the guy who was sitting on the fourth step, blocking her way.

'Hey,' she replied. Too many questions. Too many. Starting with, 'What are you doing here, Shay? And how'd you know where I live?'

'I made the guys in the pizza place tell me. Told them I'd take the models elsewhere from now on if they didn't cough the details.'

'Good to know they set a high price on betrayal. You should have thrown in a hot dog and they'd probably have given you my phone number, too.'

'Actually, they gave me that for nothing.' He had the decency to look a little embarrassed and Raine felt her heart tug. If she had Angelica Roberts' life, she could see a place for a guy like this in it.

But that was the problem, she had two lives and neither of them was really hers. Raine Storm was a figment of her imagination, created with an agenda. Raine O'Donnell was so far from the world she now inhabited that she was a stranger to her. So who was she now? And if she didn't know then how could she possibly explain it to anyone else?

'I just wanted to talk to you because I was worried.'

'Why?'

'There were a couple of guys in asking about you when I was in for my pizza tonight. Looked official. Just thought you should know.'

So much for Columbo and his sidekick's powers of discretion. Fools.

'Short guy, leather jacket, tall guy in a suit, both of them with the distinct look of stupidity?'

'Don't know about the last bit but the rest sounds about right,' he replied with a smile. His smile. God, it did things to her.

'S'OK, they found me. They were . . . friends of my dad's. Cops.'

'Your dad's a cop? Is that why Manzo's always looks like the set of *Hill Street Blues*?'

'Yeah, they're pretty protective. Like to check up on me. But those guys tonight just wanted to talk to me about his . . . retirement party.'

Where the hell were the lies coming from? She wasn't sure he actually believed her but it didn't matter. It was enough just to give him some kind of explanation.

He thought this over for a minute, then pushed himself up and took a couple of steps down towards her.

'So . . . should I ask you again?'

Dear God, you have got to be kidding me. Sick friends. DEA. Longing for normality. Double identity crisis and now the cutest guy in Manhattan asking me out. I hope you're having fun with this.

'Shay, it's . . . complicated.'

'I like complicated things.'

His lips were on hers and she knew she had to stop him immediately. She knew, but somehow she couldn't. Just couldn't. The touch of his lips, the sensation of his hands cupping her face, the exquisite warmth of knowing that someone wanted to be with her and needed her right at that moment. She'd never allowed herself this before, and much as she knew she shouldn't do it, the overwhelming need was just too much.

His tongue was probing hers, his hips pressed against hers and their breathing simultaneously sped up, becoming increasingly frantic with longing.

'I think this is where we go up to your place and you invite me to stay.'

Raine peeked up at her window and saw that the light was on. That meant that at least one, possibly two Virgin air hostesses were up there in a tiny flat and she was probably destined for a night on the couch. Somehow that seemed like it might be a bit of a passion killer.

'Can we go to your place?' The words were out before she thought it through, but she had no intention of taking them back. From somewhere near her ear, she heard him murmur, 'Sure,' then a few moments later he came up for air and stuck his hand out to hail a cab. Right on cue one slid into the sidewalk. How did he do that? She could never find a cab when she wanted one.

It didn't even bother her that the driver watched them making out in his rear-view mirror the whole way there, narrowly missing several accidents and running a red light. The guy was going to have to pull over and give himself some attention as soon as he dropped them off.

Fifteen minutes of serious lip action later they were outside his building, a brownstone on a leafy street a couple of blocks up from the pizzeria.

'Come. Now,' his words were thick with longing as he pushed open the main door, then turned immediately right along a white-walled corridor with plush grey carpeting and huge plants in every corner.

This was the kind of place she could live in.

He unlocked the door and pulled her inside, flicking on a switch as they entered. Immediately four lamps, one in each corner of the room, sprang to life giving her a chance to scope the space. It was one huge room with oak floors, white walls and a black gloss kitchen at one end. In the middle was a living area with a black leather sofa on a thick cream rug. The rest of the space was taken up with a fully equipped, high-tech photography studio.

Behind him on his right was a door. He pushed it open and they tumbled through, falling onto a bed of crisp white linens. He made love to her exactly how she knew he would, like the two of them had been together before and knew exactly what the other one wanted. Three years of foreplay was a long, long time. Words weren't necessary as they moved and twisted and came together, then broke apart as he slid down her body, kissing and licking every inch and crevice until he reached the tiny mound of pubic hair between her legs. His tongue darted across her clitoris, making her buttocks clench and her hands reached for the wooden struts at the top of the bed. She wound her fingers around them, holding on, eyes shut tight as he explored and kissed and licked her until she exploded.

The tingling hadn't even stopped when he slipped inside her and brought her once again to a climax that made her shudder. Then he flopped back on the bed, his fingers in her hair, playing with the curls.

'You OK?'

She nodded, smiling as he reached over to kiss her on the lips and nuzzle into her neck.

Normality. This was what normality felt like. A boyfriend. A lover. Someone to come home to, to make love to, someone that cared enough to have your back. She should feel warm and fuzzy, she should want to curl up and reciprocate the look of expectant happiness she saw in his eyes.

But. . . . She couldn't block the voice in her head telling her that it was a mistake. The last guy that had her back ended up dead and she couldn't handle a repeat. This couldn't happen. It just wasn't possible. There were too many secrets and telling him about her other life wasn't an option – hi, I'm your girlfriend and I'm a club freak who's on a mission to destroy one of the most important men in the city. If telling the truth wasn't an option, how would she explain her absences every night?

As his breathing returned to normal, he stroked her face, his fingers gently flowing down her cheek, her neck, her—

She put her hand over his. He didn't get the message.

'So can I stop asking you now?' he said, his eyes crinkling at the sides as he smiled.

The reply was halted by a large boulder that had formed in her throat, and to her astonishment tears slid from the corners of her eyes. She never cried. Never. There was no room in her life for self-pity or grief or complicating sadness.

'Hey, hey, don't do that. It's OK. Man, you're even beautiful when you cry.'

She wiped away the tears and sat up, aching under the pain of what she was about to do.

'Shay, we can't.'

'What?' He looked puzzled but unconcerned, obviously completely oblivious to what was happening.

'Shay.' Something in the tone of her voice struck a chord and his eyes met hers, the question hanging there.

It had to be done. There was no other way out of this. It was for the best. She knew that. The only way.

'Shay, I can't see you. There's . . . someone else.'

'What? Who?' He was sitting up now, too, and shit he was stunning. Back out. Stop speaking. Don't do this. It's not too late. Forget the other stuff. Forget Tang, forget revenge, forget Raine Storm, forget . . . Ricco. She couldn't forget Ricco. Not until this was done.

'It's kind of . . . unfinished business. With someone else.' It

235

was difficult to get this out through the stammers and the sobs and the damned boulder was blocking her windpipe.

'Shit,' he sighed. His hands came up to his face and he rubbed it for a second then ran his fingers back through his hair. 'Shit,' he repeated. 'Might have been good to know before now.'

'I'm sorry.'

'So, what? Are you saying you're still with him? In love with him?'

Oh, fuck, where could she go with this? It seemed like all she could do was nod.

'And it's not, like, over? Or gonna be over any time soon?'

'I'm . . . sorry.'

Without saying another word he got up, went into the bathroom and closed the door behind him. Raine heard the shower go on almost immediately and wearily dropped her head to her chest. This couldn't play out any other way.

She was gone by the time he came back to the bedroom.

# TWENTY-THREE

*Mei-Lin*
*New York, 1989*

'Where are Ivana and Flora tonight?' Mei-Lin took a sip of her tea as Ami flipped open a book and checked the pages inside. 'Ivana is at the Midtown Marriott with Mr Tain, Flora is over at the Holiday Vista with Mr Gallagher. I can't believe that a guy as wealthy as him will pay two hundred dollars for a girl but he won't pay more than sixty dollars for a hotel room.'

'He told me once that his wife is very frugal and she books the hotels for his business trips and checks the credit card bills. What he does with his cash when he's away is untraceable.'

Ami shook her head. 'Unbelievable. Anyway, Stacey and Ulla are still at the Hamptons with the Bulgarians and Gana and Lissa are leaving today to join Mr Kassa and his friends on the cruise. They were pretty excited about that one. Oh, and I told Mr Dolle that his business is no longer welcome and charged his credit card for the doctor's call out. Sally is going to be fine – just a surface bruise.'

Mei-Lin's eyes darkened. She'd had a bad feeling about Dolle but he'd been recommended by one of her regulars and she'd taken him at face value. She wouldn't make that mistake again.

Anyone looking at Ami now would think that she was some kind of hyper-efficient PA, as opposed to the logistical organiser of a group of girls who got paid for showing their clients a real good time.

Over the last year business had flourished. Ami had already moved into a four-bedroom apartment in a slightly better area and now she had three other girls living there, too. The rest of their girls had their own places, most of them paid for by wealthy men who liked to have them on twenty-four-hour call when they were in town. They only catered to the very rich, who could pay top dollar, and they dressed and acted accordingly. However, much as Ami did a stellar job organising the meetings, handling the finances and taking care of business, it was Mei-Lin's input that was crucial to the whole operation, since she provided most of the clients and recruited the majority of the girls. Anyone who was literally worth their weight in gold visited Reincarnation when they were in New York, and Mei-Lin had spent the last year converting those contacts into dollars. Sure it was risky. If Tang found out he'd kill her, but to her it was worth it to have a tiny glimmer of an escape route. She whispered in the ears of important men at the club, slipped cards into their pockets, spent the night with them and persuaded them to let her invite the others. Then she'd ask them to call Ami next time they were in town so that she could supply what they needed. She'd talk to the girls that came there with clients, offer them more work, then put them in touch with Ami to sort out the details.

Her approach to both clients and girls didn't always work, but she was successful most of the time and the business was expanding. The dollars were coming in, and the gods must be on her side because thankfully Tang had not discovered what she was up to.

Mei-Lin looked at her watch – a Seiko that one of her regular guys had given her on his last visit. She'd been astonished when Tang had let her keep it, but it seemed that her new, positive attitude was had impressed him enough to indulge her. If only he realised what was behind it.

Of course, if it had been an Omega or a Gucci he'd have confiscated it immediately.

'I have to go.'

She'd left Reincarnation last night with an English thespian who was opening on Broadway the following week. They'd spent the night in a huge, luxurious suite at the Sheraton and he'd been more than happy to splash out a little extra for Ami to join them. They'd made it worth his while – hours of girl-on-girl stuff followed by the best sandwich of his life. He'd left at 9 a.m. to go to rehearsals, but check-out time was eleven, so Mei-Lin and Ami had made the most of it. Tea and croissants, long baths and then a chat while sitting at the window, looking over the city, wearing white fluffy robes and slippers. In a job that was ninety-nine per cent duty and degradation, this little one per cent was to be savoured.

Ami put her pen and pad away, sat back and took a deep breath. Mei-Lin sighed, preparing herself for what she knew was coming. How many times were they going to have this conversation?

'Mei-Lin, it's time. We have eleven thousand dollars in savings, the apartment is ready and we have the contacts now. We don't need you to work there anymore.'

Mei-Lin took a sip of her tea and contemplated her friend's

earnest expression. Ami was right, in the real world she no longer needed to work at Reincarnation. They'd get by on the clients they had, and possibly even get some more. They'd make a decent life. But she didn't live in the real world, she lived in Jason Tang's, and as long as he owned her she could never leave. The only thought that got her through was that one day she'd have something on him that would create a stalemate and force him to release her.

She had hope. Lately, she'd noticed he was becoming careless. It was a subtle shift, but his drug usage was increasing and his behaviour was definitely more reckless than before. Only last week he'd thrown out a city councillor and a new boy band because they didn't want to settle up their tabs in the VIP room. It was as if he was once the person who was there to entertain and serve them, but had started to believe his own publicity, driving him to unprecedented levels of megalomania. If he continued to go down a path of recklessness and foolish decisions, who knew what could happen?

Reaching over, she took Ami's hand. 'It's not time. Until I know I can get away without having to spend the rest of my life looking over my shoulder, there's no point. I'll just be a prisoner in another way. He will fall, Ami. But until then we just have to keep preparing, so that when it all comes down I have somewhere to go.'

She didn't add her worst fear: that Tang's empire would crash and she'd be buried in the rubble. What was the point of looking at the dark side? Far better to live in hope; that was something she'd been practising since she was fifteen years old.

It was a wrench to drag herself away, but she knew she must. Hopefully they'd get to see each other again, perhaps even later that night – it was just a case of setting up a client who would be open to it.

When she got to work that evening, she realised it wasn't hopeful.

Friday nights had been quieter than normal over the last couple of months since a new club had opened on the other side of town. The usual crowd were in the VIP bar, and the only private parties that were in consisted of a band called the Steel Spikes, who were already stoned and had brought their own girls, and another band that Suzy had told her were The Bitch of Thorns. They'd been in before – four girls and a huge entourage – and tonight they had a couple of famous basketball players in their party. Suzy had told her that, too. Apparently one of them was a regular client who she saw once a month.

'Right, you whores.' Tang wasn't happy. Just after they arrived he'd had a huge fight with Ari Covet, the music guy. Mei-Lin had got to know him well over the years and she dreaded his presence. He was a sick pig, liked pain and treated everyone like shit. He'd had a screaming match with Tang over some tape he wanted to watch. This surprised her as the men were friends and Covet was a regular participant in Tang's sordid pastimes. They had come to some agreement after the dispute, but Tang had been irritable ever since and his mood seemed to be growing darker by the minute.

Mei-Lin noticed the small wooden box at the side of his desk. About eight inches by three, it looked like a Chinese antique, with flames carved into the sides and a dragon roaring on the top. His coke box. Or was it meth? Mei-Lin had no idea anymore and she certainly wasn't going to ask. All she knew was that his already dark demeanour was showing flashes of rage and instability that were extreme even for him. There were other changes, too. His appearance, once immaculate and flamboyant, now regularly showed signs of lack of care. An unshaven face. The same clothes two days in succession. A suit that wasn't pressed to perfection.

At that very second his cane flew across the room, almost spearing Suzy.

'For fu—' She cut herself off, realising that getting into a fight with Tang was never going to be a good idea.

'Get out there and drum up some business, you useless pieces of dog shit,' Tang demanded. They didn't need any prompting, they turned on their stilettos and trooped out like schoolchildren on their way from the principal's office. Mei-Lin was last in line and was almost at the door when the cane came flying in her direction, clipping her ankle.

'Not you, slut. You can stay here and amuse me. Strip. Sit there. Don't say a single word.'

He pointed to the pale blue, antique chair in the corner of the room. Mei-Lin's brow furrowed in confusion. He wanted her to strip? This was bizarre. Tang had never shown the slightest sexual interest in her or anyone else. Everyone at the club speculated on his sexuality, but no one actually knew. Mei-Lin had decided a long time ago that he was asexual. Not interested. Deprived of the emotions of lust and physical longing.

'Now!'

There was no point in arguing. She reached up behind her, pulled down her zipper and removed her dress, folding it neatly and placing it on a chest to her left. He didn't even look at her while she was doing it. This wasn't about sex, she realised. It was about amusement. Control. He was playing with her just for the fun of it. The thought held no fear for her. Let him play. She had long ago learned to deal with this kind of humiliation. There was nothing he could do to her that hadn't been done already and the only effect this had was to pour another drop into the ocean of hatred she felt for him. A little niggle set in that perhaps this was the beginning of some kind of punishment. Had he found out what she was doing? About Ami and the other girls?

'Everything.' His voice was completely deadpan. She removed her red thong and matching bra, then sat on the chair as instructed. 'From now on when you're not with clients I want you sitting there just like that. Like my new poodle.'

His words settled her concern. If he'd found out what was going on he would have been far more vicious; he would have struck out and lost his temper. No, this was definitely just some stupid game, a by-product of his insanity.

She sat back on the chair, automatically crossing her legs.

'Open them,' he ordered again, barely looking at her.

She did as the bastard said, internally repeating her mantra. One day. One day.

Tang leaned over and opened the wooden box, removed a gold straw that was clipped into the lid and snorted a line. From her angle sitting slightly behind him she couldn't see what effect it had but there was nothing obvious. How much of that stuff was he taking if it did nothing to him other than make him even more sadistic?

He picked up the phone. 'Brandy. Now!' he barked. A few minutes and a couple of lines of white powder later, Chad, one of the barmen from the VIP bar, came in carrying a bottle and a glass on a silver tray. He almost dropped it when he saw Mei-Lin, but the hint of warning as she darted her gaze to Tang and back again prevented any comment.

Tang poured a triple shot and turned to the monitors to watch what was going on. Monitor number one: a fight broke out at the front door and Vincent had a guy in a headlock. Monitor number five: in the fire exit behind the main bar a couple were having sex. He zoomed in for a moment, then back out again, as if he'd lost interest. Monitor number eleven: private room. The guys from the Steel Spikes were getting loaded, a stunning blonde woman was riding a guy with long black hair while the others took no notice at all. Monitor number twelve: in the private room next door, The Bitch of Thorns were all dancing and drinking, with one very tall girl performing a striptease on the coffee table. Tang watched for a moment before disinterest took over.

Agitated again, he poured another shot, lit a cigarette, then pulled out a calculator from his desk drawer and began punching in numbers almost manically. All the while Mei-Lin sat in perfect silence, realising that he'd completely forgotten she was there. More number punching, his hand going faster and faster, so manic that he had to just be punching in random numbers.

Suddenly the phone rang and he snatched it from the cradle. 'Wei?'

It was a Mandarin greeting. That in itself was unusual as he generally spoke only in English, even to her. He was obviously expecting the call.

She could only hear his side of the conversation and it wasn't a happy one.

'Where is it?'

'What the fuck do you mean you brought it personally?'

'I told you never to come here, you fucking pig. You were supposed to use the normal channels.'

'No, I'm not waiting until tomorrow. Bring it now.'

'I said now, or I will slice off your dick and stick it in that infested mouth of yours.'

The phone was slammed down and he checked his watch. Almost midnight. Time for his nightly phone call to his mother in Beijing. He banged out a number and immediately his voice changed to a soft burr.

'Hello, my darling mother, how are you tonight?'

'I'm afraid I can't speak for long as I have very important meetings this evening.'

'That's why I love you so much, my darling mother. I miss you every moment.'

'Yes, I have sent the Hermès. It should reach you tomorrow.'

'I know, my darling. And I you. Good night.'

Mei-Lin felt her skin crawl. In a world that was ripe with disgusting things, that was the creepiest of all. It sounded more like a man addressing a lover than a mother.

'Bastard. Bastard.' Tang was muttering to himself in Mandarin now as he reached down and opened the bottom left-hand drawer of his desk, flipped up the false bottom and removed the key. Then he got up and marched over to the farthest wall, where a picture of some French courtesan hung. He'd told her who it was once and mocked her for her lack of education, but the name escaped her now. It was an expensive painting. Priceless, he'd said. An example of Renaissance—

It moved. Only an instinctive realisation that she mustn't remind him she was there stopped her from gasping aloud as one side of the artwork pulled away from the wall, revealing a door behind it. Tang slid the key into a lock, then moved his hand to a large circular dial. He twisted it from one side to another, then back again, dialling in some kind of code. His head blocked her view, but that changed a moment later when he swung open another door, a metal one this time, and the contents of a safe were revealed. Cash. That was all she could see. Piles of cash. It was impossible to say for sure, but she thought she could also see a book of some kind, a red one, leather bound, and ... He stepped to the side, and then the real surprise became clear. Tapes. Rows and rows of tapes, and she was guessing that they weren't family-friendly movies.

If anything was going to remind Tang of her presence it would be her thudding heart, which she was sure must be loud enough for someone in the next room to hear.

Tang grabbed several bundles of cash, slammed the door shut and returned to his desk. Just as he sat down he registered her presence, as if surprised that she was there. He lifted his cane again, pressed a button on the side and a blade shot out of the bottom. He reached over and ran the tip across her breasts, leaving a fine red welt from shoulder to shoulder. 'If you tell anyone what you just saw, you will die.'

The venom in his expression, the wide, bloodshot eyes, the shaking hands, the cruel twist of his lips, all left Mei-Lin in no doubt that he meant every word. He pressed the button again and the blade disappeared, four tiny panels of a silver tip coming together to conceal that it ever existed. The cane moved down the middle of her torso and her first instinct was to snap her legs shut, but she knew that would just provoke him. Be calm. Show no fear. Don't give the sadistic prick his power. Be calm. Show no fear. The mantra went round in her head as the tip of the cane glistened in her pubic hair.

'Wider,' he said. She did what she was told, her face a mask of defiance. Be calm. Show no fear.

'Lift that pussy up.'

Tilting her pelvis back, she gave him the angle he was looking for and gritted her teeth as he pushed the silver stick inside her. The feeling of foreboding was beginning to take hold now. He wouldn't hesitate to gut her like a fish if the notion came over him, and he was so altered and agitated that it could happen at any moment.

It was going to have to stop. If she was going to get hurt, or worse, it wasn't going to be because she let this vile creature disembowel her. This had to end and it had to end n—

Before the final word had formulated there was a knock at the door. Tang slowly extricated his prop, winking at her as he did so. It took every single iota of strength she had not to shake from head to toe with rage and relief.

'Enter.' After what he'd just done to her, the sneering tone made her want to take the cane off him and stab him right through his heart.

Vincent came through the door. 'Mr Tang, there's someone here to see you. A Mr Yo.'

Tang thumped his cane on the desk, and as he did so Vincent caught sight of her. Mei-Lin was sure she saw a glimmer of ... what? Satisfaction? Amusement? There certainly wasn't an instant reaction to save or protect her. Coercing him to help with Ami had definitely made her an enemy there. Not that it mattered. He was just another one to add to a long list of people she would gladly never set eyes on again.

'So why the fuck are you standing there looking at that little cunt, then? Is that what I pay you for, to salivate over pussy?'

Vincent shook his head. 'No, Mr Tang, I—'

'Tell you what, let's make her your bonus this month. You get to fuck her on pay day. How does that sound?'

Focus on something else, she told herself. Something pleasurable. Something that would take her to a happy place. Right now, that was the sound of Tang's blood spurting from his body as the tip of his cane ravaged his arteries.

'No, Mr Tang, I—'

'I insist! Now go and get my guest before I set that rabid little creature on your cock. I've heard she bites.'

Vincent didn't say another word, just backed out slowly, unable to meet Mei-Lin's gaze again.

A few moments later he returned, walking in front of the guest. Mei-Lin didn't even look up, having absolutely no desire to see the surprise or pity on the person's face as they saw her sitting there like this.

Tang, however, was on his feet, and before Vincent had even left the room he picked up an ashtray from his desk and launched it in the direction of his visitor. 'What the fuck are you doing here?'

'But Mr Tang—'

The voice. For the first time she lifted her eyes from the floor, and the effect was like being punched in the guts by a massive force. Vincent had mispronounced the name. Easily done.

Cheung Yu stood in front of her, and even the fact that he looked mildly terrified couldn't stop the tremors that overtook her now.

Cheung Yu.

Her Uncle Cheung.

'I told you not to fucking come here. What the fuck do you think you are doing?'

There was a pause, then Cheung's head swivelled as he realised who was sitting in the corner. 'Mei-Lin?'

He said it as if he couldn't believe she was there, as if he'd he had no involvement whatsoever in selling her into this life. Bizarrely, he looked almost as if he was pleased to see her.

There was a tightness in her chest as she realised it was all too much. How much more of this could she possibly take?

'Ah, yes, of course. This is your little Mei-Lin.' Tang announced with relish. 'I do love a family reunion. Doesn't she look a little different from when I rescued her from that sewer you operated in Shanghai?'

No, she couldn't let them break her down. Gritting her teeth together once again, she regained a steely expression of defiance. They wouldn't break her. And even though all she wanted to do right now was throw herself at Cheung's feet and beg for news of her family, she knew that would be playing right into both of these men's hands.

No fear. She would show no fear.

'Sure, she looks different. Our little whore is all grown up now.'

His words changed the mood in the room, with Tang joining in his laughter. Great to see that her misery was lightening the tone. Veins spurting blood. She held on to that thought. Cheung took it as a signal to appease Tang and proceed with his purpose for being there.

'Mr Tang, forgive me for disrupting our normal procedures, but I had business in New York and decided to kill two birds with one stone.'

Cheung had business here? Doing what? When she left he was a mid-level pimp in a city of eighteen million people. What had happened in the intervening years to allow him to expand his operation to a level that involved travelling to New York? And had it really only been five years since she'd left Shanghai? It felt like a lifetime.

'Business must be good in Shanghai,' drawled Tang, almost echoing her thoughts.

'Indeed. I've now moved full time into the export business.'

'And the whores?'

Cheung nodded and Mei-Lin was incredulous. It sounded like two men having a casual conversation. He even gave the impression of a successful businessman. His hair was cut in a fashionable style, longer at the back, trimmed neatly over his ears, with a fringe that flicked to the side. He wore a long trench coat that looked to have been cut well and made from expensive fabric. Underneath that was a black poloneck jumper, a pair of smart black trousers, pressed, and hanging over black patent leather shoes. He looked like any other successful Chinese businessman in the city. It was evil masquerading as normality.

'Ah, that is still a very profitable operation. One of my girls turned out to be quite the businesswoman and has proved to be an excellent manager in my absence.'

He looked at Mei-Lin as he said it, clearly getting off on sharing his tales of success while she sat there utterly degraded.

Now sadness gripped like a vice on her heart, but not for her. His words took her right back to that stinking building in a Shanghai alley and Mei-Lin was suddenly overwhelmed by a desperate feeling of pain and loss. Jing Wei. Her beautiful, perfect little bird. Nothing would ever take away the pain of leaving her. She only hoped that Jing Wei was too ill to realise that she was on her own when she died. The hatred was rising in her again and she wanted to pounce on him, to scratch his eyes out with her bare hands. But no, that would be short-term satisfaction and she knew that would never be enough. Her next thought wasn't a fantasy scenario conjured up to get her past a painful moment. It wasn't an idle threat or an empty promise. It was a fact: one day she would kill this man in front of her and she would smile as she did so.

Tang unexpectedly interrupted with a long sigh. 'Enough of the small talk. Business. Did you bring my order?'

Cheung immediately glanced at Mei-Lin.

'Oh don't worry about her,' Tang said, realising Cheung's concerns. 'That cunt sees nothing and hears nothing. That's part of the job and she knows better than to defy me.'

This seemed to satisfy her uncle. Uncle. The word made her stomach lurch and for a second she thought she might throw up right there in front of them.

'Very well.' He reached into the inside pocket of his coat and pulled out a considerably large package wrapped in brown paper. 'I've brought—'

There was a sharp knock at the door and then it swung open. Mei-Lin watched as the tall crazy girl who promoted the Sunday night party stepped in. Storm. That was her name. Raine Storm. Very peculiar. They'd passed each other a few times since the night she had burst in and begged Mei-Lin to help her friend, but they'd never spoken since then. However, she couldn't help sensing that they had a kind of empathy. A bond.

Storm looked at her with horror.

'Sorry, Mr Tang, I just wanted to talk to you about—'

'GET. THE. FUCK. OUT!'

'But—'

'NOW!'

She slowly backed out of the door, her stare resting on Mei-Lin.

Only when the handle clicked did Cheung continue. He placed the package on Tang's desk and took a step backwards. 'Three kilos. And as always, you won't be disappointed with the quality.'

Tang lifted his cane and pierced the package, sending a puff of white powder billowing upwards. Cheung winced, then tried to cover it up with a cough. Tang didn't even notice. He delved his finger into the hole he'd made in the package and scooped up a mound of the powder, then swiftly snorted it up his nose.

Eyes closed, breathing indiscernible, he was perfectly still for what seemed like minutes before he opened his glassy eyes and stared directly at Cheung. 'You are a very lucky man, Mr Yu. Only the quality of your product compels me to forgive your lack of professionalism tonight.'

Opening the drawer of his desk, he pulled out the stack of cash, put it on top and pushed it towards Cheung.

'Take your payment, leave my club and never, ever come back here, Mr Yu. Because if you do, our business will be terminated.'

Cheung nodded, clearly disconcerted. Even her notoriously thick-skinned uncle could understand such a direct hint. Her skin was crawling with the discomfort of the situation, and for once she was fully supportive of Tang's obnoxious behaviour. The sooner Cheung was out of here the better for them all.

'Oh and Cheung, just to show that I'm an amenable man,' he was slurring his words now, making it more difficult to understand what he was saying.

'If you want to fuck that little thing before you leave, then that's my gift to you.'

Mei-Lin averted her eyes, unable to look at his face as he leered at her naked body and contemplated what he wanted to do to it. On the bank of monitors beside her, her eyes fell on one of the feeds from the private rooms, where a girl's face was contorted in pain, obviously screaming, crying and begging for help.

Right now she knew exactly how she felt.

# TWENTY-FOUR

*Stevie*
*New York, 1989*

'A Jack Daniel's and Coke, extra ice please.'

The young man who brought through the tray of drinks and glasses stared at her the whole time. She got that a lot. Everywhere she went she was recognised by fans, and much as the band appreciated every last record purchase and video request, Stevie would be lying if she didn't admit that sometimes she found the success difficult. Being the centre of attention had never come easy to her. All she wanted to do was write songs and sing them and she and Dixie were happy to leave the publicity stuff to Lou and Cally.

Of course, it didn't help in the privacy stakes that she was going out with one of the most famous basketball players in the country. Jinx had been a total revelation to her – a man that could make her laugh, make her happy, and then make love to her all night while telling her in explicit terms all the filthy, erotic things he was going to do with her. They were so alike that sometimes it scared her. In a sport that was notorious for wild behaviour, Jinx was the antithesis of the bad boy basketball player. He never smoked, not even cigars, he didn't drink, he didn't touch drugs, or gamble. He adored his family and took care of a bus load of extended relatives. He believed in fidelity and wanted a family, but only with someone he was married to for life. He was honest and thoughtful but still exciting and spontaneous. Jinx Daley was just the most grounded, together, sensationally sexy guy she had ever known and Stevie couldn't believe that she'd found him.

This was the real deal she'd been writing about in songs for a decade.

They'd even given a couple of joint interviews to magazines: the sports star and the rock star – the perfect couple.

'They're in love!' screamed the headlines of one after a ten-minute interview, snatched on the way out of a club off Sunset Strip.

Getting time together was difficult, with Stevie being on tour and Jinx playing all over the country, but somehow they made it work, coming together when their schedules overlapped, like this weekend in New York. The Thorns had just flown back from a European tour that culminated in a massive charity concert in London, playing to fifty thousand fans in Wembley Stadium last night. Decomp and the Steel Spikes were both on the bill, as was every major rock band of the last ten years. It was like the stuff of dreams hanging backstage with Guns N' Roses, Bon Jovi, Poison and – cue hyperventilation – the rock gods that were Aerosmith. But the life-defining moment for Stevie was when she stood in the wings and watched Stevie Nicks take the stage. Every dream, every fantasy since she was ten years old was realised right there and then. The only thing that could better that experience would be to get on stage with her. Next time, she promised herself. Somehow she would get Cole Presley to make it happen.

She hadn't even had a chance to speak to her idol, as

they'd been rushed out of the stadium immediately after the performance, taken to Heathrow and flown home, first class, on British Airways. Both the Spikes and The Thorns had headed to New York for a VH1 special that was due to be filmed the following day.

It had worked out perfectly. The Lakers were also in town playing the Knicks, so Jinx had been waiting for her in a suite at the Omni Park Central. They hadn't left the room for eight hours, and even then she had to be dragged out against her will. Why would they want to go to a nightclub when they could stay in, call room service and make love until dawn?

'C'mon, baby,' Jinx had slapped her butt as he jumped off the bed. 'Time to get going. Said we'd meet the rest of the guys downstairs at ten.'

'But why do we need to go?' she'd pouted.

'Because tonight's important. People to see.'

She'd thrown a pillow at him and eased herself up, groaning at the exertion on a body that was exhausted from touring, travelling and a marathon sex session with a man who was the most well-endowed guy on the Eastern seaboard. The very thought of it made her nipples stand erect again and there was a distinct tingling in the clitoral area.

Stevie had reached up to him. 'Come show me again exactly how much you love me,' she'd purred, unable to take her eyes off his gleaming, beautiful body. Every single one of his abdominal muscles looked as if they were carved into jet-black granite, his arms were perfectly formed testimonies to endless hours spent in the gym and his ass . . . oh sweet Jesus, his ass. It looked like two footballs sitting side by side. His bald head and perfectly sculpted face were the icing on her orgasmic cake. It was the body of a world-class athlete and it was right there for her to play with.

Stevie couldn't remember a single time she had ever been happier.

'Come on,' she'd said again, determined to coax him back to bed.

Laughing, he reached over, flipped the duvet back and, in a completely effortless movement, swept her up into his arms, carried her through to the bathroom and dumped her in the tub. Thankfully it was still filled with warm water from their last session, when she'd straddled him and slowly, teasingly, rode him until he came inside her, grasping her hips and gasping for breath.

The man was amazing and she loved him, and he had never given her a single reason to doubt him. When she called, he answered; when she was in town, he was there in a heartbeat, and when she was least expecting it, he'd show up at her hotel door in some random country, demanding nothing more than to be with her and love her.

This one was a keeper.

In the end, they'd made it to Reincarnation later than the others, earning them a round of applause when they walked in. They'd kicked off in the VIP room. Lou was there with Tayn Dawson, one of Jinx's team-mates. They'd hooked up a few months before when Jinx had brought him along to a gig, and to everyone's surprise it was still going strong and – drum rolls – exclusive. She was still a major drama queen, but at least the publicity and stability of a relationship was keeping her monstrous ego under control. For now.

Over on one of the black leather sofas, Cally was entwined with her latest love – Jenna Stewart, bass player with an up-and-coming LA band called Blue Tricks. The girl thing hadn't been much of a shock. Cally hated the term 'bisexual' and preferred to call it 'open-minded'. Stevie had another theory: Cally's seeds of attraction were rooted in music and anyone who could spend two hours discussing the reverberation of a D-string could make Cally come on the spot. Right now, Jenna seemed to be fulfilling the spec.

The biggest surprise in the whole hook-up department though was sitting in the corner, semi-concealed by a mass of hair: Dixie and Jude had somehow got together over the last few weeks and seemed to be making it work. Cally had performed a lap of honour of the tour bus when they'd found out and she realised that she had the sole honour of being the only member of the band who hadn't at one time been intimate with Jude's dick. It was a blessing – given that he was her uncle, that was probably a rock-and-roll experience too far.

'Babe, you look like you've been pushed up against a wall and screwed all afternoon.' Jude winked at her. What had she ever seen in him? He was harmless and kinda fun, but the last five years on the road, with the stresses and strains of running a band in a crazy world, had taken their toll and his once craggy good looks now just looked haggard. They couldn't fault his management, though. While Cole dished out the orders from above, Jude took care of all the day-to-day stuff, got them where they were supposed to be, handled all the problems and got the best deal for them in everything. And surprisingly, despite his chequered relationships with the girls as individuals, there were no bad feelings lurking out there. Although Stevie had a nagging fear that might change if it all went badly with Dixie. She was a serious chick. Quiet. Focused. Painfully introverted. There was definitely an intensity that could go the wrong way if provoked. There was always the possibility that if Jude cast her aside, he'd wake up every morning for the rest of his life, open his curtains and find her face pressed against the window.

The barman handed her the Jack Daniel's and Coke she'd

ordered and she held it as she danced at the window with Jinx, looking down on the masses below. The speaker system was just awesome, the quality of the sound pitch perfect as Bobby Brown's 'My Prerogative' faded into Madonna's 'Like A Prayer'. It wasn't Stevie's kind of music, but she appreciated it and it still made her want to dance.

'Happy, baby?' Jinx was nuzzling her ear, his hand on her ass as their hips moved tantalisingly sexily in time to the music. No one looking at them would doubt for a single second that they were insanely hot for each other.

'Uh-huh.' She smiled, slipping her hand down into the back of his jeans and digging her nails into his butt cheek. He liked it a little rough like that and the reaction was instant – a major hard-on now came between them. Laughing, Stevie threw back her head and let him lick the inches of creamy white flesh that ran from her belly button to her neck. The black halter top had been a great choice. Held together by a band that sat around her hips, it consisted of just two other strips of fabric that came up over her tits and tied behind her neck. On top of the mandatory leather jeans, the long shaggy blond hair and the kohl-lined eyes, she looked 100 per cent like the rock star she was.

Life just didn't get any better.

There was a commotion at the door and when she turned to check it out she saw the Steel Spikes had arrived. Those boys loved to make an entrance. Sly Rammer, the lead singer, was practically carrying a tiny, skinny little blonde thing who looked no more than fifteen. In actuality, it was his girlfriend Marny, who was in her early twenties and a major coke head. The poor thing was so out of it she had no idea where she was.

It was an even sadder sight when you contrasted Marny with Coco LaBiba. Coco was a legend on Planet Rock. On–off girlfriend of the genius guitarist Dax Rice, she'd also had a well-publicised affair with the lead singer of Decomp. It was an incestuous world that they lived in, where hot chicks were as much of a commodity as cash and luxuries.

Coco high-fived Stevie as she passed her. 'Hey, girl, we've got a couple of private rooms if you wanna chill with us.' They'd hung out a lot on the Decomp tour and although she had no girl-on-girl tendencies whatsoever, even Stevie had fallen a little in love with Coco. It was impossible not to. She was that rare creature – a smoking-hot babe who loved her girlfriends as much as she dedicated her life to getting it on with the sexiest guys.

'Sure, babe, like I could ever refuse you,' Stevie replied with a wink, removing Jinx's hand from inside the black fabric covering her right breast. 'I'll round them up and see you in there.'

In the end it didn't require any effort on her part. Two of the Spikes' band members, Strings and Muff, were notoriously hyperactive party animals and they moved everyone across to the adjoining private rooms with the promise of free coke, champagne and unlimited Jack Daniel's.

Lou celebrated by jumping on the coffee table and performing a striptease so erotic it even got Stevie a little turned on. Maybe she should rethink that girl-on-girl theory. In the meantime, girl-on-guy was sounding good.

She climbed onto Jinx's knee and, God bless him, he immediately took his eyes from Lou and gave Stevie his full attention.

'You know, that girl needs to work on her confidence,' he remarked drily.

'You're right. I'll have a word with her about that,' Stevie replied with a giggle. She could tell that Jinx was still just a little wired, but then tonight could be important for him.

'So who are the guys we're here to meet?' she asked.

'Martin Jones and Stan Rashe from the Sports Channel. They said they'd be here tonight so I figured hooking up with my lady might impress them.' He gave her butt a squeeze and she kissed him hard on the lips.

She knew how much this meant to him. A player's life was short and he knew he only had another year or two tops at the highest level. Some guys then went into coaching, some into property or business ventures, but Jinx had been approached with the possibility of a multi-million-dollar contract with the biggest sports network in the country. He'd been in talks with these guys for months about going to work for them as the anchor on their national basketball coverage. Screen tests, presenting training, voice coaching – he'd worked his ass off to impress them and they were getting close to signing the deal. He might not have experience in his favour, but they were buying Jinx Daley, the brand. The role model. A decade-long career as a star of the game and no scandals, no addictions, no criminal record. The fact that he was dating the sexiest rock star in the country just added to the appeal.

'There they are,' Jinx nodded his head in the direction of the door and Stevie watched as two thirty-something guys in open-neck shirts and pressed chinos headed over to them. Shit, these guys looked like Ivy League poster boys.

'Watch you don't trip there.' Her hand darted out to steady the guy in front, who was so busy watching Lou, he'd crashed right into a pile of handbags that were lying on the floor.

She pushed up off Jinx's knee and put her hand out. 'Stevie Ross, pleased to meet you. Sorry about all this craziness,' she said, gesturing to the rest of the room and getting the distinct impression that a near-naked Lou was something they could live with.

'Martin Jones,' the guy nearest her said as he shook her hand, then turned to Jinx. 'Hey, man, good to hook up. I can see why you always look like a real happy guy.'

'I'm blessed,' Jinx said with a mock salute heavenwards, 'truly blessed.'

A topless waiter appeared at their side and poured drinks for them just as they finished the introductions. They both took JDs and Stevie smiled. They were definitely trying to get their rock groove on.

'Man, is it always like this?' Stan asked, eyes wide with amazement as he surveyed the wild scene in front of him. Girls dancing, Lou stripping, people making out and a crowd of miscellaneous hangers-on that Stevie knew by sight but couldn't have named if her life depended on it – all of them whooping up a storm.

'No, sometimes it gets a bit wild,' she joked. If these guys wanted to experience serious rock-star carnage she could send them next door to where the Spikes were hanging out. There would be ankles around necks, seriously outrageous groupies and more drugs than a pharmaceutical plant could turn out in a month. Thankfully, other than Dixie's weed habit, The Thorns had never really got into that scene. Male bands could get away with the whole doped-out bad-boy shit, but The Thorns knew that a huge part of their success was how they looked, and they were far too smart to sniff or shoot themselves into sunken cheeks and hollowed-out eyes.

Stevie checked out both of their hands. No wedding rings. Either they were single or they'd slipped the bands off for the night. Either way, they were up for a good time, and by the looks they were getting from a couple of the chicks in the room, it wouldn't be long in coming. Cool. Let them get their rocks off on her scene. Then they could sign up her man tomorrow and they'd all live happily ever after. The end.

For the second time that night, she thought to herself that life was good. Real good.

The atmosphere in the club cranked up even further as the party went on, the drinks flowed, and Martin and Stan got lucky with The Thorns' wardrobe manager and one of the Spikes' groupies.

'I think your boys are having a great time,' Stevie whispered to Jinx. He grinned and kissed her, then took another slug of his Diet Coke. He never drank in season and Stevie admired his discipline, especially when he was hanging out with this wild band of reprobates.

The TV guys had no such restraint. They were both pretty far gone now, and although Martin was probably too wasted to do anything about it, the woman he was with had her hand inside his crotch, and was massaging his seemingly unresponsive dick.

Stevie, meanwhile, was loving every second. Cher's 'Turn Back Time' was playing and she and Jinx were in their own little bubble, kissing, singing, joking, just hanging out. She loved that he was so different from the rockers she spent most of her time with. Those guys lived for the drugs, the girls, the booze and the music, and everything else, including health, sleep and relationships, came far behind. That wasn't her thing. This was what she wanted. Just this.

'Well, well, if it isn't the elusive Miss Ross.'

Stevie retracted her tongue from her boyfriend's mouth and broke off to welcome the latest addition to the party.

'Hey, Ari, how you doing?' Stevie didn't need to ask. He might be wearing a two-thousand-dollar suit and have nails that were manicured every week by a Korean nail technician, but she could see just from looking at him that he was stoned out of his skin. It didn't surprise her. Over the last couple of years she'd realised that the rumours about Ari Covet were true – he was a major grade prick. In fact, she felt lucky to have escaped his wrath, especially since he'd been on her case for the last year about one thing and one thing only ...

'Can I have a word with you and lover boy next door?' A tick was throbbing on the side of his face as he spoke, making him look almost cartoonish, like the evil guy that always appeared with a gun just as the good guys/chickens/bunnies were about to escape. In hindsight, she should have realised there was a good chance he'd drop by given that the Spikes were his band. He might be LA-based, but he spent just as much time on the east coast.

'Oh come on, Ari, sit down, chill out. How about we hook up tomorrow and talk about it then.'

She didn't want to tell him that she would inevitably cancel on him, the way she had the last two times they'd arranged to meet. The simple fact was they had different aims.

Stevie wanted to be the lead singer of The Bitch of Thorns, signed to Spin Records, but for the last year, Ari Covet had been relentlessly pursuing her to go solo and sign to AC Records.

When he'd first approached her a year ago about coming over to his team she'd tried to let him down gently with a, 'We'll see what happens down the road, but for now I'm good thanks.'

Apparently that wasn't good enough for a man who always got what he wanted.

Over the last twelve months he'd become more and more insistent, to the point where he was becoming real tiresome. However, it didn't fly to piss off one of the most important guys in the industry, so she'd tried to keep it as sweet as possible given their opposing objectives. By the looks of things, charm and humour were no longer washing with Ari.

'You know what, this one can't wait. Let's go chat now,' Covet insisted.

Stevie shrugged apologetically at Jinx.

'It's OK, honey, you go. I'll hang here with the guys.'

'Actually, I think you'd be interested in what I have to say, too.'

There was a definite undertone of . . . something. Irritation? Annoyance? Impatience?

'Look, man, we're just out for a good time and this shit can wait until—'

'Jinx, it's OK.' Stevie cut him off, loving that he was being protective, but aware that this was one of those situations where it was better to go with the flow and get it over with. How bad could it be?

He'd up the offer for her to go solo, she'd say no, he'd go off with a bruised ego for a couple of months, then come back and try again. Better to just get this over and done with. Besides, the number of people crashed out was beginning to outweigh the number still partying, so it was probably time to split anyway.

They followed Ari out of the room, along the corridor and into the adjoining suite. It was identical to the one they'd just left: red walls, red carpet, huge white leather sofas, a bar on the side wall and a large TV screen high in the corner, next to the floor-to-ceiling window that allowed a full view of the heaving bodies on the dance floor below.

Stevie and Jinx flopped down on one sofa, Ari sat on the other, took out a little gold case, opened it, bumped some of the fine white powder onto the lid, then snorted it through a rolled-up fifty-dollar note. Beside her, Stevie could feel Jinx tensing up. He was a major-league athlete and always had to be aware of set-ups and stings involving that kinda shit. Not that Ari would ever pull a stunt like that. If anyone had a dodgy lifestyle that should be concealed it was the cokehead in front of her.

Eventually, his nose sated for now, Covet sat back ready to address his audience.

'Stevie, Stevie, you're fucking hot, d'you know that.'

Stevie could sense Jinx getting even tenser. Her man was a reasonable guy, but he wouldn't allow either of them to be disrespected. Time for this to be done.

'Get to the point, Ari,' Stevie said firmly.

'You know what I want, Stevie. You. Solo. AC Records. Been asking you for a year now and that's pretty special. Normally I ask once and people don't tend to refuse me.'

Stevie sighed. There was no easy way round this – she was just going to have to go for brutal honesty. 'Ari, I'm happy where I am. I'm not going anywhere.'

'But I could make you even bigger on your own. You've no idea. Cole Presley is a fucking imbecile and he has no fucking clue what he's doing. It's fucking luck and my input that have got you this far. I could make you the biggest female act on the planet.'

Stevie momentarily wondered what Madonna or Whitney would have to say about that.

'But, Ari, I don't want a solo gig. I belong with the band. And besides, I have a contract.'

'Contracts can be broken. Presley wouldn't have the balls to go up against me if I took you to AC.'

Shit this guy was delusional. Of course Cole Presley wasn't going to just let her walk out the door. The Bitch of Thorns was Spin Records' biggest act, a global phenomenon that was pulling in sales that put them in the top five per cent of the industry this year. There was no way Presley would throw her a little going-away party, present her with a goodbye gift and wish her well. It would be brutal and it would be bloody.

But that wasn't even the point. The crux of the matter was . . .

'I'll never come with you, Ari. I'm sorry.'

The next few moments of silence were only interrupted by his repetitive sniffing.

'OK, we're done here.' Jinx's patience had run out and he moved forward in the seat, prepared to leave.

'I don't think so.' Ari's tone had a finality to it that stopped them both in their tracks.

At first she thought the voices were coming from a new song she hadn't heard before. 'Oh baby. Oh baby, yes.' Then it turned too explicit for any record release. 'Fuck, yes. Oh fuck, my dick's so ready for you.'

This wasn't real. It couldn't be. This was some kind of freaky, weird trip. Slowly, almost frozen by confusion, her gaze went from Ari Covet, sitting there clutching a remote control, and refocused in the direction of the new sounds.

The TV.

The scream was out before she could stop it. There on the screen was Stevie on all fours, being fucked by Covet and giving every indication that she was enjoying it.

'What the fuck . . .?' Jinx was sitting, open-mouthed, staring at the screen.

'Ari, what . . . ? What . . . ? When . . . ?' Stevie was stammering, and before she could spit out any kind of coherent sentence, a wave of nausea overtook her and she threw up over the side of the couch.

'Oh my God. Oh my God. Jinx that's not me! That's not me! I never . . . '

Even as she was saying it she could see it was hopeless. It was clearly her. She knew it and Jinx knew it.

'When?' she screamed at Covet. He said nothing, just sat

266

there with a smug grin on that fuck-ugly face. 'Aaaargh!' Before she could stop herself she launched herself at him, her nails scoring into his face as she dealt blow after blow after blow. He acted like he didn't feel a thing, then simply pushed her back and held her by the throat at arm's length.

Like a wild animal, she carried on thrashing, punching, kicking, but nothing was landing. Suddenly she felt two arms come around her waist from behind and pull her away.

'Stevie! Stevie, enough!' Jinx's voice. He pulled her back and practically threw her onto the other sofa, then stepped forward, teeth bared. For the first time Ari Covet actually looked scared. Stevie had never wanted to kill someone more. Never. Violence wasn't in her nature but she would happily pummel this guy to a pulp.

But Jinx had got there first. His fist was pulled back and he was ready to—

'Up. Up. Up. Up.' The deafening sound of the chant cut through the room and all eyes swung to the window. Outside, on the stage, the cross was being raised holding a guy wearing nothing but a crown of thorns. An edge of hysteria was creeping into the crowd's voices now as they became more and more feverish. In the room there was a sudden shift, as their focus changed and none of them were looking downwards any more. Jinx was frozen in time, one hand still on Ari Covet's throat, the other suspended in mid air. Stevie was completely still, too, like the others she was staring up at the TV in the corner. In some kind of freaked-out fucker of a synergy, on the screen was that very cross being raised, but on a different night, with a different sacrifice.

Stevie.

'You have got to be fucking kidding me.' Jinx slumped back, exhausted, defeated, releasing Covet's throat as he retreated. Covet doubled over in a bout of racked coughing and Stevie didn't even have the presence of mind to wish he would choke. That was her up there. Her. It was on film. There was no way she could deny it. And looking at her hair, her face, she realised exactly when it had happened. The very first night. The night The Thorns came to the club with Ari after the Decomp gig at Madison Square Garden. The night their careers had taken off and they'd been put on the road to success ... by this fucking psychopath sitting across from her now.

All these years that tape had existed and she'd had absolutely no idea.

Covet finally stopped coughing, and administered some self-medication by leaning over the table and snorting another line. The smell of vomit and sweat stank up the space, adding yet another layer of disgust and horror to the situation.

Jinx turned back to her and was looking at her wordlessly, his expression loaded with questions.

'I didn't know,' she whispered. 'I swear I didn't know.'

His head moved from side to side and she could see exactly what he was thinking reflected in his eyes. 'How could you not?'

'Go ...' The word got stuck in Ari's throat as the coughing took over again. When it finally stopped, he massaged his jaw and tried again.

'Go solo and no one else has to see this. That's the price.'

'You cheating, lying fucker,' Stevie spat through the rivers of tears that were pouring down her cheeks. 'I'll never work for you! Never! Look what you did to me!'

He gave a pragmatic shrug. 'Looks like you were enjoying it.'

He didn't even see the fist coming. His whole body ricocheted to the side, his head spun like it was on a stick, at least a couple of his teeth flew out in a spatter of blood, before he crashed to the couch, out cold.

'How many more?' Jinx asked her. But it wasn't her Jinx, it was a cold, robotic guy she didn't recognise.

'What? I don't know! None! I didn't even know anything about that, I promise you. I had no idea.'

He walked over to the VCR that sat on a shelf under the TV, pressed a button and ejected the tape. Then he looped his finger into the cassette, pulled out the ribbon and ripped it to shreds.

Only when he was done did he turn to her, but his eyes were dead.

'I can't believe you never told me about this.'

'I didn't know, Jinx, I swear! You have to believe me!'

He stared at her for a second, but he was looking at a stranger.

'No, I don't.'

# TWENTY-FIVE

*Raine*
*New York, 1990*

'Are you ready for this? Do you want me to go over the drill again?'

Raine shook her head. 'Nope, I'm good. Frigging terrified but good.'

Eric Tosca tucked a gun into his shoulder holster, then took the receiver from his desk and twisted one of the knobs on the top. A high-pitched wail assaulted Raine's right ear and she howled. 'Aaaw, holy fuck!'

He snapped it off immediately. They'd deliberately used the exact same earpiece that Raine wore when she was working with the security guys on the door, a transparent coiled plastic that came out of the neck of her top and clipped into her ear. Everyone was used to seeing her with that in so it wouldn't raise any suspicions. 'Sorry, just checking you were receiving.'

'Oh, that's fine then. When my eardrum regrows I'll know it was all worth it. Tell you what, we'll call it quits if you give me one of those.' She nodded to the gun sitting tucked under his arm.

'Yeah, that's what we'll do,' Eric replied, nonplussed. 'We'll give a gun to a woman in a tutu, who doesn't work for the department, who is plastered with crime-scene tape and already covered in blood spatter. Good idea. Don't know why I didn't think of that.'

'Because Columbo isn't here to keep you on the right path.'

Tosca laughed. 'You really need to stop calling him that. It's caught on around the department and he's really pissed.'

Yes, it was wrong that this news pleased her but she was only human. Over the last year Columbo had been like an irritating mosquito she just couldn't shake. She'd met the two agents every week at least once, sometimes twice, and debriefed them on every single detail, significant or otherwise, of what was going on inside the club. The biggest development over the last year was that Tang had spun even more out of control. If he was evil before, he was a monster now. If he had a cruel streak before, he was now vengeful to the point of psychosis. If he had been erratic before, he was seriously out of it now. He was more dangerous than ever.

Right at the beginning of the operation they'd set out three targets:

1. Establish Tang's chain of supply and lock down all the players.
2. Establish where the cash was being channelled.
3. Find incontrovertible proof that he was one of the most prolific drug importers in the city.

They'd only been partially successful. Raine had managed to secure photographs and eye-witness testimonies of Tang speaking directly to his dealers in the other clubs. It seemed that after he lost Didi he decided that no one could be trusted to do the job, so took over the face-to-face contact himself. He was too tight and too paranoid to recruit another middleman. Big mistake.

However on points one and two they had made little progress. The guys at the DEA were desperate to go in, raid the club and hope that the remainder of the evidence they required was there. But it was a risky strategy, because if they hit the club hard, Tang might have time to dispose of anything important. And if there was nothing incriminating on site, then not only would Tang be alerted to their operation, he'd probably sue the shit out of them for harassment.

Lose/lose.

In the end, some genius – fairly certainly called Columbo – had come up with another plan: they were going to send Raine in first.

Tonight was going to happen in two stages. First of all, she would go in wired up, and for the first time she was going to attempt to search Tang's office. If she found anything, she was to remove it to a safe place then call in the cavalry to take Tang down. If she didn't find anything, they would go back to the drawing board and come up with another plan. The guys in flak jackets with the big guns would live to fight another day.

On paper it made perfect sense. In reality she was fifty per cent buzzed and fifty per cent freaking terrified.

As if sensing her feelings, Tosca put his hand over hers and held it for a moment. While Columbo had irritated her to the point where they'd met in a fast food joint and she'd ended up contemplating stabbing herself to death with a plastic McDonald's spoon, she and Tosca had built up a pretty good rapport. Probably too good. Their blossoming professional relationship had come to a head one night a few weeks back when Columbo was off with the flu. They'd debriefed as normal at a

Subway joint, then they'd debriefed again in bed at a hotel on 24th Street. She wondered if he'd put that on expenses.

'You ready to go?'

'Nope.'

'That's what I like, a gung-ho attitude.'

Raine rolled her eyes. 'Tell you what, why don't you go into the den of a homicidal maniac unarmed and we'll see if you whistle the "Star Spangled Banner" all the way there and back.'

Tosca didn't have time to answer.

The door slammed open and instantly the tension in the room shot up. 'OK, people, we're just about ready to roll, so let's get this one mapped out one more time,' their mighty leader commanded.

Raine began to hum the *Superman* theme under her breath. Everyone within earshot cracked up and Columbo went straight to imperious fury.

'Is this a joke? Is it? Because from where I'm standing this is no fucking laughing matter.'

It didn't take a genius to work out that his career was on the line with this operation and he was feeling just a smattering of stress.

Raine decided not to point out that she should have the monopoly on stress at the moment.

'You OK?' he asked her.

She nodded her head.

'Has Tosca checked the mic?'

'Yep, just about took my damn ear off.'

'Shame it wasn't your mouth.'

After she got over the surprise, Raine appreciated the rare moment of banter between the two of them. If there was a way to diffuse her nerves, that was it. Play it down. Play it cool. Don't think of this as the culmination of five years of her life;

just think of it as another night at the office – one that could possibly end with blue flashing lights and a whole lot of drama. She just hoped she didn't get caught in the crossfire.

To another jolt of surprise, he put his arms around her and gave her a hug. 'Good luck. OK, let's go,' he announced.

Raine didn't know how to take this newfound camaraderie. Next he'd be ... oh shit, he was just about to ...

Her hand shot out and caught his forearm. 'I swear to God, Columbo, if you slap my ass I'll sue the United States Government sideways.'

He stopped mid-slap. Letting out a sigh of relief, she hoped that stopping any other threat would be just as easy.

The club was already starting to throb when she got there. 'Hey, Raine, you want to come down and work the door tonight?' Vincent shouted over to her. That was nothing out of the ordinary. Lately Vincent had taken to asking her to help on the door on Friday and Saturday nights too – he said she looked like such a freak she had a calming presence on the crazies. Plus he trusted her judgement. Over the months he'd come to appreciate Raine's gift for diffusing trouble that would inevitably escalate to violence if he or his other guys got involved. Somehow, getting rejected by a six-foot woman drenched in fake blood was less challenging to the ego than being knocked back by a guy in a black suit. Raine was usually happy to do it since it paid cash and she could always do with a little extra. Tonight, though, she shook her head. 'Nope, you're on your own, Vin. Got people to see inside.'

Eleven o'clock on a Saturday night and the main dance floor was already busy – that was a sure sign that it was going to be packed. Climbing up the main stairs to the VIP bar was like navigating an obstacle course. At the top of the stairs she gave an update into the mike, pointing out the locations of all the dealers she could see. 'OK, Charlie Cool is over by the DJ box and he's carrying a black leather cross-body bag, Amphetamines, Es and coke. Larry Zee is on the other side of the box and those cargos have Quaaludes and Es in the pockets. Zena Jolly is outside the corridor to the ladies' toilets. No idea what she's carrying but she's selling up a storm to the trannies. JohnBoy and Delran are over by the entrance and they are definitely the main holders of K.'

The most startling thing about the view was the change in this place since the first night she'd come here. Then it was all ecstasy and hyper ravers, now there was a whole legion of meth and K zombies crawling around the edges of the floor. And it was all down to Tang and his insatiable thirst for power and profit.

The DEA had been right to come in tonight for two reasons. They needed a result pretty soon to justify the budget that had been spent on this op. And secondly, because every weekend the madness was spreading, the drugs were increasing and the criminal incidents were running into double figures, mostly thanks to the meth heads losing all sexual inhibitions and boundaries. Reincarnation had always been the go-to place for deviance and raw sex, but now it was crossing the line from consensual to seriously dangerous. Three sexual assaults in the last fortnight. One college kid dragged into the gents' toilets and raped. A dozen other incidents within 100 yards of the building at closing time every night. Statistics that were being replicated all over the city.

Tang was getting more unreliable as he spread himself thinner, too. Some nights he didn't make it into Reincarnation at all, too busy meeting his dealers and getting carried away with sampling the product himself. There had definitely been a few nights over the last few months when he'd come in seriously messed up.

Tang's time had to be over. A fate that she prayed would be sealed courtesy of the DEA.

She was just about to take the next few steps upwards when she saw something that made her stop dead in her tracks. The gasp was out before she could stop it. 'Raine, you OK?' the voice in her ear barked. 'What's going on?'

She didn't answer.

Of all the bitching nights for him to be there. Over at the back bar, surrounded by what looked like the entire cast of a Robert Palmer video, was Shay, laughing at something some bleached blonde was saying to him, then leaning in to kiss her. Ouch, that one hurt.

'Raine?' Columbo's voice in her ear rose a decibel or ten.

'It's, erm, fine,' she blustered. 'Nothing. Just thought I saw someone important, but I was mistaken.'

She shook it off and carried on up the stairs. There was no room in her head or heart for anything other than what she'd come here for tonight.

Moving into the VIP area, she nodded a hello to the guys behind the bar, then set about scoping the place. Disco Dorothy was supplying Es out of the wicker basket that she carried everywhere and even the guys behind the bar now openly sold just about any pharmaceutical a customer could want. It was carnage waiting to happen.

Over at the bar, she shouted to the nearest guy, Chad, who was paying his way through med school with his night-time work here. For the last six months he and his buddy Al – studying advanced economics – had been taking a slice of the action from the till. The Jason Tang of old would have spotted it in a heart-beat and the two guys would be queuing up at the ER to let their

276

fellow students fix their broken faces. But not now. Al and Chad had been pocketing at least ten per cent of the takings for months, and as far as she knew Raine was the only one who had spotted it. At the end of every shift their socks must be bulging, because given that their uniforms consisted of nothing but skin-tight white leather shorts, there weren't many places to hide the cash.

'Hi, baby,' Raine greeted Chad with a wink. It had always been her policy to get to know the staff and to strike up a good rapport with them. She never knew when she might need them to give her information or provide drinks or call the paramedics when Tang found out what she was up to and beat her to a pulp. She reached out and grabbed the bar top to steady herself as a wave of nerves turned her legs to jelly.

'Miss Storm, what can I get you?' The post-adolescent charm just oozed out of this one. There was a reason he never left the club alone.

'Nothing thanks, Chad, I'm cool. Listen, has Mr Tang appeared yet tonight?'

Chad shook his head. 'Nope, haven't seen him. Wasn't in last night, either.'

The fact that he almost sang that last piece of information told her that Tang's disappearance wasn't causing the bar guys too much distress. They wouldn't be sending him a Miss You card any time soon.

Raine felt a distinct tightness in her chest. This was it. This was her chance. She was really going to do this. Oh fuck. Oh fuck. She had never been so terrified of anything in her life.

Ricco. Didi. She was doing this for them and they were both with her in spirit. A horrible thought struck her, sending that bloody big boulder of a lump back to her throat. She couldn't remember what Ricco looked like. Right there, right then, she couldn't conjure up an image of him.

'I'm so sorry, Ricco.' she whispered. Just as she turned to head in the direction of Tang's office an image flooded her brain. Her and Ricco in the diner one day. She'd bunked off school early and ended up there chatting to Isa when he'd walked in all tall and smart in his uniform. How handsome he'd been. And how pleased to see her. A tear trickled down one cheek as she pushed open the door to the corridor that ran past Tang's office. Using her sleeve she pushed the tear away and turned her eyes heavenwards. 'Keep me safe, Ricco. I love you.'

More tears. Shit, what use was she going to be if she was the only undercover DEA contractor in history who had to stop halfway through an operation to call a grief counsellor?

Just to be on the safe side she knocked on Tang's door and when there was no reply she twisted the handle. Her biggest fear was that it would be locked and she wouldn't get in. Tang had the only key, but he'd been getting careless lately, his drug use and megalomania convincing him that he was indestructible. They were going to have to see about that.

When the door swung open she almost punched the air.

Inside, she closed the door behind her and headed straight for the monstrosity of a pink marble and rosewood desk. If a cardiac monitor had been connected to her right at that moment it would be announcing to the world that a heart attack was imminent.

'OK, guys I'm in,' she said to the mic that was cleverly concealed under the crime-scene tape that crossed her breasts. She appreciated the irony. 'All OK. Tang not here. In his office now.'

Pulling open the middle drawer that straddled both columns of the desk, she had a rummage around. Nothing of significance. One bag of tiny blue pills. One clear plastic tub of Es. A few wraps of coke and K. Pretty insignificant stuff.

Next she tried the right-hand drawer. Files. Bills. Lots of

them with red print on the front. Again, not a big surprise. There was no way Tang could be on top of the day-to-day management of Reincarnation when he was permanently wasted.

Top left-hand drawer. A wooden box with a dragon carved on the top. White powder inside. She kept up a steady stream of commentary so the DEA guys sitting in vans in the adjoining streets could hear exactly what was going on. 'Bottom left drawer, a book, red leather, Chinese symbols inside. Lots of them. No idea what this is. Maybe dealer info or maybe his Christmas card list.'

'Still with the wise cracks!' Columbo's anxious, irritated voice came back at her.

'Columbo, I can't see anything else. There's nothing here.'

The drawers in the huge Venetian chest against the far wall were opened and searched, but all they contained were clothes and underwear. The cupboards below held shoes, hats and – surprisingly – the biggest dildo she had ever seen. Perhaps it was better that she had no idea why that was there.

'Come on Raine, is there anything at all? There has to be something that can give us what we need. Look again.'

Columbo had graduated from 'a tad stressed' to 'borderline hysterical'. That guy should not be in a job that involved carrying a deadly weapon. He was going to end up taking someone out because they crossed him at a stop sign.

'There's nothing else here, I swear.' She opened the bar and checked behind all the bottles – nothing. The drawers in the filing cabinet were an equally disappointing waste of time, as were the mini-fridge and the stack unit that held all the monitors. Raine wished she could switch them all on and double check that he wasn't in the building, but the process of putting them on then switching them all off again would take time that she just didn't have. The longer the search went on, the more she wondered if they were going to find anything at all that they could use. Come on, Ricco, help me here. Tell me where to look.

Ricco wasn't answering.

Desperate, she moved back behind the desk. She must have missed something. Must have. There had to be something here that they could go on. Had to be. If this mission didn't succeed . . . nope, she couldn't think about that now because the only thing more terrifying than doing this was the thought of having to do all of this again.

Falling to her knees, she opened the drawers one by one again. Left, top. Nothing. Left, bottom. Nothing. Right, top. Nothing. Right, bottom . . .

'What are you doing there?'

The voice made her scream out loud.

'What happened? What the fuck happened?' Columbo screeched in her ear.

There was a split second where she considered her options. There were none.

Pushing up on her knees, her head raised above the parapet of the desk, she saw her adversary. China Girl. OK, so how did this play? Truth? Lie? Brute force?

'What are you doing there?' she repeated. Raine noted the lack of outrage or fury in her voice.

China Girl had helped her once before, but that was different – that was an emergency situation that wasn't directly connected to Tang. Rifling through his desk was a very different scenario. Suddenly a flashback. One night months before, she'd seen a Chinese dude go into Tang's office. Something looked . . . off about him. It was definitely his first time in the club and he was clearly nervous. At the time they'd wondered if he could have something to do with Tang's other operation? They knew the drugs were coming in from Shanghai so there was a possible connection. Desperate to get a better look at him, and perhaps get a handle on what they were doing, she'd burst in to try and scope out the scene, but it was futile – all she saw were two guys talking.

And China Girl sitting naked in the corner. Their gaze had met for a second and she'd seen the same loathing she felt every day reflected there.

Gut instinct. China Girl wasn't in Tang's pocket and she had a feeling she probably hated him every bit as much as Raine did.

'OK, calm down,' Raine blurted, putting her hands up in the air to signify that she wasn't a threat.

'I'm perfectly calm,' Mei-Lin replied. 'And you can put your hands down because I'm unlikely to shoot you.' How stupid did Raine feel now?

'What the fuck is happening?' Columbo was screaming now at a volume where she could probably remove her earpiece and just open a window to hear him.

'I'm Raine—'

'I know who you are.'

Raine couldn't believe how calm this woman was. There were no signs of stress or anxiety whatsoever.

Gut instinct.

Without making any sudden movements, she pushed herself up off her knees and stood up, never breaking eye contact with China Girl.

'I don't know where to start.'

'Raine! Raine! Oh fuck, she's blown, we have to go in and get her out.'

'Excuse me a second,' she said, looking at Mei-Lin before titling her head down to her chest. 'Hold your horses there,

Columbo, it's fine. I'm OK. Just a slight hitch but I don't think it's going to be a problem.'

'Ya think? Fucking get it together up there, Raine.' Columbo sounded like a man on the edge. 'Tang's car just came up the street. He'll be there in minutes. We need to know if there's anything on him so we can take him out before he gets to you. But if there's nothing there I'm not blowing this. So either find something fast or bail out.'

The decision was taken out of her hands.

Looking back at China Girl again, she peeled back the tape to reveal the hidden microphone. Still no reaction. Shit, this chick was cool.

'I'm working for the government. The DEA. Tang's a major drug importer and they want to shut him down. I need information, something to use against him. That's what I'm looking for.'

'And if I help?'

Raine had no idea how to answer that. Her experience of this kind of stuff came from TV cop shows and bad movies. 'They'll take care of you,' she blurted. 'I promise they'll take care of you.'

'What the fuck is going on?' Did Columbo really think that yelling in her ear was going to help? She pulled out the earpiece and let it dangle.

'But Tang's on his way and he'll be here soon, so you need to decide real quick.'

Come on, Ricco. I could do with some divine intervention down here. Her heart was racing, her hands were shaking. Come on, baby, come on.

China Girl nodded. 'I'll help. But you'd better keep that promise.'

# TWENTY-SIX

*Mei-Lin*
*New York, 1990*

'Bottom left-hand drawer, false bottom, key in there and other information.' Mei-Lin's calm, measured tone bore absolutely no relation to her feelings at that moment.

Was this really happening? The blood girl, Raine Storm, one of the crazies, was saying that she worked for the government? This was too insane for words. Yet ... even in the chaos she could see that this was her only chance. So many nights she'd dreamt of coming in here herself, opening Tang's safe, taking everything and disappearing, but she knew that wasn't the kind of freedom she wanted. He'd come after her, and no amount of money could hide someone for ever.

Swiftly moving round to the back of the desk, she watched as Raine pulled open the drawer and emptied everything out of it.

'Here, let me show you.' Mei-Lin was at her side now, and leaned over and flipped up the false panel.

'Holy fuck,' Raine gasped.

Mei-Lin snatched the key and moved quickly to the back wall. Stretching up, she felt round the painting for some kind of . . . there it was, right at the top, a tiny metal catch. She pressed it and the picture swung back.

She slotted the key in and turned it until there was an audible click. OK, what next? The dial. She'd given this much thought since she'd watched Tang open it and had come to the one obvious conclusion.

'Bring me the piece of paper, the tattered one,' she said urgently. Raine immediately snatched it up and brought it over. Tang's date of birth.

24.10.45.

She twisted the dial. Twenty-four left. Ten right. Forty-five left. And . . . nothing.

'It's not right,' she said.

'Bastard!' was Raine's only reply. Then a sudden thought came to her.

'Let me try the other way.'

Twenty-four right. Ten left. Forty-five right. This was it. She knew it. It had to be . . .

Nothing.

Next to her, Raine winced as her hand flew to her ear. Perhaps she should've kept the earpiece out. 'They're screaming at me that he's on his way. We are so fucking dead. Honey, we have to get out of here. Let's go.'

No. Mei-Lin couldn't move. This was it. She had freedom in her grasp and she couldn't let it go. This had to work. It had to. Think, Mei-Lin, think . . .

His mother.

'Let me see that paper again.'

'Man, you're nuts,' Raine whistled, but she held it up and Mei-Lin read the numbers written under the woman's picture. Then she read them again. And again.

29.2.24.

Her hand flew back to the dial.

Twenty-nine left. Two right. Twenty-four left.

Nothing.

'OK, that's it. We need to get out of here because if he finds us we're blown. We can come back and check it out again later.'

'No. You go if you want to, but I'm not running. I can't.' No way. She wasn't leaving. If this was going to be her chance she wasn't going to let anyone take it away and if Tang caught her then so be it. Suddenly she knew that she couldn't live another day of this existence.

'We have to.' Raine was even more insistent this time.

'No. You go.'

Raine laughed. Actually laughed. 'Aw, fuck it. Columbo is going to have a stroke.'

Mei-Lin had no idea what Raine was talking about, but she seemed to find it funny. And she was still here.

OK, the other way. Twenty-nine right. Two left. Twenty-four right.

Click.

'Yes!' Beside her, Raine punched the air. Piles of cash, piles of drugs, books, tapes – there had to be enough here for the government to nail Tang.

Raine quickly murmured. 'Columbo, we've got it. It was all in a safe. Everything is here. Get in here. What? You're shitting me! Get your guys in here now!'

Raine snatched the earpiece out again and turned to her. 'It's too late, he's in the building. We have to get out of here.'

Mei-Lin shook her head. 'You go if you want to, but I'm not leaving. If he gets here it will give him a chance to destroy this before your people arrive. I'm not letting that happen. Tell them to come.'

She completely understood the other woman's need to flee.

Tang was a dangerous enemy to have. However, he had friends in high places. What if he heard about the plans to raid the club tonight? What if one of his contacts gave him the information right now? He could burn all this stuff in ten minutes and they'd have nothing.

Raine looked at her for a second, then to Mei-Lin's surprise she smiled. 'You're fucking crazy. But I like that. OK, here's what we'll do.'

Raine picked up a radio from the desk. 'Vincent, is Tang in yet?'

'Yeah, he passed just now.'

'Vincent, I'm in his office and if he gets here he's going to kill me. I swear, Vincent, he's seriously going to kill me. There are a bunch of guys about to charge up the front steps, get them up the stairs to Tang's office quickly.'

'What the hell are you . . .?' She heard Vincent's bark come out of the handset. He actually sounded like he cared. Mei-Lin thought it best not to inform him that she was there too – if her life depended on Vincent she had a feeling she'd be flatlining soon.

'Vincent! He's going to fucking kill me!' Raine screamed, then to Mei-Lin's astonishment she threw the radio back down on the desk, winked and said, 'That should just about do it.'

'I think you're the one who is crazy, but maybe I like that, too. How long do you think we've got?'

'A couple of minutes if he doesn't stop to speak to anyone.'

'It's enough.'

A moment passed between them and then they both sprang into action. Raine dived across the desk, and snatched up the remote control for the TVs, frantically switching them on and scanning them to see where Tang was.

'There he is! West stairs. Coming up.'

Three minutes away at most.

Mei-Lin didn't listen. Instead she calmly took a cushion from the chair beside her, removed the cover and began filling it with things from the safe.

One wad of cash. Two. Three.

'What are you . . . ?' Mei-Lin responded to Raine's shock by putting her finger to her lips and pointing silently to the microphone on Raine's chest. The message was clear – don't stop me or tell anyone that I'm doing this. She could see that the other woman was conflicted but . . .

Raine covered her eyes in an 'I see nothing' gesture. Mei-Lin smiled and pushed some more money into the makeshift sack, then turned her attention to something far more important.

Tape after tape after tape followed the money. She and Ami and all the other girls were on those tapes and she was never going to let anyone else see what happened to them. This was their lives. Theirs. And now she was taking them back.

Two minutes to go.

'He's in the VIP bar. Oh shit, someone speak to him. Some fucker speak to him!'

On one of the other screens Mei-Lin could see a team of men charging up the west staircase. They were about two or three minutes behind Tang.

'We could go down the back stairs. There's still time,' Raine said urgently.

Mei-Lin shook her head. Silently, she closed the safe, replaced the painting, then darted over to the opposite wall, pulled back a curtain and dropped the makeshift bag of money and tapes down the garbage chute. That was her insurance policy. If she survived this, she would need one; if she didn't, then a garbage collector was going to get the surprise of his life.

Many nights she had dreamt of this time coming and it was

always with fear and a tightening of panic in her chest, yet now it was here she felt nothing but ice-cold calm. There was an inevitability about this moment and the only variable was how she was going to handle it.

In that split second, she made up her mind.

No fear. Calm.

One minute to go.

She turned back and sat in Tang's seat behind his desk. She would not run from him. She wanted him to know, to actually see with his own eyes that she had been involved in destroying him. If he reached her before the policemen got here then that was just the way it was going to have to be. She would rather die brave than run like a coward.

No fear. No. Fear.

Raine actually laughed aloud again. 'Oh dear God, I can't believe we're doing this. OK, China Girl, I'm with you. And if I don't make it, tell my pa I loved him. Come on, Ricco, be with us here.'

Mei-Lin assumed Ricco was one of the DEA guys and hoped that he got the message. She knew exactly what Tang was capable of and wondered if they knew it, too.

Her hands were gripping the arms of Tang's chair when the door burst open and suddenly he was there.

It took him a moment to absorb the scene in front of him: Mei-Lin sitting behind his desk, Raine Storm over on the chair next to the monitors. He didn't look great – his hair was all over the place, his face was grey and sunken and his suit looked like it had been on for days – however, she could tell by his reactions and the alertness in his eyes that he wasn't high. Good. She didn't want him to miss a single moment of this.

'Get the fuck out of my office. Now!' The atmosphere in the room suddenly crackled with tension and fury.

'No,' Mei-Lin answered calmly.

Stall him. They just had to stall him.

He took a step towards the desk, his face murderous.

'Oooh, I wouldn't touch her if I were you.' Raine this time. 'Dickhead, do you see anything familiar about me? Does anything jar your memory?'

Her calm questioning temporarily halted him and he turned to stare at her, clearly puzzled.

'Is this some sort of game? A death wish, perhaps?' He was the only one who laughed at his lame attempt at satire.

That was when Raine suddenly did something surprising. She reached inside the tape on her chest, tugged the microphone off and let it fall to the floor. Mei-Lin wasn't sure that Tang had noticed or realised what she had just done.

It didn't matter. There was no stopping Raine now. 'I wasn't going to do this but I've changed my mind. You see, we met before. Six years ago you had a man working here: Ricco Dimato. He tried to protect me and you killed him.

His face twisted into a reprehensible sneer. 'Ricco who? Sorry, I've a poor recollection for insignificance.'

Mei-Lin's heart was thudding now. So many questions, but they could wait. The most important thing was that she now understood Raine's motivation for being here.

Raine stood up, walked towards him and stopped right in front of him, towering over his head.

'Look at my face, you miserable piece of shit.' Raine pulled off the skin-coloured cap and her hair fell down past her shoulders. 'In a minute a team of DEA guys are gonna come charging in that door, but just you keep looking at me, because this is the face that's paying you back for killing Ricco. And for Didi. Don't forget me.'

'You fucking cu—'

'Shut up!' A crack reverberated around the room as Raine slapped his face.

'Raine, his stick!' Mei-Lin jumped up from Tang's seat as she saw a flash of silver come out of nowhere and suddenly it was pointing in Raine's direction.

'Touch me again, little bitch girl, and you will relive exactly what happened to your lover boy. Mei-Lin, lock that door now, then press the button on the underside of the desk.'

Mei-Lin couldn't take her eyes off the blade that was pressing against Raine's stomach, holding her against the wall. She knew what the button was for. He'd had it installed as a result of his increased paranoia, after a couple of clubs in the city had been targeted by armed robbers. It brought steel shutters down on the door and turned his office into an impenetrable panic room.

'No. You don't get it, do you? This is it – the end.' There was just the slightest tremor in her voice, but he picked up on it. Now it was Tang's turn to laugh. 'Pathetic. Pathetic whores, both of you. What do you think you can achieve? Nothing. Press the button, you cunt, or have you forgotten what I can do to you?'

'You can't do anything anymore. It's over.'

'Don't be so fucking ridiculous. No one has anything on me. Nothing. Nothing except my sworn testimony that I caught you two bitches in here trying to steal my possessions.'

'We have everything,' Raine smiled as she spoke. 'The money, the tapes. Like I said, dickshit, just remember my face.'

His eyes flicked towards the picture on the wall that concealed the safe and that's when he saw it – the frame was slightly off; it hadn't caught properly when it closed. The scream that came from his mouth was almost feral. Raine pushed forward, knocking the stick upwards and using the element of surprise to slam her fist into his face. Tang wobbled, but recovered quickly, ramming the stick into Raine's leg. She went down instantly, screaming in pain as blood spurted out, while still trying to kick out at Tang with her other foot. But he was on the move.

Pulling the blade out of Raine's leg, he pointed it in Mei-Lin's direction, striding towards her as he spoke. 'Who the fuck do you think you are? You think you can fuck with me, you useless whore?' He used the cane in a jabbing motion now, the blade on the bottom of it dripping with Raine's blood. It was getting closer to her face. Closer. Closer.

'What did you take from the safe? What? After everything I've done for you?'

'Everything you've done for me? You deserve to die for everything you've done to me and all the others. You're a monster.'

Where were the police? Where? All she could think about was Raine on the floor and getting help but she knew that if she did anything sudden he would lash out. She had to keep him talking, and that suited her just fine because she had things to say.

'You're done. And you know what, Mr Tang, I'm not. I will still be around long after they've locked you up. I'm taking over here. I'm going to be running my own business and I'll use your money to do it. Do you like that?'

Her words were coming out in short staccato bursts, but even in the midst of the unbearable tension, it felt great to say them out loud. 'I took it all, Mr Tang. All of it. Think about that when they lock you up. Think about me spending your cash, buying beautiful things. Think about me when I tell the police everything you've done. Thing about how your mama is going to feel when her little boy doesn't call anymore.'

She knew this was insane but she couldn't stop now, just couldn't.

She thought of her mother and her father, of her sisters, of Jing Wei, of Ami and she knew that so much had been taken from all of them and it could never be given back. She felt a huge wave of sadness for them all. It was too late to make those things right, but she could do something about Jason Tang. For the last five years he'd owned her, humiliated her, reduced her to a shadow of a human being. He'd controlled her life for too long. He wasn't going to control her now.

Suddenly she felt the coldness of the blade as it touched her cheek. Tang was at the other side of the desk now, reaching over it, pressing the weapon against her face while trying to grope for the panic button. She could run, back off, give in to him, but no. She would not show fear. She would not give him one more second of pleasure at her expense.

One way or another it was over.

Even when the pain came she did not wince, nor did she reach up to wipe away the blood that trickled down her face. The blade was going lower now. Lower. Moving under her chin and to her neck. For a second he stopped fumbling for the button and watched it, almost trance-like, as if he were following the ebb and flow of a naked flame.

Then he stopped, met her eyes, and she knew. She just knew what he was about to do. The blade pierced her skin again and—

'Freeze, you motherfucker! Don't fucking move!'

A body came flying in through the open door and crashed into Tang, taking him down with a deafening thud and a woman's scream. 'You're on top of me, you fucking idiot!'

Mei-Lin watched as Raine kicked out with her non-injured leg, catching Tang's head. The man dressed all in black who was on top of Tang didn't notice, he was too busy wrestling the cane from Tang's hands and then flipping him over so he was face down. Suddenly, there were a whole lot of other people in the room too. Vincent was there, chalk white and obviously confused; he stood immediately to the left of the door, not sure what his role should be in all of this. Another man dressed in black was on the floor next to Raine now. 'Raine, are you OK? Where's the blood coming from? What happened?'

'Tosca. You're. The. Worst. Fucking. Detective. Ever,' she said between gasps. The man on the floor smiled, slipped his belt off and tied it round Raine's leg. 'She's fine, boss,' he announced. Mei-Lin wasn't sure who that was directed at.

Meanwhile, the guy on top of Tang was wrestling cuffs onto his wrists and spitting out some words about ... actually Mei-Lin wasn't at all sure what he was saying. Everything seemed hazy now. Confused. More men were arriving and it was all so ... busy. And loud. And warm. It was suffocating. All she wanted to do was go to sleep.

The guy on top of Tang wrenched him up and headed for the back fire exit door, the one that led down the stairs and out to the alley. 'You, you and you, come with me,' he barked, and three of the men in black followed him, dragging Tang with them. As soon as the door opened, cool air filled the room and Mei-Lin realised that she could breathe again. Then the shaking started. From her head to her toes, every single bit of her began to vibrate and her heart began to thud in her chest.

Suddenly, an arm went around her and pulled her close, 'Hey, don't worry. I'm Agent Tosca and we're going to take real good care of you,' he said softly before turning to the other guys still positioned at the door. 'Where the hell are the paramedics?' he yelled.

Right then two things happened. The eternal thump, thump,

thump of the music in the club stopped, and they could hear shouts of objection then a loud voice booming through the speakers. Mei-Lin couldn't make out what it was saying but she guessed the police were clearing the club. The second thing that happened was that two men in medical uniforms rushed in carrying large boxes. One immediately went to Raine and the other fell to his knees beside Mei-Lin and snapped open his kit.

'OK, let me see this.'

He worked quickly and efficiently, pulling a large white gauze pad out of a paper packet and pressing it to her face. He repeated the process and she soon felt the pressure against her neck, too. After a few seconds he eased the one on her face back off. Tired. She was tired. Just wanted to sleep. 'Ma'm, stay with me. This is gonna hurt like hell, though, and we're going to have to get you to the hospital for some sutures.' There was kindness in his face and eyes – not something she was used to seeing in a man who was touching her. She could feel the pad being eased back off her neck now too. 'Definitely need sutures here, too. Just missed the jugular. You've been lucky, ma'm. Real lucky.'

The giggle caught in her aching throat, then escaped before she could stop it. Suddenly she was laughing, real proper laughter, tears sliding down her face as she roared like she'd never done in her life before. She was laughing and crying and shaking and . . .

'It's OK, it's OK, this is all normal. You've had a massive shock and the adrenalin is going to make you feel real weird for a while.'

'You OK up there, China Girl?'

Raine pushed herself up on her hands, while the medic tended to her leg.

It took a few moments for Mei-Lin to compose herself

enough to answer, but eventually she regained the power of speech. 'Yes. The medical man here says I'm lucky.'

She could see in Raine's eyes that she understood.

'Well, honey, I don't know about you, but I haven't felt lucky for a real long time. Maybe he's right. Maybe it's time for a change.'

Mei-Lin nodded, wincing as the pain in her face and neck began to throb.

'OK, guys, get this room sealed and get ready to start bagging.' Tosca looked around. 'Raine, didn't you say you'd got the safe open?'

Mei-Lin felt a twinge of fear.

'Yeah, but we had to slam it shut because you cowboys let Tang get here before you. It's over on that wall there, behind the naked French chick.'

Tosca felt around the frame, found the same clip Mei-Lin had located earlier and released the canvas.

'This is the key and these are the numbers,' said Mei-Lin, hastily jotting the code down on a piece of paper on Tang's desk, then handing it over to Tosca with the key.

He took both and within seconds the safe swung open, revealing the piles of cash, drugs and the books.

'Well, I'll be damned. It has to be all here.' He pulled out one of the leather-bound books and flicked through it, then snatched his radio from his belt. 'Boss, this is Tosca. We'll be back at HQ in twenty and I've got Tang's journals. But if we're going to find Tang's supplier before he gets wind of this, we'll need to get this stuff translated pronto. Like tonight.'

Tosca was still listening to the reply in his earpiece when Mei-Lin interrupted. 'What information do you require?'

Tosca looked at her quizzically. 'He's been pulling stuff in from Shanghai. I need to know who's sending it.'

'Cheung Yu. 3452 Hau Teng, Shanghai.'

Grinning, Tosca picked up his radio again. 'Boss, target is Cheung Yu. 3452 Hua Tong, Shanghai. Repeat Cheung Yu. 3452 Hau Teng, Shanghai.'

He clicked off the radio. 'Thank you. After you've been checked out at the hospital, you'll have to come with us and tell us everything you know. I'm sorry. I know you probably just want to go home.'

Mei-Lin shook her head. 'That's OK. I'm happy to tell you, but I want to know that you will take care of me, that Raine's promise will be kept.'

'It will be.'

'Then I also have journals. Notes. Everything that happened in here, the people he met with, the ones who helped him, the places he went to. Everything.'

Tosca's eyes lit up like he'd just been handed a lottery cheque.

'But only if you keep the deal.' Mei-Lin added.

Tosca turned to Raine. 'Hey, hero, did you promise anything else that I should know about?'

'Yeah, two weeks in Bermuda on the government. Hey, what do you think you're doing with that?' Raine blurted as the medic next to her prepared a stretcher.

'Ma'm, we need to get you to hospital.'

'Fine,' she replied, making it clear that it was anything but fine. 'But I'm not getting carried out of here. No way. Hey, China Girl, you up for walking?'

Mei-Lin nodded.

'Apologies, guys, she's always a pain in the ass. Just let her do what she wants.' Tosca again.

Mei-Lin paused to allow the medic to fasten the white bandage that he'd wrapped around her head and neck to secure the dressings. When he was done, he helped her to her feet.

296

Each of them had a paramedic and an armed cop to support them as they climbed down the back stairs and out into the alley. The lights from the massage parlour were blinding, and she tried to ignore the crowds of people who were gawping from every doorway and window. At the end of the alley, when they hit the main street, the chaos jumped to a whole new level. Mei-Lin had never seen anything like it. There were blue flashing lights everywhere. Ambulances, cop cars, even a fire engine. Dozens of police and guys in black padded suits. There were even a couple of policemen on horses on the periphery. Road blocks had been set up and in the middle there were over a thousand people – revellers from the club – being allowed to leave in ones and twos by policemen with clipboards. Flashbulbs were going off everywhere and a helicopter hovered overhead.

One ambulance sat over to their left and Mei-Lin realised they were being taken to it. They were almost there when Raine stopped dead, almost causing Mei-Lin to crash into the back of her.

'Raine?' It was a confused voice and it came from a man standing with a camera in a nearby doorway.

'Shit, what happened? Are you OK? Can I . . . '

'There's nothing you can do, Shay,' she cut him off. 'I'm sorry.'

The paramedics helped them into the ambulance and one of the cops bolted the door. They heard him shout out to the other one, 'I'll ride up front and you follow.'

The other cop shouted back his agreement.

The medical guy who had been so sweet to her climbed into the back with them, settled Raine onto one bed and helped Mei-Lin buckle herself into a seat opposite. He then pulled down a flip-up chair and buckled in, too.

The wail of a siren started up and suddenly they were moving.

This felt so surreal. Like a dream. She had come in to work tonight expecting just another run-of-the-mill evening, and now Tang was in custody and she was in an ambulance on the way to hospital. No matter what happened next, no matter whether they jailed her for prostitution or put her on a plane back to China or kept their promise to take care of her, the most important thing was that Tang was locked up and she was free.

She felt the warmth of another hand and realised that Raine was reaching out to her. She clasped her fingers around hers.

'Thank you,' Raine said. 'This would never have happened if you hadn't helped me.'

Mei-Lin shrugged. 'I hated him. He made every day of my life a nightmare. I should be thanking you.'

It was over.

The two women smiled at each other for a moment, both of them with eyes brimming with tears, before Raine pushed herself up on one elbow.

'Hey, nice ambulance guy, is that a phone there?' she pointed to a white receiver set into the wall.

'Yeah, but I'm not allowed—'

'Look, don't you think we've had a really bad night? So far we've caught a very bad guy, been stabbed, been dragged down four flights of stairs, our pictures will be over all the papers tomorrow and now we're sitting here, in pain and probably scarred for life. The least you can do is let my friend here use the phone to contact a loved one and let them know that she's OK.'

Mei-Lin wasn't entirely sure where this was going, but she had a fairly good idea.

She turned her very best pleading expression on their saviour.

'Please. My sister will be so worried. I must just let her know and I promise you I'll never tell anyone that you let me use it.'

The guy was squirming now, and Mei-Lin was afraid he wasn't going to go for it when he rolled his eyes and grinned at her.

'Two minutes.'

'Thank you so much,' she whispered, oozing gratitude.

'Yeah, thank you,' Raine echoed. 'Oh and Mei-Lin? Don't forget to tell her to take the garbage out.'

# TWENTY-SEVEN

*Stevie*
*Los Angeles, 1990*

The coffee tasted bitter as it hit her tongue and Stevie took a deep breath, letting the cool morning air clear her head. A couple of joggers ran by and raised their hands in greeting, smiling as she waved back at them.

Every morning, the same routine. She reached over for the toast that was in front of her and took a bite, watching as a yacht sailed into view on the horizon. It was impressive, but not the biggest boat on view.

Marina del Rey. She still had no idea why she'd come here after it all happened, but she'd been searching for anonymity and this was where she'd found it. No one knew her here, no one had ever tracked her down. As far as the world was concerned she had just vanished into thin air, never to be seen again.

Her former band mates knew a slightly different story. The morning after the meeting with Ari Covet in Reincarnation she'd resigned from the band. If he was going to come after her like that there was no telling what he would do to them. She couldn't let that happen – couldn't put them in the firing line because of what she'd done. The girls were furious, shocked, horrified, but she hadn't even given them time to vent their anger, she'd just left. A few months later her lawyers received a letter stating that she was in breach of contract and all payments were being withheld. Turns out Jude hadn't protected her interests in those initial contracts after all. There was a clause in there that said if anyone quit they forfeited all future royalties. It amounted to millions of dollars but she didn't care. They could have it.

She was just glad that The Bitch of Thorns had recovered. Initially there had been a massive wave of speculation about what had happened, letters by the sack load from desperate fans, TV documentaries examining her life, and the music magazines buzzed for months with rumours and gossip. No one even came close.

However, now that The Thorns were back on top, all the focus was on them. MTV even did a special on their resurrection now that Leeane Star had taken her place as lead singer and was stomping up a storm at gigs all over the country. She was definitely making an impact. Record sales were holding steady and The Thorns were good for another few years of international success.

However, Stevie Ross's career was over.

And it was only a matter of time before the world knew why. She only hoped that when they found out the truth, Cally, Dixie and Lou would forgive her and understand that she had to leave so that she didn't contaminate them with Ari Covet's filth. His poison.

But then again, how could she expect them to forgive her when the man she was in love with couldn't?

Losing her career and the money she was owed was a crushing blow, but it didn't come close to Jinx walking out of her life that night. She understood. She did. When his sports show had launched ten months ago, she'd watched with pride as he breezed on to camera, a complete natural. She'd read somewhere that he'd been signed to a five-year, ten-million-dollar deal. She was happy for him. He'd come out OK. After that night, she hadn't watched the show again, though, what was the point of rubbing salt into the wounds?

In the days after she'd left, she'd called Covet constantly, trying to reason with him and begging him to destroy the tapes and cut her free, but the answer was always the same: sign as a solo and he'd burn the tapes. She couldn't do it because she could never trust him. Guys like that had no heart. None. All he cared about was the bottom line, and if he had to destroy her in the process, well that was just collateral damage. He would hold those tapes over her for the rest of her life, using them as leverage at every turn, expecting her to accede to his every demand. The thought made her feel physically nauseous. There was no getting away from this. She was an animal trapped in a cage and there was no way out.

However, if it was just her that he was destroying she could handle it. She could somehow find the strength to get through that, to find a shred of comfort in the fact that she knew the truth. But the fallout would be far, far, greater than Stevie's dignity. The release of those pictures would destroy her mother's life.

How could Ella Ross show her face at the day-care centre and look after other people's children when her own daughter had done things like that? How could she walk into church and deal with everyone talking about what her daughter had done? How could her mom ever look at her face again after seeing those images? How could her brother face his team mates and the crowds at the game, knowing they'd all seen his sister doing those things? Ari had told her what he would say – that she came on to him and had sex with him to get her band on the Decomp tour. People would believe it. And even if her mom and Matt didn't, their lives would be tarnished by this for ever.

That was what hurt the most. If she had an ounce of bravery in her she would go to her mother and tell her everything, but she couldn't. How could she willingly break her mom's heart? How could she expect her family to believe that she was innocent of all this? She'd seen the tape. It looked like she was a willing participant.

So she'd waited. And waited. Desperately hoping that Covet would lose interest and realise that the world didn't care about Stevie Ross any more. This was purgatory. Limbo. But while he was still out there with those tapes, she could only hope that if her profile faded to obscurity, he'd give up when it got to the point that no one cared who she was or what she'd done.

That hadn't happened yet.

Every month Ari Covet still contacted her legal people, repeating his offer of solo representation and asking her lawyer to pass on the message that Stevie was already aware of his terms and he was fully prepared to adhere to the points that came out of their previous negotiations. Every month the deadline he gave her passed with no publication and she'd realised that he was playing with her. The sick bastard had always been a sadist and now he was getting a kick out of her pain, probably watching those tapes every night, jerking off while thinking about her living her life in fear.

That thought made her blood run cold. How much longer was he going to wait? It had been a year now and nothing – nothing except waiting for the day that she would pick up the *National Enquirer* or one of the other tabloids and see that she was all over the front pages, doing vile things with that disgusting piece of crap.

The thought made her want to die.

'Morning, Stephanie, how are you doing today, sweetheart?'

Mrs Gullan from next door leaned around the partition that separated their balconies. Stevie's heart flipped every time she did that, convinced that one of these days she'd fall right over. She already had a broken relationship, a decimated career, a sex scandal and the loss of her whole life on her mind, the death of a senior on her conscience would tip her right over the edge.

'Good morning, Mrs Gullan. I left your newspaper outside your door.'

Another routine. Every morning Stevie jogged to the market, picked up fresh fruit and newspapers and delivered half to Mrs Gullan.

'Thank you, my darling. You take such good care of me. You're such a lovely girl. I bet your mamma is so proud.'

As Stevie smiled, her eyes filled up, but Mrs Gullan didn't notice. She'd already moved on to the next stage of her morning – a large dose of *Good Morning America* and an even larger dose of prune juice.

She wondered what Mrs G would say if she had any idea who she was. Short haircut, back to her old name, no make-up, a pair of thick glasses and a baseball cap when she went out – it had been remarkably easy to disappear. She visited her mother once a week, brushed off leaving the band as being down to creative differences, her choice, and told her she was absolutely fine – just needed some space. Her mother had obliged, sending her away with food, making her promise to eat more. Stevie always said she would and they both pretended to believe it.

Other than that, Stevie lived a solitary life. People just went about their business around here. Built in 1965, the marina was home to eight thousand people and five thousand boats, crime was low and other than when the mist settled over the water, the weather was great. It was half an hour away from her mom's house, half an hour from downtown Los Angeles and a million miles from the world she used to live in.

Life was simple.

There had been enough money already in the bank for her to buy this condo outright, with plenty left over to live on for another decade if she kept it low key. Situated at the end of one of the marina's seven jetties, the space had a large open-plan lounge/kitchen, two bedrooms and a view of the water through the floor-to-ceiling windows that ran around three sides of the apartment. It was the closest thing to living on an island without leaving the mainland and it suited her just fine.

In the afternoons she'd sit with her guitar on her balcony, watching the little ones play with their Mexican nannies while mothers with expensive hairstyles topped up their tans on sun-loungers nearby. In the evenings she'd grab a sandwich and some salad and watch the couples walk up and down the water's edge, hand in hand.

Sometimes she'd wander down to the beach with her guitar and a pad and write a new song, or just play whatever her soul needed to hear. Sometimes people threw down a dollar when they were passing; she'd lost count of the number of strangers who'd told her she sounded just like that girl from the rock band. She'd smile and say she wished she was.

And all the time she was waiting. This was the calm before the storm, and every day she wondered if it would be the day that the clouds would break.

She leaned over the balcony and shouted round to Mrs Gullan. 'Mrs G, I'm going up to the farmer's market at Venice this afternoon. Can I get you anything?'

Her neighbour appeared with curlers in her hair, one half of

305

her face fully made up, wearing a pink robe with feathers around the neck.

'Ooh, thank you, dear, that would be lovely. Mr Kominski is popping by today for a poker lesson and I do like to have something in for him.'

Stevie tried not to wince. Mr Kominski had been coming for a poker lesson every week since she'd moved in, and going by the sounds that came from the apartment while he was there, he was now an expert in attaining a royal flush.

'How about I pick up some salad stuff and maybe some nice ham. I'll leave it outside the door about two o'clock.'

Mrs G reached round and pinched her cheek, setting Stevie off on the whole 'silver fox crashes to her death' scenario again.

Stevie picked up her glass and plate and headed back inside.

No one would ever believe a former wild rock star lived here. The floors were solid wood, stained white, with thick, shaggy cream rugs in the lounge and bedrooms. The solid walls in each room were a soft ivory and completely bare, pushing the eye towards the view at every turn. The kitchen was a soft cream wood with a light oak counter top. The whole effect was one of light and calm and serenity, the perfect antidote to the tumultuous panic and fear that was with her from the moment she woke up in the morning until she fell asleep, exhausted, knowing that she would wake up several times in the night covered in sweat.

Through in the bedroom, she showered, then pulled out an old pair of faded jeans and a white T-shirt. Plumping down on the cream bedspread to dry her hair, she flicked on the TV, intending to switch to the music channels so that she had some sounds while she was getting ready. The face that filled the screen changed her plans.

An Asian man, hair unkempt, a black eye, bruising on his cheeks, a row of numbers running across his chest.

It was weird. She couldn't put her finger on how she knew him, but he seemed bizarrely familiar.

Reaching over for the remote again, she turned up the volume and then sat, crossed-legged, a little line evident in the furrow of confusion between her eyebrows.

The screen flicked to a video now, a night-time scene of chaos. What was it? A bomb? Some kind of terrorist thing? The newscaster's voice ran over the top of the film, a jerky piece of camera work that had clearly been shot from a helicopter.

This was the scene in a New York street this morning as officers from the drug enforcement agency conducted a surprise raid on the infamous Manhattan venue, Reincarnation. Once the hangout of glamorous movie stars and musicians, the club has increasingly been the subject of controversy in recent months, with accusations and rumours of drug use and public displays of indecency.

Stevie realised that she had stopped breathing. Public displays of indecency. Was this it? Were they about to flag up a clip showing her doing those ... things? There was a sudden sensation of a band around her chest, squeezing it tighter and tighter and ...

The camera zoomed in now to two women being helped from the club. The smaller woman's face was partially covered by a bandage, but Stevie definitely recognised the taller of the two. She couldn't remember the name, but the whole crime-scene tape and blood thing was unmistakable. Every time she'd been at the club that girl had been in the VIP room and Stevie hadn't been able to take her eyes off her. The camera panned out wide again, showing scenes of mass hysteria as clubbers were

307

forced to remain in some kind of makeshift pen while the police spoke to them.

The DEA have so far refused to comment on the details of the case, but it is known that Jason Tang, prominent businessman and son of former Chinese envoy to the United Nations, Tai Yi Tang, was taken into custody and charged with twenty-seven contraventions of US law, including importing banned narcotics, drug dealing, money laundering, tax evasion and fraud. A spokesman for the Chinese embassy in New York refused to make any comment at this time. A full statement is expected at a press conference later this afternoon, where it's hoped that the scale of this operation and the ramifications for the city will become clearer. In the meantime, speculation is rife that material contained within the building may incriminate many more members of New York society and government. CBS news will be running a full update tonight at 9 p.m.

No, this couldn't be happening. Stevie bent double with the physical pain that was piercing her stomach, making her want to throw up. This was exactly like that night, that horrible, vile night when Covet had showed them the tape for the first time.

Was the nightmare going to get even worse?

She'd thought this through a thousand times, every day, every hour, it was all that had occupied her mind for the last year. The movie of her and Covet was obviously shot in Reincarnation, but was it Ari who had set up the camera or was it some kind of system in the club? Surely it had to be the former? There was no way a club with the kind of people that frequented Reincarnation would get away with filming their guests. Dear God, she knew of an ex-president who'd been there on at least one occasion.

Covet was still threatening her with the tape, so he obviously still had it, but what if there was a copy at the club, too? What if right now, this minute, members of some government organisation were sitting in a viewing room watching her having sex? Bile rose from her stomach and she really wanted to be sick. Just suppose . . . suppose there was a copy there, how would that play out? The police would recognise her for sure, so would they get in touch? Would they leak it to the press? Go straight to her lawyer? If this shit went to court, would they play the tape there? Would her mother have to stand by as the whole of America watched reports of what she'd done on the night-time news?

Fuck, how had all this happened to her? A year ago she was on top of the world, in love with the man of her dreams, and happier than she ever thought it possible to be. Now it was all over and every day was spent in abject misery and terror, just waiting for the world to end.

No more. She couldn't take any more. She couldn't breathe. Couldn't get any oxygen into her lungs. If this was what her life had become then she would rather it was over, and she was the only one who could end it.

Stevie got up, went into the kitchen and pulled opened the door of the unit under the sink. There it was. She'd thought about it many times before, but had never had the courage to follow it through. Now she realised that the hell she was living in couldn't be any worse than the one that was waiting for her.

Her family would be better off with her dead. Covet would have no reason to release the tapes and there must be some legal thing that would stop them being shown in court.

Never speak ill of the dead, isn't that what they said?

If she was gone her mom could hold on to the memories of who she was – Stevie Ross, musician, songwriter, success. The

309

girl who lived a decent life with the principles Ella had instilled in her. Someone to be proud of.

The rope caught on some bottles of kitchen cleaner as she pulled it out. It had only ever been used to tie down the balcony furniture when a storm was on the way, but right now she had a different use for it altogether.

The steam from her shower had cleared when she went back into the bathroom. She'd had this room remodelled when she'd moved in. There were natural stone tiles on all the walls and gleaming black granite on the floor. The tub was against one wall and across from it was the WC, a hanging glass sink and a shower, enclosed on all four sides by glass panels. She swung open one of the panels and stepped inside, then threw the rope up and over the chrome shower head that protruded from the wall.

She didn't even think. Not about the consequences or the options or what would happen next. All she knew was that she couldn't take another day of fear. She couldn't take another day of worry. She couldn't face the thought of disgracing everyone she loved.

If that was going to be her life, it just wasn't worth living.

# BOOK THREE

# AFTER THE DOORS
# CLOSED . . .

# TWENTY-EIGHT

*Raine*
*New York, 1991*

'You cold? You look cold. Turn the collar of your jacket up.'

'Pa, stop fussing, I'm fine. I promise.' Raine punched her dad playfully on the arm and he feigned injury.

'Yeah, well sue me. I'll pay you out of the funds the DEA have set aside for my future well-being.'

They both laughed and carried on walking down 7th Street. This was her favourite time of year. The beginnings of winter, when the trees were bare and you could see your breath in a little cloud every time you exhaled. The only problem was that it played havoc with her leg, making her limp just a little more pronounced than usual.

After Tang stabbed her, the physiotherapists had told her there was a real possibility that she would limp for the rest of her life, but she was determined to prove them wrong. Every spare minute she'd trained and exercised and massaged, and now, on a good day, it was barely noticeable. However, on a day like today . . .

'Ricardo Dimato came to see me yesterday.' Raine clutched his arm just a little tighter. 'He told me what you did.'

'Yeah, well. No biggie.'

'Seemed like a pretty big deal to me.'

'Least I could do,' she shrugged, causing her dad to sigh.

'Raine, you have got to stop beating yourself up over this. Nobody blames you.'

'I get that, Pa.' She was speaking so quietly that he had to strain to hear her. 'But the thing is, I still blame myself.'

It was a tough call whether telling her pa or Mr and Mrs Dimato the truth had been the toughest thing about the last year. Both of them had been way harder than helping to take down Jason Tang.

Her dad heard the news first, alerted by a cop who recognised her at the Reincarnation bust. She'd only been in hospital half an hour when he'd stormed through the doors and flew to her side, getting right in the way of the doctors and nurses who surrounded her bed.

'We're going to have to ask you to leave, sir, while we take your daughter into surgery.'

Ripped tendons, torn muscles and a wound requiring a train track of sutures – nothing life-threatening, but a medical priority nonetheless.

He'd been right there waiting for her when she woke up.

'Hi, ma darlin',' he whispered. 'Your mom was here but she had to get back for mass.'

Her first act of recovery was to roll her eyes and he admitted now that that's when he knew she was going to be fine.

'I killed him, Dad.'

Pat O'Donnell shushed her. 'Honey, no one died. Tang's locked up. Everyone is still alive. Look, it's the anaesthetic, it's just weirding you out, babe.'

314

'Not Tang, Dad, Ricco. I killed Ricco. It was my fault.'

Slowly, in the voice of the truly haunted, she told him the whole story and watched as he alternated between rage, sympathy, fury and despair.

'Why didn't you tell me, Raine? I coulda helped you. I'm a cop, for Christ's sake.'

She'd shook her head. 'Because I couldn't risk you getting hurt too, Pa – by him or by what I'd done.'

He'd cried at that point. They both did. For a long, long time, just holding each other, both of them feeling helpless that they couldn't sooth the other one's pain.

However, when all the conflicting feelings died down, he was left with an admiration that his daughter had dedicated six years of her life to avenging what happened to Ricco and had been successful in the end. Sure, he would have done it differently and would have counselled her in a different way, but he understood her argument.

That's why, a week later, he'd gone with her to visit Ricardo and Caroline Dimato and told them every detail of what had happened to their son. They were distant cousins of her mother, so Raine had known them all her life, but she realised right there in their lounge that day that there was a reason Ricco Dimato had turned out to be such a decent man. They'd listened to every word, about how she'd been in love with him, followed him to the club, and what had happened then and since.

Caroline cried and Ricardo pulled his wife closer.

'Thank you for telling us,' he'd said, his voice loaded with sadness. Raine almost wished they would shout and scream and tell her how fucking evil she was, but no.

'I'm sorry. I'm so, so sorry.' She didn't feel like she had a right to cry in front of them. She had caused this to happen. She was the reason they were reliving the pain of losing their son, an emotion that must be magnified now they knew it could all have been avoided.

The only consolation they could give was that Danny Docherty, the cop who'd recruited Ricco to work at Reincarnation and covered up the truth after he died, had been tracked down to the door of a Vegas strip joint and persuaded to testify. A deal had also been made with Vincent March, the head of security at Reincarnation, who was prepared to admit that he saw Tang stab Ricco, and that he then carried out Tang's order to move the unconscious Raine from Reincarnation to the alley she woke up in. He would also confirm that Tang then ordered him to back up Docherty's story that Ricco had died breaking up a fight. Together with a review of all the physical evidence, the DA figured there was a good chance of nailing Tang for the murder.

The Dimatos absorbed this news in the same dignified way that they'd listened to everything else. When Raine was finished, she stood.

'I will never expect you to forgive me,' she told them softly. 'He was the most incredible man I'll ever know and I'm so sorry for being the reason he was taken away from you.'

She turned to leave and was almost at the door when Ricardo spoke. 'Raine, you listen to me.'

The tears glistened in his eyes, as she turned to face him. He was staring at her, but the whole time he stroked his wife's head as she cried against his shoulder.

'We knew when Ricco joined the police force that this could happen. He knew that, too. Taking the job at Reincarnation was a mistake, but we all make them. You did, too. It breaks my heart every day that he is gone, and I wish that you had told us before now what really happened, but we accept your apology.'

Outside on the sidewalk, she'd fallen to the ground and cried hopelessly, until – for the first time since she was a child – Pat O'Donnell had physically picked her up and carried her home.

A few weeks later, she'd received a letter from Mrs Dimato, with three photographs enclosed, all of them showing Raine and Ricco. She didn't even remember two of them being taken. One in the diner, both of them laughing, looking at each other with undisguised affection. The other of them playing baseball, when Ricco had tackled her to the ground and then tickled her to buy time until his team could strike her out. The other was a picture at a family wedding where they sat next to each other, his arm casually slung over the back of her chair, the two of them deep in conversation. They were beautiful. Priceless. Snatched moments in time that she wanted to hang on to for ever.

There were only four words on the note that came with them. 'He loved you, too.'

A week had passed before she could get out of bed. Thankfully one of the air hostesses had moved in with her boyfriend and the other was on a training course in London, so they weren't there to witness Pat arriving, thumping on the door and threatening to break it down unless she got up and let him in.

Now, months later, Pat was still concerned about her and drove into the city to see her twice a week. 'So how much cash you got left?'

'Pa, don't ask that kinda stuff.'

The DEA had been generous with compensation. They'd given her a few monthly interim payments to cover the period she wasn't working, and then just a couple of weeks ago she'd received a letter from their lawyers. In order to avoid any possible litigation, they'd awarded her fifty thousand dollars, without prejudice and with no liability. Raine had given forty thousand of it to the Dimatos to set up some kind of scholarship or prize in Ricco's name. The rest she'd put to one side and was planning to use for rent and living expenses until she found a new job. At least now that one of the air hostesses had moved out, she had a permanent bed.

'Any luck with the job?'

She shook her head. As soon as the wound on her leg had healed, she'd gone back to the pizzeria, but it had been too painful to stand all day. Plus, given that her name and face were all over the newspapers now, she'd become a bit of a curiosity, with some people stopping by just to point and stare.

'I don't know, Dad. Working in the club and the pizza joint is all I've ever done. I'm qualified for nothing.'

Immediately she'd said it, she wished she could take the words back. From the moment she started school, Pat O'Donnell had drummed into her the importance of education, qualifications and getting a great job, and she knew the fact that she was now twenty-four, with absolutely no career options in front of her, saddened him terribly.

'You could always come back across the bridge and go back to school.'

Her laughter cut off his flow. 'Come on, Pa, you know I'd go crazy. It's just not me.'

He stopped, put his arm around her and hugged her close. Only then did she peek over his shoulder and realise that they were back where he'd parked his car earlier in the day.

'OK, ma darlin', but you know where we are if you need us. You'll find your way.' Pat's Irish accent always crept in when he was emotional.

'Stop worrying about me, Pa. I'm a tough cookie.'

'I know that, love. And I'm proud of you.'

318

As the car pulled out, he wound down the window and shouted, 'See you Wednesday!'

With a toot of the horn he was gone, leaving her with a familiar recurring feeling of awe that he could still love her after everything she'd done.

Raine checked her watch. Two o'clock. There was nothing to rush home for, so she decided to walk a little further. Eric Tosca would be over later, but not until his shift finished at eleven. At first he'd popped in to check on her mostly, she suspected, at the behest of Columbo, who was terrified she'd go to the press or a lawyer and explain just how she managed to get stabbed while carrying out a task on behalf of the DEA on his watch.

It was just a friendly thing. Casual. Neither of them mentioned the one-night stand they'd had before the bust and it hadn't seemed right to repeat it until months later, just before he was about to leave, when he leaned over and kissed her. Ten minutes later they were having sex on her kitchen table. That's how it had been ever since. He'd drop in once a week or so, they'd have great sex, some laughs, then he'd leave. A couple of times he'd floated the possibility of it being something more after Tang's trial was over, but she'd avoided the issue.

Right now he made her feel safe. He held her when noises outside in the dead of night spooked her. Calmed her when she woke up feeling fine for thirty seconds, then slumped when the whole thing came back to her.

He was a nice guy, but she knew she wasn't going to spend the rest of her life with a man who was married to a job that could stop him coming home at night. He was determined to make it to the top in law enforcement, and while she admired his commitment, life as the wife of a cop wasn't for her – not if it didn't involve Ricco.

At least that was what she told herself in daylight hours. At night when she couldn't sleep, the demons would come and she knew that she could never have any more than a casual thing with Tosca because he also reminded her of what had happened. He was connected to the nightmare, a symbol of what loving someone had cost.

The cold was beginning to nip her fingers and she couldn't feel her toes, but she kept on walking, her limp occasionally earning glances of curiosity from passers-by. It didn't bother her. She was still alive and that was all that mattered. Actually, it was more than that – she was alive and free, the shackles of revenge finally having been wrenched from her. It was more than she could say for Tang.

He was still in custody awaiting trial and his buddy Cheung was just down the hall. In a massive stroke of luck, he'd been picked up at JFK just as he was about to board a flight to Shanghai via Dallas and Tokyo. Turns out he'd come over on a shopping trip for new customers, in an effort to make more money out of the supply route he already had going to Tang.

According to the DA, the trial would kick off early in the New Year, so she had a few more weeks to wait. It was fine. She had nowhere else she needed to be more than watching Jason Tang pay for everything he'd done. For Ricco. For Didi.

Didi hadn't reacted at all when she'd told him what had happened. No change. But his mother had been quietly happy that Tang would be punished, even if it meant that she might hear things about her son that she could live without knowing.

'Hey, lady, any change for a coffee?'

Down on the sidewalk on her left-hand side a homeless guy sat in a doorway with all his worldly goods crammed into what looked like a large dog basket. It was a pitiful sight.

She took out ten dollars and watched as his eyes lit up. 'Have you eaten today?' she asked him.

It was obvious by his reaction that he hadn't. It was also obvious that eating wasn't his priority. She handed over the cash.

'Do me a favour, buddy. Spend that on whatever you like,' she pulled out another ten and gave that to him too, 'but spend this one on something to eat.'

He saluted her and she laughed before walking on. A few yards further along the sidewalk she realised where she was.

The doorway on her left. The road on her right. The dilapidated building that sat facing her, decaying in the December winds.

Reincarnation.

It was a sorry excuse for a venue now. There were slates missing from the roof, the front had been vandalised with every colour of spray paint and every gang insignia in the city and the signage pronouncing that it was New York's top nightclub had been decimated.

It was a tragic sight. No matter what had happened in there, it had once been a glorious and glamorous venue that gave New Yorkers somewhere fabulous to go and now there was nothing left.

According to those on the scene, no other nightspot had taken its place. So many clubs had shut down in the last few years: Area, Danceteria and, of course, the legendary Studio 54 would be mourned for ever. The Limelight on West 20th Street was one of the few clubs still doing a good trade.

Every fibre of her being missed that part of her life. She missed the excitement and the drama and the buzz. She missed the glamour and the crazies. She even missed the late nights and the relentless problems. Her club career might have been born out of a desire to avenge Ricco's death, but it became more than that. It became her life.

Now that was gone, and for the first time she admitted to

321

herself that she wanted it back. That was who she was, and without that world she felt like only half a person.

Oh, dear God. How was she going to break this one to her dad?

A massive reality check dawned on her. There was no point in upsetting Pat because it would never come to anything. Sure, before this happened she had a good reputation and people around the city that knew the industry viewed her as a maverick character who could bring in business and run a door. But no nightclub owner in the country would touch her now that she'd been the pivotal player in a scandal that brought down the most influential guy on the New York club scene. Her association with law enforcement would be with her for ever, and let's face it, no club was ever going to be drug free. No one would let her past their front door in case someone smoking weed in the washroom put them on the radar of the DEA.

'Hey, lady, you OK?' It was the homeless guy from along the street, walking past her clutching the biggest hot dog she'd ever seen. 'That kinda food will kill ya,' she told him, laughing. 'Yeah, I'm fine. Just . . . thinking.'

'Must be a long thought. You've been there a mighty long time.' He shuffled back down to his doorway with his calorific intake for the day.

For the first time she noticed that darkness was beginning to fall and checked her watch again. 5 p.m. Shit, where had the afternoon gone? She'd been walking for miles, standing for hours and her leg was beginning to throb like hell. It was still another twenty minutes to get home from here.

Halfway there, she changed direction.

This idea she had in her head was burrowing deeper and deeper and she knew that there was no moving on from it until she'd done something about it, talked it through, looked at it rationally and really drummed into her mind why it was the worst damn idea she'd ever had.

There was only one other person who would understand where she was going with this and who could relate to what she was saying.

She just hoped her friend was up for a visitor.

# TWENTY-NINE

*Mei-Lin*
*New York, 1991*

Mei-Lin watched as Ami got ready to go out, pulling on an exquisite Balenciaga dress and slipping her feet into beautiful Versace shoes. Anyone seeing her for the first time would assume that she was the daughter of a diplomat or a very wealthy businessman. The last thing she looked like was a hooker out to give some rich guy a real good time.

'Did Ivana call in?' she asked. Ami finished applying her Chanel lipstick then nodded. 'Yes. Mr Gregoriov has extended their trip for another three days. You know, I think he seriously has feelings for her. That's the fifth time he's booked her this year and the trips are getting longer and more lavish.'

Mei-Lin pulled a gold brocade pillow under her head and rolled onto her side. It was always her natural reaction to cover that side of her face. The scar had faded considerably, but it was still a perfect line that ran from her cheek to her chin, then commenced again at the top of her neck and ended in a round circular scar about three inches further down. A scarf could cover that section, but the one on her face was impossible to conceal.

'What does Ivana say?'

'That she'd marry him tomorrow if he asked, because he's seventy-four, a billionaire and he has such a small dick there's no possibility that she'll ever have to put up with any discomfort.'

Mei-Lin giggled despite the crudeness of the conversation. If the clients ever heard them speak like this she was sure they would be shocked and outraged.

'OK, my lovely, I'm off now. Mr DeLossa hates to be kept waiting and no doubt he'll have popped his pill right on schedule so that he is ready for me the moment I walk in the door. What is it with lawyers that they always have to be so precise?'

She leant over and kissed Mei-Lin on the exposed cheek.

'Are you sure you're going to be OK? What are you planning to do?'

Mei-Lin held up a book that was on the bed next to her. Judith Krantz's *I'll Take Manhattan*.

Her reading coach had told her that she must read something every day, but she found the books that they provided at school far too dull. Someone had suggested she visit a library and the moment she'd stepped into the New York Public Library on 40th Street she'd been overtaken by a spectacular sensation of awe. It was not only the most amazing building she'd ever seen but there were more books there than she'd ever imagined had been written.

It had become her sanctuary and her entertainment. Television didn't interest her – she couldn't quite grasp the point of watching other people living their lives – but books were a whole different story.

During the day she studied business topics using books designed for young students. It would take her a long time to catch up, but she was a quick learner and her progress in the afternoon classes in mathematics and English had been dramatic.

She also read the classics that her tutor recommended. Mark Twain, Henry James and T. S. Eliot were all on her list and she was steadily making her way through their works. However, the biggest revelation had occurred on the subway when she'd noticed that two different women were both engrossed in a book called *Dazzle*. She'd asked the librarian for it the next day and it opened up a whole new world.

After her baptism by *Dazzle*, she'd gone back and read every one of Miss Krantz's books and was now midway through what she thought might be her favourite.

'I'll be fine, I promise. I'll see you later and try to call if you're going to be out overnight.'

Mei-Lin knew that Ami understood the worry, even though, in this case, it felt unnecessary. Mr DeLossa was a long-standing client who tipped well and liked it kinky but not sadistic. In a business where there were many dangers, he wasn't one to fret about.

However, the dark shadow of Jason Tang nestled in the corners, occasionally flaring and causing Mei-Lin's breath to quicken. He was a powerful man who still had many contacts. The government liaison officer reminded her every week that Tang was behind bars and wasn't stupid enough to do anything that could jeopardise his case even further.

That was one point of view, but she would be stupid to ignore the fact that she was a witness against him and that his case would be stronger if she wasn't around to tell her tale. Would this ever really be over? Or was Jason Tang always going to be a demon that haunted her?

Shaking off the thought, she picked up her book, determined to take her mind off her fears.

Ami was only gone ten minutes when the doorbell went. Mei-Lin smiled as she padded out of her bedroom and headed for the door. How many times in one week was that girl going to forget her keys and have to dash back for them?

Perhaps it was best that she had been forced to move from the bed. She was getting sleepy before and would no doubt have dozed off after a few pages. Now she could go and have a bath and climb back into bed with some hot tea, ready to read long into the night. It had taken her many months to adjust to the fact that she had choices about how to spend her time, and she had discovered, to her great surprise, that the thing she loved doing most was lying still.

Hand on the door knob, she was about to swing the door open and laugh at her friend when force of habit made her peek through the spyhole. They'd already moved twice because journalists had got hold of their address and pursued her relentlessly, offering ever-increasing amounts of money for her side of the Jason Tang story.

It took a moment for her eye to adjust to the light and ... no, it couldn't be. She opened the door to see that her eyes had not been deceiving her.

'Raine?'

The taller woman bent down and hugged her. 'Come in, come in.' Mei-Lin ushered her into the hallway and through to the lounge.

'Nice pad.' Raine observed and Mei-Lin knew she was right. Sometimes she couldn't believe that she lived here. They'd been so lucky to find it, guided by a gentleman who had been one of Ami's clients for a couple of years. He owned many properties throughout the city and had been glad to offer them a discount on this basement conversion in an Upper East Side townhouse. It had a tiny garden at the back and three small bedrooms that led onto an open-plan lounge and kitchen. But the most crucial feature was the fifty per cent discount he gave them on the rent in return for Ami placing herself at his disposal for one afternoon a week. Ami felt it was a price worth paying.

'Sit down, please,' she gestured to the red chenille sofa in front of the fire. 'How did you know where we lived?'

'I persuaded Eric Tosca to tell me. For a detective, he's rubbish at resisting interrogation.'

Mei-Lin laughed. Raine always had that effect on her. They had met on many occasions after Tang's arrest and sat through countless interviews and legal proceedings. They'd even shared tea and confidences in the breaks between men in suits probing them for details.

However, that had never stepped up to a full-blown friendship. Both women were too battle-scarred and had too much to deal with in their own lives to make time for forging new relationships. Mei-Lin liked and trusted Raine – her removal of the money and tapes had never been revealed. Suddenly she had the beginnings of a queasy feeling in her stomach. Was that why Raine was here now? Did she want Mei-Lin to confess? Or did she want a cut of the cash? Her jaw set into a hardened expression. If Raine was about to pull a stunt like that she was going to have a battle on her hands.

'Would you like tea? Water?'

Raine shook her head as she kicked off her boots and stuck her feet in the direction of the fire. 'I hope you don't mind, but they're frigging freezing.'

'You walked here?' Mei-Lin asked, incredulous. 'From where?'

'Fourteenth Street.'

Mei-Lin was puzzled. 'But why? Were there no cabs?'

'I was thinking.' Raine answered simply, as if that explained everything. 'Do you ever miss it?'

'Miss what?' Mei-Lin sat on the corner section of the sofa and pulled her feet up underneath her, starting to relax a little.

'Miss the club.'

'No, of course not!' The anger in her voice was unmistakable. How could Raine ask that? That place had been a living hell for her and she associated it with nothing but pain and anguish. Miss it? She hoped it would burn to the ground and that she could be there to watch the flames destroy every inch of it. 'There is nothing about that life or that club that I could ever miss.'

Raine groaned and sat forward, then reached down to pull her boots back on. 'Mei-Lin, I'm so sorry. Of course, you're right and I really didn't mean to upset you. I'm sorry if I have. This was a mistake. Stupid mistake. Sometimes I feel like I'm going crazy with all of this and today must be one of those days. Forgive me.'

She was on her feet now, pulling her jacket back on while walking towards the door.

'Raine, wait. Come back. Tell me what all this is about.' Despite the difference in their size, Mei-Lin's hand on Raine's arm stopped her dead and when she spun round Mei-Lin could see that there were tears in her eyes. That alone was a surprise. In all the time she had known her, throughout all their dramas and pain, she had never seen Raine shed a tear.

Reluctantly Raine returned to the sofa and Mei-Lin gave her time to compose herself by going off to make two mugs of coffee. She was acquiring quite a taste for the bitter Americano, although she preferred the lightness of her green tea.

By the time she got back to the sofa Raine's eyes were dry and she was much calmer.

'So tell me,' she prompted as she handed over the steaming mug. 'What has upset you so?'

'I walked past Reincarnation today and, Mei-Lin, I don't know what happened but I was suddenly . . . I was . . . Oh fuck,

329

I have no idea what I'm doing. I miss it. I just miss it. Not that fucker Tang and all the shit stuff, but the rest of it, you know. And I realised that . . .'

The tears were flowing again and as quickly as they dropped Raine was wiping them away with her sleeve. 'I think I want to open a new club. Not one like Reincarnation, but one that takes all the amazing things that were there and puts them in a safe place away from a psychotic fucking maniac.'

'You're crazy, Raine. Why would you want to go back to that?'

'But it's not going back, it's going forward. Mei-Lin, what else can we do? Who would employ us? Are we supposed to just put our heads down, crawl away and forget any notion of making a success of our lives?'

A realisation suddenly dawned. 'You said "we"?'

Raine looked at her, puzzled. 'What?'

'You said "we". You are talking about this and you said "we". Did I misunderstand?'

Raine slowly shook her head and a half-smile appeared through the tears. 'Did I not mention that bit?'

'What bit?'

'I think we should be partners. And I think we should find a way to open our own club.'

No. No. No. No. No. No. Every one of Mei-Lin's senses screamed their objections. That world was poison. Toxic. It had almost killed her and it was a miracle she was still sane. To even contemplate going back would prove that last statement wasn't true. She couldn't. Couldn't.

'Just think, Mei-Lin, it would be the biggest "fuck you" to Jason Tang that there could ever be. The two women he hates, the ones who are responsible for destroying him, go on to become successful in the world he once ruled.'

There was nothing to say to that, but she would be lying if she didn't admit that there was a glimmer of truth there.

But she couldn't. Just couldn't.

'What else will we do with our lives? I found myself thinking today about getting a job as a cashier in a coffee shop. Is that it? Is that supposed to be the extent of my ambitions at the age of twenty-four? I want to be a success, someone who achieves something amazing, and the only thing I'm good at is running a nightclub. What about you? What's the deal with you? Do you have plans? Do you know what you're going to do?'

Reluctantly, she shook her head. 'The DEA have promised me a green card and no criminal charges, so I will be able to live and work here legally. Doing what? I have no idea.' It was something that had kept her awake on many nights. What did the future hold for her? This was her second chance at life and she already had a fair idea of where it was going. She and Ami had settled straight into a working routine. Mei-Lin balanced her studies with running the admin and logistics for the girls – without actually associating herself with it in any way, of course – while Ami pitched in on some of the details but spent the majority of her time with clients.

That side of the business was definitely over for Mei-Lin. She couldn't imagine that anyone would want to pay a lot of money to spend the night with a notorious former sex slave whose face was scarred by her previous owner. However, that wasn't the crux of the situation. The truth was that right now she couldn't imagine ever allowing a man – or woman – to put their hands on her body ever again.

So where did that leave her? As a professional madam for the rest of her days? Eventually some journalist somewhere would cotton on to it and there was the potential for carnage to be wreaked on her life all over again.

Her past and lack of education ruled out anything solid or respectable. Her face ruled out anything dependent on beauty. So where did that leave her? Nowhere.

It was a few seconds before she realised that Raine had started speaking again. 'Do you have any wine? I suddenly feel that need to get seriously loaded. But please don't let that put you off my proposition – I'm a nice drunk.' Mei-Lin laughed and padded into the kitchen, returning with two glasses, a bottle of white wine and a bottle of water. She poured the wine for Raine and still water into the other glass. Alcohol held no appeal for her. It didn't take a psychologist to realise that after all that had happened she had issues with not being in control.

A large slug of wine refreshed Raine's vocal chords and she returned to her pitch. 'Mei-Lin, you were there every day, too. You know what it's all about, what goes on, how to deal with the girls and the VIPs. And you're so organised. I've seen how you handle everything. I think we'd be a great team. Picture how it could be – you and I, running our own place, calling the shots and making the profits. We could create something really incredible. So fan-fucking-tastic that everyone in New York would want to go there. I know we could do it.'

Raine's desperation seeped into every word, but Mei-Lin could see that there was more than that involved here. There was passion, belief, excitement, enthusiasm ... Raine actually believed that this was an incredible idea that could transform their lives and she honestly wanted Mei-Lin to be a part of it.

'All this would take money. A lot of money.' Mei-Lin couldn't believe that she was saying this, that she was even entering into a discussion that indicated she saw potential in the idea.

A deep breath from the other side of the sofa. 'You're right. I promise you, Mei-Lin, this isn't why I've come to you. And if you say no, I will never, ever disclose anything that happened or was said to another living soul. You have my word.'

Mei-Lin believed her, so she sat back and let her carry on.

'I saw the cash you took from the club; there must have been a hundred grand there. I don't want a penny of it. Tang's money is nothing to me. But if we did this we could use it as capital. We could take out a loan and use that money to guarantee the payments, that way we're not actually touching his money.'

'I don't understand.' It wasn't really surprising. Bank accounts were completely alien to her. Only she and Ami knew that the money she took from Tang was currently lying in a hollowed-out floorboard under the hearth of the fire. 'So there is a way to borrow the money that would not involve using that cash?'

'We'd only use it to show the bank that we have a fall-back if we default on the loan. Look, Mei-Lin, I promise you we would get the best lawyers to protect you, and even if you decide you don't want to use that money, we will find another backer. The important thing is that you and I do this together and we make it work.'

There was a long, long pause as Raine realised that she had said everything she needed to say and Mei-Lin realised that she needed to think this through. The seconds stretched to minutes and still neither of them spoke. Raine looked exhausted now, head back, eyes closed, and Mei-Lin could see that her hand was subconsciously rubbing her thigh where the knife had entered her.

They had been through a lot together, she and Raine O'Donnell, and that could never be forgotten. In a way they would always be part of each other's lives, always be connected.

Something in Mei-Lin stirred at this thought. She had no family and her only real friend was Ami. Here was someone who believed in her and wanted to work with her, someone who Mei-Lin knew was unfailingly loyal. Hadn't Raine already proved what she would do for her friends?

There was something comforting in that, something that Mei-Lin suddenly realised she wanted to be a part of. Tang had made her strong. The fact that she had survived his treatment had proved to her that there was no challenge she couldn't conquer – and opening a new nightclub might just be a mountain she could climb.

'Raine?'

There was a slight jump as Raine snapped out of her semi-doze. 'Oh God, did I nod off? I'm so sorry, Mei-Lin, it's just that I haven't been sleeping and it was the wine and the ... honey, I'll go. I'm so sorry for bursting in on your night and being a complete maniac.'

'I think I will accept your offer.'

Raine had one boot on and one boot off when she paused and turned to face her.

'You mean it?'

Mei-Lin nodded.

'Oh holy fuck, I love you!'

Raine launched towards her and enveloped her in a crushing hug.

They talked long into the night, every hour that passed making the insane idea even more of a reality.

'The only problem is that in the beginning we will still be associated with Tang and the court case, so I think we need someone else to be part of the team,' Raine said sometime around dawn.

That didn't sit well with Mei-Lin. She already had trust issues, and to bring in a stranger would be too unsettling.

'Who?'

Raine shrugged. 'I don't know. I was thinking someone who

already has a profile, someone people instantly associate with glamour and fame. Madonna would be perfect but she wouldn't touch something like this unless she had full control. Maybe someone like Tala DiVinci – her career has gone down the pan since that sex tape of hers found its way into every video store in America. That had to hurt.'

*That had to hurt.* The thought recovered a long-buried memory and an image flashed across Mei-Lin's mind, sending a chill through the rest of her body. That night . . . it was one of the sickest things she had ever seen. The way they treated that poor girl was less than human. She suddenly had a thought she couldn't suppress. 'I have an idea about that. What about . . . '

The doorbell rang, cutting her off mid-sentence. As soon as Mei-Lin opened the door, Ami burst through in a bubble of happy chat. 'Oh I'm so glad you're up because I forgot my keys and I didn't realise it until I was already there and it was too late to come back. I was afraid I was going to wake you and you know that I hate to do that and . . . Raine! Oh my goodness, I'm sorry, I didn't know we had a visitor.' She plonked herself down on the end of the sofa and began taking off her shoes. 'So. What did I miss?'

# THIRTY

*Stevie*
*Los Angeles, 1991*

The incessant buzz of the door intercom woke her but she pulled a pillow over her head and ignored it. It would just be a delivery for one of the other tenants or some workman wanting access to the inside of the building. Those guys drove her nuts, buzzing at all times of the day and night. Is that not what the building superintendant was for?

Eventually it stopped and she sank further under her duvet. Maybe today she wouldn't bother getting up. What was the point? All she ever did was wake, scour the papers and television for any news concerning the Reincarnation case, Ari Covet or The Bitch of Thorns and then go back to sleep again. The constant feeling of nausea and the crippling anxiety never left her any more.

In fact, the only thing that marked the passing of one day to another was Mrs Gullan's requests for produce from the market. Stevie didn't mind. At least it forced her to get out of bed and gave her something to focus on other than constant dread.

Even her mother was losing patience with her. Ella had

survived much hardship in life, worked three jobs, been a single mother, raised two kids with no money and never once succumbed to self-pity or misery. So as her wealthy, talented daughter retreated further and further into a reclusive state, Stevie knew her mother was finding it more and more difficult to deal with her. She'd mentioned Prozac twice on her last visit, only for Stevie to insist she didn't need anti-depressants. She didn't add that what she needed was a fucking big gun and someone to shoot that bastard Ari Covet. Sometimes she wondered if Ella would feel differently if she knew the truth, but it didn't matter because she was never going to tell her.

A loud crack reverberated around the room making her lift her head from under the pillow. What the hell was that? She looked around her – nothing – then dropped her head back down. Oh God, another poor kamikaze bird. It didn't happen often but every now and then one would fly right into the glass windows, not realising they were there.

Crack.

Holy crap, was there a whole squad of them? Groaning as she moved, she reluctantly pushed herself up, swung her feet onto the floor and went to check it out. As she slid back the balcony door, she checked the ground, expecting to see two specimens of fowl flat on their backs with their feet in the air. Nope, nothing.

'Erm, Stevie Ross?' The voice was female, uncertain and hesitant, and her first reaction was that either a fan or a journalist had tracked her down. Neither option appealed in any way. She was just about to duck back inside and return to bed when the voice hitched up a notch on the anxiety scale.

'Stevie, is that you?'

Stepping forward onto the balcony, she put her hand up to her eyes and squinted against the sun as she looked down ten feet to the sidewalk below. The sight that awaited her was probably as unlikely as she could ever have imagined.

Two women: one very tall, quirky, long dark hair and huge sunglasses. The other small, Asian, impeccably dressed in black Capri pants and a twin set cashmere cardigan and jumper, her hair piled high on her head like some kind of oriental Ivana Trump.

Wasn't that . . . Good Lord, it was!

'Stevie, can we talk to you?' The taller of the two women spoke again. She'd read every detail of Tang's court case, so she felt like she'd known Raine O'Donnell for years. Raine O'Donnell and Mei-Lin Yan, standing here under her balcony shouting up to her. This was about as surreal as it got.

The sickening feeling suddenly returned to her gut. If they were here then maybe this meant that she was about to get dragged into the case. So it had happened. The tapes must be out there. Perhaps they'd seen them. Did their lawyers have them? Were they here to tell her they were going to be used in court? A whole mess of tangled thoughts collided in her head and she felt a wave of nausea rise from her stomach. Suddenly she bent over at the waist and retched, throwing up over the balcony.

'Well, that went well,' she heard Raine say to Mei-Lin. 'I'm just glad she wasn't a few feet further forward.'

There was an edge of humour in her voice, and as Stevie found the strength to straighten up she smiled awkwardly. 'Sorry, I think I must have . . . ate something bad.'

'Look, can we come in? Only this sun is melting the make-up off my face and I'm dressed for New York, so I'm sweating out here. It's not a good look.'

Now that her eyes had fully adjusted to the sunlight she could see that Raine was wearing jeans, a thick cream cable-knit sweater, black leather boots and a coat that reached her knees. It was seventy-five degrees out.

Two options: Say yes, let them in and face this. Say no, go back inside and torture herself with fear and worry for the rest of the day, week, year.

'Come around to the door and I'll let you in.'

'Hallelujah.' Raine again. She definitely seemed to be the more outspoken of the two.

Inside, Stevie did a quick detour to the bedroom, slipped out of her vomit-stained pyjamas and pulled on some grey cotton track pants and a white T-shirt. The greasy hair and bloodshot eyes she could do nothing about, but it was a slight improvement.

The buzzer rang again and she pressed the door-release button to allow them in. While they made their way up from the entrance, Stevie flicked the switch on the coffee maker and pulled three cups out of the cupboard, ignoring the pile of dirty crockery already stacked up in the sink. She really had to get this place cleaned up.

The coffee had just begun to percolate when there was a knock at the door.

'It's open,' she shouted. 'Come on through.'

Suddenly they were there – Raine O'Donnell and Mei-Lin Yan in her apartment – clearly trying their very best not to react to the fact that it looked like a bomb had detonated and probably smelled worse.

'Can I use your bathroom? Got a thing about peeing on planes and New York was a long time ago.'

'Sure, over there, the door on the right.'

Raine headed off and Mei-Lin stood there, clearly nervous, stuck for anything to say. The scar. Now that she was up close she could see the scar down Mei-Lin's face and she felt a wave of sympathy. According to the newspapers, Mei-Lin had been abused by Tang for years, forced to have sex with anyone he chose. Her own experience was different, but for a second she felt such an empathy that she wanted to put her arms around her and sob.

'Hey, what happened to your shower? It's dangling in mid-air,' Raine asked as she reappeared.

Stevie shrugged. 'Long story.' Just as she needed to get the apartment cleaned up, so she needed to get a maintenance guy in to fix the shower, but she wouldn't. It had been broken for a year and she'd left it like that as a reminder of the low point she had reached where she'd actually tried to take her own life. Thank God for Mrs G. The force of dropping off the stool had bent the shower head so that it dangled down and her feet hit the floor in an instant. Unfortunately she'd cracked her head against the tile wall and knocked herself out as she fell.

Fortunately, the shared inlet pipe for the shower had cracked under the force, sending water pouring through Mrs G's wall. After watching every episode of *Murder She Wrote*, Mrs G fancied herself as Angela Lansbury and had sensed something was wrong. She was over the balcony in minutes, and by the time Stevie woke up she was lying on the couch with a compress on her head and a sore neck where the noose had left a friction burn on her skin.

Mrs G had stayed with her for three days and not once did she ask why Stevie had done it. She just cooked for her, cleaned the apartment and held her when she cried. She moved back to her own place only after she'd solicited a solemn promise that it would never happen again. Stevie had kept her word and every time she climbed into the tub instead of standing under the shower, she remembered the promise and decided to live another day.

'How did you find me?'

The two women turned to each other, a questioning glance passing between them. Eventually Mei-Lin answered.

'I, erm, knew your brother. We, erm, got together back when . . .'

Raine interjected when it was clear that Mei-Lin wasn't going to get past the discomfort. 'She had a thing with your brother when he used to come to the club, it's best that you don't know the details, but when she called him he freaked out and would have promised her his firstborn child to get her off the phone. He gave her your address instead.'

Mei-Lin recovered. 'I know us turning up like this must be a very big shock for you, but we would like to talk to you about something important.'

Stevie wanted to throw up again. Here we go. This was it. This was the moment she was going to slip to a whole new level of hell.

'We have a proposition we'd like you to consider.'

'What?' Stevie didn't understand. Raine leaned over the kitchen counter and took one of the freshly poured coffees. 'Thanks. My mouth feels like I've been chewing sand. That red-eye was brutal.'

This was all way too weird. After handing one of the other cups to Mei-Lin, she picked up the third one and motioned for them to move over to the white glass dining table. There Raine pulled out one of the chrome and white leather chairs and waited until the others had done the same.

'A proposition?'

'OK, so first of all, I know this is going to sound completely crazy because we don't know you and you don't know us, but we think we might be able to do something together.'

'We've met,' Stevie blurted it out. 'At Reincarnation. Or at least I saw you there. Both of you, I think.'

The temperature in the room dropped a degree as the three of them privately acknowledged their connection to the club and the memories that threw up.

'I've followed the case ever since.'

Raine nodded thoughtfully. 'Then that's probably a good place to start. If you know what's going on then you'll know that we're going to trial soon, but we're all over every newspaper and TV show and it's having a huge impact on our lives. All we want to do is move on and start a new chapter.'

None of this was computing with Stevie yet. What did any of this have to do with her?

'We're pretty much unemployable and we want to get back to work, so we've decided to go into business together.'

Wow! That came out of nowhere. Yet . . . she could see these two working together. They had a natural rapport, a comfort in each other's presence. Stevie almost felt a little jealous of their bright eyes and positivity.

'We're going to open a new club. We thought about doing it on the site of the old Reincarnation, but that was just too weird, so we're looking for new premises and we hope to get moving on it real quick. The Tang stuff is looming over us right now, but the idea is that the club is ready to go as soon as possible after the trial ends.'

OK. Good for them. Stevie still didn't understand what any of this had to do with her.

Mei-Lin took over now, smiling at Stevie as she spoke. 'But we think we need another partner and we wondered – forgive me because I know this will be very shocking to you – we wondered if you would consider it.'

*What?* Stevie looked from one to another, then back, like a spectator at a tennis match. This had to be a joke. Had to be. The punch line was going to come any minute now. But no.

Nothing. Just two expectant expressions and a loud slurp as Raine drank some more of her coffee.

'Me? But . . . why?'

Raine looked around her. 'Please don't take this the wrong way, but it doesn't look like you're doing anything else at the moment.'

Stevie felt her eyes fill with tears.

'Oh fuck, I'm sorry. I'm so sorry. I didn't mean to upset you.'

Stevie shook her head. 'It's OK, it . . . happens.'

'What she *meant* to say', Mei-Lin reprimanded Raine with her eyes, 'is that we know you are no longer with your band and we wondered if you would be open to a new opportunity. Raine and I bring very different experiences to a management team, but we have identified areas where we feel we are not sufficiently qualified. We need a third partner, someone who is very famous and who has the kind of appeal that will pull in the crowds without us having to spend budgets we do not have on marketing. We need someone who can be a spokesperson for the club and who will ensure that the music and the entertainment is the best it can be. We need . . . someone like you.'

The tone of Mei-Lin's voice rose at the end, leaving the conversation hanging on a note of gentle questioning.

Too stunned to move, too shocked to speak, it seemed like minutes before Stevie reacted. Eventually she came to life when two huge fat tears spilled from her eyes and ran down her face.

'I'm so sorry, I'm a mess.'

'That's OK. We're quite often messes, too,' Raine said softly.

'Th . . . thank you for the offer. I still don't quite understand why you want me, but I'm sorry I can't accept. There are . . . problems, issues at my end that need to be sorted or . . . oh, I don't know what the hell I'm saying. I just can't come to work with you, I'm sorry.'

Her chair fell back as she bolted for the bathroom. There she slid to the floor and sobbed, weeping like she hadn't done for a long, long time. What was going on? She didn't understand any of this. None of it. All she knew was that it was reopening wounds and making her hurt and she didn't want to feel all that stuff again. She didn't want to think about the old Stevie and the life she had because it was gone now. The band was gone, Jinx was gone and every hope and dream she'd had for the future was gone, and there was no way to fix it.

The cold tiled floor was no relief as she lay there, unable to stop the pain until . . .

When she woke up she realised first of all that she'd fallen asleep and secondly that she was freezing cold. Shivering, she climbed to her feet, the events of the morning coming back to her in stages. That had to be a dream, surely. Perhaps this was it – perhaps the strain of the last two years was kicking in and she was losing her mind.

That was it.

She was going crazy.

Losing it.

Maybe it was time to take Ella up on the Prozac idea.

But still she was afraid to open the door. She chided herself for being so stupid. If it was a dream then it was over, and on the million-to-one outside chance that Raine O'Donnell and Mei-Lin Yan really had been in her kitchen this morning, they'd be long gone by now.

Slowly she eased the door open and was met by the aroma of fresh coffee and something else. It took her a few moments to pin down toast and lemons.

'Hey, how are you feeling?' Raine was behind the kitchen counter, drying a coffee cup with a towel.

'F-f-f-fine. I think.'

'I hope you don't mind but we made ourselves busy while we were waiting for you.' A glance over at Mei-Lin explained the lemons. She was clutching a mop, standing next to a foaming bucket of water, and as Stevie scanned the room she could see that the floors were gleaming with moisture. It was also obvious that the apartment had been cleaned, tidied and polished to the most sparkling state it had been in since the day she was handed the keys.

'Oh no, please don't cry again.' Raine sounded panicky. 'Come and sit down and let us feed you and talk to you. I think we completely fucked things up this morning.'

As if in a trance, Stevie crossed back to the dining table and slid into a chair. In seconds there was a hot cup of coffee in front of her, a mountainous stack of toast and a bowl of orange slices.

'Sorry, we had to work with what you had. Do you never shop?'

'Things have ... slid lately,' Stevie said quietly. 'Look, this is all just a bit surreal for me. When I woke up in there I was sure I'd been dreaming that you were here.'

Mei-Lin joined them now, pulling off a pair of pink rubber gloves as she sat down. 'You are very lucky that you were allowed to sleep in peace. Raine thought that perhaps you'd an ... *accident* ... and was ready to break the door down to get you out.'

'What stopped you?'

Raine shrugged. 'I don't know if anyone has ever mentioned this, but you snore.'

For the first time the three of them laughed and then fell into a semi-comfortable silence as they drank their coffee. Stevie took a piece of toast, suddenly feeling ravenous. She couldn't remember the last time she had actually felt hungry.

'OK, so maybe we should start again and try to explain ourselves a little better this time. You can see why we need a spokesperson.' As soon as Raine stopped talking she took a chunk out of a piece of toast.

Stevie held her hands up. 'Really, there's no need. I'm very flattered and I'm sorry about the whole passing-out thing this morning,' she motioned to the bathroom, 'but I'm wasting your time here. I can't accept your proposition because there are ... *issues* that I need to sort out before I can move on with my life. Huge issues. Things that I can't fix or control.'

A hand came over hers. 'We know about the issues.' Raine nodded to Mei-Lin, who reached into a bag that was lying under the table before coming back up and pushing a small cassette across the white Formica.

Stevie stared at it, her face twisted with fear.

'Is that ... ?'

Mei-Lin nodded. 'It's a tape from Reincarnation of you with Ari Covet and then going up on the cross later that same night.'

The scream that emerged from her throat was deafening. So they had it. They had a copy of the tape and they'd brought it here to prove ... what?

'How did you get that?' So many questions. She had so many questions that they were tripping over each other in her head. Was this a blackmail attempt? Were they in with Ari Covet? Had he sent them? Was all that stuff this morning just bullshit to get her back out in public? What did they really want from her? Who else had a copy and what were they planning on doing with it?

Mei-Lin stepped up with the first answer. 'This is the only copy.'

'It isn't,' Stevie argued. 'Ari Covet has one, too.'

'No, he doesn't.'

'But he told me ...'

'He's bluffing.'

Stevie couldn't believe what she was hearing. 'He can't be.'

'He is.'

*No.* How could she believe this? After all this time, every waking minute of hell waiting for Covet to blow this thing wide open, it turns out he didn't have a copy of the tape? How could that be possible?

'How can you know that?'

Mei-Lin shifted uncomfortably in her seat. 'I don't know anything about the night that this was recorded – I think I was engaged elsewhere that evening and had no knowledge of it until Covet came back a few weeks later and he and Tang watched the tape together. I'm sorry if this is difficult.'

'No, it's OK. Please go on.' She had to know.

'Over the next few months Covet came back many times and he and Tang would get loaded while watching the tape. It was like Covet's own personal porn flick. Sometimes he would have other girls there while it played, sometimes not. However, I can assure you that none of them were ever in a condition to remember what went on in those rooms.'

'Are you sure?'

Mei-Lin nodded. 'I'm positive. No one else had any lasting knowledge of you being on that tape until the night that you were in the club with your basketball friend.'

Stevie felt a swift kick to the solar plexus. Would the pain of losing Jinx never go away?

'Covet came into Tang's office that night. I was there and witnessed this. Tang was messed up and demanded I sit in the office with him. Covet showed up and asked Tang for a copy of the tape. He was refused. Tang was a very paranoid man. He would record everything that went on in those rooms, sometimes with the client's knowledge but mostly without, but he never allowed anyone to have a copy because the club was too easily identifiable. He did however agree to allow Covet to play the video in one of the private rooms. You know the rest. You were there.'

'But how do you know?'

Mei-Lin's eyes went to the floor. 'Because I saw everything. Tang started to watch the events in your room but passed out before Ari Covet showed you the tape. However, I saw the whole thing. I heard him blackmail you. I saw your friend rip the tape out and destroy it and I saw you leave. I should have helped you, but it was impossible. I'm so sorry.'

'Oh my God.' Stevie couldn't believe what she was hearing. Was this for real? It was so incredible, so way out there that it was difficult to take in, but instinctively she knew that Mei-Lin wasn't lying. So Covet didn't have a copy after all. If this was true then the only copy was sitting right in front of her.

Her eyes fell on the table.

'I can promise you that this is the only copy,' Mei-Lin said softly. 'Tang copied everything involving celebrities to a master and this is it. To protect the others that he also recorded, I've deleted everything else except your segment, not because I wanted to cause you more pain, but because I wanted to prove to you that what I've said is true.'

There was nothing, nothing that could happen to her right now that could astound her more than what this sincere, beautiful woman was telling her.

'Can you wait here for a few minutes please? It's not that I don't trust you, it's just that . . . I have to know. I have to see it for myself.'

'Of course,' Mei-Lin replied. Raine was silent throughout the whole exchange.

In the bedroom, she popped a copy of *Road House* out of her VCR, and slipped in the tape. After three seconds she knew it was authentic and snapped it back off.

This was it. Two years of grief and a life destroyed and now she had the end in her hands. She walked back into the lounge and nodded.

'So now what?'

Raine spoke this time. 'Stevie, we didn't bring this here for any other reason than to give you closure. That's yours now. Destroy it. Do with it whatever you wish. We just wanted you to know that this problem was over for you.'

Stevie sat down again and brought her knees up under her chin. 'Two years. He's been holding this over me for two years.' The tears were falling again now and Raine got up and came to her, slipping an arm around her and holding her close. They stayed like that until the sobbing stopped. She was going to have to do some serious eye repair after today.

Raine reached out and picked the tape up again. 'So that barbeque out on your balcony – seen any action lately?'

Stevie shook her head. She'd used it once, when she'd first moved in, to make some steaks for her and Mrs G, but it had lain dormant ever since. Until now.

Wordlessly she rose and collected some matches from a drawer in the kitchen, then, followed by the other two, she went out to the barbeque and lit it. They watched in silence as the tape crackled, melted and burned.

When it was just a pile of plastic mush on the grill, they scraped it off, took it back inside and dumped it in the sink. She would saw it into little pieces later just to be entirely safe, but she knew, truly knew, that the nightmare was over.

But where did she go from here?

Raine poured another coffee then delivered it with another

hug. 'I know this must be hard for you. Do you want us to leave now?'

It was on the tip of her tongue to say yes. It had been so long since she'd been around other people that she was finding it strange to see them in her apartment, in her personal space, but she realised that she didn't want them to leave yet. It was comforting. Soothing.

'No. Can you stay for a while?'

'Do you have a spare room?'

Stevie nodded. 'Over there, the third door.'

'Excellent, because we're not flying back until tomorrow and I haven't got the strength to go looking for a hotel. Do you have wine? Mei-Lin, I think I'm developing a drinking problem.'

Mei-Lin giggled and it was impossible not to join in. 'I think you are,' she said. 'I blame the drama.'

'I don't have any wine but my neighbour will have a bottle. Hang on a second.' Stevie went out onto the balcony, then used a brush handle to lean around to Mrs G's window and give it a couple of taps.

Mr Kominski appeared wearing nothing but a towel. Good to see those poker lessons were still coming along nicely. He slid back the door and smiled as if there was nothing out of the ordinary about the situation.

'Mr Kominski, I'm sorry to bother you but does Mrs G have a bottle of white wine I can borrow?'

'Sure, sweetheart, just give me a minute.'

He returned with a bottle straight from the fridge and handed it over.

'Having a celebration?' he asked with a smile.

She was about to answer no, but then realised what she was doing and nodded her head.

'Mr Kominski, you're absolutely right. It's a celebration.

A huge, big-assed, completely insane celebration, and I intend to have a real good time with it.'

He was still laughing when she went back inside.

'Anyone want to see a seventy-four-year-old man wearing nothing but two-day stubble and a towel around his waist?'

'Hell, no,' Raine replied, clearly horrified at the prospect.

Stevie plonked the bottle down on the table, then pulled three glasses out of the cupboard.

'OK then,' she said with a laugh that had begun at her toes and was now working its way upwards. 'In that case we'd better make this last.'

She'd taken her first sip when she realised it still didn't feel right. The others immediately sensed her discomfort.

'What's up?' Raine asked, clearly confused. 'Is it the wine?'

'No, it's the . . .'

Her speech left her as the thoughts that were running through her mind allowed the tremors to take hold of her body again. This moment of levity with these two women was all very well, but she couldn't do this, not while he was still out there stalking her, determined to make her suffer. Before she could change her mind, she snatched the phone from the table in front of her and dialled a number that was ingrained in her mind.

'I'd like to speak to Ari Covet. This is Stevie Ross.' Beside her she heard Raine inhale sharply, and Mei-Lin's hand came to rest on her shoulder.

He was on the other end of the line almost instantly.

'Well, well, well, if it isn't the prodigal rock star.'

She wondered how long he'd been waiting to use that line.

'So, you've finally seen sense and decided to come to Uncle Ari then. Well done, sweetheart. Better late than never.'

His voice made her nerve endings scream. She hated him.

She hated him so much for everything he'd cost her and done to her. She had to do this. Two years of being a victim was long enough. Ari Covet wasn't taking another minute of her life.

'I'm coming nowhere near you, you prick. Listen to me carefully because I'm only going to say this once. I'm sitting here with the only copy that exists of that night in Reincarnation.'

'But there's another one that—'

'Shut the fuck up, we both know you're lying.' Suddenly she knew it was true. With the benefit of clarity she could hear the lack of conviction in his voice.

'The copy I have has just been burned to a cinder. That means there is no trace of what happened and nothing for you to hold over me.'

Silence, then a loud sniff from Covet. She could picture him bent over his desk, snorting up another line.

'We're done. If you contact me again I'll take out a restraining order. If you break that, I'll have you jailed. My lawyer is sitting next to me and we are taping this conversation. You tried to blackmail me and it didn't work. I never want to see your face or hear your voice again. If you do anything, I mean *anything*, that is to the detriment of me, my career or my family, I will see to it that you spend thousands of dollars and hours of your time in court. Let's make it simple, Ari, as far as you're concerned I don't exist. And Ari? I hope you rot in hell.'

In her profession she'd heard many incredible lyrics, listened to countless unforgettable melodies, but Stevie Ross had never heard anything as incredible as the phone receiver going down after she'd reclaimed her life.

Her future belonged to her again. She wasn't going to waste it.

# THIRTY-ONE

*Raine*
*New York, 1992*

'OK, guys, blast them,' Raine shouted into the darkness. Like some kind of biblical scene, her whole world was suddenly transformed by a kaleidoscope of light, basking her in a golden glow that was almost saintly. Until she opened her mouth.

'That is fucking killer!' she shouted, punching the air.

Up in the heights above the dance floor, suspended from the metal rigs that spanned the ceiling, the lighting technicians hollered and clapped. She hadn't been easy to work for, she knew that. She an image in her mind of every detail of this club and only perfection would do, but man, it felt great when it all came together to make something mind-blowingly incredible. And this lighting set-up was definitely mind-blowingly incredible.

'Thank you so much, guys – I can't tell you how much I appreciate it. You know you're all on the guest list for the opening, everything on us, right?'

More hollers and claps from above. She couldn't wait to see how sixty-five-year-old Bernie from the Bronx, currently suspended up there above the centre strobes, liked mingling with the assortment of clubbers, dancers and celebrities that were already lined up to attend. He'd be telling his grandchildren about this night until the end of time.

Four weeks. Four weeks until opening and she still couldn't believe how much they'd achieved in the last six months. Since Stevie came on board it had been a rollercoaster of activity, drama and excitement.

The first challenge had been finding the club. They wanted something smaller than Reincarnation, but big enough to generate a seriously hot atmosphere. In the end, the tenacity of Pat O'Donnell's detective skills had found it for them. He'd somehow managed to pull together a list of every disused church, cinema, theatre and club in the whole of Manhattan and he and Stevie had visited them all. Nothing felt right. Too big. Too small. Wrong location. Too much money required to make it work. Then, after three weeks of searching, he called her up.

'Darlin',' I don't want to dance on anyone's grave, but there's a club in Soho that's about to find itself in difficulties real soon.'

'How soon?'

'Tonight. About midnight. And there's no arguing with this one. I'm guessing it'll be up for rent by Monday morning.'

He didn't need to explain. By next morning it was all over the local news that King Wong's Funkatron had been stormed by the cops. A meth lab had been discovered in the basement and everyone who was in any way connected with the operation was now desperately trying to use their one phone call to track down a bail bondsman.

By the following Friday Raine, Mei-Lin and Stevie had taken on the lease. The building was perfect. It had begun life as a church before becoming a dance hall in the fifties, then lying derelict for twenty-five years until someone – presumably King

Wong – had blown a serious amount of cash converting it into a psychedelic rave house.

The decor was shocking, the toilets were nauseating and the smell of illicit narcotics permeated every corner and crevice, but the fundamentals were there. The size was perfect (five hundred capacity), the remodelling required was purely cosmetic and it was in an area that was fine for night-time trade, with plenty of passing cabs.

Perfect.

Once they'd accomplished that first step, the rest had been pretty plain sailing. They'd visited a banker who was no stranger to at least four of Mei-Lin's girls and Stevie had explained that she was throwing in a hundred grand of her own cash, therefore giving the operation a certain legitimacy, and they'd drawn up a legal agreement so that two thirds of the funds would be repaid to her in the first year of operation. They weren't worried. Privately they all knew that the money from Tang's safe was there as a back-up, so if it all went horribly wrong Stevie would get that cash and they'd all walk away without losing anything except the legacy of a man they all despised.

It was a tight budget, but the return of Stevie Ross was generating more publicity than a two-hundred-thousand-dollar marketing campaign, Mei-Lin was utilising every contact her girls had to squeeze out discounts and complimentary services, and Raine was focused on spending money only where it would really count.

It was all going so well she could hardly believe their luck.

The pager on her waistband reverberated and she pulled it up to see the screen. Mei-Lin. The smile was automatic. Since they'd begun working together she'd realised what an amazing person China Girl really was. She never got flustered, never reacted to drama and she had a core of steel that could handle any situation that arose. Her dad had warned her that it was now common knowledge on the streets that Mei-Lin was behind a high-class hooker operation, but for Raine it wasn't an issue. She had complete confidence in Mei-Lin being smart enough to make sure she was squeaky clean. There was no way she was going to allow the United States Government to retract her green card. Nope, she had absolutely no concerns – or moral judgements – about her friend and partner. To her surprise, her dad didn't either. Mei-Lin might have an unsavoury reputation, but her dad understood how she had got to that point and appreciated she was now going to be legit. That was enough for him.

On the way through to the office she passed Stevie and did a double take. 'Hey, baby, you look great.' Her hair had grown long again and she was in full rock-star uniform of black skinny leather hipsters, black vest, black skyscraper boots and silver bangles that went all the way up her left arm. A Dolce & Gabbana bag bounced off her ass as she walked and her weekend-in-Miami tan added the final touches to make her absolutely breathtaking.

Stevie blew her a kiss. 'Have to run, babe. *New York Post* at one o'clock then over to *Harper's* at four. See you at dinner?'

Raine nodded. 'Le Cirque, eight p.m.' It was all part of their PR strategy. Every evening the three of them ate together in restaurants frequented by the paparazzi. It didn't matter that they usually only had a budget for a main course and water. All they needed were the paps to snap them as they left and run the pictures the next day with details of their imminent club opening.

Stevie's 'see you there' was partially swallowed by the banging of the door behind her.

Raine pushed through the fire doors and then turned into

the office on the immediate right. Mei-Lin was sitting behind the desk, so she plumped down on the orange and yellow sofa that sat against the pink wall to her right.

'We are seriously going to have to redecorate this place – I swear it's burning my eyes.'

'No budget,' Mei-Lin replied with a smile, echoing Raine's most-used phrase of the last month.

'So what's up?'

'I think we have a problem. Our liquor licence has been put on hold.'

What? No, this couldn't be happening. The liquor licence was all sorted out and in the process of being granted. The club had a previous licence so that made the process smoother. The representatives from the Division of Alcoholic Beverage Control had already been to reinspect the premises, the girls had filled out all the relevant application forms, they'd paid the fee, satisfied all the other requirements and were under the impression that it was now just a matter of a rubber stamp being put on a dotted line.

'How could that happen?'

'Officially they're saying that it's still pending . . . ' She pushed a letter across the desk in Raine's direction. 'But unofficially I hear the new mayor has blocked all new applications. The police have shut down seventeen clubs in the last fortnight. This new guy is on a mission to cut crime and hit clean-up targets, starting with us.'

'Holy fuck.' She exhaled loudly. 'This can't be happening. Not now. Without the licence we can't open. What are we going to do, tell people to bring their own vodka?'

While Mei-Lin always dealt with every problem in a measured, controlled way, Raine was getting ready to punch a hole in the wall.

'Bastards. Bastards. There must be something we can do. Do we know anyone in the mayor's office?'

Mei-Lin shook her head. 'I've already checked and no. It seems that particular department has escaped us. My girls tend to avoid getting near anyone too high up on the legal authority ladder.'

This couldn't happen. No way. Think. Think. Who could she call? She pulled back her wild mane of jet-black hair and secured it at the back of her neck with a band that had been around her wrist. Who? Eric Tosca was already out of the equation; their non-romance romance had fizzled out as soon as she became a woman with a mission to open a club. It was mutual. She didn't have the time and he knew it would be bad for his career in the long run to have close connections with someone in that world. Anyway, Eric had no pull outside the DEA and the regular NYPD.

Think. The mayor's office. They must know someone who would know someone who would know someone who could help. That was the way this city worked.

It might have been her imagination, but she was sure she could feel damp patches begin to form under the arms of her white T-shirt.

'This guy must have a seriously small dick if this is the kinda shit he's pulling to make himself feel big. Who is he anyway?'

'His name is . . . ' Mei-Lin lifted the newspaper in front of her. 'May-or May-er. Did I say that correctly?'

Raine's heart went out to her. Even now she still worked on her reading and writing skills every day and hated to get things wrong.

'Mayor Mayer? No wonder he's got an ego issue, he's probably sick of the jokes already and . . . Mother of God, let me see that.'

She was up and at the desk before Mei-Lin could react. One minute later she had a plan. Two minutes later she'd rescinded her earlier assertion that he couldn't help, called Eric Tosca at the DEA and threatened him with bollock amputation if he didn't provide certain information. Four hours later she was sitting on the steps outside New York City hall, the building that housed the mayor's office, having ascertained from Tosca that the new mayor liked to be seen jogging around his kingdom at 5 p.m. every evening.

Right on cue a tall guy in grey sweats emerged from the front doors, flanked by two heaving hulks with earpieces. What kind of ego trip was this? She was sure the prick could have used one of many back doors but there he was, running the gauntlet of his minions while they stopped to stare. Raine stood up and timed her approach so that she was right at him by the time he reached the bottom step.

'Mr Mayer.' One of the bodyguards snarled at her, but they kept on running.

She started to jog alongside – not ideal in jeans and scuffed-up black leather biker boots. 'Mr Mayer, can I talk to you?'

The bodyguard snarled again, and for a moment she thought he was going to reach for his holster gun and take her out.

Jack Mayer, however, was far too smooth for that. For the first time he looked at her, adopting a campaign smile and a tone of voice so smooth it could induce retching.

'Honey, I'm a little tied up right now but I've always got time to hear what the voters have to say. Just call my office or drop me a line and I'll get back to you.'

Classic fob-off. She didn't want to do this, she really didn't. OK, maybe just a little, but the asshole was leaving her with no choice.

The nerves in her bad leg screamed in outrage as she speeded up so that she was just a few feet in front and then turned to give him a full view of her face.

'Mr Mayer, I need to talk to you now. My name is Raine O'Donnell and I grew up in Brooklyn. I believe you used to fuck my mother.'

# THIRTY-TWO

*Mei-Lin*
*New York, 1992*

Mei-Lin savoured the warmth as Ami folded her arms around her and held her tightly. 'It's over now, Mei-Lin. It's over.'

They stood like that for a long time, just holding each other, drawing strength and support. It had been the longest week already and there was still so much more to happen.

The court room had been every bit as excruciating as she had anticipated. The only blessing was that the DEA lawyers had secured an agreement to let her testimony be given in private. No press, no public gallery, no cameras. They couldn't keep the main players out, though. Her Uncle Cheung had refused to make eye contact with her at all, instead doodling on a pad the whole time she was on the stand. But Jason Tang had sat there through every single word, smiling like a proud daddy as his girl recounted every indignity, every criminal act, every single damning thing she'd seen or been forced to do while working in his employment.

Every day she'd told herself that she wasn't afraid of him, and she truly believed that to be true, but to see him there, back to

361

his old perfectly groomed, outwardly respectable self had shaken her somewhere deep in her soul.

Ami had stayed away from court – it didn't do to put someone with her occupation in the public eye – but Raine had been there with her every minute, willing her on, keeping her strong.

She was just glad that it was over. Every month the trial had been adjourned again and again, as Tang's legal people used every trick in the book to find something they could use to help him. Eventually they'd had to concede the evidence was too overwhelming. Eye witnesses. Forensic evidence. Hours of video and tapes that Raine had secretly filmed of Tang setting up his illegal activities. Communications between Cheung and Tang. Phone records. Meetings. It was a catalogue of crime, and that afternoon when the jury had retired to consider their verdicts, the prosecution was deeply optimistic.

This was America. He had broken their laws. He was going down for a long, long time.

It was that simple and she intended to be in court the next day to hear him condemned to a lifetime behind bars without possibility of parole, with Uncle Cheung trotting along right behind him. His drug-smuggling charges were fewer and less severe, but nonetheless the prosecutors had assured her that he was looking at twenty years before parole.

She'd take that.

In the meantime she had work to do, with the biggest night of her life in front of her. In a schedule that was surely designed by the gods of irony, the court case had finally ended on the day their club was set to open.

Mei-Lin disentangled herself from Ami and checked her appearance in the full-length mirror that sat against the office wall. Budget or no budget, she'd splashed out to redecorate the room in a muted tone of soft pale grey, with a charcoal carpet and an ornate mirror with a pewter frame that nearly covered one whole wall. Set against the black desk, matching filing cabinet and the pale cream leather sofa against the other wall, she felt the room reflected their personalities perfectly: strong, stylish, classy with a hint of softness.

'I don't think I've ever seen you look more beautiful, Mei-Lin.'

Smoothing out invisible creases on her white floor-length gown, she tried to see herself through Ami's eyes. How different she looked from the young girl who had landed in New York years before. Her dress was a floor-length, one-shouldered silk Dior sheath, with a split that rose to her right hip, decorated with chains of crystal beads that fell from the neckline across the front, catching the eye as they reflected the light. It was the most beautiful thing she had ever seen and required no further adornment, other than perilously high silver sandals and diamond studs in her ears. Her hair was pulled back into a chignon – the only aspect of her look that was giving her second thoughts.

'Those scars say that you survived,' Ami whispered, reading her thoughts.

Mei-Lin nodded. She was right. The scars were part of her story and she wasn't going to hide them.

The door swung open and Raine strutted in, throwing her arms around her from behind.

'Wow, you look like a beautiful doll! I might have to stop being your friend – I can't handle the comparisons.'

The two women sat at opposite ends of the female spectrum. Mei-Lin with her tiny, delicate features and understated manner, and tall, loud, outrageous Raine, who thrived on life and all its craziness. Tonight she looked spectacular – her hair blown out like Diana Ross's in a wild bundle of curls. She too was wearing white – they'd decided this would be their theme for the night – but had chosen a high-necked, full-length, long-sleeved, body-skimming Lycra dress that was split at the back to allow her to walk. Almost every inch of her flesh was covered, yet Mei-Lin didn't think she'd ever seen anything so overtly sexy. Raine's body was a silhouette of perfection, with her voluptuous breasts and hips and tiny waist and ass. She was glorious.

'Are you ready?'

Mei-Lin nodded, then reached for Ami's hand. Ami shooed her away. 'No, you must go only with the other two. It's what people will want to see.'

Mei-Lin felt like her heart may burst. There had been a lot of speculation about her relationship with Ami, but the truth was that they were the closest of friends, bonded together without any of the other complications people added. Theirs wasn't a sexual relationship; it was more – they were family, sisters in life. Perhaps her feelings would one day change, but right now sex was not something she ever wanted to experience again.

'Where is Stevie?'

'Meeting us out by the back door. The script is that we go out the back door, into a limo, drive around the block, then enter via the red carpet at the front. I just hope that people start to turn up. What if they don't? What if in an hour's time there's just the three of us on that dance floor, looking like idiots singing along with Whitney to "I'm Your Baby Tonight"? It'll be tragic.'

Mei-Lin reached out and took her hand. This was so typical of her funny, volatile, erratic Raine, the one who panicked, shouted, laughed loudest and always came through in the end. When she'd somehow managed to attain their liquor licence, they'd all given her a standing ovation.

'Raine, you must stop. Everyone will come, the night will be spectacular and we will celebrate later.'

'I know, I know. I think I'm just ... did you see that bastard's face in court today? They way he grinned at us? The way he looked like he knew something we didn't? It's rattled me. I know I shouldn't let him get to me, but ... Argh! I just need to shake it off. C'mon, China Girl, let's go open our club. Jason Tang can go screw himself ... which is exactly what he'll be doing unless he gets an enthusiastic, open-minded cellmate called Bubba.'

That was so Raine – covering her fears with jokes. Mei-Lin reached out and took her hand as they pushed through the double doors in front of them and carried on down the corridor. Through the wall in the main dance area Haylo cranked up the first song, Michael Jackson's 'Black Or White', and they could hear by the noise levels that the room was already starting to fill up with invited guests. Tonight was a strictly ticket-only affair, and the guest list had been one of the most difficult things to decide on. In the end, they'd tried to find an eclectic balance of people from the worlds of music and movies, dignitaries, TV stars, regular clubbers, sports guys, college kids from the nearby NYU and everyone else they could think of that they wanted to impress, keep on side or encourage to return.

As they approached the back fire exit, they saw that Stevie was already there. Her dress was completely different from the others, a spider's web of glistening white chords that draped and twisted, creating an illusion of complete nudity underneath. She pointed to an imaginary watch on her wrist.

'Am I not supposed to be the totally unreliable rock star person who turns up late for everything?'

Mei-Lin smiled as they came together in hug, slipping her arms around both of their waists and feeling them do the same to her. They put their foreheads together in the middle, no words were necessary to convey what they were feeling. After a few moments they all stood up, shaking out their emotions. This was it.

'OK, girls,' Raine said, exhaling deeply.

'Let's go launch Manhattan.'

The limo's engine was already running as they climbed in and held hands for the three minute journey. As they turned the corner to the front of the building, Raine screeched with excitement.

'Yes! Look at all those people!'

There had been a few pockets of teenagers hanging out in the street outside all day, drawn there by the rumours that everyone from Tom Cruise to Jon Bon Jovi to Madonna was going to show up. But in the last half hour the numbers had swelled and there were literally hundreds of people gathered behind the velvet ropes, barriers that Raine had ordered in an act of optimism.

'It's like a freakin' gig!' Stevie exclaimed.

Mei-Lin said nothing, just concentrated on her breathing and on savouring the moment. This was her life now and she was so, so grateful but there would always be a part of her that felt . . . broken. She was a woman with no family, no one to remember her birthday or to tell her stories of her childhood and ancestors. She had occasionally wondered if her parents knew of Cheung's arrest and fate, but of course they would not. They had no knowledge of such things as television or newspapers. All they had in life was their crops and each other and the memories of a daughter who had gone off one day to save them from starvation. She had no idea if they were even alive or dead and Cheung had refused to give her any information, even when specifically requested through her lawyers.

No, it was done. If they were still in their home in their village, perhaps they would talk of her occasionally, but she would be dead to them by now. After what had happened to her life over the last ten years, she knew that was for the best, because that way the stain of her dishonour could not spread.

'Look, Mei-Lin! Look!' Stevie pointed up towards the middle of the building, right beneath where the spires of the old church left the roof and stretched towards the sky. On the front of the building, there was one word, blazing in lights like a Hollywood movie sign. MANHATTAN. They had been through every name imaginable, but the moment the word had escaped Mei-Lin's lips they all stopped and stared at each other, running it over their tongues, thinking it though.

MANHATTAN.

It was perfect. It was settled there and then, and it was only later that they realised it meant different things to all of them. For Mei-Lin it was inspired by her favourite book, for Raine it signified her upbringing and for Stevie it evoked the gig that began her career.

The limo drew to a halt, and Joe, their head of security and recruit from the former staff at Reincarnation, stepped forward and opened the door, then reached in to help them out one by one.

The crowd cheered with the appearance of Raine and Mei-Lin, but the noise levels doubled when Stevie emerged last. They stood in a line, holding hands, while a riot of photographers snapped and shouted. Mei-Lin knew this was the kind of stuff that sold newspapers – the club promoter who worked undercover for the DEA, the hooker who turned on her evil boss and the fallen rock star who had returned from obscurity – it didn't get more controversial or intriguing than this.

Calm. No fear. Calm. She repeated the mantra in the midst

of the chaos, smiling until her jaws hurt, her heart racing with happiness that something so incredible could come out of something so horrific.

Another massive cheer went up as another car stopped and Giles Corcoran – direct from his eleventh stint in rehab – emerged with Dimitri Krakov, both of them sporting a stunning blonde on each arm, courtesy of Mei-Lin. A free night's company and a lifetime membership of the club had been a small price to pay for their attendance. Right behind them, Brody Revel and Donnie Cray arrived, neither bringing girlfriends. Instead they both had very glamorous older ladies on their arms. They went everywhere with their mothers these days. Since their last movie together tanked, they'd been busted again for drugs and their rumoured sexual dalliances had decimated their box-office appeal. Consequently they were trying to revive their fortunes by targeting the family market.

Mei-Lin had personally called every single star she had ever entertained and assured them that they were welcome. The fact that some of them may have interpreted her call as a loaded invitation, and possibly taken the hint that non-arrival would not be appreciated, said more about their personal fears than anything else. She'd known they would come, some looking for publicity, some looking for excitement and some wondering if their names would be dragged into a scandal if they refused. Della Voight alighted from the next car. The band Meteor Blue from the limo after that.

'Jesus H. Christ, my jaws are killing me.' Beside her, Raine spoke through gritted teeth and a mega-smile that never moved. 'Keep those grins on, girls. Just a few more minutes.'

Mei-Lin beamed towards the crowds. The atmosphere crackled with anticipation and she couldn't help but smile at the excitement and exhilaration on the faces of the young girls behind the ropes. A tug of sadness pulled at her heart again. She and Jing Wei should have had that kind of childhood, but instead it had been taken from them and . . .

Still. She stopped perfectly still and searched the crowd for . . . there it was again. A face that was so beautiful, so familiar yet so strange . . . Jing Wei. Jing Wei was staring at her and as their eyes met she smiled then . . . No. It wasn't Jing Wei. Of course it wasn't. The girl disappeared into the crowd and Mei-Lin braced herself against another wave of sadness, thinking how much her little cousin would have loved this spectacle. The tears glistened in her eyes but she refused to let them fall. Tonight her emotions were just getting the better of her and she was carrying the spirits of everyone she loved too close to the surface of her heart.

Shanghai, her family, Jing Wei, Cheung, Tang and everything else about her past was gone now. Her life was her friends, her business and Manhattan. It was a new life that started that night. And if Manhattan was her future, she was going to make sure it made up for the past.

# THIRTY-THREE

*Stevie*
*New York, 1992*

'Man, that was so amazing. I'd forgotten how good it felt. Does that make me sound like an egotistical jerk?'

'Yep,' Raine replied, 'but you're in good company because I want to go right back out there and get me some more love.'

Amazing. This was the kind of rush that usually required great sex followed by a crowd of forty thousand people chanting your name. 'I'm gonna go and see if I can track down my mom. I made the mistake of telling her we'd invited Robert De Niro and he's her favourite actor of all time. It's best if I get to her before Mr De Niro's security have to peel her off him.'

'Yeah, like mother, like daughter.' Raine whistled with a grin.

Stevie playfully smacked the back of her head. 'Hey, that was Charlie Sheen. And he was definitely giving me signals.'

Still grinning, she headed out of the office and towards the main hall, her stomach still flipping with adrenalin. She thanked God every day for sending these women. Her life not only had focus again, she had friends, and she was having more fun with this than she'd had in way too long.

As soon as she pushed through the huge steel doors, the rush of the vibe almost made her reel back. The place was going seriously wild, and she could see that they were pretty close to capacity already. Raine had done an incredible job with the design. She'd stripped everything back to the wood, tearing down the false ceilings to reveal a huge, majestic vaulted roof with a dramatic cupola in the centre and original artwork that was inspired by the work of Michelangelo.

That had set the theme for the rest of the design: Manhattan rises to heaven. Every wall was painted with a different black-and-white view of the New York skyline, so that standing alone in the middle of the room felt like being dumped right in the middle of Times Square in the fifties.

The lighting was spectacular and could transform the room from a summer day to a Hitchcock movie at the flick of a switch. But it was the action up above that totally took her breath away. The upper level of seating, used for congregational overflow in the old days, had been transformed into a VIP section that was only accessible by two glass lifts from the lower floor. The revellers on the ground floor could watch as their favourite stars ascended to heaven, but when the VIPs got up there, their privacy was assured by their biggest expense – a glass window that allowed everyone upstairs to look out, but was tinted so the visibility was only one way.

The biggest stipulation from all three partners, though, was that there were no other private rooms. None. They wanted full visibility of what was going on in their club and none of the hobbies enjoyed by Tang would be tolerated. No visible drug use. No public sex. No humiliation. No filming. No one's life was ever going to be destroyed by something that happened at Manhattan.

Loving the gimmick, she used her thumb to open the lift to

the VIP room. Everyone who was permitted to enter had their thumb print taken on their first visit and was free to come and go after that. The prints were connected to a database so anyone could be deleted at any time if they misbehaved. They were all about having fun, but they weren't going to be slow to use the delete button if anyone, famous or not, got out of hand.

Up in the VIP room the air was thick with perfume and cigarettes. People watched her as she crossed the room. No matter how many interviews she gave claiming that the reason she left The Thorns was because she was simply exhausted and needed a break, people were still intrigued about the disappearing rock star.

'Mom! You made it!' She rushed over to the window, where her mother was standing chatting to another middle-aged woman who had also upped the glam stakes for the night. 'This is my friend, Sadie, I hope it was OK to bring her.'

'Of course it is, Mom, you can bring anyone you want!'

'Really?' her mom replied.

'Of course.'

'OK, so now's probably a good time to tell you that I brought someone else, too, then.'

Ella gestured over Stevie's shoulder, so her first reaction was to turn and . . .

Jinx.

Almost three years after he'd walked out of her life, Jinx Daley was standing in front of her, big, black and so damned beautiful that the only thing she could do was stare.

He wasn't saying anything either.

They stood looking at one another, neither of them willing to start, until the feeling of being suffocated started to shut down her breathing.

She couldn't do this.

Turning, she pushed her way through the crowd to the elevator, then cursed as she discovered it wasn't at this floor and she would have to wait. Panicking, she realised she should have used the back stairs.

'Stevie, stop.' He didn't yell or sound demanding, it was just a quiet, soft plea.

She could handle this. She could.

'Don't blame your mom, I asked her to bring me. I want to talk to you.'

'Why? Is your wife not listening these days?'

Oh yes, there was the irony. A year after he left her he'd married a lawyer called Juliet, who had left him after she was caught banging a client with a chain of restaurants and alleged mafia connections.

So much for him staying away from scandal and maintaining a squeaky-clean family-values image. He'd been sharing blow jobs with a guy who whacked people one Sunday a month just for fun.

'It was a mistake,' he said.

'Really? I didn't think you made those. Didn't think anyone was allowed to make a mistake in your world. Thought that was when you fucked off and left them, even when they begged you to stay.'

Where the hell had that come from? It was as if a torrent of rage had filled her gut and now it was spewing everywhere, hitting anyone in its path. She was so fucking angry. Why had he left? Why hadn't he helped her? Why hadn't he given her one chance, just one fucking chance to explain?

He was just gone.

'I'm sorry, Stevie. I really wish . . . '

She really wished she could listen to him, but that whole rage thing was still in charge of what came out of her mouth. 'You know what, Jinx. I don't care. For the first year I cried, for the

373

second year I waited, but now I really, really don't care. So if you'll excuse me . . . '

The lift finally opened beside her, but he put his arm across, barring the way. 'Move your arm and let me past,' she told him through gritted teeth.

He didn't budge. 'Stevie, c'mon, I just want to—'

'Move your arm,' she repeated, staring straight at him, her face a mask of defiance.

'Stevie . . . ?' he was pleading now and, oh shit, she had to get out of here because if he looked at her like that again she would melt.

'Hey, asshole, she said move your fucking arm.'

There was a pause as she tried to make sense of what had just happened. Then she took one step inside and waited as the doors closed before turning to face Cally, who was standing there in the lift looking like the fierce, gorgeous, bisexual rock goddess she now was, complete with a crooked grin that sat behind the cigarette dangling from her lips.

Stevie suddenly realised that she had no idea how this was going to go. None. She'd bailed out on The Thorns, totally let them down, and even though they'd maintained the same huge success, she knew that there was no forgiving what she'd done.

'Is this going to end really badly for me?'

Cally shrugged. 'That depends. Are you gonna sing Patsy Cline?'

Stevie shook her head, fighting the urge to cry, her eyes never leaving Cally's.

'Then I guess we might be cool.'

When the lift doors opened at the bottom, Stevie grabbed Cally's hand and pulled her down the side corridor to the office. Thankfully it was empty. The minute they got inside, she threw her arms around her.

'I can't believe you're here. I can't believe you're actually here.'

Cally eventually broke off the embrace and kicked back onto the sofa. 'Sorry. You're giving me a hard-on.'

Stevie burst out laughing. How much had she missed this? So damn much.

'How's ... how's ... how's ... ' Stevie couldn't get the words past her mouth.

'The rest of the band?'

She nodded.

'Lou's still a pain in the ass and Jude and Dixie got married.'

'You're kidding me!'

'Nope. I was the bridesmaid, on account of the fact that I was the only one who'd never seen his dick.'

'I know I've no right to say this, but I miss you guys so much.'

There was an awkward pause as the obvious question hung in the air.

'Wanna tell me why?'

Deep breath. Did she? So many times she'd thought about telling them, but had stopped, knowing it was a road to disaster. What would they have done? Stormed Ari Covet's office and threatened to kick the crap out of him if he didn't hand back the tape? Back then, she'd figured that course of action would only have ended one way: he'd have released the tape to spite them, and then if he was feeling twisted enough he just might have turned on them, too. He was a powerful man in the music industry and he could make life real hard, even for acts that weren't signed to his label.

But now? There was no tape. There was no reason for him to hurt them.

'Ari Covet.'

'What? How?'

'Remember the night of the gig at the Garden? We went out after?'

'Reincarnation?'

Stevie nodded. 'I didn't know it then, but he drugged me, raped me, filmed it . . .'

She wouldn't cry. She would not.

'Then the last time we were there he showed me the tape and threatened to release it if I didn't sign solo with him.'

Cally's eyes blazed fire.

'I couldn't . . . do it. But I couldn't stay with you guys and risk bringing the band down, so I left. And waited.'

'I'll fucking kill that prick.'

'You'll have to join a long line. But it's done. Over.'

'And the tapes?'

'My partners here got the only copy for me. Turns out he didn't have it at all. That's the kind of sadistic pig he is.'

'You can't let him get away with that.'

Stevie nodded. 'He won't. But right now he's not my priority. I had to get my life back first.'

'Man, I wish you'd told us all of this. We were seriously pissed off with you for a long time.'

'I get that.'

Two years of barriers had taken two minutes to come down again.

'So how's Leeane working out?'

'Nightmare. Total wacked-out nightmare. That's why I'm here – looking for her. She goes off on benders for days, misses gigs, cancels shows, turns up naked and in jail.'

'Sounds like a pretty good rock singer.'

'Yeah, but not when she's in your band.'

Oh she wanted to say it. She wanted to say it so badly but she wouldn't. Especially since . . .

'Cally, I think you just found her.'

She pointed at the top monitor on the wall, one of eight that showed different angles in the club. This was a very different set-up to Tang's place. This wasn't voyeurism or entrapment; this was security, pure and simple. The door. The bars. The fire exits.

Back to the camera that covered the door. There was Leeane Star, clearly off her face. Even without sound they could see that she was arguing with the security guys because they didn't want to let her in due to the fact that she seemed to have misplaced every item of her . . .

'Oh shit.' Cally sighed. 'Well, at least she isn't in jail.'

# THIRTY-FOUR

*Raine*
*New York, 1992*

So this was what being on top of the world felt like. Raine stood at the front of the VIP bar and looked down on the crowd below. One scan of the room and she already saw things that no one else would see. There was a fight brewing just below the DJ box – two guys were at the pushing stage but one of their buddies was standing with a bottle that had trouble written all over it.

She pulled the radio out of her pocket. 'Hey, Mike.' The hand of the security guard nearest the problem immediately sprung to his ear. 'Two o'clock, white guys, look like a Don Johnson tribute act, just about to kick off.'

Right at that moment her prediction panned out and the first punch was thrown, but Big Mike had the two of them by the neck and on the way to the nearest fire escape before it could escalate.

'Karl.' Her word had the same effect on the security guy at the back of the hall, standing just inside the main entrance. 'There's a female about thirty feet to your right. Pink handbag.

Ridiculous shoes.' Karl smiled at this. 'She's dealing out of that bag. Tell her she needs some fresh air and then tell her to spread the word that she and her friends aren't welcome here.'

Karl nodded and she watched as he calmly made his way to her then walked her to the door.

The next thing that caught her eye required no intervention. A tall redhead. Killer figure. Bikini top and mini-skirt. Making out with one guy who clearly had no idea that at the same time she was groping the balls of the guy behind him. There was something to be said for multi-tasking.

The crowd, she realised, was perfect. They'd got the balance just right, a mix of the upmarket, the posers and the guys that were just out for a good time. There was none of the seediness or danger of Reincarnation. There was no malice or sinister intent sitting behind the vibe. This was pure glamour, and it was all about the music, style and class.

This was the kind of club she'd dreamed of and it felt amazing. There was a part of her that actually wished Jason Tang was there now so that he could see what they'd done. That insidious little freak could never have achieved anything as cool as this.

The thought of him made the hairs on the back of her neck stand up. She'd anticipated that once all of this was over her feelings for him would be cushioned by triumph but no, the hatred still burned bright, even more so now that the full extent of his actions had come out in court. Before, she'd known that he was evil, but now she knew that it was more than that. The guy was truly psychotic, he would stop at nothing to hurt those who displeased him and didn't have a shred of conscience or a limit on the pain he inflicted. He wasn't someone to ever be on the wrong side of, and much as she knew the evidence was overwhelming, she'd sleep just a little better when the jury delivered a guilty verdict and locked him away for a very long time.

Enough. She chided herself for letting dark thoughts steal the moment. Tang had already taken enough. Inhaling deeply, she forced herself to return to the light, to the moment right there and then and the club that had healed them all.

It was a sensation.

This just didn't get any better. Except . . . someone over at the back bar caught her eye. Shit, she couldn't believe he was here. Another problem that hadn't been addressed yet. She pulled the radio out again. 'Sorry, Mike, not your night tonight. Guy on the left, standing with two skinny chicks. Can you bring him up here and don't take any arguments off him?'

Mike nodded and seconds later he was on his way with someone who clearly wasn't pleased about being ordered around. She watched them come up in the lift and then she moved back to a quieter corner, screened off by a mirrored partition, where they wouldn't be overheard or watched. These little booths had been her idea – mirrored dividers to allow the stars to look at themselves while having a bit of privacy, but still in the midst of the VIP area so that nothing illicit could take place.

By the time Mike had delivered the guest he was looking mighty pissed off.

'You came,' she said.

'You invited me,' he replied. 'Although, I didn't realise that getting dragged away from my friends was part of the deal.'

Raine glanced out of the window towards where he'd been standing.

'There's no way you were having a good time with them anyway. Chicks that skinny must be way too hungry to have a sunny disposition.'

His laugh sounded so good, and he looked incredible. White shirt, black pants, expensive shoes, and hair that was just the right side of messed up. He'd kinda grown out of the whole hobo look and had emerged looking like someone from a Dolce & Gabbana advert. She'd battled with herself over whether or not to invite him, but in the end she hadn't been able to stop herself. Even now her motivations weren't too clear to her. Did she want him to see how well she'd done? Or did she want to know what he was doing now? Or did she want to look into his eyes and see if there was still . . .

'OK, here's the deal,' she said in a matter-of-fact voice. Shit, was she going to do this? Really? Two voices were fighting it out in her head – one telling her to shut the fuck up and the other saying that . . . well . . . hadn't she done that before? Didn't she already know what happened when you didn't have the courage to say what was on your mind? For the rest of her life she would regret not being up front with Ricco. Always.

That was the voice that won out.

'Shay, I love you.' She said it like he was a stranger who had stopped to ask directions. Romance had never been her thing. One day she had to do something about that. He cleared his throat and opened his mouth to speak but she cut him off.

'I know I'm a complete nightmare and I'm sorry about the whole double-life thing . . . '

He raised one eyebrow at that, making her shrug.

'But I had . . . reasons.'

'I've been following the court case. I'm sorry about Ricco.'

'So you know the reasons.' To her surprise, hearing Shay say his name made her windpipe constrict. She paused for a second to recover then went on, 'But the thing is that I'm sorry I didn't tell you the truth and I'm doing it now. There isn't a day since I met you that I haven't thought about you, the night we spent together was incredible and I really hope that you haven't gone and got yourself married to one of those plastic females you hang out with because if so you'll have a miserable life. And you'll be hungry. A lot.'

Why wasn't he saying anything? Why? She wasn't expecting declarations of undying love, but he could at least say—

'Are you finished?'

She nodded.

He leant down and he kissed her, a slow, delicious, gorgeous kiss that made her want to pull him down and do things to him that the management of the club had expressly forbidden.

Fuck the rules.

But after far too short a time he stopped.

'Raine, I'm only going to do this if there's no more shit. Seriously. I fell in love with you the first year we met but I'm a straightforward kind of guy and I can't do the drama. If we're together, we're together and I don't want to have to worry about you packing up and leaving in the middle of the night.'

'I only did that once.'

'It was once too many.'

'I'm sorry.'

'Accepted. But don't disappear on me again, OK?'

She nodded, reaching up to kiss him, just as a voice came through her earpiece.

'Boss, you're needed back at the office.'

Breaking off from the kiss, she turned her head and spoke into her radio.

'No.'

'Sorry, boss, not reading you. You're needed at the office. Code Red.'

'You have got to be fucking kidding me.'

'What are you talking about?' Shay had no idea what was going on.

'I have to go. I'm sorry.'

His eyes widened and he took a step backwards, his hands going up in front of his chest.

'Raine, I'm not doing this. Forget—'

'Come with me. Come. Now.'

Despite wearing six-inch heels and a tight dress that only allowed twenty-inch strides, she moved quickly to the back door, pushed through, then began to descend the four flights of stairs to the ground floor.

'I don't plan this, Shay, I swear. I promise I won't leave but I can't promise that it won't be like this sometimes.' She was gasping for breath, spitting the words out between exhalations.

Code Red. Danger. Something heavy was going on. Shit, she knew this would happen. Tang. He'd done something, found a way to fuck with them. She should have killed the bastard in the office that night, taken that stick off him and rammed it through his heart. Any jury would have bought self-defence. Now she had everything she could want but she would spend the rest of her life looking over her shoulder in case he found a way to attack them.

On the ground floor they ran along the corridor, then burst into the office to a waiting audience and complete silence.

Mei-Lin. Stevie. Eric Tosca. Columbo.

Every one of them looked like they were about to attend a wake. Behind her she could sense Shay, standing just inside the doorway.

'What's happened? What is it?'

Oh no, it could only be one thing. Her chest started to tighten unbearably.

'Is it my dad? Is my dad OK?'

Eric Tosca answered immediately. 'Raine, your dad's fine.'

'Then what?'

Mei-Lin's eyes were red and she looked like she'd aged ten

years since the beginning of the night. Stevie was looking at her with absolutely undisguised sympathy.

Columbo, resplendent in a shiny suit, spoke up, running one hand through his hair as he slumped against the desk.

'They've disbanded the jury.'

'What? How? How can they do that?'

'Special dispensation from heaven.'

'So what? A retrial? Oh fuck, are we going to have to go through all of that again?' No wonder Mei-Lin looked so devastated – giving evidence in this case had almost killed her.

Columbo shook his head.

'They've abandoned the trial, too. The Chinese government stepped in and came to some arrangement with our masters. Right now Tang is on a diplomatic flight back to Beijing. They're saying that he will be charged as guilty there and punished accordingly, but I don't hold out much hope considering his father's position in the government there. Cheung will stay here. Ten years, no parole, his lawyers plea-bargained, the DA accepted.'

No. No. No. No. This couldn't happen. It couldn't. After everything they'd been through, right now that bastard was sipping champagne on some private fucking jet on his way back to Beijing where his mamma would be waiting for him on the tarmac and he'd be welcomed like some kind of returning hero. How could this happen. How?

Tosca took a step towards her, arms outstretched, but she put up her hand.

'Don't come near me. Just don't.' Her tone brooked no further argument. She knew she was being harsh. These guys had worked damn hard to get Tang and they would be as crushed as she was, but there was only one person she cared about right now.

She moved over to Mei-Lin and put her arms around her, and immediately China Girl let out a piercing scream of pure pain.

Raine couldn't do anything but hold her until she'd stopped. No one else said a word, everyone was lost in their own disappointment and despair.

After minutes had passed she looked searchingly at Columbo. 'Is there anything we can do? Anything at all?'

'Nothing. It's out of our hands. The decision's made. Apparently the Chinese are returning four American political prisoners in return for US co-operation in this case. The press statement will go out tomorrow saying that he's guilty and will serve out his sentence in Beijing.'

'Bullshit! You know that's not true – you just said it yourself,' she lashed out.

He nodded, every movement steeped in regret.

'Then this will never be over,' Mei-Lin said quietly, 'because one day Tang will come for us.'

'He won't, Mei-Lin, he can't come back to the US and he's not stupid enough to stir up more trouble. If anything happened to you guys he'd be the obvious suspect. The Chinese Government wouldn't stand for any of that shit.'

Raine just hoped he was as confident as he sounded.

Mei-Lin wasn't buying it, though.

'If that's what you believe you don't know Tang. This isn't over. One day he will come after us, I promise you.'

# BOOK FOUR

## THE SPOTLIGHT NOW
## SHINES ON MANHATTAN . . .

# THIRTY-FIVE

*Mei-Lin*
*New York, 1992*

The elevators were delivering stars to the upper level every few minutes as the crowd on the dance floor went wild for Nirvana's 'Smells Like Teen Spirit'. Mei-Lin watched from the balcony as the young people danced with wild abandon and not a care in the world. That is what life should be like at their age – dancing and laughing and surrounded by friends. Sometimes she felt like the oldest twenty-four-year-old in the world.

But then, many of them would give anything for her success. Manhattan had been full to capacity every single night since it opened, attracting an amazing crowd and garnering a reputation as the most glamorous club in the city. They'd made it. Out of something horrific had grown this amazing blessing. That paramedic had been right – she'd become a lucky girl.

Out of the corner of her eye she noticed some friction in the VIP room to her left. She slid through the glass door and stood back, watching what was going on. It was club policy that one of them had to be on the upper floor at all times. People came here for the music, the glamour and the vibe, but they also came because they were intrigued by the three women behind the music.

She caught the eye of the bartender and nodded, letting him know that she had things under control. He moved his hand away from the section of the bar that concealed the alert button, a system designed to let security know if anything kicked off. So far they'd had nothing more than the occasional drunken actor collapsing in a stupor, but this looked like it could ramp up into something a little more dangerous.

Levo Howard, the lead singer of Meteor Blue, was sprawled on a sofa with two blondes, one of whom was trying to leave. Mei-Lin recognised them as working girls – not hers, but regulars on the circuit. They were more than welcome here as long as they didn't tout for business in her club.

One of the girls was clearly upset, but every time she got up to leave, Howard grabbed her and pulled her back down again. It was getting heated, as she alternated between begging and anger. The next time she tried to move he lunged at her, snatching her thin satin top and tearing it with the force of his pull. Mei-Lin was in front of them in a second. He didn't even register her hand until it locked on to his. 'Leave her.'

Her voice was deadly calm.

'What the—'

'I said leave her. Touch her again and I will break your arm, and I do believe that you need that to play guitar.'

He immediately dropped his arm to his side and Mei-Lin had to stop herself from smiling. The benefit of being Asian – everyone believed her when she threatened them, figuring she was accomplished in some kind of deadly martial art.

Mei-Lin turned to the girl. 'Go now,' she said calmly. 'You're welcome back any time, but for tonight it's best that you go.'

'Thank you,' she said, eyes moist, grabbing her bag and heading for the lift before anyone changed their mind. 'You, too,' Mei-Lin told the other one, who clearly had no intention of following her friend. Where was their solidarity? Reluctantly, she struggled to her feet, balanced on her six-inch Perspex platforms and stumbled off, muttering something under her breath.

Mei-Lin replaced her on the couch.

'Mr Howard, we seem to have got off on the wrong foot. I'm Mei-Lin Yan.'

He looked at her warily. He knew who she was, everyone did. The club, the scars, the legacy of the Tang case and the trial – she was famous in this city now.

He opened his mouth to speak but she immediately brought her finger to his lips and shushed him.

'Don't talk, just listen. You are a guest in my club, that is like being a guest in my home. I take offence very easily, Mr Howard. Right now I'm offended by the way that you just acted. Touch any woman in my club like that again and I will become so offended I might have to act. Purely in the name of social responsibility, you understand.'

She smiled sweetly, stood up and walked away without another word, meeting Stevie as she alighted from the lift.

'Hi, Babe, anything happening?'

'Nothing serious. Levo Howard's on a warning.'

Stevie rolled her eyes. 'Urgh, I hate that dickhead. Lou banged him once on a tour bus – he gave her crabs. OK, I've got this. Wanna go grab a cup of that green stuff you drink?'

It took her twenty minutes to reach the office, stopping on the way to check that Raine was OK on the door. That was her domain and one of the other reasons the club was so successful: Raine had an inherent instinct for who should get in and who shouldn't, for the troublemakers and the dealers. Manhattan belonged to all of them, but it was Raine's baby.

As soon as she reached the calming surroundings of the pale grey sanctuary, she flicked on the kettle, and then stood with her back to the wall, eyes closed. She didn't even hear the door open.

'Raine said you would be in here.'

Ami's voice was thick with concern as she crossed the room and wrapped her arms around her, wafting the intoxicating aroma of Chanel No. 5. When Ami finally released her, she stood back and looked at Mei-Lin for a second, her brow furrowed with concern.

'Mei-Lin, you have to tell me what is going on in your mind. Is it Tang? Are you afraid?'

She was about to launch into a tirade of bravado when she suddenly stopped.

'Yes, part of me is afraid. I would be foolish if I were not.'

It was true. Only an idiot would underestimate Tang, no matter how much the authorities assured them that he would not act against them. It would come, she was sure. That day would come because their success and a need for revenge would eat at Tang until he acted on it.

It would come. She just had to be ready.

But this feeling was more than that. It was . . .

'Empty. Ami, I feel empty. Look at all that I have achieved and yet, other than you and Raine and Stevie, I have nothing. I don't care about the money or the fame, I just need . . .'

She didn't have the answers. What did she need? Love? A man or a woman to lie with? Something to fill her days with meaning?

'You need your family.'

Mei-Lin felt like she'd been slapped. Her family were long

gone and Ami knew that. How could it be anything other than the way it was? That part of her life was over and there was no way of going back. She would be a stranger to them now. Perhaps they even knew what she had become and were shamed by her. She was about to give Ami a hundred reasons why she was wrong, but the beautiful Japanese girl in front of her spoke first.

'I understand why you are afraid of Tang. There is much there to fear. But Mei-Lin, when it comes to your family the demon is yours. You do not know how they will react, how they will be. And until you have visited them, the only thing you are afraid of is the unknown. And you, my friend, are stronger than that.'

Mei-Lin booked her flight the following morning.

# THIRTY-SIX

*Stevie*
*New York, 1992*

'OK, Stevie, let's go. Action!'

There was total silence in the room as the crew switched into their roles.

Her face streaked with make-up, her hair matted and wild, Stevie crawled along the floor and scrambled towards the balcony.

She just hoped that the tremors in her hands and body added to the authenticity of her performance, as opposed to giving away the truth: that she was completely terrified.

Taking on this acting role had seemed like a great idea at the time. *Disco Drug* was to be set against a backdrop of the New York narcotics scene in the eighties, a cautionary coming-of-age tale about a young guy who ran away from his Midwestern home and found the family he never had amongst the night people, the crowd that lived their lives in the bowels of the club scene.

Raine hadn't spoken to anyone for two hours after she'd read the script, she just sat there, ashen, before telling Stevie that she had to do it. Stevie knew why. If she was at a loose end on a Tuesday night sometimes she would tag along when Raine visited Didi. No change. Always no change.

On Raine's request alone she would have done it, but if she were honest there was more to it than that. Manhattan reigned supreme in the club world but Stevie knew that could change in a heartbeat. Another club could open. The crowd could lose interest. Someone could sabotage their success. She knew that the other two worried every day about Jason Tang, but he wasn't on her radar. She'd already had her life ruined by one psychopath and that was about as much pain and stress as she could handle.

They'd all done an amazing job getting the PR and press coverage that was required to launch the club, but keeping it in the public eye was a different story. *Disco Drug* would help. It was directed by Lee Versy, the hottest guy in the movie world right now, fresh off the back of his global hit movie about Vietnam. He was renowned for being controversial, cool, edgy and a genius – and those were labels Manhattan should be associated with.

There was a personal agenda there, too. If this was the movies, her life would be all wrapped up in a bow right about now. Redemption equals new beginning equals triumphant heroine equals happily ever after.

This wasn't the movies, though.

There wasn't a morning she woke up that she didn't thank God for her second chance, but she had a nagging feeling she was meant to do more. Manhattan was part of her now, but there was still room for the performer in her, the creative side that needed to be out there, putting on a show.

Perhaps acting could be that thing. Singers transitioned on to the screen all the time and perhaps this was where she was meant to be. Here, crawling along the floor, looking like something from Michael Jackson's 'Thriller' video.

She reached the balcony and scrambled on top of it.

This was her role. The first girlfriend, the one who got too far into the drug scene, who couldn't handle what it had done to her life, who crawled up on to a balcony and ...

Arms wide, eyes closed, Stevie stopped perfectly still, then silently, gracefully let herself fall forward to her death.

Versy had offered her a stunt double for the fall but she had declined. Now, as she slammed against the inflated safety balloon, the impact knocked the wind out of her lungs and she lay there gasping for breath.

Only when the safety team pulled her off did she realise her pain was nothing to do with the fall. The biblical pose. The vulnerable female. The suicide. The filming. It was all much too real and her brain made associations she had never even considered.

It hurt.

It really hurt.

'Man, that was amazing!' Versy, with his little John Lennon glasses and his Grateful Dead T-shirt, was beside her now and clearly stoked. 'The depth of that performance was incredible. Your face. Your pain. Man, we could almost touch the desperation up there. You sold it, baby. You sold the story. You got to that place and you showed that there was no coming back from it.'

Stevie tried to get a hold of her shudders and regain her power of speech.

'Th-h-h-an-ks.' It was all she could manage and even that threatened to open the floodgates to a whole new river of pain.

'Listen, I've got another movie shooting straight after this one. A twisted love story. Older, predatory, twisted guy, young, naïve girl. Svengali-type deal but with needles, nudity and a jail sentence.'

Stevie didn't even stop to hear the rest. There were some scenes in life she had no need to re-visit.

Her film career was over.

She was going to have to find some other way to get her creative kicks.

If her life was a movie, she suddenly knew exactly how she'd want the next scene to play out.

# THIRTY-SEVEN

*Raine*
*New York, 1992*

'Oh crap, I've just remembered something.'

Shay stopped dead on the top step. 'Tell me that you haven't just remembered you're already married.'

'Nope, better than that.'

He thought for a moment. 'Nope, I've got nothing. Shoot.'

'Last time I was on these steps I was waiting for the mayor so I could blackmail him into giving us our liquor licence.'

Shay groaned. 'I think I'd have preferred it if you were already married. Are we going to get arrested in here?'

'There's every possibility.'

He grabbed her hand as they ran up the rest of the stairs. 'I must be crazy. Certifiable.'

It had been a spontaneous decision to get married. Big white dresses and floral arrangements were the stuff of Raine's nightmares so weddings had never been on her priority list. But with Shay it was ... different. She wanted him to know that she was serious about this. And besides, given that he spent every day surrounded by specimens of beauty, she wanted to have a legal stamp on him just to let the vultures know where he stood.

Not that she was worried on that score. If Shay was going to hook up with an incredible beauty, he'd have done it before now, instead of holding out for an unusual-looking Irish Italian with a big mouth and hair so huge it deserved its own zip code.

Stevie and Mei-Lin met them at the top step and they headed up to the marriage bureau, leaving convention at the door. The groom was the closest thing to normal, wearing a suit and an open-neck shirt, but there was not much that could be said about the bride's knee-high white boots and white crocheted mini-dress, other than that she'd succeeded in her wish to channel Barbra Streisand circa 1968. Her bridesmaids, on the other hand, appeared to bystanders to be the rock singer, Stevie Ross, and an exotic Bond girl – stunning, scarred and dressed head to toe in black. 'So were you guys involved with her blackmailing the mayor?' Shay hissed in the elevator.

Raine shushed him, but it was too late.

'You didn't!' Stevie said, wide-eyed. 'The liquor licence?' Mei-Lin asked.

Shay took up the baton. 'Do you, Shay Smith, take thee, Raine O'Donnell, in sickness and health and criminal indictments . . . ' he said, cracking the others up.

These were just two of the things Raine loved about him – he made her laugh her ass off and her friends thought he was great.

Sometimes she couldn't believe she got so lucky. After the trial there had been a couple of months when she'd struggled to keep her head up, living in constant anxiety about Tang's next move. But as time passed it became clear that he'd retreated into the sidelines. Word had come back that he was serving time in a prison near his parents' home, or some bullshit like that. Raine had realised then that she had to get a handle on the worry, relegate it to a place where it didn't overshadow the rest of her life. It would always be there, sitting just out of sight, but in the meantime she had so many other things to be thankful for. Starting with the man she was about to marry. And her friends. And her family. And Manhattan.

Her Manhattan. She loved that place. Six months after opening it was everything she'd ever dreamt of in a club. Every night brought famous faces and glamour and less trouble than any city nightclub should ever expect. She suspected that was due mainly to her connections with the DEA and her father's influence. Just like back in the Manzo's days, her dad had spread the word and the local judiciary put just a little extra effort into looking out for his daughter. The situation was also helped by the fact that she had very publicly put herself at risk in order to bring down a bad guy, and was happy to provide the officers with an endless supply of coffee and sandwiches.

Raine Storm seemed like another lifetime ago. Raine O'Donnell, however, had got real lucky and she never forgot it.

'Hey, ma darlin', I was about to send out a search party.' Pat greeted them at the door of the marriage bureau and took the hand of the woman next to him before folding his daughter into a group hug. He'd been devastated when Maria had left him for Father O'Flynn in a scandal that had rocked the parish, but the last six months had healed the pain. As had the Maureen O'Hara lookalike who was standing there with tears running down her face.

'Oh, Raine, you look so beautiful,' Isa told her.

'Thanks, Ma.' It had seemed like a perfectly natural progression. Isa had always been more of a mother to her than Maria O'Donnell had ever been.

'Right, come on, we need to get in there.' Pat put his crowd-control training to good use and began ushering them through.

'But where is . . . ?' Mei-Lin this time, looking anxious, but then her expression relaxed as Ami ran down the hall and took her hand.

Inside, the marriage official was keen to get started.

'Hang on, hang on,' Raine ordered. 'OK, Stevie, go.'

Stevie launched into the beautiful, emotional words of 'Evergreen', as Isa and Pat cried, Mei-Lin and Ami smiled, and she and Shay danced in the aisle, eyes locked, smiles beaming.

She was starting anew with this man and it was time to leave all of her sadness behind. She'd visited Didi last night and told him she was getting married but, well, no change. That was fine. She would still go to visit him every week in the hope that one day there would be. There wasn't a day went by that she didn't think about Ricco, but she couldn't live her life punishing herself for his death. If he really had loved her, she could only hope that he would be happy now for her to move on.

It was time. After a lifetime of lies and subterfuge, Shay Smith was going to make an honest woman of her and she was going to let him.

Stevie sang the last line and even the marriage official joined in the applause. This would give him something to tell the wife over dinner.

The ceremony got started and they both faithfully repeated their vows to the soundtrack of Isa sniffing into her floral handkerchief.

'Ladies and Gentlemen, by the powers vested—'

Brrrrrrrrrrrrrrrrrrrrrrrrrrriiiiiiiiiig.

'What the hell . . . ?'

'I'm sorry, but that's the fire alarm. We have to evacuate immediately!'

Raine grabbed his arm. 'Do the next bit. Hurry up. Just say it.'

'By the powers vested in me by the United States government and the State of New York, I now pronounce you man and wife. Now can you please make your way immediately out of the door and through the fire exit on your right.'

They weren't listening. 'You remember when I said I don't do drama?' Shay prompted her.

'Yeah, well I think you might need to revise that statement.'

# THIRTY-EIGHT

*Mei-Lin*
*Shanghai, 1992*

The humidity hit her the minute she took the first step from the plane. It had been a long journey. New York. Vancouver. Shanghai. She appreciated that Raine had upgraded her flight to first class, but she had to admit it had been a wasted expense as she had eaten and drunk nothing, nor had she spoken to any of her fellow passengers.

A driver holding up a card with her name on it was waiting for her when she reached the arrivals hall. Shanghai airport may be the gateway to the world, but it was still many years behind the cosmopolitan organisation of other airports she'd travelled through. Porters slept on trolleys, people wandered into zones that in other airports would be forbidden and construction work was evident all around her. Yet none of that mattered, because all she could see, smell and feel right now were the memories of her childhood and they were threatening to overwhelm her.

Coming here had been a mistake. What had she been thinking? She should never have listened to Ami. How could it possibly be a good idea? She should have let sleeping dogs lie.

She looked up at the departures board and saw that there was a flight to Hong Kong scheduled to depart two hours later. She could take that, maybe even spend a few days shopping in Hong Kong, and then go home loaded with new clothes. But those things meant nothing to her.

'Miss Yan?' The driver looked at her quizzically, using his powers of deduction to assert that the only female left in the arrivals terminal was the one he was waiting for. He pretended not to stare at the scar that lined her face and she acted like he wasn't making it very obvious that he couldn't take his eyes off it. That was just part of everyday life now and it honestly no longer bothered her.

'The car is right outside,' he said, using a Shanghainese dialect that she struggled to remember.

In the cab – an air-conditioned Mercedes that charged a fraction of the price it would have cost in New York – the driver attempted to speak to her, but she made it clear she would prefer not to chat. After five minutes in the car she realised that closing her eyes was the wisest course of action. No one stuck to lanes. Lights were on in broad daylight. The roads were packed with vehicles that wouldn't be deemed roadworthy anywhere else. There didn't seem to be any general rules of the road. It was a free-for-all. A sudden thought struck her – how ironic would it be if she travelled all this way back to see a family that she left as a child but was killed in a car crash caused by a man on a moped carrying two dozen live chickens? Yes, keeping her eyes closed was probably the best course of action.

When she opened them again she realised she'd fallen asleep. 'How far?' she asked the driver.

'Maybe fifteen minutes.'

The nerves in her stomach tightened. Calm. No fear. Calm. No fear.

However, the mantra that had protected her from the very worst kind of evil was having no effect now.

The surroundings here held no visual familiarity for her at all. As a child she had barely left the land her family worked and never travelled, not even to nearby towns. Over to her right she could see masses of people, bent over, working the fields. Old men and woman, strapping boys, young children, mothers with babies on their backs. This was the life she should have had. She would never know whether it was the right one for her, but it would have been better than the one she was given.

Anger settled in with the nerves, not at her parents – they only did what they had to for all their sake's – but with Cheung and Tang. She tried to sweep away the negative energy, but it was tough to shift. Of course it had been a risk travelling to the country where Tang now lived. The powers of his family stretched far and wide. But if anything that had given her an extra incentive to come. She knew deep inside that Tang would one day seek revenge. It might be today. Maybe tomorrow. Maybe many years from now. If he got his way then she had no doubt she would die, and she realised she couldn't leave this earth without first facing the situation that awaited her now.

Her parents had no idea that she was coming and she had no idea what they would know of her life. Had Cheung told them terrible things? Had they been informed of the occupation that had supported them throughout her teenage years? Were they ashamed of her? Dishonoured? Angry?

The word 'stop' stuck in her throat only because she knew she had come too far to turn back. Suddenly something she recognised. 'Turn here,' she told the driver. 'At the tree there. Then straight down the track until you see the house.'

A few moments later he stopped. She was home.

405

As soon as she climbed out she could see that something wasn't right.

The house looked even shabbier than she remembered, neglected. Always basic, her mother had at least kept it clean and tidy, but now there were branches coming from windows and the doorway was overgrown with bushes. No one lived here.

She sank to her knees and ignored the driver's curious stares. They were gone. The tears flowed down her face and she clutched her stomach where a physical pain had taken hold. What had happened to them? Had they died? Moved to the city? Been torn from their house by an irate landlord or a corrupt government official? Where had they gone?

'Hello?'

A beautiful girl, a teenager, was suddenly standing in front of her and a jolt of electricity shot through Mei-Lin. This creature, staring at her with undisguised curiosity, was so . . . familiar. It took a second for her to realise why. It was like looking at her reflection when she was fifteen years old.

'Ling?'

The girl shook her head. 'No. I'm Suyin. Please excuse my rudeness but who are you?'

'I'm. . .' Her words failed her. 'I'm . . .'

A jolt of recognition. 'Mei-Lin?' Her sister's mouth opened wide with surprise but she could only nod in response.

Then, to her utter astonishment, Suyin began to laugh. 'You must come and come quickly, for I'm not being accused of telling tall tales when Mama and Baba hear about this.'

'Where is the house?'

Suyin pointed across the field to a concrete shack, as cosmetically basic as the one beside them but much larger.

'Come in the car.' But Suyin shook her head. 'I will run, but thank you.' Such perfect manners. Mama and Baba had taught her well. 'Then I will come with you,' Mei-Lin told her.

She turned to the driver, who was watching all of this as if it were an opera for his entertainment.

'Can you please bring my luggage round to the house over there?' He nodded, and for a brief second she wondered if the last she would see of him would be the back of his car as he tore away with her suitcases en route to market to sell them.

But no. He knew that a tip and the promise of a return journey were far more valuable.

Grateful that she had worn flat ballet pumps, she tore across the field after her sister, both of them shrieking with uncontrollable excitement. She was no longer twenty-four, now she was fifteen again and completely oblivious to the dangers of the outside world.

There were about forty feet away when a figure appeared at the doorway.

'Suyin! Suyin! Stop that insufferable noise immed—'

Her mother's words descended into a scream, bringing her father rushing from inside.

He took a step towards her and Mei-Lin stopped and waited before he opened his arms and she ran towards them.

Later that evening she realised that for the second time in her life she had watched her father cry and not understood his reasons.

The afternoon had passed in a blur of tears, and declarations of love, but there had been no discussions as to what had happened to her in the years since she left. They hadn't asked and she knew it was because they didn't want to discuss it in front of her sisters. There were some things a child should not see or hear and she knew that more than anyone.

After a dinner of rice and eggplant, Suyin and Ling wailed

with outrage as their parents sent them to bed. 'It's so unfair,' Ling stomped and Mei-Lin smiled. Unfair. If this was the extent of the unfairness in her beautiful sister's life, then the gods were smiling on her.

'Come, let us sit outside.' Her mother had barely let go of her hand since she arrived and she took it again now, guiding her out to a hand-made table to the right of the house. Mei-Lin slid onto one of the benches beside it.

When her father joined them a few minutes later, there was a silence, an excruciating pause that came loaded with fear and dread.

Eventually her mother's sob broke through the barrier like water bursting through a dam. 'Mei-Lin . . . ' Her voice was a strangled wail and her father instantly put his hand out to calm her. It was time. Mei-Lin knew it was time to tell them the truth and she prayed that it was the right thing to do. If she was going to come back into their lives then there could be no more secrets, even if it meant that she disgusted them, even if they could never look her in the eye again.

'Mama, Baba, I am so sorry. I am so sorry for what I am about to tell you because I know it will break your hearts, but you must know. Uncle Cheung—'

'We know.'

At first she wondered what her father had said, so quiet was his voice. Her mother sobbed again, rivers of tears pouring down a face that was ravaged by anguish.

'We know what he did.'

'But how?'

'Many months after you left, the family of Lee Sing Si from across the river allowed Cheung to take her to a new job in the city. Her body was found a few weeks later, battered so that it was almost unrecognisable. She was only identified because she had a letter from her mother folded in her shoe. When the officials came here to tell her parents, her father gave them Cheung's details and told them about her job caring for children in Shanghai. No such family existed and the address Cheung had given them was false. He has never been seen from that day to this. We knew, Mei-Lin. We reported you missing immediately. The public security bureau told us that they suspected he was selling girls for . . . for. . . .'

He couldn't say it and she realised that she didn't want him to.

'It's us who must apologise to you, Mei-Lin. There isn't a night since then that your mother hasn't cried or that we haven't prayed for you to come back to us. We didn't know, my daughter. We truly thought that we were doing the right thing, giving you a better life and providing for the twins at the same time. I'm sorry, Mei-Lin. There are no words to say how sorry.'

This time she was the one to comfort him. 'Father, please don't. I never blamed you or Mama and I know that you would never have sent me with him if you had realised . . .' Still, she couldn't say it.

'He sold me to a man who took me to America. I will tell you about that in time, my parents, but right now there are two things you must know. Cheung is in prison in America. He was caught and he is being punished for what he did to all of us.'

A tiny ray of light flickered in her father's eyes, a glimmer of satisfaction that some kind of justice had been delivered.

'The other thing I must tell you is the most painful of all. Our cousin, Jing Wei . . .'

Her mother sobbed again, buckled over, tortured by things no mother should ever have to face.

'Jing Wei is dead. Many years ago, when she was barely more than a child.'

Their tears flowed long into the night and many times over the next few days, until it was time for Mei-Lin to leave. They planted a blossom tree for Jing-Wei in front of the house, in the sun, where they would see it every day.

When the taxi returned to collect her, she had no luggage, leaving everything for her sisters, together with many promises. Yes, she would come back and yes, she would find a way for them to visit her in America. Somehow she would make it happen.

Travelling back to the airport, Mei-Lin thought of the ancient proverb that said a journey of a thousand miles started with a single step.

For her family the healing had just begun.

# THIRTY-NINE

*Stevie*
*Los Angeles, 1993*

'Hey, Stephanie, are you keepin' that barbeque? Only Mr Kominski likes himself a bit of steak on poker nights.'

There were so many things wrong with that statement. So many.

'You can have it, Mrs G. Just take it. And anything else that you'd like, too.'

The only sadness that packing up the Marina del Rey apartment had for her was that she would miss Mrs G. 'Thanks, lovely. And I know I should call you Stevie, but Stephanie just seems more natural for me.'

'That's OK. You can call me anything you like.'

Mrs G's shock when she realised who she had been living nextdoor to had been hilarious. By the time she'd made the first trip back from New York, her hair had grown, she'd ditched the glasses and of course she'd been in every magazine and newspaper courtesy of their relentless drive to get publicity for the club.

After a late-night arrival, Stevie had made it onto her balcony early the next morning, and the noise of her coffee cup on the glass table had alerted Mrs G to her presence. The familiar head had come around the dividing wall. 'Stephanie, is that you? I . . . for the love of God!'

Stevie watched as it all clicked into place. If ever there was a morning that Mrs G almost went head first over the balcony, that was it.

This trip, she'd been fantastic at helping Stevie pack, even swearing blind that the occasional tears that welled up in her eyes were caused by hay fever.

By the end of the day they were done, the guys from the storage company had everything in their van and the cleaning team had finished, leaving the apartment ready for renters to move in the next morning. There was absolutely no point in keeping this place lying empty when she was based full time in New York now. Having houses on both coasts was great in theory, but not this home. Other than the incomparable Mrs G, there were too many bad memories here, too much pain. It was time to move on from that.

New experiences. New home. New life.

Time to get back to the club and start making plans for 1993. Christmas had been crazy and seeing in the New Year with five hundred invited guests had been incredible. It had been the best Christmas since the one she'd spent with Jinx and . . . argh! Why was she thinking about him?

OK, so she missed him, but her life was good and it was busy and she didn't have time to sweat it.

She'd left New York on New Year's Day, trying to get over to LA, sort out her stuff, then return before the post-holiday lull was over and they were back to a capacity crowd every night.

It made sense to make the break now, close the chapter, and over on the east coast she would start looking for somewhere to buy. Living in a rented loft in the Village was fine, but it was time to find somewhere she could make her own and really put down roots.

Manhattan had been the best thing that had ever happened to her for many reasons, but one of the unexpected surprises was that it had been a great investment. The hundred thousand dollars she had put up had already been recouped and it was providing a steady income that was more than enough for an apartment somewhere great, maybe around Battery Park or up near Mei-Lin on the Upper East Side. She might even get a dog. Hey, that would be cool. For years she'd wanted to buy a pup, but life on the road was too unfair for an animal. Now that she was no longer with The Thorns and was going to be settled in the one place, perhaps it was time to think about it.

She headed over to the Cheesecake Factory at the beach to meet her mother for dinner before going off to the airport. She'd offered Ella the apartment she'd just vacated, but her mom much preferred the townhouse Stevie had bought her when The Thorns were riding high. It was a couple of blocks back from the beach, but Ella was settled there and regularly announced that she wasn't moving 'unless Robert De Niro came calling for her'. If Ella kept this up, Robert De Niro would be calling for a restraining order.

They kissed and then sat at a table out on the patio, overlooking Mother's Beach, so called because the lack of tide made it perfect for the children that flocked there.

'So have you heard from—'

'Jesus, Mom, I haven't even ordered a drink yet.' Stevie laughed.

Ella had the courtesy to look embarrassed, but only for a few seconds before she regrouped and came back with a second wave of attack.

'I don't get it, Stevie. That man loves you. He comes to see me every time he's in town and he never forgets birthdays and Christmas and—'

'Mom, we broke up for a reason.' Stevie sighed. She couldn't have this conversation again. She just couldn't.

'But what could possibly be so terrible that you couldn't fix it? I mean, I know he went off and married that lawyer, but that was a rebound thing, Stephanie. Rebound.'

Her mother always used her birth name when she was irate. This was ridiculous. Totally crazy. She was an adult, a successful musician, a partner in the best club in New York and her mother was still trying to run her relationships.

'Mom, some things just can't be fixed and Jinx and I fall into that category. You've got to stop trying to run my life. Jinx and I are over. Period. Done. So ... Oh shit, Ma, tell me you haven't invited him here tonight because I think I'll put myself up for adoption if you have.'

Ella's pursed lips refused to comment and Stevie swore under her breath.

'That's enough of that, Stephanie, and no, I haven't invited Jinx here tonight. Although I now wish I had. He's better company.'

Stevie tossed a bread roll at her mother and they both laughed. If she ever became a parent she was going to make sure that she interfered in her adult children's lives, too. She'd blame it on family genes.

'So are you going to come out to New York for your birthday?'

It was only a few days away but her mother still hadn't told her what her plans were. Now she shook her head. 'I'm sorry, honey, but your brother is here ...'

'Favourite.'

'He is not my favourite! But he is here and you know that

you'll be at the club every night, so I think it's better if I just stay in LA. He's promised to take me out to some sports awards show. Jinx will be there.'

'Mom, you're incorrigible.'

Over the last few months in New York she'd dated a little, had a few one-night stands, hooked up with some guys she'd known before, but ... nothing. No spark. No longing for them on the nights that they weren't there.

Maybe that was just the way it was going to be. She'd only ever loved one man and perhaps nothing would ever match up to that. What a depressing thought – another fifty years of Ella trying to get them back together.

She was thinking about him again! Why did this keep happening? This was her mother's fault, spreading her obsession on to the unwilling. Jinx was history and it could never be any other way because the truth was that she would never trust him again. Every time she looked at his face, every time they made love, every time she needed to know that she could count on him, no matter what, every time she needed him, she would wonder if he was going to bail out.

Enough pain.

Her mother had finally got the hint and didn't talk about Jinx again for the rest of dinner.

They'd asked for the bill by nine and the town car she'd ordered to take her to the airport was waiting outside. She squeezed her mother tightly and gave her a kiss. 'See you soon, Mom. Maybe you can come out for Valentine's? I'll see if I can get you an inflatable Robert De Niro.'

Ella laughed as she took her key from the valet and climbed into the white BMW convertible Stevie had bought her for her last birthday.

There was barely any traffic on the journey to the airport, so twenty minutes later they pulled up outside the terminal and Stevie jumped out, throwing her bag over her shoulder. She always travelled light.

On the way to check-in she stopped to buy a magazine and a book in case she couldn't sleep on the flight. *Vogue. Marie Claire. Harper's. Rock Out.* Yep, that would do, she decided, pulling it out of the stand. She hadn't read anything about . . .

The front page. The picture staring at her. The headline: ARI COVET CLOSE TO DEATH. Full story page three.

Frantically, she flipped the cover over. More pictures.

MUSIC MOGUL CLOSE TO DEATH AFTER

ROCK STAR WEDDING

### Exclusive insider eyewitness accounts and photos by Bobby Sofranko

The wedding of Steel Spikes singer Sly Rammer and his girl-friend of eight years Marny Tucker was thrown into chaos by the collapse of head of AC records, Ari Covet. Covet is believed to have suffered a stroke and is presently in a critical condition in Cedars-Sinai Medical Center. A representative from AC Records issued the following statement yesterday morning:

*It is with deep sadness that we confirm the illness of our founder and president Mr Ari Covet. The current status of his condition is extremely serious and we have put our trust and faith in the medical professionals at Cedars-Sinai, who are currently working to ensure Mr Covet receives the best possible care. We would also like to thank the general public, Mr Covet's associates and the stars of both the music and movie industries who have been so thoughtful in sending their condolences and prayers.*

416

According to insider reports, Mr Covet collapsed just moments before the ceremony. However, organisers and guests were unaware of this as he left the wedding area after complaining of feeling unwell.

Gilly-Ann Strong, personal make-up artist for supermodel bridesmaid Coco LaBiba, revealed that the situation only came to light when paramedics arrived on the scene after being alerted by a member of the catering staff. This was shortly after the bride and groom had completed their vows. 'I saw everything,' said a traumatised Ms Strong. 'He just fell over right in front of me and I immediately rushed to his side and put him in the recovery position. I then called to staff and informed them that medical help was urgently required. But I'm not a hero, I only did what anyone else would do.' The following photographs of Mr Covet, taken by an anonymous source as he fought for life, show the gravity of the situation.

Stevie was shaking so hard it was difficult to read the small print. Ari Covet was close to death. She only wished that she were there to finish the job. Her eyes began to sting and she reached into her bag for a pair of sunglasses. It totally contradicted her theory that all people who wore sunglasses when not in direct sunlight were idiots – but this was an exception.

She just needed to get from here to the plane without throwing up or having to speak to anyone. Ari Covet was sick. He was dying. He didn't have much longer to live. The thoughts buzzed around in her head and she realised that she wanted to talk to someone who knew, who understood what had happened to her.

The air hostess showed her to her seat – first class, row one – and she asked for a blanket. Sleep. She needed some sleep, some time to process this. Was it justice? Was this some kind of divine retribution for what he'd done? Or was the fact that he could die at any minute an escape for him, a chance to conceal his true nature and crimes from the world?

This wasn't how she wanted it to play out. She wanted him to pay, to suffer like she had done. Like she was still doing.

'Anyone sitting here?'

Shit, that was all she needed, someone in the seat right next to her. Why the hell did airlines do that? The whole of the first class section was empty, yet they'd allocated the seat right next to her to . . .

'Has anyone ever told you that people who wear sunglasses inside are complete dicks?'

. . . Lou.

Her first reaction was to pull off the glasses. Lou's reaction was violent.

'*Nooooo*, put them back on! Dear God, the horror!'

Lou grinned and punched her on the arm just as Cally and Dixie appeared and slid into the row behind them.

Stevie didn't miss the shocked looks that passed between the three of them. This was going to be seriously awkward. She'd only been in their company once since the split and that was the week after the opening of Manhattan, when Cally had brought them all in, minus Leeane Star, who'd escaped indecency charges by checking into a rehab facility in Kansas. Stevie had no idea what Cally had told them, but no questions were asked and it seemed like the bad feeling was over. That was good enough for her.

However, seven hours on a flight might be just too much to ask of the ceasefire.

'Guys, is this going to be weird? I don't mind moving to another seat. I'm really not interested in getting into what happened. It's in the past and it needs to stay there.'

'No, it's cool,' Cally told her.

'You sure?'

Another nod.

'Lou? Are you going to use that pillow as a weapon while I sleep?'

Lou laughed and punched her arm, just a little too hard for Stevie's liking.

'Much as that would be fun, it would kind of defeat the purpose.'

'What purpose?'

'The purpose of our trip to New York.'

Stevie was confused. What did punching her have to do with going to New York? Shit, were they going there to see their lawyers? To instruct some legal thing against her? To . . . to . . . Nothing else sprang to mind.

'We were coming to New York to see you.'

'Why?'

'Because we were wondering how you would feel about rejoining the band.'

Maybe the puppy would have to wait, because she'd just been given a shot at the happy ending she'd hoped for . . . just as long as she kept one eye open if she fell asleep next to Lou.

# FORTY

*New York, 1993*

New York Globe – *21 December 1993*

The stars are expected to turn out in style tonight for the first anniversary celebrations of top New York nightclub Manhattan. Since it opened its doors exactly one year ago today, the venue has played host to famous names from across the globe and garnered a reputation for glamour and excess. It was also the source of much controversy when it was the principal location used in the movie Disco Drug.

Manhattan owners Raine O'Donnell, Mei-Lin Yan and Stevie Ross last night paid tribute to the clients who have frequented the nightspot, saying, 'We are incredibly proud of our club and we owe a huge debt of thanks to everyone who has supported us throughout these amazing twelve months. And thank you to the city of New York, because only in this town would three women be able to achieve so much in such a short time in such a crazy industry. Tomorrow night, the cocktails are on us!'

It's thought that the celebrities taking the Manhattan bosses up on that offer will include such luminaries as Calvin Klein, Jackie Collins, Janice Dickinson, Diana Ross, Jack Nicholson, Dimitri Krakov, Tala DiVinci, Leeane Star, Madonna, Sylvester Stallone, Christie Brinkley and Bruce Willis.

Full details and photographs of what promises to be a spectacular event will feature in our Saturday edition.

# FORTY-ONE

'I haven't been this excited since Sean Penn felt me up on the back fire exit.' Raine covered her grin by taking another sip of pink champagne as she waited for the inevitable chorus of outrage.

Right on cue, Stevie's jaw dropped. 'He did not!'

'Oh, OK, so he didn't,' Raine admitted glibly.

Stevie wasn't letting it go. 'How many times have I told you to stop exaggerating and making things up?'

'A million. You're right. I'm sorry.' She paused. 'It might have been Jack Nicholson.'

The three of them laughed and one by one put their glasses into the middle of their huddle.

Raine offered up the toast. 'Here's to Manhattan and to us. To think they said we'd never make it in this town.'

'That's the worst James Cagney impression ever,' Mei-Lin teased.

Raine nodded. 'I know. Sean Penn taught me.'

After a few moments their laughter subsided and Stevie spoke up, her voice choked with emotion. If her fans could see her now they'd barely recognise this softly spoken, all-American blonde as the biggest female rock star of the decade.

'I just want to say thank you. I'd never have made it without the two of you.'

Mei-Lin leaned over and softly kissed her cheek. 'You would always have made it. It just wouldn't have been this great.'

The others nodded. Mei-Lin continued to speak, her perfect Revlon Red lips an exact colour match of the stunning, floor-length red cheongsam that skimmed her petite frame. 'You know, when I came to this country my heart was broken, but now, finally, I feel that it is whole again.'

Stevie's eyes filled with tears and even Raine executed a very pronounced gulp.

Stevie summed it up. 'We all needed each other. And I love both of you so much.'

In the distance, a bell started ringing. Raine sniffed loudly and cleared her throat. 'That's the "Too Much Emotion In Here" alarm. I had it fitted especially for tonight,' she joked.

Before the others could reply, the phone rang. Raine was closest to it.

'This had better be good because you're interrupting a memorable moment.' Her sing-song voice oozed happiness and excitement.

'What?' In a split second her face changed. Another bell started to ring, then another. All three heads swivelled to the fire-alarm board on the wall behind them. It was lighting up like a Christmas tree.

Raine slammed the phone down.

'We have to get out of here. There's a fire on the east side, the west, the basement . . .' Another light on the board. 'And shit, there's one above us, too.'

Despite the urgency of the situation, none of them moved.

'This is it,' Mei-Lin whispered. 'He's coming for us.'

As trickles of smoke crept in around the doorframe, no one argued.

Raine was the first to move.

She snatched up her radio. 'Joe? Karl? Who's got ears out there?' Joe's voice came back first. 'Boss, we're getting people out. There are fires at the front door, the east and west fire exits, but the back one is clear. We're taking them out there.'

'Everyone's getting out!' she relayed to Mei-Lin and Stevie.

'Not everyone, Boss!' Joe again, his voice coming through the earpiece. 'We can't get up to the VIP level. The lifts have gone out and the board is registering a fire on the back stairs. We don't know if they can get past it.'

Raine didn't even know how to repeat that to the others. This was their first anniversary, a huge party and everyone they loved had been invited and given access to the VIP room upstairs.

The Bitch of Thorns were here, ready to play their first gig since Stevie rejoined the band.

Pat and Isa were here, celebrating the last night of their honeymoon.

Mei-Lin's parents were here. Oh God, her parents! Their English was non-existent – how would they even begin to understand what was going on?

Stevie's mother and brother were here, too.

How could they have been so stupid? They'd gathered everyone they loved in one place and given Jason Tang the perfect opportunity to wipe out their lives.

How could this have happened? Ten minutes ago they were celebrating and now . . .

'Raine, we have to get out of here.'

Shay! Where was Shay? She'd asked him to take photographs

of the club tonight, people shots that would preserve the occasion. He'd be OK. He was smart. He'd get to a door. He had to.

'Mei-Lin, can you breath? Come on, we have to move!'

Raine grabbed a bottle of water from the table, tore strips from the bottom of her dress and soaked them, then they covered their mouths and opened the door to a thick wall of black smoke.

'Get down! Crawl!' They followed Raine's instructions and went to the left, desperate to make it the thirty yards to the front door. They were halfway there when they realised it was hopeless. The heat was getting more intense, so they were obviously going towards a fire source. Fuck.

Raine spun round and headed back the other way, her eyes stinging. Mei-Lin and Stevie copied her, taking what seemed like ages to get back to the door of the office, where they'd started. They made it in and slammed the door. Raine grabbed the fire extinguisher, then pushed the desk back, climbed on top and used the bottom of the extinguisher to smash the small grate that sat high on the far wall. It wasn't big enough to get anyone out, but it would give them some breathing space until the heat got them. The thought didn't cheer her.

'We're going to have to go the other way and try the side exit,' Stevie yelled.

Raine nodded and grabbed their hands. 'I love you,' she whispered.

They soaked the cloths again, pressed them against their mouths and opened the door. This time the heat was even worse and there was no light at all now, just an empty void of pitch black. 'Feel the wall,' she gasped.

They started crawling, pushing themselves along, terrified to breathe because every inhalation burned deep inside them. Raine felt her knees burn. Stevie felt her throat closing.

Mei-Lin thought she might suffocate before she got another . . . she stopped. There was no more movement in her. No more energy to go on.

A hand pushed her from behind and forced her to keep going. Keep going. Keep . . .

A light. A tiny glimmer of light that was getting closer and closer.

Raine moved faster and faster, overtaking Mei-Lin, knowing that she had to get to the door and get it open. It was hard to tell in the dark, but she thought she'd got there first. She reached up and pushed the bar but it wouldn't move. This fire exit led to a back alley and no one had been in it for months. Raine groped out and felt someone near her. Stevie. Perhaps both their weights would do it. She couldn't speak, couldn't see and she was so exhausted that she knew they were only going to get one shot at this. Pushing her arm against Stevie's back, she pulled her up, placed her hands on the vertical bar, put hers next to it and then roared and pushed. There was a loud crack, then the doors swung open and the two of them fell out, gasping, into the night. Two. Fuck. Without giving it a second thought Raine dived back in. She didn't have far to go. Only a couple of yards inside the door Mei-Lin was crawling towards them.

Raine dragged her out, both of them rolling into the alley. Raine pulled the cloth from her nose and mouth. 'Are you both OK?' she croaked. They nodded.

Shay. Her dad. Their families. If the lifts were down there was only one way out of the VIP bar and that was down the back stairs. Joe had said it was blocked by a fire, but if they'd got past that . . . Please God let them have got out. If she had this right they would exit just round the corner. The wails of sirens were blaring now. Close. Almost there.

She pushed herself up and, using the wall for support, moved along the side of the building until she reached the edge and fell round. The first face she saw was Shay's. Behind him, covered in dust and soot, some coughing, some lying dazed on the ground, were people she knew had been upstairs in the VIP bar. They'd got out. Some of them at least. But where was . . . 'Shay, where is my dad? My dad!' she screamed, choking with pain. No, she couldn't lose him now. That bastard Tang couldn't have taken him from her. Her dad and Shay were everything and she should have protected them. She'd known this would happen, she was waiting for it. 'Dad!' she screamed. 'Dad!' Shay was beside her now, his arms around her, trying to calm her and hold her tightly, but she struggled for air. 'Dad! Shay, help me! Where's my . . . dad!' The hulking figure of Pat O'Donnell was unmistakable as it staggered towards her, being supported under one arm by the tiny figure of Isa. She sank to her knees and howled with pain and relief. They were safe. Her dad, Isa and Shay were safe. And that was all she needed to know before she passed out on the cold floor, completely unaware that Mei-Lin had just stepped over her.

Mama. Baba. She had to get to them. After all these years she'd found them again and brought them here and now they could be taken away. She couldn't let that happen. Her eyes fell on the doorway and on the people pouring out of it. She could see Raine's dad and stepmother and she knew that they had been looking after her parents so surely they must—

'Mei-Lin!' The voice was her mother's as she staggered into view, her father right behind her. More people came after them, but at that moment all she cared about were the two people she was holding. They were crying, shaking, but they were alive. Jason Tang had not taken them from her again. He had not destroyed their lives. He hadn't succeeded.

She closed her eyes, opening them again only when the stinging became bearable.

That's when she saw her. The Asian face that she'd seen in the crowd on the night the club opened. She was coming out of the fire exit, the last one, looking around her and . . . lock. Their eyes met and Mei-Lin saw it. Hatred. Then a smile. The girl turned around and ran right back into the building she'd just escaped from.

Mei-Lin passed her mother's sobbing body over to her father and found the strength to rise to her feet. Every step was excruciating, every breath hurt, but she kept going. She had to know, had to see . . .

She was halfway up the stairs before she caught sight of her, almost at the top of the stairs, only feet away from re-entering the VIP bar.

'Jing Wei!' she shouted.

The girl stopped and turned around, and Mei-Lin saw immediately. This wasn't her beautiful, innocent Jing Wei, her little bird who had relied on her so much back in Shanghai. This was another girl, an angry one, seething, spitting and looking at her with undisguised hatred.

'Jing Wei?' She was vaguely aware that they had to get out of there. The flames were darting from the doorway now, ready to follow them back downstairs to the open air. 'But how . . .?'

'Why are you following me?' the younger girl screamed. 'Why? Leave me! Leave me like you did last time.'

'But . . .'

This didn't make sense. None of it made sense. How could Jing Wei be here?

'You left me!'

She was screaming now, her face contorted with rage and

pain. Mei-Lin took another couple of steps upwards. She was ten feet away from her now.

'I didn't leave you, Jing Wei. They told me you were dead.'

'Liar! Cheung told me. I know you left. He took care of me. Made me better.'

This was insane. The rantings of a crazy person.

'We were a team. He loved me! You couldn't stand it, you jealous bitch!'

Mei-Lin couldn't breathe and this time it was nothing to do with the flames that were getting hotter every second.

'Jing Wei, I was never jealous. They told me you were dead, he sold me to Tang. I would never have gone if—'

'Liar!' she screamed again. 'Stop lying! You wanted him and when he came to America you kept him here. I want him back! Give him back to me!'

'Jing Wei, Cheung is in prison. He was caught—'

'Liar!'

'Did you do this? Did you start the fires?'

She already knew the answer. It wasn't Jason Tang. It was Jing Wei.

Her cousin stopped and smiled.

'He's all I've got, and I'll never let you have him.'

Mei-Lin didn't see the foot coming until it connected with her chin and sent her hurling backwards. Three steps. Four steps. Five . . . She bounced downwards, the pain in her head excruciating.

Cloudy. Everything was cloudy, and all she could see was . . . Jing Wei. Little bird. Her little bird was smiling and walking backwards towards the door. Now all she could see were the flames and . . . darkness. She didn't know if the scream was only inside her head.

'What was that? Who was it?' Stevie didn't even feel the

pain of the gravel on her knees as she crawled towards the other fire exit. Had she really just seen that? Had she really seen Mei-Lin go back inside the building? Why would she do that? No, it didn't make sense, but she had to go and find out.

'Mei-Lin!' she screamed into the darkness.

'Stephanie!' The voice came from beside her and then came the force of her mother's arms being thrown around her. 'Oh, baby, I thought you were still in there. I thought you were dead. I thought . . .'

'Ma, stop! Stop! Where's Matt? Where is he?'

'He's there, honey, right over there with Cally and Lou. They're out. They're all out. Everyone's going to be OK.'

Stevie knew different. She grabbed Ella's arms and prised them off her. 'Mom, Mei-Lin is in there. She went back in. I have to get to her.' She pulled away and headed towards the door. '*No!*' Ella shouted. 'Stevie, no!'

Mei-Lin. She had to get to Mei-Lin. Five feet. Four.

From her left a hand rushed towards her, scooping around her waist and pulling her to the side until she landed on something soft. 'Thank God. Thank God. I couldn't find you.' Jinx. He was holding her and crying and now he was saying her name over and over.

'What are you doing here?' This was so confusing. Why? Why was he here?

'Your mom . . .'

'Stop.' She put her hand over his mouth and stopped him. All she needed to know was that he was safe. And so was her mom and her brother and Raine and . . . Mei-Lin. She had to get to Mei-Lin.

'Jinx, Mei-Lin went back in there, she went back upstairs. Jinx, help her, please! You have to help her.'

He was on his feet before she'd finished, running towards the open doors and disappearing inside.

Stevie screamed and screamed and screamed. What had she done?

The ambulance crews were arriving now, men with stretchers, putting masks on people, talking to them. Where was he? 'Someone help him! Someone help him!'

People were looking at her now, screaming and crying. She had to go to him. Scrambling to her feet she took a step, fell. Up again, another step. She fell. 'Miss, you have to lie down, you're hurt.'

She pushed the medic's hand away. 'I have to help him. I have to get in there.' She'd done this. She'd killed Jinx. She'd sent him back in there to die. Oh God, the pain. She couldn't breathe. Couldn't breathe. But she had to get in there, had to find him.

'Miss you're not going anywhere. It's too dangerous. The stairway is collapsing and we think everyone's out.'

'But they're not! They're not!'

She tried to pull away, but his hold was too tight. Then her legs gave way again and she fell to the ground, on her knees, and . . .

He was there. Walking out of the doorway, carrying Mei-Lin, coming straight towards her. He'd done that for her. For her. When she needed him he'd been there. And that was all she needed to know.


The whole area was awash with uniforms now. Paramedics pulling oxygen masks onto soot-stained faces and pressing dressings onto wounds.

'Can you hear me? Can you open your eyes?' Raine heard a voice cutting through her sleep. She could hear him but her eyes were so heavy. So heavy. 'Raine, come on, baby, open your eyes.' Shay. Her Shay.

431

'Come on, Raine, you can do it.' Not Shay now. Eric. It was Eric.

It took every bit of strength she had, but she pushed her eyelids open to see that she was right. Shay on one side, Eric on the other. All kinds of weird. A dream. Must be a dream.

'Stay with us, Raine, stay awake. Come on, Raine, you can do this.'

She could do it. Pushing open her eyes again, she looked at Eric. 'Tang,' she croaked. 'Tang did this.'

Eric was shaking his head. 'He didn't, Raine. That's why I'm here. I came to tell you that he can't hurt you any more. Tang's dead. Heroin overdose last night. They found his body in his cell this morning.'

'But . . .'

This didn't make sense. If Tang was dead who had done this? Had he ordered it before he died? Or was it nothing to do with him at all? She didn't understand. Answers. There had to be answers.

The paramedic slipped a mask onto her face and she felt a blast of oxygen hit her lungs. Slowly, she pushed herself up on one elbow and saw the carnage around her. Bodies everywhere. But they were all alive. 'Stevie,' it came out in another croak, and just feet away her friend, her face and clothes black with ash, smiled back at her.

'Mei-Lin's OK, too,' she said. 'She's right over there with the medics, but they say she'll be OK.'

'Stevie, Tang is dead. He's dead!'

'So who did this?' Stevie stammered, but she was immediately interrupted.

'He's dead?' Mei-Lin's voice.

Raine nodded. 'He's dead, Mei-Lin. It's over.'

Nothing was certain now. The club was destroyed, they were

battered and sore and there were questions that she didn't have answers to. But everyone had made it out and they still had their lives and their futures with the people they loved.

Most importantly of all, Tang did not.

The monster was dead.

He was gone.

And that meant one thing.

It really was over.

And their new lives could begin.

# EPILOGUE

*New York, 1994*

'Move up! Move up, fat lady coming through. And Shay Smith if you roll your eyes one more time I will kill you, and I'll get off with it because I'm hormonal and a former undercover government agent.'

There were times in life when Shay knew it was best to keep his mouth shut – many, he'd learned – and this was definitely one of them.

They trampled several pairs of feet before sliding into their seats beside a very amused Stevie.

'Glad you don't like to make a big entrance. I'd hate everyone to be staring at us, what with me trying to keep a low profile and all.'

Raine looked around her to see dozens of pairs of eyes watching them. 'Obviously the action on the court isn't enough to keep their attention.'

In a fine example of comic timing, a roar swept the stadium and the crowd went wild.

'There are reasons that I don't earn my living as a psychic.'

Raine took a huge bite of her hot dog, thereby stopping

herself from uttering any more inanities. What had happened to her? She used to be a smart, switched-on, super-fit career chick who kept on top of every detail of her life while running the top nightclub in New York.

Now she was an inflated, hormonal, exhausted, cranky career chick who still ran the top nightclub in New York. She checked her watch. Half an hour and then they'd have to head to Manhattan to get set up before opening. She'd finally given in to Shay's pleading to stay away from the door. They didn't get much trouble, but you never knew when some crazy would kick off, and at eight months pregnant she was a slow-moving target these days.

'Wanna bit?' Raine held out her hot dog to Stevie.

'Will you be upset if I say yes?'

'Devastated. I'm only offering out of politeness.'

'Then no, I'm good.'

It felt great to be doing normal stuff, Stevie realised. The last year had been crazy, what with the tour and pitching in at the club when she was in town. Oh, and then there was the not-too-insignificant issue of her forthcoming nuptials to Jinx Daley to consider. Ella hadn't taken her nose out of bridal magazines since the night he proposed. It had been a rough road, but they'd made it to the finish line in one piece.

They watched the game in silence for a while, until the closing minutes of play, when Jinx ran up the court, swept round three players and scored.

'Touchdown!' Raine shouted. Shay buried his head in his hands.

'I only do that to piss him off,' Raine whispered in her ear.

'I know, babe. I know.'

What had she ever done without Raine O'Donnell in her life? There was no one who made her laugh like Raine and no one more loyal or more outrageously defensive of her friends. Although, trying to stop her bitch-slapping Lou into submission was getting harder every time they met.

The final claxon sounded and Jinx turned to wave as he ran off the court. He'd catch up with them later at the club.

As they got up to leave, Stevie realised this place didn't bother her any more. Madison Square Gardens – where she'd launched her career and first met Ari Covet. He was nothing to her now. Dead. She could honestly say she never gave him a single thought. He'd taken enough time from her.

The limo ride back to the club was straight and fast, right down 7th Avenue, and they crossed the threshold of Manhattan twenty minutes later, dropping Shay at his and Raine's new home on the way. The two storey Greenwich Village loft with a studio on the ground floor had seemed like a great idea when they'd bought it. Two weeks later, when they discovered she was pregnant, she wasn't so sure. Getting kids up and down in that rickety old elevator was going to be a treat.

When they got into the office, Mei-Lin was already there, immaculate as always in black leather thigh-high boots over black jeans and a silver jumper that slid off one shoulder as she moved. She'd come in early to do some organisation for the weekend. Being a co-partner in a nightclub and running a network of twenty-five stunning girls kept her pretty busy. People judged, but she didn't care – her girls worked for her through choice and they earned good money with full benefits. They could walk away any time. It was up to them if they chose not to.

Stevie leaned down to hug her. 'Hey, baby, how was today? Rough?'

Mei-Lin nodded. 'Pretty much.'

'What are the docs saying?'

Mei-Lin took a deep breath. She'd spent the whole day with the doctors at the secure facility that housed Jing Wei and the diagnosis was complicated. Post-traumatic stress. Stockholm Syndrome. Underlying personality disorders. Paranoia. Pyromania. Turns out that arson had already claimed the brothel in Shanghai just weeks before Jing Wei travelled to the US. The authorities there had no evidence to connect her to the crime, but the suspicions were obvious.

She was just grateful that a sympathetic judge had acceded to her pleas not to deport her, but to keep Jing Wei in the US, as long as her bills were met by Mei-Lin. It was a small price to pay. The thought of her rotting alone in a Chinese facility was too much to bear.

'It's not your responsibility, you know. You did everything you could,' Raine said softly.

A sad smile crossed Mei-Lin's face as she shrugged. 'I know. But do you still feel responsible for what happened to Ricco?'

'Every day.'

'Then we both have our ghosts.'

They understood each other perfectly. It was one of the things that had made them so close, sisters from a different mother, different culture, different continent, but sisters all the same.

'I'd lean down and hug you, honey, but with a sudden weight displacement like that, the baby could drop right out of me like a stone.'

'Hey, did I tell you that my mother is dating?' Stevie informed them both.

'Who?'

'Dixie's dad. He owns the pub in Santa Monica where we played our first ever gig. I'm not sure if my mom is in love or just permanently wasted on Guinness, but she seems happy. They met when we played the Bowl last month.'

'Go, Ella. I hope you told her to use protection.'

Mei-Lin and Stevie uttered a simultaneous 'Eeew.'

Raine ignored them, slipping right into business mode.

'Did the new lighting system arrive today?'

Mei-Lin nodded. 'Apparently so, but I haven't had time to test it yet.'

'Come on, let's check it out.'

The three of them went into the main hall and stopped in the middle of the dance floor.

'Haylo, you back there?'

Their DJ stuck his head up over the top of his booth. Raine really didn't want to know what he was doing back there. Last time she strayed behind the stage there was action involving three French girls and a linebacker from the Washington Redskins.

'Haylo, can you slam on the new lights – we just want to check them out.'

There was a moment of stillness and then bam!

The whole room was flooded with rays of white lights, shooting from a hundred different angles in the ceiling, every one of them coming together to bathe them in an almost celestial glow.

The effect was breathtaking. It was more than just a dance floor in a nightclub. This felt like being in the centre of the world. Their world.

Manhattan.